Irish author **Abby Green** ended a very glamorous career in film and TV—which really consisted of a lot of standing in the rain outside actors' trailers—to pursue her love of romance. After she'd bombarded Mills & Boon with manuscripts they kindly accepted one, and an author was born. She lives in Dublin, Ireland, and loves any excuse for distraction. Visit abby-green.com or email abbygreenauthor@gmail.com.

Clare Connelly was raised in small-town Australia among a family of avid readers. She spent much of her childhood up a tree, Mills & Boon book in hand. Clare is married to her own real-life hero, and they live in a bungalow near the sea with their two children. She is frequently found staring into space—a surefire sign that she's in the world of her characters. She has a penchant for French food and ice-cold champagne, and Mills & Boon novels continue to be her favourite ver books. Writing for Modern is a long-held dream. 'are can be contacted via clareconnelly.com or at her Facebook page.

Also by Abby Green

Awakened by the Scarred Italian
The Greek's Unknown Bride

Rival Spanish Brothers miniseries

Confessions of a Pregnant Cinderella
Redeemed by His Stolen Bride

The Marchetti Dynasty miniseries

The Maid's Best Kept Secret

Also by Clare Connelly

Redemption of the Untamed Italian
The Secret Kept from the King
Hired by the Impossible Greek
Their Impossible Desert Match

Crazy Rich Greek Weddings miniseries

The Greek's Billion-Dollar Baby
Bride Behind the Billion-Dollar Veil

Discover more at millsandboon.co.uk.

THE INNOCENT BEHIND THE SCANDAL

ABBY GREEN

AN HEIR CLAIMED BY CHRISTMAS

CLARE CONNELLY

MILLS & BOON

First Published in Great Britain 2020
by Mills & Boon, an imprint of HarperCollins*Publishers*
1 London Bridge Street, London, SE1 9GF

The Innocent Behind the Scandal © 2020 Abby Green

An Heir Claimed by Christmas © 2020 Clare Connelly

ISBN: 978-0-263-27843-9

MIX
Paper from
responsible sources
FSC™ C007454

This book is produced from independently certified FSC™ paper
to ensure responsible forest management.
For more information visit www.harpercollins.co.uk/green.

Printed and bound in Spain
by CPI, Barcelona

THE INNOCENT BEHIND THE SCANDAL

ABBY GREEN

I'd like to dedicate this book to Annie West, who is not only one of my favourite romance authors but also, I'm honoured to say, my friend. We sold to Mills & Boon around the same time, and our first books hit the shelves within months of each other.

Since those first books she has provided support, much-needed advice and friendship. Not to mention inspiration! She helped ease my path into becoming a writer and took the terror out of navigating a whole new world.

Thank you, Annie, this is for you. xx

CHAPTER ONE

Paris

HE WAS THE most beautiful man Zoe Collins had ever seen, and that was some realisation when she was currently surrounded by some of the world's most physically perfect men and women at one of Paris Fashion Week's biggest shows.

He was sitting in the front row, so he had to be important.

Aware that she was staring, Zoe dragged her gaze away and looked around the vast ballroom that had been transformed into a fairy woodland scene, with real trees down the centre of the catwalk. The air was scented with the expensive perfume of the hundreds of guests milling around while they waited for the show to start.

Her heart was still pounding from the adrenalin rush of what she'd just done.

She'd been outside the Grand Palais, taking pictures of 'influencers' as they went into the show, and by pure fluke she'd noticed one of the catering staff outside a door, having a cigarette. When he went back inside he'd left the door ajar, and Zoe had seized the opportunity to get into the inner sanctum.

She knew that if she could actually manage to get into 'the pit', where the official photographers lined themselves up at the end of the catwalk, she would be able to try and convince them that she was one of them. Even though she wasn't. At all. She was a self-taught amateur photographer.

There was no way she would have got accreditation to be in here officially. As it was, some of the other photographers were looking at her suspiciously. She hunched forward, letting her shoulder-length hair hide her face, and hoped they wouldn't notice that she had no official lanyard.

Excitement buzzed under her skin. She'd never been at a fashion show before, and it had always been a dream of hers to see the spectacle up close. Along with the dream becoming a bona fide fashion photographer. For as long as she could remember she'd escaped into glossy magazines and pored for hours over the fantastical editorial created by the industry's best photographers, editors and stylists.

But breaking into a tight-knit industry like this was akin to climbing Everest without oxygen. Next to impossible without contacts or experience.

She knew she shouldn't draw attention to herself, but she couldn't resist looking at the man again. When her gaze found him her pulse-rate skipped and her heart beat a little faster.

He had more than just good looks, she realised. There was an air of impenetrability about him. He was talking to no one. Looking at no one. Glancing down periodically at his phone. Totally relaxed, yet primed. Interested, but not showing interest. Aloof.

She guessed he was tall, just from the way he dominated the space around him. He had broad shoulders, a lean body. Very short hair—almost militarily short. Dark under the lights, but not brown, or black. More dark blond.

But his bone structure alone had Zoe lifting the camera to her face, almost without realising what she was doing. And when she looked through her viewfinder her heart stopped altogether.

Close up, he wasn't just beautiful—he was breathtaking. High cheekbones, deep-set eyes. A mouth that promised decadence and sin. Firm contours. Sensual. A hard, uncompromising jaw that a shadow of stubble only enhanced.

There was a faintly olive tone to his skin. And then

his head turned and his eyes connected directly with hers through her camera. She froze. His eyes were mesmerising. Dark grey. Cold. Cynical. Guarded.

Zoe acted on instinct. Her finger came down on the button and the camera made a clicking sound as it immortalised his image for ever.

But before she could even take the camera down from her face there was a blur of movement, and then she was being grabbed by her jacket and hauled up and out of the pit full of photographers.

'Who the hell are you and why are you taking pictures of me?'

Dimly, Zoe recognised the fact that his voice matched the rest of him. Deep and authoritative. Slightly accented. She also recognised that he was much taller than she might have guessed. Well over six feet, and towering over her own far less substantial five foot four.

His eyes raked her up and down. 'Who are you? Where's your accreditation?'

'I...' She faltered, all the bravado that had led her in here dissolving. She swallowed. 'I don't have any.'

She vaguely heard muttering from the other photographers and guilty heat climbed up over her chest to her face.

'Look, I'm sorry. I saw an open door and I just—'

'Thought you'd enter illegally?'

Zoe spluttered. 'Well, that's a bit extreme, isn't it?'

He put his hand on her arm and pulled her out of the photographers' area and along the front row towards the main doors, on the opposite side of the room from where she'd entered. Her face burned with humiliation. Who the hell did this guy think he was? Acting like judge and jury? Crashing a fashion show was hardly the crime of the century!

Zoe could see people tucking their legs out of the way as

they passed, and noted several iconic famous faces assuming looks of disgust and horror as she was all but hauled out.

When they were on the other side of the main doors she pulled free. She could see security guards approaching, but the man put up a hand and they stopped. She looked up, breathless. Adrenalin rushed through her system, and something else—something that felt disturbingly like excitement.

'Who *are* you?' She rubbed her arm, even though he hadn't hurt her at all.

He didn't answer, just reached for her camera, lifting it over her head before she could stop him.

She reacted instantly, reaching for it. 'Hey, that's my camera. You can't just—'

But a hand planted squarely on her upper chest, holding her back, stopped her words.

She watched in dismay as he easily accessed and scrolled through the pictures, presumably finding the one of him, and the ones she'd taken outside.

He closed one hand around the camera and took his other hand down from her chest. 'I'll take this. You can go.'

Zoe went cold inside. 'But you can't just take my camera—that's my property.'

Her most precious possession.

It had belonged to her father and it had gone everywhere with her since that awful—

She spoke rapidly to push down unwelcome memories. She didn't need those now. 'Are you Security? You can wipe all the pictures. I don't care. Just please give me back the camera.' She put out her hand. Panicking.

The man's voice was incredulous. 'You don't know who I am?'

She looked at him. She wasn't all that up to date on pop culture or gossip magazines, but she was fairly sure he wasn't an actor or a singer. Although he did look vaguely familiar. Maybe he was a male model. He certainly had the looks. Although there was something raw about him—as if he would never do anything so submissive as pose for a photograph.

'You're *not* Security?'

'I'm Maks Marchetti.'

He looked at her. She looked at him. Shock spread through her body.

Maks Marchetti.

He arched a brow. 'The Marchetti Group? We own the fashion house whose show you just crashed.'

Zoe could feel the blood draining south from her face. Faintly she said, 'I know who you are.'

The reason she hadn't recognised him was because he was the most reclusive of the three Marchetti brothers, who had inherited the business from their father on his death some years previously.

The Marchetti Group was at the very top end of exclusive, and had become even more so in the years since Marchetti Senior's death. It owned every major brand in the world—and if they didn't own it they were busy acquiring it. The brands they didn't own weren't worth mentioning.

And this man was a Marchetti. Which meant he could buy and sell everyone in that room.

She could hear music starting now. Presumably the show was kicking off. That dark grey gaze was unnervingly direct. He seemed unconcerned that he was missing the start. Zoe recalled that sense of aloofness she'd picked up from him.

'Shouldn't you be inside? If you could just give me back the camera I'll go and you'll never see me again.'

Maks Marchetti looked down at the woman in front of him, more transfixed than he liked to admit. At first glance she was pretty average. Average height, average weight and build. Slim. Petite, actually. But there was something about her that kept him looking—that had caught his attention when he'd looked over and seen the camera raised to her face, pointing directly at him.

She had honey-blonde shoulder-length hair. Finely etched brows. A delicate jaw. Straight nose. Her eyes were an arresting shade of green and blue. Aquamarine. Pretty.

More than pretty, actually.

But she had a scar—an indentation that dissected her top lip on one side, almost an inch long. There was another scar too, that ran from one upper cheekbone to under her hairline. They piqued his interest.

As if sensing his gaze on her, she ducked her head and her hair fell forward, covering her face. 'It's rude to stare.'

Maks had to curb an impulse to reach out and tip up her chin so he could see her. She was a complete stranger.

'It's rude to trespass.'

She looked up again, those eyes flashing green. They were long-lashed. She wore no make-up that he could see and her skin was flawless. Apart from the scars. It was the colour of pale cream roses with a hint of pink. It made him wonder what she would look like in the throes of passion. Would her eyes turn a deeper green when she was aroused? Would her cheeks flush a deeper pink?

An unexpected jolt of lust caught him by surprise. More than a jolt. Actually, she wasn't just pretty. She was beautiful—but in a way that crept up on him. He moved in a world that celebrated beauty so much that he'd almost become inured to it. But she had a kind of beauty he'd never seen before. Understated. Captivating.

Dio. What the hell was wrong with him?

He took a step back. 'Leave now and I won't have you prosecuted for trespassing.'

She went pale.

He ignored his conscience. 'We don't allow paparazzi into our shows.'

Her mouth opened and he noticed her lips. Wide and lush. Soft. Tempting. His eye was drawn to that intriguing scar again.

'I am *not* paparazzi.'

She'd drawn herself up, her whole body quivering as if she was indignant. Maks had to hand it to her: she was a good actress. He ignored the way he wanted to drop his gaze down over her body and study her more thoroughly. There was a distinct hum in his blood now and he did not welcome this distraction. Or attraction…

'Well, I'm afraid that sneaking into one of the biggest shows of the season, with wall-to-wall A-list guests, makes me a touch suspicious. And in any case this is not up for discussion.'

Maks Marchetti looked over her head and made a gesture. Zoe turned around to see two beefy security men approaching them. She swivelled back to Marchetti. 'Look, please, I didn't mean any harm. I'm really not paparazzi.'

But her words fell on deaf ears.

Marchetti said over her head, 'Please escort this young woman out. Make sure she doesn't ever get into another show again.'

Zoe's mouth fell open as her arms were taken on each side, lightly but firmly. She glared at Marchetti. How had she thought he was beautiful? The man was cruel and cold.

'Seriously? You're blacklisting me?'

Now she wouldn't get in even if she had a lanyard. Her dreams of breaking into the lower echelons of the fashion photography industry were going up in smoke.

The security guards started to lead her away. She saw her camera dangling carelessly from Marchetti's hand. 'What about my camera?'

He held it up. 'You lost it the moment you trespassed. Goodbye. I hope we don't meet again, for your sake.'

Zoe was being propelled backwards, and she knew she should turn around. She didn't even know this man and she'd gone from thinking he was gorgeous to hating him all within a few seismic minutes. But she couldn't tear her gaze from his.

And, worse, there was a feeling of...*hurt* at what he'd said. That he hoped they wouldn't meet again. What on earth was that about?

It galvanised her to say, 'Well, for what it's worth, Mr Marchetti, you're the last man on earth that *I* ever want to meet again.'

He lifted a hand—the one without her camera. He even let his mouth tip up at one corner. *'Ciao.'*

Maks watched the security men take the woman outside and disappear. It was crazy, but for a moment he'd almost wanted to go after them and tell them to let her go.

And do what? he scoffed at himself. *Look at her some more?*

He shook his head and went back into the show.

He watched it from the back of the room, barely taking in the rapturous applause at the end. And, even though he'd just watched some of the world's most beautiful women parade down a catwalk in front of him, he couldn't seem to get a pair of long-lashed aquamarine eyes out of his head.

He went still inside, though, when he realised that he hadn't even taken her name. She'd distracted him that much. He scowled. Just as well he'd ensured she wouldn't gain access again. He didn't need distractions like her.

Maks looked at the camera in his hand. It was an old Nikon, probably about twenty years old, and a bit battered. There was a bin nearby, and he knew he should just throw it away and put that brief encounter out of his head, say good riddance to the whole encounter. He wouldn't see her ever again.

A few hours later, Zoe looked broodingly out of the window of the train as it arrived back into London. Early autumn had been sunny in Paris, but London's late-afternoon skies were leaden and did little to elevate her mood. Every time she thought of that last image of Maks Marchetti, smirking and saying *ciao* with her camera dangling from his hand, she wanted to scream—or cry.

To her horror, tears prickled behind her eyelids. How could she have lost her beloved father's camera like that? It was probably at the bottom of a rubbish bin by now. Wiped clean of all pictures. Memory card destroyed.

Absently she touched the scar above her lip. It was that camera that had given her the scar. Both scars. When their car had crashed seventeen years ago, killing her parents and her younger brother. She'd been eight. Ben had been five. Her parents had been in their prime.

She'd been holding the camera in her hands and her father had looked back at her for a moment, telling her to be careful with it. And then… Then the world had exploded in a ball of fire and pain and her life had changed overnight. She'd become an orphan. She and the camera were the only things that had survived the crash.

Zoe took her hand down from her mouth and squeezed her eyes shut, as if that might block out the unwelcome memories. She did not need to go there now. She went there enough in her dreams and nightmares.

She opened her eyes again and forced emotion out. It was entirely her fault she'd lost her father's camera. She shouldn't have been so impulsive. If it hadn't been for that other photographer telling her that if she could get into an actual show then she might have a real chance to make some decent contacts then she wouldn't even have thought of it.

A frisson ran over her skin when she thought about the man. Maks Marchetti. He'd been so…intense. Overwhelming. She had to acknowledge now that, in spite of the stress of the situation which she'd found herself in—entirely her own fault—she'd felt alive in a way that had had nothing to do with the adrenalin running through her body.

He'd looked at her scars. Everyone did after a few seconds, when they registered them. She was used to the skin-prickling moment when eyes widened and then narrowed, followed by a quick look at her eyes to see if she'd noticed. Then a guilty or apologetic smile. Embarrassment.

Zoe knew she was lucky. Her scars weren't *that* disfiguring. But when Maks Marchetti had looked at them she hadn't felt the usual sense of invasion. She'd ducked her head because, disturbingly, she'd felt something else— awareness.

Zoe went cold inside. The same kind of awareness that had led her into trusting someone who had betrayed her trust. Who had almost done a lot worse than just betray her trust.

The train slowed down and Zoe clamped down on her rogue thoughts again, welcoming the sight of the station ahead.

She wasn't as naive as she had been before. Now if a man affected her she was doubly wary, because she knew how awareness, or desire, could hide the truth about someone until it was almost too late.

The train drew to a stop inside St Pancras Station.

She couldn't help wondering, though… If she knew better now, then why did she feel a sense of loss at the fact that she'd never meet Maks Marchetti again?

It was ridiculous. Right now he was presumably at a glamorous after-party, while Zoe was headed towards the labyrinthine Tube system to get back to her tiny East London flat. Their worlds couldn't be further apart. She was scarred—on the outside and the inside. He was not.

She'd learnt her lesson in attempting to infiltrate a world that was not open to her. The truth was that her love of photography was just a hobby—a hobby that was now getting her into trouble. The prospect of it ever becoming anything more seemed further away than ever. In the meantime, she had a living to earn.

Two weeks later, London

Zoe's arms ached, and her face ached even more from fake smiling. Her tray went from heavy to light and then heavy again, in relentless rotation, as she passed around glasses of champagne to the glittering *crème de la crème* of London's most famous and beautiful.

In an ironic twist of fate, the catering company she worked part-time for was catering a fashion event. The launch of a new head designer at a famous fashion house. It was being held in their flagship shop on Bond Street. And the label was owned by the Marchetti Group, of course.

Zoe felt the back of her neck prickle, but brushed the sensation away. She blamed it on her hair being tied up—a rule of the job. She always felt more exposed when it was up. Exposed, and then guilty for feeling exposed. Her scars were a reminder, after all, of the incident that had defined her life.

She told herself off for feeling paranoid. Maks Marchetti was in Paris. He was hardly likely to turn up at every event the group presided over.

Pushing him firmly from her mind, she turned and faced the other way for a bit, hoping her tray would lighten soon. And then she spotted someone across the room and her blood ran cold. A tall man. Broad. Short hair glinting dark blond under the lights. He wore a steel-grey suit, a white shirt open at the neck. He was holding a half-empty glass of champagne carelessly in one hand. His head was bent towards a tall, statuesque red-haired woman who was wearing a very short, very sparkly green dress, who had the longest legs Zoe had ever seen.

It was him.

As if sensing Zoe looking at him, he lifted his head and those all too familiar dark grey eyes met hers before she could even move. His gaze narrowed. Recognition dawned and his expression turned icy.

Zoe could practically read his lips. *What the hell is she doing here?* He said something else to the woman, never taking his gaze off Zoe, pinning her to the spot, and then came towards her, putting his glass down on a table.

She couldn't move. Like a deer caught in a car's headlights. He stopped right in front of her. She'd convinced herself over the last couple of weeks that he couldn't possibly be as beautiful as she remembered. But he was. Devastatingly so. Even if he was horrible and cruel.

'How did *you* get in here?'

'I'm working for Stellar Events.'

He made a rude sound. 'A likely story.'

He put his hands on the other side of her tray and the glasses wobbled precariously. Zoe came out of her shock. 'Hey, watch it. I *am* actually working here.'

'I don't think so. Give me the tray and get out of here.'

Zoe glared at him. 'No, I'm just doing my job. You can't chuck me out every time you see me.'

She gave a tug of the tray at the same moment that he relaxed his grip and stumbled backwards under the weight of it, losing her balance. As if in slow motion she watched the tray tip up towards her and then the inevitable trajectory of about a dozen glasses, full of sparkling wine, falling towards her and then crashing to the artfully polished concrete floor, spraying wine in an arc around them.

A second afterwards there was a collective sharp intake of breath and then silence. Zoe stood in shock, the front of her shirt soaked. Wine had splashed up into her face.

She stared at Maks Marchetti. He looked grim. There was movement near them and Zoe's boss appeared in her eyeline. An officious man in a suit, he'd been stressed already, and now he looked ready to blow completely. His face was red.

Zoe held the tray to her chest like a shield. She started to say, 'Steven, I'm so sorry—

'Stop talking. Clean this up and then see me in the kitchen.'

He made a motion to another waiter Zoe didn't know and he rushed over with a brush and pan. Someone else arrived with paper towels.

Zoe couldn't look at Maks Marchetti again. She bent down and started picking up the bigger pieces of glass, sucking in a breath when she pierced her finger.

Suddenly Marchetti was beside her, taking her hand, looking at the blood. 'Leave the glass. You'll hurt yourself.'

Zoe pulled her hand back, shocked at the zing of electricity that raced up her arm. She glared at him. 'As if you care. Just leave me alone, will you? You've already caused enough trouble.'

She ignored the pain in her finger and continued to pick up the glass. When she stood again, her face burning with humiliation, Marchetti was gone.

She went back to the kitchen, where her boss was waiting for her. She put down the tray full of bits of broken glass and he handed her an envelope. His rage was icy, but his face was even redder now.

'Do you have any idea who that was?'

Zoe's stomach sank. This wasn't going to end well. 'Unfortunately, I do know who that was.'

'What on earth were you doing, tussling over a tray with him?' He waved a hand, as if he didn't even want to hear her answer, then said, 'Maks Marchetti is one of the most important people in the fashion and luxury industry. And not only that, but his brother Nikos is here too this evening.' He handed her an envelope. 'I'm sorry, Zoe, but we can't keep you on this evening—not after this. We won't be contacting you again.'

Zoe's mouth dropped open. She started to formulate her defence and stopped. Nothing she could say would reverse this. They wouldn't forgive her for this public humiliation.

Before he left, Steven glanced at her hand. 'You're dripping blood everywhere. Clean yourself up, please, and leave.' Then he swept out.

Zoe looked at her hand stupidly. At her cut finger. Numbly she searched for and found a first aid kit, and cleaned the cut and put a plaster on her finger, wincing as it throbbed. She welcomed the pain. Damn Maks Marchetti anyway. Now she *really* hoped she never saw him again.

But unfortunately that was not to be the case. When she stepped into the street from the staff entrance a short while later, she saw a sleek low-slung silver car by the kerb. The door opened and a man uncoiled his tall, lean body from the driver's seat.

Maks Marchetti.

She started walking away, but he kept pace easily beside her. She was aware of her worn black trousers, white shirt—still damp from the wine—and her even more worn leather jacket. Flat shoes. Backpack on her back. She couldn't have been less like one of the women in that glittering space. And why did that even matter to her?

She stopped and rounded on Maks Marchetti. 'Look, what do you want now? I've been fired—isn't that enough for you? The last time I heard, streets were public spaces, so I don't think I'm actually infringing on hallowed Marchetti Group property now, am I?' She stopped, surprised at the depth of emotion she was feeling.

Maks put up a hand. To her surprise, he looked slightly... sheepish. He lowered his hand. 'I owe you an apology.'

Stupidly, Zoe said, 'You do?' And then she remembered what had happened. 'Yes, you do, actually.'

'I didn't mean for you to get fired. I saw you across the room and I...'

Maks trailed off, rendered uncharacteristically inarticulate for the first time in his life. He hadn't been able to get the woman in front of him out of his head for the past two weeks. She'd dominated his waking and sleeping moments.

When he'd spotted her across that room he'd been so surprised to see her that any kind of rationality had gone out of the window. He'd even forgotten that he'd come to the grudging conclusion that she wasn't actually paparazzi.

The truth was that she'd got to him. On some visceral level. From the moment he'd seen her camera lens pointed straight at him, provoking an extreme reaction. Not everyone would have reacted the way he had. His brother Nikos would have smiled and posed.

For Maks, though, camera lenses represented an intrusion of his privacy, and he'd spent the last two weeks wondering if he'd massively overreacted. A knee-jerk reaction to old trauma.

Yet when he'd seen her this evening, the mere sight of her had sparked that visceral reaction again. A need to see her up close juxtaposed with a need to push her away. And this time she hadn't even had a camera.

Because you took it.

Whatever it was about the way she made him react, he knew he couldn't let her walk away again. As much because he owed her this apology as for other, deeper and less coherent reasons.

Because you want her, whispered an inner voice.

He ignored it. She'd taken her hair down, but it couldn't hide her exquisite bone structure or delicate beauty. Or the scars. The one above her lip and the other one at her cheek. He wanted to reach out and trace them.

He curled his hand into a fist.

Abruptly he asked, 'Why did you sneak into the fashion show in Paris if it wasn't to take shots of celebrities and sell them?'

She swallowed. 'Do you believe I am not paparazzi?'

He nodded once. 'I looked through your photos. Street fashion shots. Landscapes. Architecture. People.'

Him. Zoe felt exposed again when she thought about focusing on his face that day two weeks ago.

His gaze lingered on her face now, intent. He looked at her scars. But, disconcertingly, like the last time, it didn't bother her as much as it had when she'd noticed people clocking them as they'd taken drinks from her tray at the event just now.

He was waiting for her response.

She sighed. 'I made an impulsive decision to sneak into the show when the opportunity presented itself. I've never been to a fashion show before, and they fascinate me. I was hoping that I might make some contacts with other photographers…break into the industry somehow. That's all.'

'You want to do fashion photography?'

Zoe squirmed a little. She'd never really articulated this to anyone before. 'It's something I've always been interested in, yes. But there's no way I'm remotely qualified.'

'Meanwhile you're working as a waitress?'

She shrugged self-consciously. 'Among other things—

childminding, cleaning offices, teaching English to refugees… Although I'm not paid to do that.' She stopped talking, suddenly aware that she was babbling about her peripatetic career. And to Maks Marchetti, who must be one of the richest people on the planet.

Suddenly awkward, she stepped back. 'Thank you for the apology. I'm sure you're required back inside. I should get going.' Zoe turned around.

'Wait.'

She stopped. Her heart was beating out of time. She felt breathless.

Maks Marchetti came and stood in front of her. To her surprise he said, 'Can we start again?' He held out a hand. 'I'm Maks Marchetti.'

Zoe knew she should just her head and step around him, saying something about having to get home and then put him out of her mind for good. But at that moment he smiled, and her breathlessness turned into asphyxiation. All good intentions turned to dust.

She had no defence for a smiling Maks Marchetti.

He'd been gorgeous from the moment she'd laid eyes on him, but he'd been aloof, and then condemnatory. Intimidating. She hadn't actually seen him smile. Not even when he'd been across the room at the event with that woman. But now he was smiling and he was…utterly irresistible.

Zoe had to force herself to breathe. She was feeling dizzy. And against every better judgement she found herself putting out her hand before she could stop herself. 'Zoe Collins. I'm Zoe Collins.'

Marchetti wrapped his hand around hers and that jolt of electricity zinged up her arm and into her blood. This time she didn't pull away. She couldn't.

He said, 'Zoe. It suits you. It's spiky.'

That gave Zoe the impetus to pull away. She almost cradled her hand to her body, as if she'd been burned. The air between them was charged. Zoe barely noticed people passing by. Traffic on the street. The warm early autumn evening. The dusky sky.

Her mouth tipped up ruefully. 'I'm not normally spiky. You seem to bring out the worst in me.'

Marchetti's smile faded. 'You lost your job because of me.'

Zoe made a face. 'It's not that big a deal, I only did a few jobs for them a month—if I was lucky.'

He looked at her for a long moment. And then he said, 'Still, I'd like to make it up to you. Will you join me for a drink?'

CHAPTER TWO

ZOE LOOKED AT him. 'A drink? Like…' She wanted to say *Like a date*, but stopped herself in time. The thought was too outlandish. Ridiculous. Maks Marchetti was feeling guilty, that was all.

He said, 'A drink. Like a way for me to apologise for being heavy-handed, not once but twice.'

See? Not a date.

As if she was anywhere close to his league, with her very ordinary looks and scars.

Zoe felt something drop inside her. He was being nice, that was all. 'Thank you—really. But you don't have to. It's fine. And I did trespass on your fashion show in Paris, so you were within your rights to throw me out.'

And confiscate my camera.

She felt a pang of pain when she thought of that.

Maks Marchetti said, 'It's not just to apologise, though. I'd like to take you for a drink to get to know you better. You…intrigue me.'

Zoe's brain seized. She intrigued him? Her, Zoe Collins, who wasn't remotely interesting. Not really.

'I…' She trailed off when she saw flashbulbs popping behind him, where one of the A-list celebrities was leaving the venue. She gestured. 'Shouldn't you go back? Isn't that your event?'

Marchetti didn't even look. 'I've shown my face, seen who I needed to see.'

Zoe shook her head, fiercely trying to push down the excitement that had flared. *She intrigued him.*

'Mr Marchetti, that's your world and this is my world.'

She gestured towards a nearby bus-stop. 'Thank you again for the offer, but it's probably not a good idea.'

Before she could take a step back he grimaced and said, 'It's Maks. *Mr Marchetti* reminds me of my father—never a good thing.'

Why? Zoe wanted to ask. But couldn't.

Then he frowned. 'Do you have a boyfriend at home?'

Zoe knew it would be the easiest lie and then she would be able to walk away, never to see him again. But something rogue inside her made her shake her head. 'No. I live alone. I am…alone.'

She hadn't meant it to come out like that, but as she said the words she felt a familiar sense of hollowness inside her. A chasm that she'd tried to fill with intimacy before, which had been a huge error of judgement.

She'd shied away from any kind of intimacy since. But the thought of walking away from Maks Marchetti right now was causing an almost physical resistance inside her. A little voice cajoled her. *It's just a drink—how dangerous could that be?* Except Zoe had a sense that, while she felt she could trust Maks Marchetti on a physical level, on an emotional level it would be a whole other story and one she hadn't really considered.

'So?' he asked. 'What's stopping you?'

It's just a drink.

Now Zoe felt ridiculous. She was projecting way too much onto what she was sure was just a polite overture, even if he had said she intrigued him.

'Okay, then. Yes, I'd like that.'

Maks wasn't prepared for the relief he felt. Most women he asked out were all too eager. Zoe had looked as if she was considering his question from a million angles before coming to her decision. Not what he was used to, but then he sensed nothing about this woman would be usual.

He said, 'I know a place not far from here. I'll drive.'

She looked at his car and seemed to go slightly pale in the dusky light, but then she said, 'Okay.'

Maks sent a quick text to give notice of their arrival, and as he drove he noticed that Zoe's hands were tight on the backpack on her lap.

'You're a nervous passenger?'

She flicked him a quick glance. 'Something like that.'

'You don't drive?'

She shook her head. 'No. Living in London, I don't really need to anyway.'

That was the platitude trotted out by most people who hadn't learned to drive and who lived in London, but Maks sensed there was something more to it.

'Don't worry,' he said. 'I'm an excellent driver.'

She flicked him another glance. When she saw his face she smiled and let out a small chuckle. 'I guess that shouldn't surprise me.'

Maks smiled back. He felt ridiculously buoyed up, to have defused her tension.

After a few minutes he pulled to a smooth stop outside an anonymous-looking townhouse. He unclipped his seat-belt as a valet came around to his door. 'This is a private club. I hope that's okay?'

Zoe did her best to sound nonchalant. 'Sure.'

Someone opened her door and she got out, her legs feeling slightly wobbly as they inevitably did after a car journey—even a short one. Maks hadn't lied, though. She'd felt cocooned in his car, and he'd driven with total confidence and competence.

For someone who was as hyper-alert as she was in cars, she'd almost let go of her alertness for a moment. A disconcerting sensation to admit to.

Maks joined her where she stood on the pavement. He

indicated a set of steps that led up to a huge oak door. There were no markings on the building and Zoe sensed the exclusivity.

She moved forward and went up the steps, very aware of the man just behind her. As she got closer to the door she wondered why this moment should feel so momentous. She really didn't want it to. She didn't want to attribute anything special to this...date. She was sure it would be a one-off. And she told herself it wasn't as if she was in the market for anything more—not with her woeful track record...

The door opened and a sleek uniformed woman stood back to let them enter. 'Miss Collins and Mr Marchetti, you're very welcome. Shall I take your coats?'

Surprise that the hostess knew her name had Zoe hesitating on the threshold for a second. Then Maks's hand touched her back. It was barely noticeable through two layers of clothes, yet it burned like a brand.

As Zoe followed Maks's barely discernible prompt to move forward into the hushed space, she knew with a sense of doom that she was in trouble. Because this felt momentous, and there was nothing she could do to quash it.

'What do you think?'

Maks looked at Zoe's rapt face as she took in the surroundings of the private club. She was looking up at a massive chandelier lit with hundreds of fake candles that flickered with a surprisingly realistic effect. He wanted to tuck her hair behind her ear so he could see her better. And then he wondered what the hell he was thinking. He never usually indulged in moments of PDA, even minute ones. They tended to be misconstrued.

Zoe said, 'It's...very decadent. It reminds me of a boudoir.' She glanced at him quickly. 'Not that I've ever been in a boudoir.'

Pink tinged her cheeks. He wondered if she kept her hair down to hide her scars.

He looked around and made a face. 'It's a bit over the top, and about five years out of date. We're redecorating soon.'

She looked at him. 'You own this place?'

'It's part of our portfolio,' he said carelessly.

'Is there anywhere you *don't* own?'

He looked at her. 'Plenty…but we're working on it.'

'Total world domination?'

He smiled minutely. 'Something like that.'

They looked at each other for a long moment and eventually she broke the contact. 'Why are there curtains on every booth?'

She was looking at the long heavy velvet curtains, currently drawn back from their own booth.

'So that they can be pulled across if one wants privacy.'

She frowned. 'But why—?'

And then she stopped suddenly, the pink in her cheek deepening as she obviously thought it through.

'Oh.'

Oh, indeed.

It was a long time since Maks had seen a woman blush and it had a direct effect on his blood. Making it surge. He shifted in the seat.

A waiter approached at that moment, with a tray containing a bottle of champagne in an ice bucket and two glasses. When the waiter had poured the champagne and left, Zoe said, 'Is this really necessary? This isn't a date.'

Maks handed her a glass and looked at her as he said, 'Isn't it?'

Zoe's heart palpitated. Maks was so close she could see that his eyes were lighter grey around the edges. His jaw was stubbled.

He tipped his glass towards hers. *'Salute.'*

After a moment she clinked her glass on his and it gave a melodic chime. 'Cheers.'

She took a sip of wine and it fizzed against her tongue, igniting her taste buds, leaving a crisp, dry taste in her mouth.

'Your accent…you're not English?' he asked.

Zoe tensed. She wouldn't have expected him to notice that. He was foreign himself. She shook her head. 'No, I'm Irish. But I've been living here since I was eighteen.'

'Do you have family in Ireland?'

She shook her head quickly, instinctively shying away from more questions. She deflected the attention to him. 'You're Italian?'

'Half-Italian, half-Russian. My mother was Russian.'

'And you have…brothers?' Zoe knew he shared control of the Marchetti Group, but not much more than that.

He nodded. 'Two half-brothers. And one half-sister on my mother's side. She was the result of an affair my mother had with an American bodyguard. One of her many affairs while married to my father.'

This was said with no intonation of emotion, but Zoe sensed the undercurrents. 'Are you close to your brothers and sister?'

A muscle pulsed in Maks's jaw. 'My brothers and I didn't grow up together. It's only since our father died and we took control of the company that we've got to know one another better. So, no, I wouldn't say we're close, but I am very close to my sister.'

'How old is she?'

'Sasha is twenty-five.'

The same age as Zoe. It sounded as if his parents' marriage had been volatile, which would have undoubtedly brought him and his sister together.

Afraid that he would ask about her family again, Zoe asked, 'Did you spend time in Russia, growing up?'

He took a sip of champagne and shook his head. Zoe noticed his hands. Masculine. Long fingers. Strong. A shiver of something that felt like longing went through her.

'Not really. My mother's family cut ties with her when she married my father and he got his hands on her inheritance. It was his modus operandi—fleecing his wives of their fortunes to fund his own ambitions.'

She was surprised at his honesty.

As if reading her mind, he said sardonically, 'I'm not telling you anything that isn't available online.'

'So where *did* you grow up?'

'Rome and Paris, mainly.'

At that moment they were interrupted by a young woman in a trouser suit, hair tied back. She looked at Zoe. 'Sorry to interrupt,' she said. Then she looked at Maks as she handed him a small bag. 'This is it, sir.'

He took it. 'Thanks, Maria.'

The girl left and Maks handed the slightly bulky-looking bag to Zoe. 'This is yours.'

She took it and her heart thumped as she felt the weight and shape of it. She looked at Maks as she opened the cloth bag and took out her camera. The rush of relief was almost overwhelming. As was the surge of emotion.

When she'd gathered herself she looked at him. 'I thought you would have thrown it away.'

'I almost did...but something stopped me.'

'I'm glad you didn't.' Her voice was husky.

'It's important to you. Clearly.'

She nodded. 'It belonged to my father. He was a photographer...among other things.'

'Would I have heard of him?'

Zoe avoided answering directly by saying, 'He died a

long time ago—that's why this camera has such sentimental value for me.'

'You're a good photographer. Did you study?'

She shook her head, self-conscious now. 'I'm self-taught.'

'So you sneaked into that show to try and get some experience.'

Shame lanced her. She put the camera down. 'Look, I'm so sorry—'

But he cut her off, saying gruffly, 'When I saw your camera pointing at me I overreacted. I don't tolerate invasions of privacy well. My sister and I...we were constantly hounded by the paparazzi while we were growing up, thanks to our parents' very public affairs, fights and then divorce.'

'I'm sorry to hear that.'

Maks shrugged. 'It came with the territory.'

'How old were you when they divorced?'

'About fifteen. My mother is on husband number three now.'

Maks's voice was hard and flat, brooking no further discussion. She could empathise with that. There was a lot she didn't want to talk about either.

She picked up the camera again. 'Thank you for this. It means a lot.'

'Why did you take a photograph of me?'

Zoe felt heat rise into her face. She forced herself to look at Maks, even though she was squirming inside. She felt defensive under that cool grey gaze. 'I'm sure you don't need me to tell you you're a good-looking man.'

'There were infinitely better-looking men than me there that day.'

Zoe could have debated that point. She shrugged, trying to feign a nonchalance she wasn't feeling. 'You caught my eye... Everyone else was looking around, looking for attention, but you looked…contained.' Zoe winced. How could she articulate the way he'd sent off such an aloof vibe…?

Maks's mouth twitched. 'I don't tolerate small-talk well. Inane conversation, talk of the latest trends… I like to make my own judgements.'

His gaze narrowed on her and Zoe felt breathless all over again. A hazard with this man.

He said, '*You* caught my attention.'

Her heart thumped. 'But… I'm nothing special.'

Maks knew she wasn't fishing for compliments. She sounded genuinely perplexed.

'I haven't stopped thinking about you for the past two weeks. I kept your camera. I looked through your photographs. There are none of you.'

'Why would I take pictures of myself?'

'You're beautiful.'

Her expression shut down, and she avoided his eye. 'You don't have to say things like that. I know I'm not.'

Once again Maks fought the urge to tip up her chin, make her look at him. 'You might not be seven feet tall and have the kind of outlandish traffic-stopping looks that models have, but, yes, you're beautiful.'

Zoe glanced at Maks suspiciously. But he wasn't laughing at her. She'd been given compliments before, and she'd found herself soaking them up like a flower responding to the sun's rays, but soon she'd realised they were empty compliments, used to manipulate her.

This felt different. Which made it dangerous. Because she'd extricated herself from a situation with an ex-boyfriend who had been infinitely less in every way than the man in front of her.

Maks Marchetti left Dean Simpson in the dust. So how

much more damage could a man like Maks do, if she left him in?

She didn't want to answer that, because on the other side of fear was something she didn't want to acknowledge: *hope*. She'd allowed herself to feel hope before and had learnt a harsh lesson. Did she really want to risk that again? No.

'Look, I'm under no illusions. Your industry celebrates perfect beauty, and we both know that I do not come close to that ideal. Not with a scarred face.'

Maks cocked his head to one side, looking at her. His gaze moved over her face and she felt hot again. She cursed herself for drawing his attention like this. She'd hoped mention of her scars, of the fact that she wasn't perfect, might act as a deterrent. Remind him that she only intrigued him. Nothing more.

'Perfection is overrated. Believe me. I'm far more interested in beautiful flaws. Everyone is flawed, Zoe, but most just hide it underneath a pseudo-perfect exterior.'

Zoe's breath hitched. She really hadn't expected to hear him say something like that. His words resonated deep inside her, where she held exactly the same sentiments.

Before she could respond, Maks was reaching for her hand and holding it up. Electricity short-circuited her brain.

He was frowning. 'Your finger—is it okay?'

She looked at her hand stupidly and saw the plaster over her injured finger. She wasn't sure if it was throbbing now because of him or because it hurt. She couldn't pull her hand back.

'It's fine. It wasn't a deep cut.'

'Still, it was my fault you hurt yourself.'

Zoe forced herself to move her hand away. 'Honestly, it's fine.'

She took another sip of champagne, hoping it might calm the hectic beat of her pulse. She would never have expected someone like Maks Marchetti to prove to be so…perceptive. And the fact that he'd kept her camera and returned it kept emotion bubbling far too near the surface.

She needed to take a breath. Get her bearings before she lost all sense of reality. Before he could speak again or, worse, touch her and scramble her brain.

'Would you excuse me for a minute?' she asked.

Maks said, 'Of course.'

He motioned to one of the staff, who came over and showed Zoe where the restrooms were. She went inside and leant against the closed door for a moment, wondering if it would ever be possible to be in this man's company and not feel dizzy.

She chastised herself as she pushed away from the door. She wouldn't be seeing him again. Stupid even to go there.

She went over to the sink and ran the cold tap, putting her wrists underneath the water and then splashing some on her face. She stood up and looked at herself critically. Her face was flushed, her eyes far too wide and awed-looking. Her hair was down and tousled—and not in a good way.

Her leather jacket looked worn, and her shirt still showed a damp stain from the spilled wine. Zoe groaned. She most definitely was not sophisticated—or beautiful. Especially not when compared to the women she'd been serving wine to at the event. The man needed his eyes checked. Perhaps he only found her interesting because she was so different to everyone else in his milieu? He was just jaded.

She battled against the fizz in her blood that spoke of too many dangerous things—excitement chief among them.

She couldn't indulge this heady moment any longer.

Maks watched Zoe return to the table. The lines of her body were tense and her eyes were avoiding his. He knew instinctively even before she opened her mouth what she was going to say.

She stopped at the other side of the table and finally looked at him. 'This has been lovely. Thank you for the drink, but I really should be going now. I have to work in the morning and I don't live near here.'

Maks had to curb every urge he had to persuade her to stay. Not something he was used to having to do. She reminded him of a fawn, ready to bolt. She was resisting this…this thing between them, and he was more intrigued than ever.

He said, with a carelessness he didn't feel, 'Sure, no problem. I'll give you a lift home.'

Her eyes grew wide. 'Really, there's no need, I'm all the way over in East London. It'll be far quicker on the Tube.'

Maks looked at his watch. It was after eleven p.m. 'And more dangerous,' he said. 'I insist. The roads will be quiet now. It won't take any longer.'

She looked as if she was inclined to argue, but eventually said, 'Okay—if you're sure it's not out of your way.'

It was. Massively. But for the first time in a long time Maks felt energised, and there was no way he was letting this woman slip through his fingers again.

'It's not a problem.'

He stood up and led the way out. The hostess behaved with utter discretion and showed no hint of surprise even though they'd only arrived a short while before.

Back in the car, Zoe gave him directions and Maks drove away from the Bond Street area. He could see her hands clasping her bag again out of the corner of his eye. She was tense.

To distract her, he asked, 'Why did you leave Ireland? By all accounts the country is thriving. My brother has a house there and his wife is Irish. They have a baby son.'

Just saying those words sent a fresh jolt of shock through Maks. He was still coming to terms with the fact that his playboy brother Nikos had recently discovered that he'd fathered a child and was now married.

The thought of being careless enough to find himself having to consider marriage for the sake of a child made Maks go cold. No way would he subject any child of his to the prospect of a dysfunctional marriage, and he didn't know any other kind.

Beside him, Zoe shrugged. He welcomed a diversion from thoughts of his brother and babies and marriage.

'I wanted to travel and explore the world outside of Ireland.'

'Have you been anywhere else?' Maks glanced at her and saw that her hair had swung forward again. He had to stop himself from pulling it back. He hated not being able to see her face.

'A little…around Europe. Not as much as I'd like.'

Maks, having become used to reading people and situations ever since his parents had waged their psychological warfare, guessed that Zoe wasn't giving him the whole story. But he wouldn't push. For now.

A companionable silence fell in the sleek car as it easily ate up the distance between the fashionable centre of London and the far less salubrious area where she lived. Zoe hated to admit how comfortable she felt. She wasn't used to comfortable silences with men. Although admittedly she didn't have much experience…

'It's the next right and then immediately left,' Zoe said quickly, realising they were practically at her door. 'This is fine.'

Maks pulled to a smooth stop in a space between two cars. 'You live here?'

Zoe bristled slightly, imagining how the tall, scruffy house must look to him. 'Yes. My flat is on the top floor.' *Her tiny, one-bedroom flat.*

Maks undid his belt and opened his door, getting out. Zoe had to scramble to catch up. He was already at the bottom of her steps.

He put out a hand. 'Your keys?'

Zoe looked at him. 'I can let myself in. This is fine—you can go now.'

He shook his head. 'I'm not leaving until I know you're safe.'

She let out an exasperated sound. 'This area is probably safer than where we just were! It's a tight-knit community.'

'Zoe.'

She shivered at the way he said her name, with a slight hint of an accent, an emphasis on the 'Z', making it sound exotic, and at his insistence on seeing her safe.

His hair glinted under the moonlight and he looked almost otherworldly against the very humdrum backdrop of houses. Yet he wasn't getting out of there as quickly as he could. Rushing back to his rarefied world.

She dug into her bag and held out her keys, saying a little huffily, 'You're being ridiculous.'

He took the keys and went up the steps. She followed him. He opened the front door, which didn't stick the way it usually did for her. Then, instead of giving her the keys, he said, 'Lead on.'

Zoe rolled her eyes. 'You asked for it—there are five flights and no lift.'

But of course who was out of breath when they got to the top? Not Maks, who was showing no signs of strain. Zoe could feel the heat in her cheeks and beads of sweat on her brow, the lack of breath. Except she couldn't be sure if that was from the exertion or knowing he had been right behind her the whole way up.

She turned around at her door and held out her hand. 'My keys, please. I'm safe now.'

Maks held on to her keys. 'How do you know there isn't an intruder inside?'

Zoe wanted to stamp her foot. 'I'm sure there isn't.'

Maks arched his brow. 'You're really not even going to offer me some water before I make the long trip back down to the bottom?'

There was a glint of devilry in his eyes that completely dissolved Zoe's resistance. She grabbed the keys out of his hand. 'Fine—you can assure yourself that I'm totally safe.'

She turned around and opened the door and pushed it open, turning on the light at the same time. The soft glow illuminated the tiny room, with its sofa covered in a colourful throw and the plants by the window, which was open a crack to let air in. Photos covered every available wall space.

Zoe turned around, expecting to see horror on Maks's face at such a rustic basic room, but he was stepping over the threshold, his eyes taking it all in, not looking surprised. Looking…interested.

At the last moment Zoe remembered her manners. 'I don't have anything alcoholic, but I can offer you some tea or coffee?'

'Coffee would be great, thank you. Black, no sugar.'

No frills. Like the man.

Zoe went into her tiny galley kitchen, off which was the even smaller bedroom and bathroom. She made the coffee, glancing through the hatch to see what Maks was up to. His hands were in his pockets and he was staring at the photos on the wall.

The fact that he was here, in her private space, should feel…overwhelming. She'd never felt entirely comfortable when Dean had been here, which should have been an alarm she paid heed to. But Maks being here…it didn't feel intrusive, or uncomfortable. She felt safe.

She brought him his coffee and he took the cup, barely glancing at her. 'Who is this?' He pointed to a black and white picture on the wall. It was of a young girl with a huge smile that almost eclipsed the horrific scars on her face.

Zoe held her own mug of coffee in both hands. 'That's Fatima. She's a refugee from Syria. I do some work with the Face Forward charity.'

Maks looked at her. He was frowning. 'That was set up by Ciro Sant'Angelo, no? To help people with scarring?'

Zoe nodded, feeling self-conscious of her own scars. 'Do you know him?'

Ciro Sant'Angelo was an Italian billionaire—she wouldn't be surprised.

Maks looked back at the picture. 'Our paths have crossed. I admire what he's doing. This is a great photo.'

'Thank you.' Zoe felt ridiculously pleased at his praise.

He looked at her. 'If it's not too personal a question, how did you get your scars?'

Zoe had no time to school her expression or hide. She'd absently tucked her hair behind her ears. So she couldn't escape Maks's intense gaze, demanding the full truth. Behind him, on a shelf, she could see the framed photograph of herself and her family, taken before that awful—

A lump rose in her throat and she spoke quickly to counteract it. 'It was a car accident.'

'Is that how your father died?'

Zoe nodded quickly, pushing down the emotion. 'And my mother and little brother.'

Maks frowned. 'How old were you?'

'Eight.' Her voice was clipped. Abrupt.

'That's why you were tense in the car? Why you don't drive?'

She nodded.

There was a silence. And then, 'Zoe... I—'

She cut him off, dreading his pity. 'It's fine. You don't have to say anything. It was a long time ago. It was an accident.'

My fault.

Feeling far too exposed now, on a million levels, Zoe took the coffee cup out of Maks's hand and took it back to the kitchen, not caring that she was slopping coffee on her floor.

'Like I said, I have to work tomorrow.'

She came back into the living area and went to the front door, opening it. She avoided looking directly at Maks, which wasn't the easiest thing when he took up so much space.

'Thank you for dropping me home.'

'I take it you're asking me to leave?'

His tone was dry. She glanced at him, suddenly afraid that he wouldn't take no for an answer, even though instinctively she felt safe with him, which was something she didn't really want to analyse.

But he didn't look angry. He appeared unconcerned that she was being so rude. She felt contrite. 'Yes, look…sorry. It's been a long day.'

So why didn't she feel tired? Why did she feel as if she was full of fizzing anticipation and a breathlessness that was becoming far too familiar in his presence?

Maks looked at Zoe. She was tense again. Reminding him of that fawn, ready to bolt.

He walked towards her and saw how her hand tightened on the door handle.

'Okay, I can take a hint. I'll leave… But before I do I want you to be honest with me.'

She looked up at him and Maks had to stop himself from staring at her soft mouth.

'What do you mean?'

'You feel it too, don't you? This...energy between us. Chemistry. Desire.'

Colour spilled into her cheeks even as she shook her head. When she spoke she sounded breathless, and it had a direct effect on Maks's body.

'No, I don't... I don't think I do.'

Maks smiled, because it was a long time since he'd had to seduce a woman. 'Liar.'

Now Zoe looked bewildered. 'Why are you interested in me?'

'Why are you so suspicious?'

'Because I'm just...nothing special. And I'm not looking for compliments.'

'I know,' Maks said.

'I'm just normal. Nothing extraordinary.'

'Your pictures aren't *"just normal"*. You have a talent. And you're beautiful. I want you, Zoe, more than I've wanted anyone in a long time.'

Her cheeks glowed. 'You're very direct. Has anyone ever told you that?'

A memory flashed into Maks's head of his mother, her face contorted with fury, her hand coming out of nowhere to slap him across the cheek, her spittle hitting his face as she said, *I owe you nothing.*

'On a rare occasion,' Maks said dryly, pushing down that rogue memory of the time when he'd confronted his mother about her woeful mothering skills.

Zoe looked up at Maks Marchetti. She couldn't believe he'd just told her he wanted her. *Her.* Boring, ordinary Zoe Collins.

But he didn't think she was ordinary, or boring.

It was too seductive...too much. She could feel secret parts of herself that she'd exposed before wanting to unfurl and bask in this man's dynamic presence. *Dangerous* to want those things. Because she'd wanted them before and she'd paid for it. For her naivety. For her vulnerability.

But, in truth, Dean Simpson hadn't really had the power to truly wound her. She'd had a lucky escape. Whereas this man… She sensed a level of danger that she would be wise to heed.

He looked as immovable as a massive stone statue. But treacherously, in the same moment she could acknowledge the danger, she also felt it dissipating, to be replaced by temptation.

Desperation gripped her at the thought that he might see how tempted she was. She needed to nip this in the bud now—prove to Maks that he was delusional. Surely if she could prove that he'd leave, and then she could get on with her life and forget that she'd ever met him?

As if you could forget a man like this, taunted an inner voice.

It was a taunt that turned her desperation to panic. Panic strong enough to make her step closer to him and say, 'I'll prove to you that there's really nothing between us.'

A glint came into his eye. 'Go on, then.'

CHAPTER THREE

ZOE KNEW HE was issuing a challenge, but she had no option but to follow it through now. She sucked in a breath and stepped even closer. Maks made no move to touch her. She reached up, putting her hands on his shoulders, coming up on her toes.

He was so tall, so broad. Every part of her tingled with her awareness of him as a virile male in his prime.

That had to be all it was. She was only human. It couldn't be desire uniquely for *him*. And he would soon realise that she really didn't hold any appeal for him.

She reached up as much as she could, her hands gripping his shoulders, and pressed her mouth to his before she could lose her nerve.

But the nerves, the sense of panic, the desire to prove him wrong…all was incinerated in a flash of electric heat as soon as her lips met the firm contours of his mouth.

Zoe was vaguely aware that she'd intended this to be a quick physical transaction, merely to prove Maks Marchetti wrong. But she couldn't move. *Didn't want to.* Her lips clung to his in a timeless moment when everything was suspended on a breath…which she finally let out like a sigh against his mouth.

It was a sigh of resignation, a sigh of futility, a sigh of recognition that the hectic throbbing pulse of her blood wasn't just because she was a human reacting to a virile male. It was because something in her resonated so deeply with something in him that she would never be the same again.

She could feel the sheer whipcord strength of his body

but she was still not close enough. She wanted to move against him, let all that heat and strength envelop her.

Of their own volition her lips opened, as if they literally couldn't bear to keep shut. Breath flowed. Her tongue-tip moved forward, seeking to taste. But she had barely touched the seam of his mouth when she suddenly realised what she was doing and pulled back, as if stung.

Maks Marchetti was looking at her. She realised that she was still clinging to him, reaching up, straining to get closer. She pulled her hands off him and stepped back so suddenly she almost fell.

Her cheeks burned. She ducked her head and let her hair fall around her face. She was terrified to look at him again and see his expression. Terrified to get confirmation of what she'd set out to prove—that he couldn't possibly want her.

She'd failed miserably in proving she didn't want him, though. She'd been clinging to him like a monkey, and she was sure he'd only been seconds away from having to physically remove her—

'Zoe... I can practically hear your thoughts, they're so loud.'

She looked up before she could stop herself. His eyes were glittering, almost silver now. His mouth was quirking. This was even worse. He was *laughing* at her.

Zoe stalked over to the door and pulled it open. She didn't look at him again. 'I think you should leave now.'

He came over and the door was pushed closed again. But Maks was still in the room. Zoe looked at him. He was shaking his head. No quirking mouth now. Deadly serious.

He reached out and tucked a lock of her hair behind her ear. And then he moved closer. The air grew thick and heavy. His hand was still in her hair.

He said, 'May I?'

Zoe's heart beat fast. He hadn't left. He wasn't laughing at her. He was looking at her mouth as if mesmerised and now…at her eyes. She had nowhere to hide. She just nodded.

He made a total mockery of her clumsy kiss by taking her face in his hands and tilting it up to his with an assurance born of experience and mastery. She could feel the rough abrasion of his palms and fingers against her jaw and cheeks. Rough, not smooth. Evidence that he wasn't as civilised as he looked.

His mouth touched hers, lightly at first, as if testing… Zoe held her breath, afraid to move in case he stopped. Their breaths intermingled. He kissed the corner of her mouth, taking her by surprise. And then the other corner, where the scar dissected her lip.

Her legs felt weak. She had to lock her knees to stay standing.

And then his mouth settled over hers completely, and she had to close her eyes against the burning intensity in his for fear that he might see the effect he was having on her.

His mouth was hard, but soft, coaxing a response that she couldn't hold back, giving it as instinctively as a flower gave itself to the power of the sun. She opened her mouth on a sigh that turned into a shiver of excitement when Maks's tongue touched hers, demanding more, demanding everything.

Zoe had been kissed before. She'd even enjoyed it— until she hadn't. But this went beyond mere enjoyment. This was…elemental. A conflagration burning her up from the inside out, leaving no cell untouched or un-scorched.

Time faded away. All she was aware of was the hectic beat of her heart and the pounding of her blood. She strained to get closer to Maks, winding her arms around his neck.

And then he broke the kiss.

Zoe opened her eyes with effort. She was dizzy. She re-alised she was all but plastered to Maks and that his hands were on her waist, helping to support her.

Her breath was choppy. Shakily she took her arms down and moved aside, dislodging Maks's hands.

'I think that's proved the point,' he said.

Her brain felt sluggish. She felt undone. 'The point…'

'That there's chemistry between us.'

Was that what it was called?

Zoe's whole body was throbbing. She wanted Maks to kiss her again, to stop talking. She knew she didn't want to think about what was happening here, because that would be way too scary.

He took a step back. Her belly lurched. 'Where are you going?'

'You want me to stay?'

'I—'

She stopped. For a moment she'd almost said *yes*, and as the full realisation of that sank in—how quickly she'd forgotten what had happened the last time she'd allowed a man close—sanity cooled her heated brain.

'No, I don't want you to stay.'

'Even if you said yes, I'd still leave.'

Zoe looked at him. She was surprised, and not liking the little voice that whispered inside her head. *He's differ-ent. This is different.*

'Why?'

Maks took a step closer again. 'Because I can see that you're not ready. You're skittish. Something has happened to you. You don't trust me.'

It took a few seconds for Zoe to absorb that, and when she did his words landed in her belly like a cold stone. *'Something has happened to you. You don't trust me.'* She felt totally exposed now. In a way that she'd promised herself she wouldn't ever again.

Zoe folded her arms. 'You think you see a lot, Mr Marchetti.'

He smiled, but it was rueful. 'I'm good at reading people. A lesson I learnt at the hands of selfish and self-absorbed parents.'

She didn't want to know that about him. She didn't want to think of him and his sister dealing with their parents' bitter divorce.

She went to the door and opened it.

Maks said from behind her, 'Give me your phone.'

She turned around. 'Why would I do that?'

'Because this doesn't end here. But I'm going to leave the ball in your court.'

Torn between wanting to shut down that arrogance and wanting to know what he meant to do, Zoe made a huffing sound and then went to her backpack and pulled out her phone. She handed it to Maks, who took it and punched in some numbers. He handed it back, and somehow she resisted the urge to check it. There was something about his confidence that was as irritating as it was seductive.

He went to the door. She felt that lurch again—as if something very primal inside her objected to him leaving.

She walked over. He was already on the other side of the door.

'I look forward to hearing from you,' he said.

Zoe held on to the door. 'You might not hear from me at all.'

He looked at her for a long moment. 'I think I will. And then you'll tell me what happened to you.'

The thought of telling him of her humiliation made her go cold. It helped her to stiffen her spine and say, 'Goodbye, Maks.'

He shook his head as he backed away, his mouth quirking up. '*Ciao,* Zoe.'

He turned, and he'd disappeared down the stairs before she could say anything else. She closed the door only after she'd heard the door close downstairs, and then the powerful throttle of his car's engine.

She got ready for bed in a bit of a stupor, still slightly stunned at everything that had happened this evening.

She'd lost her job.

In fairness, it hadn't exactly been her main source of income. Truth be told, she didn't have a main source of income. She was an expert in doing lots of things and committing to none. Not even photography. Because committing to something meant showing some kind of vulnerability, risking a massive fail or, worse, pain and loss.

Zoe scowled at herself in the small bathroom mirror. And that was why she didn't need to invite a man like Maks Marchetti into her life. Because he saw too much and he made her feel too much. And not just physically. That impulse she'd had to ask him to stay scared her even now. It had been so immediate. Visceral. And he was a stranger.

But you want him in a way that's different—

She clamped down on painful memories. She'd confused desire with being able to trust someone before. But that kiss had blown any kind of understanding of desire she'd had before out of the water. What she'd experienced had been child's play. This was the real deal. Earthy, raw, out of control. She knew instinctively that Maks Marchetti was a man who would demand nothing less than total surrender. And that was something Zoe couldn't imagine giving. To anyone. It would ask too much of her.

She looked at herself critically. Pyjamas buttoned up to the neck. Face scrubbed so clean that her scars stood out in pink lines. Superficial scars that hid far deeper scars.

Maks Marchetti would soon forget all about a woman who had intrigued him just for a moment. She wouldn't be using his number and he wouldn't be knocking on her door again.

'What?' Maks growled at his assistant without turning around from where he stood at the window of his London office.

The city was spread out before him, with the Thames snaking between iconic buildings and under even more iconic bridges, but Maks couldn't have cared less.

All that had consumed him for a week now was, *Why the hell hasn't she got in touch with me?*

Zoe Collins. The woman he'd shared probably the most chaste kiss of his life with, and yet it had left an erotic imprint that lingered in his blood, waking him every night with his body aching for sexual fulfilment.

'Um…boss, it's the fact that you're meant to be overseeing that shoot in New York at the moment…'

Maks turned around to face the young man. He arched a brow. 'And clearly I'm not?'

Because he was loath to leave London in case she called. When he never normally made decisions based on a lover who wasn't even a lover. *Yet.* The thought that she might never be a lover evoked an almost violent reaction inside him.

He would know her.

'They've decided to reschedule and relocate to St Petersburg, in the hope that you can attend while you're there for your meetings.'

Maks should feel slightly chastened by the fact that one of the world's biggest fashion houses cared enough about his opinion to reschedule an advertising campaign to suit his schedule, but he didn't. He was filled with a sense of resolve.

'Tell them I'll be there.'

And I won't be alone.

No matter how he had to do it, he would have Zoe Collins by his side and in his bed.

Zoe packed her bag as the people left the classroom. One of the young women turned around at the door and came back, surprising Zoe with an impromptu hug.

Zoe hugged her back, and smiled. 'What's that for?'

'Just to say thank you. You don't know how much it means, you helping us find our way in this new life.'

Zoe blushed, embarrassed. 'Don't be daft. If I wasn't here someone else would be.'

The girl shook her head. She was serious. Too serious. She'd seen awful things. She'd lost her entire family.

'Maybe, Miss Collins. But you are the one here, helping us, so thank you.'

Zoe's heart constricted as she watched the young woman in the headscarf walk out. She couldn't imagine not being here to help these people. Teaching English to newly arrived immigrants was such a basic thing, and the sense of reward she got from it made her feel guilty enough that she was happy it was on a voluntary basis.

She was about to leave when her mobile phone pinged with a message. She frowned and picked it out of her bag. Not having close family or friends meant that she wasn't used to receiving the casual messages everyone else took for granted.

She unlocked her phone to see a text from…

Her heart stopped. *Him.*

Hi Zoe…

She texted back,

How do you have my number?

I made sure I called myself from your phone when I put in my number, so I knew I'd have it.

Zoe's heart was palpitating. All week he'd haunted her waking and sleeping moments. A dozen times she'd almost deleted his number and then stopped herself at the last moment.

She typed back.

I would have called you if I was interested.

An answer came almost immediately.

Oh, you're interested.

Zoe wanted to scowl, but it turned into a grudging smile. She couldn't deny the rush of excitement. And also a treacherous sense of relief.

Before she could think of how to respond to that he sent another text.

I'm outside, waiting for you. Interesting place.

Zoe nearly dropped her phone. She looked up, suddenly terrified he'd be lounging in the doorway, smirking at her. But it was empty. He could hardly mean...

She walked out of the room with her bag, down the corridor of the local community centre. Not the prettiest building in the world, by any stretch of the imagination, and certainly not the kind of place for a man like—

He was here.

Zoe stepped outside the main doors to see Maks Marchetti, lounging against the same low-slung car he'd been driving a week ago. Except this time he was dressed more casually, wearing dark trousers and a dark grey long-sleeved top. She didn't have to inspect it to guess that it was probably cashmere, and it clung to his muscles far too lovingly, leaving little to the imagination.

Zoe felt self-conscious in her worn jeans and T-shirt, worn under an even more worn V-necked jumper. Scuffed trainers.

She walked over. 'What are you doing here?' She sounded accusing and winced inwardly. This man precip-itated extreme reactions in her.

'I got bored waiting for you to call and sought you out. You'd mentioned teaching English, and it wasn't hard to find out where some local classes were listed.'

Zoe hated to admit that she was impressed. 'You could have just called me.'

He shrugged. 'It wouldn't have been as much fun.'

She looked around the very ordinary car park in dis-belief. 'As much fun as visiting East London again? You need to get out more.'

Maks chuckled. 'Perhaps I do.'

He stood up straight, reminding Zoe how tall he was. How powerful. How that mouth had felt on hers. Hot. A wave of desire made her legs feel momentarily weak.

'I've been invited to the opening of a photography ex-hibition this evening. I thought you might like to come with me.'

Zoe hadn't expected him to say that. Curiosity got the better of her. 'What exhibition?'

'Taylor Cartwright's latest work.'

Zoe sucked in a breath at this mention of one of Amer-ica's foremost landscape photographers, who had died re-cently, and said, almost to herself, 'It's been sold out for months...'

'Would you like to come?'

She was torn between jumping at the opportunity and her wariness at the thought of spending more time with a man who made her skin prickle with heat and a million other disturbing things.

Zoe looked at him suspiciously. 'And after the exhibition? Then what?'

'That's up to you. I'd like to take you for dinner, maybe a drink, or I can drop you home.'

Remembering that kiss, Zoe said quickly, 'I can make my own way home.'

'Whatever you wish.'

Maks looked at the woman in front of him. If his blood hadn't been humming just from being near her again he might have wondered why she had such a unique effect on him, but he wasn't capable of wondering about anything right now. He felt as if he'd scored a victory merely because she hadn't said no, and because she hadn't ruled out dinner or a drink.

The fact that he hadn't had to work so hard to seduce a woman *ever* was also not something he cared to think about right now.

Zoe couldn't have been less dressed to impress, but all he could see were those huge aquamarine eyes. Her hair was down, which he was guessing was her default, so she could hide behind it if she wanted to. It made him want to pull it back, so he could see her face more clearly. He barely noticed her scars. He was more distracted by her soft lips, and the erotic memory of how they'd opened under his mouth, the taste of her...

He cursed silently when his body responded.

'Okay. I'd like to come, thank you.'

Maks almost didn't hear her, he was trying so hard to get his body under control. 'Good. That's...good.'

Zoe made a face, and she suddenly looked shy. 'Would

you mind if I stopped by my flat to change, though? Just
for five minutes.'

Maks shook his head. 'Of course not. Let's go.'

A couple of hours later he was wondering why he'd been
surprised when Zoe literally had only been in her flat for
five minutes before re-emerging.

He looked at her across the gallery.

She'd changed into figure-hugging leather trousers and
a soft V-necked cream sweater, under a dark grey jacket.
Clothes designed not to draw attention. To blend in. Like
the way she used that fall of honey-blonde hair to hide her
face—most of the time.

She had a tomboyish style that made him want to see
her dressed in long falls of silk and satin that would cling
to her body and reveal those slender curves. That pale skin.

She was staring intently at a large photograph of Yo-
semite, the national park in America. His mouth thinned.
Another first—a woman who wasn't utterly absorbed with
him. Either feigning it or otherwise.

As if reading his mind, the woman beside him said, 'I
like her already. She's not clinging to your arm as if she
can't walk by herself or simpering about the latest nail
varnish colours.'

Maks looked at his sister and said dryly, 'Sash, if I
wasn't so emotionally barren you could really hurt me
sometimes.'

His sister snorted derisively but Maks ignored her. It
had been a bad idea to ask her to come. She was too astute
for her own good.

Zoe knew she couldn't keep pretending that the photos
held more fascination for her than the man she could see
behind her through the crowd, reflected in the glass over
the black and white image.

He was talking to a woman. Tall, slim. A dart of something hit Zoe in the solar plexus. A jolt of possessiveness. Which was ridiculous. They'd kissed once! He was obviously only interested because she wasn't falling into his arms like an overripe plum.

Steeling herself, Zoe turned around and walked back over towards Maks, whose dark grey gaze was unnervingly intent on her.

She took in the woman beside him. Something about her was familiar, but she knew she'd never seen her before. She was wearing nondescript clothes, a shirt and long skirt, as if she was trying to hide. Long hair…dark blonde. And she wore glasses. But Zoe realised that woman was extraordinarily beautiful. She was just trying to hide it.

Something about that resonated inside Zoe. The sense of a kindred spirit.

Maks gestured to the woman. 'Zoe, I'd like you to meet my sister, Sasha.'

His sister. A knot unclenched inside Zoe.

She put out her hand, smiled. 'Nice to meet you.'

Sasha shook her hand, smiled, and Zoe was nearly bowled backwards. She wasn't just beautiful. She was stunning.

'You too,' she said. 'I was just telling my darling brother—'

'Sash, didn't you say you had someone to meet?'

His sister's grey eyes danced mischievously. 'No…but I can take a hint. I hope we meet again, Zoe.'

Zoe watched her walk away, fading into the crowd. She turned to Maks. 'You didn't have to send her away.'

Maks took her arm. 'Oh, yes, I did. She was bound to embarrass me—it's her life's mission.'

Zoe's heart clenched. She'd had a younger brother. He would have been twenty-three. Would he have ribbed her like Sasha did Maks? Her heart ached.

Maks was looking down at her. 'Ready to go?'

Zoe nodded quickly, afraid he'd see the sudden melancholy in her eyes. She worked so hard not to think of those things. 'Thank you for this. I enjoyed seeing the photos.'

She didn't mention that Taylor Cartwright had been a mentor of her father's when he'd been young, travelling around North America and taking his first photographs.

Maks led her out of the gallery onto the street. Summer was tipping into autumn and there was the faintest chill in the evening air, a sign of things to come.

Zoe shivered slightly. Immediately Maks said, 'Are you cold?'

His solicitude melted the cold around her heart. She shook her head. 'No, I'm fine.'

'So, can I take you for dinner? There's a place not far from here.'

Seeing Maks with his sister and touching on the past again had made Zoe feel vulnerable. She didn't want to be alone. But she knew that was just an excuse.

She looked up at Maks. 'Sure, I'd like that.'

He smiled and, like his sister, it transformed his face, turning him from gorgeous into devastating.

He took her hand and led her to his car. She found that her usual anxiety around being in a car didn't surface when she was with him. He drove so competently, not trying to show off. He didn't need to. He oozed confidence.

Within ten minutes, Maks was driving down a quiet mews street.

Zoe frowned. 'Where are we?'

'Mayfair.'

He pulled to a stop outside one of the houses. It had dark brick and black-framed windows. It looked discreet and exclusive. She wondered if this was another private club.

As if reading her mind, Maks said, 'This is my London townhouse.'

Zoe looked at him. She opened her mouth, but then she

realised that he hadn't actually specified where he was bringing her. He'd just said, *'There's a place...'*

'That's rather underhand of you.'

'I promise my intentions are very honourable. If you feel uncomfortable in any way, I'll take you wherever you want to go.' He made a crossing his heart motion.

Zoe didn't trust him for a second. But it was more that she didn't trust herself, if she was totally honest. She unclicked her seatbelt and watched as Maks uncoiled his tall frame from the driver's seat to come round and help her out.

She was more intrigued than she liked to admit to see where he lived.

The door opened as Maks approached as if by magic. A middle-aged Asian man dressed in dark trousers and dark long-sleeved top greeted Maks.

'Hamish, I'd like you to meet Zoe Collins.'

The man stepped forward at the door, smiling and holding out his hand. 'You're probably wondering how I came by a name like Hamish? I was born and brought up in Scotland when my parents emigrated there from Vietnam. I'm Maks's housekeeping manager. Please, come in.'

Zoe was charmed by him and his soft Scottish burr. 'Nice to meet you, Hamish.'

She walked into a sleek marbled hallway, decorated in tones of dark grey and silver. Understated. Elegant.

She heard Hamish say, 'I'll park the car, boss. Angie said dinner will be ready in about twenty minutes.'

'Thanks, Hamish.'

Maks came and took Zoe's hand again. She must have looked dumbstruck. He led her down the hall and into a sumptuous but again understated reception room. He let her hand go and walked over to an exquisite walnut drinks cabinet. It looked like a piece of art, not furniture.

'Would you like a drink?'

Suddenly Zoe relished the prospect of some fortification. 'A glass of white wine, if you have it?'

Maks came back with a glass of perfectly chilled white wine. He had a tumbler of what looked like whisky. He lifted his glass. 'Cheers. Welcome to my home.'

'Cheers.' Zoe took a sip of wine, appreciating the dry crisp taste.

'Please—sit, make yourself comfortable.'

Zoe looked around. There was an assortment of low couches and footstools set around glass tables covered in the latest coffee table hardbacks. Except these actually looked as if they'd been thumbed through, their edges slightly frayed.

She chose a seat on its own and watched as Maks sat down on a couch at a right angle to her, resting one arm along the back. Utterly relaxed. Yet full of taut crackling energy.

'You have a beautiful home,' she said.

Maks looked around. 'It's probably not what you were expecting.'

Damn his perceptiveness. 'I'm that easy to read?' she asked.

'It's refreshing. I'm used to people freezing their emotions with enough chemicals to put an animal to sleep for a year.'

Zoe couldn't stop a huff of laughter. 'I have to admit I would have expected something less…discreet. Maybe a penthouse apartment.'

Maks made a face. 'That's more my brother Sharif's style. He likes to be far above mere mortals, high in the sky.'

Zoe took a sip of wine. 'What's he like?'

'Driven.'

'What about your other brother… Nikos?'

'He used to live like a nomad, keeping apartments in

our various hotels. But all that looks to change now that he's married and settling down. A wife and baby don't really go with a nomadic lifestyle.'

Zoe's insides tightened. Marriage. A baby. *Family.* Her worst fear. Her most secret dream. She shut it down. She'd vowed never to put herself at risk of feeling that loss and pain again, no matter what moments of yearning she felt.

Maks swirled his drink. 'What about you? What kind of home would you aspire to live in?'

Zoe felt like pointing out tartly that she was perfectly happy where she was, but she knew no one could claim that. It was damp, dingy, and surrounded by concrete jungle.

But before she could say anything she was assailed by the memory of a house in Ireland… Dublin. On the coast… high above the Irish Sea. With acres of green lawn. A big golden house with windows like shining, benevolent eyes. Flowers blooming along borders. A shaggy dog.

Her mother, standing on the steps, calling, 'Come on, you two. It's time to go…'

And then her father, lifting her up so high she could hardly breathe, swinging her around and then down, into his arms…

She'd felt so safe. So loved. So happy.

'Zoe? Are you okay?'

She blinked and saw Maks sitting forward, frowning. 'You've gone as white as a ghost.'

Zoe swallowed down the memory. It usually only came in dreams that turned into nightmares. 'I'm fine. I just…'

What had they been talking about?

She forced a smile. 'I don't know where I'd like to live… I hadn't really thought about it. I'm happy where I am.'

Maks was relieved to see some colour come back into Zoe's cheeks. For a moment he'd been afraid she was about faint. She'd looked stricken.

A light knock came to the door. It was Hamish. 'Dinner is served when you're ready.'

Maks watched Zoe stand up, graceful. She walked out ahead of him, following Hamish, and he noted the unconsciously sensual way she moved. A cynical part of his brain kicked into gear. Was it really unconscious? Or was he so jaded that an act of wide-eyed innocence had him hooked like a gasping fish on a line?

Even if it was an act, he told himself, it didn't negate the fact that he wanted her more with each passing moment. And he was confident that as soon as he'd had her she'd lose her allure and her air of mystery. He didn't want to explore her mysteries. He just wanted to explore *her*.

CHAPTER FOUR

ZOE LEANED BACK and wiped her mouth with her napkin. She hadn't eaten such a delicious meal in a long time. Maks's personal chef, Angie, had served up a simple roast chicken and in-season vegetables, followed by the lightest, zingiest lemon tart Zoe had ever tasted.

Angie came back in to clear the plate and Zoe looked at her. 'Seriously, that was sublime. I wish I could cook like that.'

Angie smiled and looked at Maks. 'I like her—she doesn't behave as if the staff are invisible.'

Maks sent a glower at Angie, who left the room smiling, totally unperturbed. Witnessing Maks's easy and egalitarian interaction with his staff made Zoe feel off-centre. Once again, it wasn't the way she would have expected someone like him to behave.

Maks stood up. 'Come into the lounge for some coffee?'

Zoe stood up. 'Sure.'

Dinner had passed easily. Too easily. They'd conversed about topics as diverse as Irish history, politics, and the latest Marvel movie. It turned out they were both Marvel movie buffs.

But there was still an uneasiness she couldn't shake. She'd trusted a man before—someone she'd known since she was young. And he'd betrayed her heinously and almost violently.

She knew even less about Maks, and yet her instincts were telling her she could trust him. That he wouldn't harm her. Physically. Dean had hurt her physically—or had tried to. But he hadn't left any deep emotional wounds. Zoe sensed that Maks posed a wholly different threat.

'What are you thinking about?'

Zoe turned around from where she'd been looking at the books on Maks's shelves, with her coffee cup in her hand. He was sitting on the couch again, sipping from his own steaming cup, looking so gorgeous that he took her breath away.

She came over and sat down on a couch opposite, with a small table in between them. She noted how a gleam came into those silver eyes, as if he knew exactly how skittish he made her feel. How achy…how needy. But also how scared.

Maks kept his eyes on her and put down his cup. He stood up and came around the low table, sat down on the couch near her.

Zoe's insides somersaulted. She desperately searched for something to say.

'What Angie said…about people thinking the staff are invisible…who was she talking about?'

Great—now he'd think she was fishing for information on his girlfriends.

Maks said, 'I host dinner parties here sometimes.'

'I guess I know what she means…most people are dismissive of those in the service industry.'

Maks winced. 'Or they get them fired.'

'That too.'

Zoe couldn't think straight. Couldn't seem to remember what she'd been worried about. Maks was close enough to touch. To smell. To want. Every part of her clamoured to be closer.

Damn him. Why wasn't he taking the lead?

Maks shook his head, a small smile playing around his mouth. 'Your move, Zoe. If you want me, all you have to do is show me. It's not complicated. I can hear you over-thinking this from here.'

Zoe wanted to scowl. But even before she knew she'd made the decision she'd put her coffee cup down on the low table and scooted closer on the couch. She couldn't *not*. The clamour in her body had become a sizzle.

She was fixated on his mouth. She reached out and touched it experimentally with her finger, tracing the shape…

Maks was burning up. He wanted to grab Zoe's hand and tug her all the way into him until he could feel every curve of her body pressed against him. Until he was drowning in her sweetness.

But he held back. Something told him that her reticence wasn't an act.

For a moment he had a jolting moment of wondering if she might be—

But that dissolved in a rush of heat when she leaned all the way forward and pressed her mouth to his.

Maks's mouth was firm under Zoe's. Her breasts were pressed against his chest. It felt like a steel wall. A *warm* steel wall.

His mouth wasn't moving.

Zoe was in too deep now to pull back. Her brain cells were melting. She pressed closer, angled her head slightly. She opened her mouth and let the tip of her tongue explore the closed seam of Maks's mouth.

And that was when she realised the level of Maks's restraint, as he put his hands on her arms to haul her up and even closer, so she was sprawled across his chest, letting him take her weight.

She lifted her head, looked down, aware of her hair falling around her face. For once she wanted to push it back, so she could see him. He did it for her, tucking it behind her ears. It was a surprisingly tender gesture amidst the inferno building in her blood.

It had never felt like this with—

Maks caught her head and pulled it down, so their mouths touched again. Except this time there was no doubt who was the instigator. Even though he was under her, Maks controlled and dominated the kiss with an expertise that made Zoe's heart race.

He opened his legs so she was between them, her lower belly pressed against the place where the evidence of his arousal was hard. As hard as the rest of him.

Except his mouth was soft now, coaxing her to be bolder, more daring. To use him. She funnelled her hands through his hair, holding his head, exploring his mouth as if she'd never kissed a man before. And she hadn't...not like this. Not as if she was an adventurer in a new undiscovered land.

Zoe was killing Maks with a thousand tiny innocent kisses. With the most chaste foreplay he'd ever indulged in. Either she was a wanton seductress who knew exactly what she was doing and was laughing at him for his restrained response, or she really was as gauche as her kisses.

Except gauche kisses had never turned him on like this. He had never been so close to climax with his clothes on.

He moved her so that she lay under him on the couch, looking up at him with those huge sea-green eyes, her hair tumbled around her head, cheeks flushed, mouth plump and moist.

He gritted his jaw when his erection pressed uncomfortably against his trousers. His thigh was between her legs and he moved it subtly against her, seeing how her eyes widened at the friction.

He lowered his mouth to hers again, to find it open, willing. She put her arms around his neck. His chest expanded. He explored the seam of her top above her trousers, delving underneath to find bare silky skin, pushing it up until he encountered the lace-covered swell of her breast. Small, but perfect. Plump.

He squeezed her flesh gently and she gasped into his mouth. A little hitch of breath that ramped up his arousal to excruciating levels.

He tugged on her lower lip, biting gently as he pulled down the lace cup of her bra, his knuckles brushing against the soft swell of her breast. He pulled back and looked down. Her breast was perfect. Her nipple small and hard... pink. He couldn't resist, bending his head and exploring that hard tip with his tongue, feeding her to himself as if she was a succulent morsel...

Zoe was drowning in heat. Sensations were piling on top of sensations so fast she couldn't breathe. Maks's mouth was on her breast, tugging, licking, and it was the most exquisite form of torture she'd ever been subjected to.

Then he was pulling up her top and exposing both breasts to his hands, his mouth.

Zoe's head rolled back. His thigh was between her legs, where she ached. As if he knew exactly what she wanted he moved subtly, so that the sensation spiked like a sharp knife-point.

It was too much... She couldn't get her head around how fast things were moving. In spite of all her rationale, telling herself this was different—way different from what had happened before—she suddenly felt trapped. Very aware of Maks's weight on top of her, holding her down.

She put her hands against his chest and pushed, but he didn't move. Panic flared, eclipsing pleasure. She pushed harder.

Maks pulled back, his eyes molten, cheeks flushed. *'Che cosa, cara?'*

He wasn't even talking English.

Panic was making Zoe fight for breath. 'I can't... I can't breathe.'

Maks reared back. 'Zoe? What is it?'

She scrambled up and back, drawing her knees up to her chest. She shook her head. Already the waves of panic were receding, leaving her feeling cold and ridiculous. This wasn't the same situation.

'I… I'm sorry. It was just all going so fast… I felt trapped.'

In contrast to hers, Maks's clothes looked a bit rumpled but were still on. She felt dishevelled. Awkwardly, she straightened her clothes.

Maks got up and went over to the drinks cabinet. He came back holding two glasses.

He handed her one. It held dark golden liquid. 'Here, take this.'

She took a sip, watching as he threw the liquid in his own glass back. She winced inwardly. The drink had a warming, numbing effect.

He sat down, giving her plenty of space. 'What was that, Zoe?' Maks looked pale. 'Did you think I was going to…to force you?'

She shook her head, an immediate and visceral rejection of that rising up inside her. '*No.* No. Not at all.'

She couldn't think straight when he was looking at her like that. She put down her glass and got up from the couch, pacing away from Maks. Walking to a window that reflected back her own image. It was dark outside.

She owed him an explanation. At no point had she really felt unsafe or pressured. It had been her own demons.

She turned around. 'Someone else did, though. My ex-boyfriend. I trusted him and he…'

Maks surged to his feet. 'He raped you?'

Zoe looked at Maks. His face was stark. She shook her head. 'No, but he almost did. I managed to stop him, get him out of my apartment.'

The memory of that awful night made Zoe shiver. The awful full, ugly truth of why Dean had sought her out again.

'Who was he?'

Maks's voice was like steel. In that moment she had a premonition of what it would be like to face a far less benign Maks. She'd faced him once before, when they'd first met.

'Someone from my past. It doesn't matter. He's gone now. He's not in this country.'

Maks was finding it hard to absorb everything Zoe was telling him. She looked so vulnerable, standing on her own, arms folded tight across her chest. The thought of someone forcing themselves on her made him feel sick. But also livid. She was so petite. Slight... He wanted to go over to her, but he felt she wouldn't want that. Not yet.

She lifted her chin. 'The truth is that...as you may have already guessed... I'm not that experienced. In fact not experienced. At all.'

Maks frowned. 'Are you saying that—?'

'I'm a virgin, yes.'

Her words were quick. Clipped. His instinct had been right. A swell of something that felt like possessiveness rose up inside him. Primal. *Mine.* And relief to know she hadn't been subjected to a terrible assault.

She said, 'So, I know that that'll probably change things.'

Maks focused on Zoe. 'Change...how?'

She suddenly looked unsure. 'Well, you won't...you can't find that attractive.'

Maks's body begged to differ. 'Really? And why would that be?'

'Because you're experienced...and I'm not. Most men don't find inexperienced women a turn-on.'

'I'm not most men.' Now Maks folded his arms, bristling at the thought that she was comparing him to her ex. Her bullying abusive ex. He could see her throat work as she swallowed.

'So...what are you saying?' she asked.

Yes, Maks, what are you saying? That you want to be this woman's first lover and risk all the emotional entanglements that come with that?

Maks forced the heat haze out of his brain. He had to be careful. He normally steered well clear of situations like this. He had to let Zoe know the kind of person he was.

'I'm saying that you being a virgin is not a turn-off.'

Quite the opposite, in fact. The thought of being the first man to witness Zoe in the throes of passion was seriously sexy.

'But,' he added carefully, 'I'm not interested in a relationship. I don't do happy-ever-afters, and after my experience with my parents I have no desire to recreate that toxic scenario in marriage. You need to know that.'

Zoe looked at him for a long moment. There was no discernible expression on her face, which unnerved him. He'd believed her to be as easy to read as a book.

She seemed to hug her arms around herself even tighter and she said, 'That's the last thing I'm looking for. Believe me.'

He did. There was something stripped away in her voice, leaving it bare and compelling.

Then she said, 'I think I'd like to go home now.'

Maks was surprised at the strength of the feeling of rejection that rose up inside him at the thought of her leaving, but he forced himself to say, 'Sure. I'd take you home, but I'm over the limit. I'll have Hamish drop you back.'

The fact that Maks was willing to let her leave so easily made Zoe feel all at once relieved and disappointed. She'd just humiliated herself spectacularly by revealing she'd been abused in a relationship, and then told Maks how inexperienced she was. And, damn him, he hadn't reacted the way she might have expected.

She was learning that this man didn't do anything she expected.

But the fact that he was so willing to let her go told her that he was done. As he'd said, he didn't do relationships. And he obviously suspected that, as a virgin, she'd want more from her first lover. Even though she'd denied it.

Zoe just wanted to leave now, and take her humiliation with her. She was about to protest that she didn't need a lift but, as if connected with his boss telepathically, Hamish appeared and started to put on a light puffer jacket.

'It's no problem to give you a lift home, Zoe.'

She couldn't help feeling that Hamish had done this before—sprung into action to help Maks dispose of a woman he was no longer interested in. She followed Hamish and turned at the front door to face Maks. She felt awkward. Why had she blurted all that out? She could have made something up.

She forced a smile in Maks's general direction. 'Thank you for this evening. I had a nice time. It was lovely to meet your sister—she's nice.'

'She liked you too. Goodnight, Zoe.'

Zoe had to restrain an impulse to study his face and imprint it on her brain for ever. And somehow she knew she didn't need to do that. He would be hard to forget.

After Hamish had dropped her at her flat, Zoe sat on her bed feeling deflated. Hollow. She opened up her laptop and did what she'd been reluctant to do before, because that would have meant she was interested.

She searched online for Maks Marchetti.

As she might have expected, compared to his two brothers, not much came up for Maks at all. There was a handful of pictures of him with women, all stunningly beautiful and accomplished. Which made his interest in Zoe even more unlikely.

There were no salacious kiss-and-tell stories—unlike

a recent one involving his older brother Sharif. Nor were there screaming headlines as there were about his other brother settling down, speculating about how long it would last.

Zoe saw some pictures of Nikos with his new wife. She was a tall redhead, and Zoe realised that she looked familiar. She was the woman Maks had been talking to at the fashion event where she'd met him again.

She shuddered to think of being in the public eye like that and felt sympathy for Nikos's wife, who didn't look completely comfortable in the photos.

There were some older pictures of his parents—his father was tall and dark, very masculine. His mother was tall, almost taller than his father, and very, very beautiful. Blonde with grey eyes. Maks's grey eyes.

Zoe winced when she saw the hundreds of images of Maks and Sasha when they were younger. Coming out of a palatial villa in Rome. Going to school with security guards. Skiing. On beaches. Nowhere had been safe from the paparazzi, it would seem.

One picture caught Zoe's eye. Maks was in swimming trunks, on a beach. He looked about sixteen, tall and rangy, his body only hinting at the adult power and strength to come. He had his hand out towards whoever was taking the picture, his face twisted in anger.

Zoe saw there was a girl behind him, looking fearful, embarrassed, in a one-piece swimsuit, all gangly limbs and braces on her teeth. She looked hunted. *Sasha.*

No wonder he hated the paparazzi so much.

But, compared to his brothers and his parents, Maks had since become a veritable recluse. Evidently he and his sister did all they could to avoid the limelight now, and who could blame them if they'd been hounded like that?

Zoe pushed the laptop away and lay back on her bed.

She'd effectively turned Maks off tonight, even if he had been enough of a gentleman to say otherwise.

She told herself she was relieved. Maks was a force of nature. A man who would demand nothing less than everything she had to give. Yet she couldn't ignore the ache at the thought of never seeing him again.

Zoe realised now that she'd never been entirely honest with herself where her ex-boyfriend was concerned. She'd convinced herself that she'd desired him, but it hadn't been desire. Because now she knew how that felt.

It had been loneliness. Pure and simple. A weak need for intimacy. Weak, because she'd always vowed not to let anyone close enough to become important to her.

She'd only let Dean close because she'd known subconsciously that he couldn't affect her. But Maks did affect her. So it was a good thing that it was over before it had started.

A wave of heat went through her body just from thinking about how it had felt to be in his arms. His mouth on her flesh. And it hadn't just been the physical response he'd unleashed—it had been the other, more tender responses. Emotional responses. The instinctive need to open up. Trust him.

Zoe got under the covers of her bed and pulled a pillow over her head. As if that could help her ignore the sense of loss. She told herself over and over again that it was a good thing Maks wasn't interested in pursuing this—*her*—further, until she finally fell asleep.

When she woke, bleary-eyed, the next morning, to the persistent silent buzzing of her phone she had to shake her head to make sure she wasn't still dreaming. Numerous missed calls from Maks and three texts.

I'm outside, let me in.

Zoe? Are you there?

Zoe, if you don't let me in in the next ten minutes I'm calling the police.

Zoe scrambled to call him back. 'I'm here… I'm here.'

'I have coffee and cakes.'

'What are you doing here? I thought…' She trailed off.

'Can we discuss this over coffee? And by the way it's raining. I'm getting wet out here.'

Zoe looked out of the window. The rain was lashing. She put down the phone and got up, and pressed the buzzer to release the door downstairs. She heard it open and close. Footsteps. And then Maks appeared outside her door. Huge. Broad. And very wet. Drops of water clung to his hair and his short jacket. He was holding cups of takeaway coffee and a bag of what looked like pastries.

His scent hit her nostrils. Musky and masculine. Expensive. She really wasn't dreaming. He was here. Twelve hours after she'd thought he'd said good riddance.

'Can I come in?'

The smell of fresh coffee hit Zoe's nostrils then and she almost groaned. How did he know she couldn't function before her first coffee in the morning?

She stood back and he walked in and she saw the extent of how wet he was.

'I'll get you a towel.'

She went to her tiny airing cupboard and took out a towel, bringing it back and handing it to Maks, who had put the coffee and cakes on her table.

'Thanks.'

He shrugged off his jacket and draped it over a chair. Zoe took in the fact that he was wearing worn jeans and a light long-sleeved top. Muscles moved as he rubbed his head briskly.

She became very aware of her loose pyjama bottoms

and singlet top, putting her arms around her chest. 'I'll just…get changed.'

'Here, take this with you.' Maks handed her one of the coffees.

Zoe grabbed it and ran, still in shock that he was here. When she was in her bedroom—mere feet away, but thankfully behind a door—she breathed out and took a sip of coffee, hoping that might restore a sense of reality.

It didn't. She had the quickest shower on record, dried her hair and dressed in a pair of jeans and a loose, oversized shirt.

When she went back out to the living area Maks had the photo of her family in his hand. They were all pulling funny faces. Her insides clenched. Hard.

He looked around. 'This was you and your family?'

She nodded, longing to take the picture from him.

He put it back on the shelf. 'What happened after the crash? Who brought you up?'

Zoe kept her voice neutral. 'I went into foster care. Both my parents were only children with deceased parents. There was a great-aunt on my father's side, but she didn't want to take me in.'

'That must have been rough.'

Zoe shrugged and avoided Maks's eye. 'I don't remember much about that time, to be honest. I was lucky. I only had two foster homes and they were kind families. I know some kids who went through many more and had bad experiences.'

Like Dean, her ex. Zoe clamped down on thinking about him. It only invited comparisons to Maks and the knowledge that Maks was so much more dangerous for all sorts of different reasons.

She looked at him. 'What are you doing here? I thought last night… I thought I wouldn't see you again.'

He frowned. 'Why?'

Zoe's face grew hot. 'Because I'm not experienced.'

'I told you that didn't matter to me. I thought you needed space. I didn't want to crowd you after you told me what happened to you.' He walked closer. 'Make no mistake, Zoe. I want you. That hasn't changed. And I've told you that I'm not interested in anything permanent. But if you don't want to explore this chemistry between us, tell me now and I'll walk away. I don't beg and I don't play games.'

I'm not interested in anything permanent.

That should reassure Zoe, because of the lessons she'd learnt at the hands of personal tragedy and also her ex-boyfriend.

Her head told her to say she wasn't interested. But first, that would be a lie. And second... The fact that Maks had turned up here this morning, that he *still wanted her,* in spite of her lack of experience... She couldn't fight her overriding impulse to stay in his orbit for a little longer. In spite of knowing better.

She took a breath, felt her heart pounding wildly. 'I don't want you to walk away.' *Yet.*

Maks had to hide the rush of triumph. He closed the distance between them, but stopped just short of touching Zoe. 'I have to go to St Petersburg today for a few days,' he said. 'For meetings and to oversee a fashion shoot. Come with me.'

Maks saw the shock on Zoe's face.

'St Petersburg? That's in Russia.'

He bit back a smile. 'That's geographically correct.'

She made a face. 'But I can't just...leave.'

'You have a passport, don't you?'

'Yes, but—'

'What commitments do you have this week?'

She folded her arms and looked at him. 'One is to find a new job.'

The novelty of a woman who wasn't rushing to acquiesce sent a thrill of anticipation through him. 'All the more
reason to come away with me for a few days. I owe you for
getting you fired.'

Zoe suddenly looked less spiky. 'I do actually have other
commitments. I mind a neighbour's child a couple of days
a week, and I do some work for a contracting firm, cleaning offices.'

Maks shook his head. 'I can arrange for your neighbour
to have substitute childcare. And as for the office-cleaning
job… I refuse to believe that's what you need to do to survive, Zoe. You are young, beautiful and talented. You can
have the world at your feet if you want.'

Zoe's chest tightened at Maks's words. She knew very well
why she preferred to operate on the fringes, and she felt
the sting of shame that she didn't have the courage to take
up more space. How was it that this man she barely knew,
who was from a world elevated well above hers, could see
something in her that she didn't even dare to articulate to
herself? It was unnerving.

She admitted sheepishly, 'I don't have any cleaning
shifts lined up this week.' She saw a glint of what looked
like triumph in Maks's eye and said quickly, 'But I won't
go anywhere until I know that Sally's childcare is sorted.
I can't let her down.'

'More champagne, Miss Collins?'

Zoe looked up. She'd been staring out of the window at
a carpet of fluffy white clouds under a blue sky. She shook
her head at the steward. 'No, thanks, I'm okay.'

But she wasn't okay. She was still reeling from the speed
with which Maks had managed to secure childcare for her
neighbour—childcare that she was happy with—and had
then spirited Zoe and her one small suitcase out of her

shabby top-floor flat, across London to a private airfield and this sleek silver jet, which was now flying somewhere high above Poland, according to the pilot.

Maks was in a seat across the aisle, long legs spread in front of him while he simultaneously spoke on his phone and typed into his laptop. He'd excused himself when they'd got on board, saying, 'I have some calls to catch up on—make yourself comfortable.'

Zoe couldn't imagine ever feeling *comfortable* in Maks's presence. Fizzing with electricity. Alive with anticipation. Reckless. Heady… The champagne wasn't helping her to feel any less reckless. Or heady. And definitely not comfortable.

What exactly had she even agreed to? An affair? Just because she'd said she'd come with him? Would he expect payment in kind in bed?

Her mind shied away from that. Maks was too controlled, too sophisticated. Too proud. As he'd said from the beginning, she intrigued him, and she was sure that sense of intrigue would fade very quickly once he'd spent more time with her. *Once he'd slept with her.*

Zoe shifted in her seat as a pulse between her legs throbbed at the very thought of him—

'What are you thinking about? You look almost…guilty.'

Zoe's head swivelled around to Maks so quickly she almost got whiplash. She hadn't realised he'd stopped talking on the phone and had put away his laptop. She felt guilty now—which was ridiculous.

'I'm not thinking about anything special.'

The pulse between her legs throbbed again, as if to mock her, and she pressed her thighs together. Maks's gaze dropped for a second, before resting on her face again. She scowled. This ability of his to read her mind was seriously irritating.

Wanting to get his attention off her far too obvious

thoughts, she said, 'So what are these meetings in St Petersburg?'

Maks sat back. 'The Marchetti Group has an office in Moscow, but we're interested in the untapped potential of Russian designers, a lot of whom originate in St Petersburg. We're interested in developing the city as another growing fashion hub—not just for designers but for brands.'

'Where was your mother from?'

'Originally St Petersburg, but she moved to Moscow with her father after her mother died and he remarried.'

Zoe thought of the pictures she'd seen. 'She is very beautiful.'

Maks's face became impassive. 'Her whole life revolves around her looks. They're as much of a currency to her as money is.'

'Your sister is beautiful too.'

Maks's gaze narrowed on Zoe. 'You noticed that she hides it away?'

Zoe nodded.

Maks's mouth twisted. 'Our mother couldn't handle having a beautiful daughter who might eclipse her, so she did her best to undermine Sasha's confidence. It's probably the worst thing she's done.'

Zoe felt that tug of empathy for his sister again. 'Maybe she'll surprise you and come out of the shadows when she's ready.'

Maks looked at her and his eyes saw far too much. He said, 'Maybe she will.' And they both knew he wasn't talking about his sister.

CHAPTER FIVE

ZOE WALKED THROUGH the series of palatial rooms that made up her suite at the Grand Central St Petersburg Hotel, right in the centre of the city. As soon as they'd arrived at the hotel, to an effusive welcome from the manager, it had become clear that she would have her own suite. She wasn't sure what she'd expected, but she was ashamed to admit that she'd been feeling slightly trepidatious that Maks would have booked them into the same room.

They were in adjoining suites, though. So, while she had her own space, she was very conscious that a mere door separated them.

The drive from the airport to the hotel had taken them past some of the city's stupendously beautiful domed cathedrals and palaces. Zoe itched to explore, and see the city through the lens of her camera, which she'd brought with her. But for now she was enthralled by the vast suite, and if hers was this impressive she could only imagine what Maks's must be like.

She found the bathroom, laid out in cool marble and gold furnishings that should have looked tacky but didn't. And beside the bathroom there was a dressing room. The rails and drawers were empty and her small suitcase looked a bit pathetic. It highlighted how out of her depth she was in this situation. She had no idea how to play the part of a rich man's...companion.

She giggled at that, and her giggle had a tinge of hysteria. *Companion* sounded so Victorian, when the feelings Maks inspired within her were anything *but* Victorian.

The suite's doorbell chimed at that moment, low and melodic. Zoe sobered up again. She made her way back to the main door and opened it. Maks was on the other side, leaning against the doorframe with an insouciance that came from being born into this world. She couldn't control the wild rush of her blood to see him again. She was as pathetic as her little suitcase.

'How do you like your rooms?'

Zoe feigned a nonchalance she was far from feeling. 'Oh, you know... I think they're adequate for my needs.' Who was she kidding? She could fit her entire flat into the suite about ten times.

Maks smiled, not fooled for a second. 'Good. Let me know if you need anything more than...adequate.'

Zoe looked at him suspiciously, expecting to see a smirk around his mouth, but his expression was innocent.

Then he glanced at his watch, and back to her. 'I've been invited to a couple of social events while I'm here. I'd like you to join me.'

Trepidation rushed back. 'What kind of events?'

'No need to look so wary. They're nice things. I've been invited to the gala opening night of the St Petersburg Ballet Company. They're performing *Swan Lake* tonight. At the Mariinsky Theatre—one of Russia's finest.'

As a child, Zoe had been obsessed with ballet and, the Christmas before they'd died, her parents had taken her to a performance of *The Nutcracker*. She hadn't been to a ballet performance since then, and every instinct screamed at her to say *no,* to curl up somewhere and avoid the painful memories.

But something else inside her—something new—resisted the urge to protect. To avoid. She was a grown woman now. She could handle a ballet performance, surely?

She shrugged. 'Okay...sure.'

Maks slanted her a dry look. 'Your enthusiasm is bowling me over here, Zoe.'

She blushed. 'No... I mean, that would be lovely.'

He didn't know the demons in her past. In her head. But then she thought of something else, something far scarier.

'I don't know if I have anything suitable with me to wear.'

She'd brought her one and only smart black dress, but that felt woefully inadequate for what was presumably to be a black-tie event?

'There are boutiques in the hotel. I'll have a stylist meet you and help you to choose a couple of dresses.'

'A couple?'

'There's another event at the end of the week—a showcasing of new designers.'

'Oh…' Zoe bit her lip. Her finances didn't run to buying the kind of dresses that would be for sale in luxurious hotel boutiques. 'Thanks, but maybe I can take a look around the local shops?'

Maks stared at Zoe. He wondered if she was for real. She looked so awkward…conflicted. He was used to women from his own milieu, who already owned a wardrobe of suitable clothes, or the kind of woman who would have jumped at the chance to obtain some free clothes on his tab. He should have anticipated this. He was too cynical.

'I don't expect you to pay for the clothes. I've invited you here and I'm asking you to these events.'

Her face grew redder. 'But I won't accept that. I'm not a charity case.'

His conscience kicked hard. 'I know you're not. Think of it as a loan. We'll have the dresses cleaned and sent back before we leave.'

'You're sure?'

'Of course—no problem.'

An hour later, still feeling uncomfortable, Zoe was standing in one of the hotel's very sumptuous boutiques with a stylist who was looking her up and down critically.

Imagining all sorts of meringue confections, Zoe said quickly, 'I'm not really a girly girl. I don't want anything too fluffy or flashy. Dark colours would be good. Simple, discreet...'

The stylist, blonde, tall and beautiful, smiled and said in a charming Russian accent, 'Mr Marchetti warned me you'd probably say that.'

Indignation flashed through Zoe. 'Oh, he did, did he? What's the brightest coloured dress you have in here?'

A few hours later Zoe was severely regretting her impetuous behaviour. She looked at herself in the mirror and a svelte, groomed stranger looked back at her. In a bright canary-yellow dress. It had a low neckline, small capped sleeves, and hugged her breasts and torso. It fell from her waist in a swathe of material.

Above her hipbones were two small cut-outs, revealing her pale skin. She'd been about to protest when she'd tried it on in the boutique, but when she'd seen it in the mirror she hadn't been able to get the words out to say no. It reminded her of a fairy tale dress, and she'd stopped thinking of fairy tales a long time ago... But not today.

A couple of women had arrived before she'd been able to leave the boutique and had proceeded to do things to her hair and face. And now...

Zoe's chest hurt. She wasn't a stranger to herself at all. That was the problem. She looked like an old picture she had of her mother. Her hair was down but in sleek waves, heavy over one side. Red lips. Her eyes looked huge and very green.

She was too distracted to think of her scars and wonder if they marred the picture.

There was a knock at her door. Too late to change now, or to make excuses. Or worry about her scars.

Full of emotions she'd successfully kept locked up for

years, Zoe turned and picked up the small matching bag and wrap. She hoped Maks wouldn't see how exposed she felt.

But when she opened the door every last thought, concern and emotion was incinerated to dust. Maks Marchetti in a classic black tuxedo was simply…breathtaking. Like… literally. She couldn't breathe. The suit was moulded to his powerful body, as if a tailor had lovingly made it especially for him. Hugging muscles and accentuating the width of his chest.

She was barely aware of his grey eyes sweeping up and down, or the way his jaw clenched. Somehow she remembered to suck in oxygen as she raised her eyes to his face with an effort. 'Hi.'

He was shaking his head, 'You look…stunning, Zoe.'

Zoe was still in too much shock to take that in properly.

When he held out his arm and said, 'Shall we?' she put her arm through his and let him guide her down to the lobby, where people turned and stared at them.

She felt as if she was floating. The dress swirled around her legs as she walked—slightly gingerly in the high-heeled sandals. A car was waiting outside and the driver held open the back door, closing it behind her when she was in. Maks got in on the other side. They were cocooned in soft leather and tinted glass, making the world outside seem very far away.

The streets in St Petersburg were very wide. Summer was tipping into autumn, and Zoe noticed golden tinges on foliage appearing everywhere. She could only imagine how beautiful it would look when autumn descended fully.

She was trying to avoid looking directly at Maks. It was like looking at the sun. His beauty burnt her retinas.

They turned a corner and drove alongside a canal. 'I didn't expect so much water,' Zoe remarked.

'St Petersburg has been likened to Venice, with all its canals and the River Neva. There are over three hundred bridges here.'

She shifted in her seat, feeling acutely self-conscious beside Maks, thinking about all those other women she'd seen him with in photographs. Looking far more comfortable than she felt right now.

'Zoe?'

'Hmm?' She kept looking resolutely out of her window, as if the architecture of the city was keeping her utterly enthralled.

'Zoe, look at me.'

She bit her lip, wishing for a second that she had some glasses that would turn Maks blurry, so she wouldn't have to take in his sheer gorgeousness. She turned around and steeled herself, but nothing could help. The fact that he was close enough to touch...*smell*... Zoe gritted her jaw.

He reached out and pushed back her hair a little. 'You don't have to hide, you know. You're a beautiful woman.'

She thought of how she'd insisted the hair stylist leave her hair down and immediately felt defensive. 'I'm not hiding.'

Maks took his hand away and she felt contrite. She wasn't used to compliments, even though she knew this was probably just part of Maks's repertoire. Nothing special.

'I don't mean to sound short. The truth is that I've never worn an evening gown before. I've never had occasion to. This is all just...new to me.'

'You didn't have a school prom? Or whatever they have in Ireland?'

Zoe shook her head. 'It's called the Debs—and, no... I left Dublin after my final exams...before the Debs.'

She'd been eager to leave behind sad memories and forge her own life, to follow in her father's footsteps to London and beyond. Put some distance between herself and the ever-present grief. Even though it had been a wrench to leave Dublin, it had felt like the right thing to do.

'You look stunning, Zoe. Really.'

She felt ridiculously shy. 'Thank you. So do you.'

Maks reached for her hand and held it. He brought it towards his mouth and pressed a kiss to her knuckles. Everything in her clenched in reaction.

He looked over her shoulder. 'We're here.'

The car had stopped and she hadn't even noticed. There was a red carpet and lots of beautiful people walking into an impressive nineteenth-century building—one of Russia's foremost classical theatres.

Maks got out and helped her out of the car, keeping hold of her hand as he led her towards the entrance. Photographers lined each side of the red carpet, yelling in Russian. She recognised Maks's name being called.

He ignored them, walking past all the other people posing and preening. Zoe didn't mind. She was only too eager to escape the flashes of light. It was very intimidating.

But not as intimidating as the interior of the building. It was breathtaking. As if they'd stepped back in time. Vast spaces and high ceilings. Elaborate plasterwork and chandeliers. Zoe felt dwarfed—especially beside Maks.

Maks was very aware of Zoe's hand in his. It felt small. Delicate. But strong at the same time. A little voice asked him what he was playing at. He never usually indulged in PDAs, or went to these elaborate lengths to seduce a woman. *A virgin!*

Normally he shied well away from any woman who didn't understand how things worked. His lovers had a good time and moved on. No promises, no demands. No games.

That was how Maks had managed to keep such a low profile in comparison to his brothers. And a low profile suited him fine. He didn't have Nikos's need to scandalise the public—albeit he was doing it less now—or Sharif's desire to make everyone bend to his will. He was happy to take a more laid-back role, cultivating and managing the Marchetti brand and its fashion wing, restoring vital respect after the damage inflicted by their father, who had died in the arms of his latest lover. A sordid detail they'd managed to keep from the press at the time.

So any connection with a woman beyond the purely superficial was anathema to Maks. He had a close relationship with his sister and that was all he needed. She got it—she understood—because she'd also witnessed the bitter chaos of their parents' marriage and divorce. Neither of them wanted a replay of that drama in their lives.

And yet here he was…holding Zoe's hand and feeling protective. *It was her first time in an evening gown.*

Maks had been having doubts earlier, wondering if he'd done the right thing, inviting her to St Petersburg—but then she'd appeared in that dress and he'd forgotten every whisper of doubt.

The fact that she'd chosen yellow had punched him in the gut, because he'd known immediately that she'd done it purely to surprise him and was probably feeling self-conscious.

He looked down at her now. The dress showcased her body—her small waist and gently flaring hips, the modest swells of her breasts. Maks remembered how they'd felt in his hands, under his tongue, and his body surged into hot life. As if he had no control over it.

Her gaze was lifted to the ceiling, rapt. The sleek hair and make-up only enhanced what he'd seen that first day. He found it almost impossible to see her scars now, and not because they were covered. They were too deep to hide, but she eclipsed them.

He squeezed her hand. 'Okay?'

She looked at him, and for a second he saw something

unguarded in her eyes, but then she pulled her hand out of his and said brightly, 'Yes, fine. This place is…amazing.'

Maks curled his hand into a fist and put it into his pocket, feeling strangely off-centre. He hadn't expected that. Then he mocked himself. He was concerned that Zoe might expect too much or get hurt, but at every step of the way she demonstrated her independence. She might be innocent, but she wasn't naive.

Zoe hadn't known that Maks could speak Russian, although it made sense, his having a Russian mother. He was speaking it now, to another man, at the drinks reception before the performance started.

She had to admit that Maks speaking Russian was seriously sexy. As if he wasn't already sexy enough. And she couldn't fault him for excluding her. He'd introduced her in English to his acquaintance, but the other man had apologised profusely and claimed his English was not good.

Zoe didn't mind. She was happy to people-watch and revel in the fact that she wasn't the one serving the drinks on this occasion. She knew it wouldn't last long, so she was enjoying it while she could.

They were soon moved to the main auditorium, and when they went into their private stall Zoe stopped in her tracks. She'd never seen such magnificent opulence in her life. There were at least four tiers of seating around the auditorium, reaching high into the gods. The ceiling was frescoed with angels and cherubs dancing around a spectacular central chandelier.

'Wow…' was all she could manage.

Maks said, 'My mother was here on a shoot once, and for some reason she brought myself and Sasha with her—which was not usual. We were normally left with the nanny. I remember seeing it for the first time and being blown away.'

Zoe looked at Maks. They were in a private booth, just

to the left of where the main elaborate box was situated, facing the stage. Maks had told her it was the box reserved for local officials.

'You seem very comfortable here in St Petersburg.'

Maks shrugged. 'In spite of my mother I have an affinity with Russia. I guess it's where my roots are. And I have always loved the Russian writers, whereas Sasha prefers the French classics.'

'It's nice that you're so close.' Zoe felt that pang again, thinking of her lost brother.

Maks's mouth quirked. 'She complains that I'm over-protective, but she's my baby sister.'

'My brother would be twenty-three now. I often think about him and wonder what he'd be like.'

Maks took her hand just as the lights went down. 'I'd wager that he'd be a lot like his sister. Independent, passionate…'

Zoe was glad the lights had gone down, Maks's words had affected her more than she liked. She knew she should pull her hand away from his as an expectant hush settled around them, but she couldn't.

Then the curtain went up and Zoe forgot everything around her—even Maks—as the powerful music and the performance swept her up in a lush and magical embrace.

'You enjoyed it, then?'

Zoe scowled at Maks and saw him smirk. They were in the back of his car, leaving the Mariinsky Theatre behind. She'd been bawling like a baby at the end of the performance, and she knew well that her overload of emotion had come more from the memories it evoked than the actual performance itself—which had been spectacular.

'It was amazing. Thank you. Although I think all the work the make-up artist did has probably been washed away.'

Maks looked at her. 'You look perfect.' Then, 'Did people comment on your scars when you were growing up?'

Zoe was taken aback by the abrupt question, but she also appreciated it. She hated it when people looked at her scars but said nothing.

Absently she touched the one at her lip, tracing the indentation. She dropped her hand. 'Sometimes, in school, they called me Scarface.'

'Children can be cruel. Were you ever tempted to try and get rid of them?'

Zoe looked at him. 'With plastic surgery?'

He nodded. 'Not that I think you need to—at all. But I could understand the temptation…for an easier life.'

Zoe shook her head. But then her conscience made her admit, 'I thought of it when I was younger. In secondary school. But I knew I couldn't be so weak.'

Maks turned to face her. 'Weak?'

Zoe resisted the urge to touch the scar above her lip again. 'They're a reminder of what happened. Of what I did.'

'What you did?'

'I was looking at the camera in the back of the car—it was my father's prized possession. He was telling me to be careful…he took his eyes off the road for a second… and then…' *Bam.*

Maks shook his head. 'Zoe, you weren't responsible for the accident. You were eight.'

Old wounds ached. 'I distracted him. If I hadn't had his camera…'

'Accidents happen. They're tragic. Senseless. And usually the sum of a lot more than just a father taking his eyes off the road for a second. You can't hold yourself responsible.'

Zoe couldn't escape Maks's grey eyes. On a rational level she knew he was probably right. But on a deep cellular level, where her trauma lay, it was hard to believe what he was saying. The guilt had been such a constant companion in her life.

The car had pulled to a stop not far from the theatre. Zoe looked outside, welcoming the distraction. She could see water glinting under the moonlight. 'Where are we?'

Maks was enigmatic. 'You'll see.'

He got out and came around to help her out of the car. Zoe sucked in a breath of surprise, all painful recent thoughts fading back where they belonged. There was a small boat with a glass roof bobbing on the canal. Candles flickered inside, and Zoe saw a table set for two. A waiter dressed in a suit. Waiting…

'We're going on a boat?'

'A little late-night dinner while we take in the sights.'

Zoe was speechless.

Maks took her hand and led her down some steps, where a man helped her on board. She took off her sandals after wobbling precariously in her heels. The boat was small but enchanting. Maks was pulling out a chair, and bowed towards her like a maître d'. She sat down, and the boat starting moving gently along the canal as staff served them chilled champagne and a selection of Russian food.

Zoe realised she was starving as she tried delicious kebabs, dumplings filled with meat, puff pastries filled with cheese and then, of course, the ubiquitous caviar on small pieces of crusty bread. It tasted salty and sharp and she washed it down with champagne.

'Do you like it?' Maks asked.

Zoe wrinkled her nose. 'I think it might grow on me.'

She was feeling light-headed from the wine, and then dessert was served—delicious blinis filled with chocolate syrup.

While they were winding their way along the canal Zoe asked about various landmarks and Maks told her what they were. One in particular caught her eye, an elaborately domed and turreted cathedral, floodlit.

'That's the Church of the Saviour on Spilled Blood. It's where Tsar Alexander the Second was assassinated.'

Zoe shivered at that gruesome image.

'We'll go and see it tomorrow. The interior has beautiful mosaics.'

Her heart leapt. She ignored it. 'Don't you have meetings? Please don't feel like you have to babysit me. I don't mind looking around on my own.'

Once again Maks wondered what he was doing—actively upsetting his own hectic schedule—but the truth was that watching Zoe's reaction at the ballet had been more engrossing than anything he'd experienced in a long time. He was used to people hiding their emotions or reactions. He was jaded and the people around him were jaded.

'It's fine,' he said. 'It's a fashion shoot tomorrow. I'm sure they'll survive without me.'

When Zoe woke the next morning, dawn was breaking outside. She stretched in the massive bed. She was alone. She wasn't sure what she'd expected last night, but she'd assumed Maks would expect her to go to bed with him.

She'd certainly been feeling susceptible after that surprisingly thoughtful boat trip and dinner. When they'd got off the boat he'd insisted on carrying her to the car, because she'd still been barefoot. But when they'd returned to the hotel he'd delivered her to her door and said, 'I'll collect you for breakfast.'

Zoe must have looked confused, or something worse, because he'd snaked a hand around her neck, his thumb brushing her jaw, and said, 'We're taking this slow, Zoe. There's no need to rush.'

She'd watched him walk away, totally conflicted and

reeling at his unexpected chivalry, but also wondering why he wasn't trying to rip her clothes off.

Maybe he'd gone off her? Or maybe he was well aware of his effect on her and was priming her, so that when he did seduce her she'd be begging him.

She turned and buried her face in the pillow and tried to ignore the ache of frustration in her lower belly—a wholly new sensation.

She flipped over on her back again. With Dean it had been more about the connection they'd had since they were teenagers, in the same foster home. He'd been the first boy to kiss her. When she'd left Ireland she'd broken up with him, and it hadn't been that much of a wrench. After all, they hadn't even slept together. He'd pushed for it a couple of times, but something had always held her back.

She'd been surprised at the level of affection she'd felt when he'd appeared in London, asking to see her. She knew now that she'd confused that emotion and her desire with a loneliness that she hadn't wanted to acknowledge.

And Dean had taken advantage of that to sneak under her skin. Convincing her that there was still something romantic…sexual between them. But, as had happened in the past, when he'd pushed for intimacy something inside her had clammed up. She hadn't wanted it.

He'd backed off the first couple of times, but then… that last night…he'd grown angry. Accused her of teasing him. Grown violent. Revealed his real reason for coming back into her life.

Zoe shut the memory out.

Dean was gone. Thankfully she'd managed to get rid of him before he'd done anything serious to her. But she wouldn't forget his horrible, nasty words and the sense of betrayal that had taken her breath away. *'Frigid, stingy bitch.'*

The phone by Zoe's bed rang and she seized the opportunity for distraction.

Maks. Her pulse skipped a beat.

His voice was deep. Sexy. 'Morning. Are you awake?'

Zoe lay back, a delicious sizzle of anticipation in her gut. 'I am now.'

'Be ready in ten minutes. I'm taking you for breakfast.'

She smiled into the phone. 'Has anyone ever told you you're very bossy?'

'Frequently. Now, move.'

'These *pyshki* are the best in St Petersburg.'

Zoe looked at the doughnuts. She had thought she was full, after the lavish breakfast served in one of St Petersburg's most ornate and oldest cafés, but now her mouth watered again. If she wasn't careful she'd have to be wheeled back to London.

'Here, try one with the coffee.'

Maks handed her a plate holding about five doughnuts and then a coffee. Zoe dutifully took a bite, and as the flaky sweet texture melted on her tongue she moaned. She took a sip of coffee—the perfect accompaniment to the sweetness.

She looked at Maks, casual in dark jeans, top and jacket. His jaw was stubbled, as if he hadn't been bothered to shave that day. It made him look more dangerous. *Sexy.*

She helped herself to another small doughnut. 'So, where to now?'

She was surprised at how much she enjoyed just spending time with Maks. He was easy company for someone who made her insides knot with need whenever he looked at her.

'I thought we could—' He broke off and picked his ringing mobile phone out of an inside pocket. He answered it. 'Yes?' He frowned. 'Okay, tell Pierre I'll be right there.'

'What's up?' Zoe asked.

Maks made a face. 'I have to go to the fashion shoot. Our very temperamental famous photographer is freaking out because his assistant has got a bug and couldn't come in.'

Zoe was shocked at the level of disappointment she felt. 'Oh, that's okay. You should be working anyway. I can go back and get my camera and look around the sites myself.'

'Come with me. You said you were interested in fashion photography.'

Zoe was shocked. 'I couldn't… I mean…really? Would that be okay?'

Maks shrugged. 'Why not? Probably be good for you to see an egotistical maestro in his natural habitat and use it as a lesson in how not to be.'

On the way over to the shoot, excitement fizzed in Zoe's belly. 'Why do you hire people like this photographer if he's so horrible?'

'I didn't want to hire him—the brand insisted. But I'm not suffering people like him for much longer. There's no need to behave like a petulant child, no matter how talented you might be.'

Zoe agreed.

They arrived at a street that was cordoned off by Security, who let them in. Their driver parked up at the back of a long line of trucks and Winnebagos. There was even location catering. Zoe was totally intimidated by the sheer scale. For *one* fashion shoot!

Maks held her hand and led her to the other end of the street, where it opened out into a small square circled by tall neo-classical buildings in varying pastel hues and elegantly crumbling splendour. Zoe appreciated the aesthetics immediately, and could see why this location had been chosen to shoot the models, who were wearing vibrantly modern monochromatic clothes.

Maks went straight over to where a group was huddled

around a tall man with long hair, who looked furious. He saw Maks.

'About time, Marchetti. What are you going to do about this? I have no assistant! I can't be expected to work without help.'

Maks's voice was completely relaxed, but a thread of undeniable steel ran through it and Zoe noticed how people's eyes widened. 'This is an unforeseen event, Pierre. How can we make it right and get on with the shoot?'

'Get me an assistant! Right now!'

Zoe had only the barest premonition before Maks squeezed her hand and said, 'Pierre, I'd like you to meet Zoe Collins—your assistant for the day.'

Zoe's mouth dropped open. She looked at Maks, who was looking at the photographer, daring him to disagree. The other man looked at Zoe and sputtered, 'But…who *is* she? Your latest girlfriend? Does she know one end of a camera from the other? This is out—'

'Yes, she does. She's very talented, actually, and actively looking for experience.' Maks's calm voice cut through the photographer's outraged bluster. 'So what will it be, Pierre? Are we going to delay the shoot further or will you let Zoe assist you? Do I need to remind you we only have this location for one day?'

There was no doubting who was in control now.

Pierre looked around, as if to find support, but everyone just looked fed up and eager to get started. Eventually he huffed and said, 'Fine—but I'm warning you. If she can't keep up, I'm leaving, and you can use her to take the shots. I'm sure the brand would love that.'

Zoe heard Maks say something rude under his breath. Pierre was looking her up and down. He rattled off a list of things he needed and, knowing that this was an opportunity that wouldn't come along again, Zoe let go of Maks's hand and went over to where the equipment had been laid out.

CHAPTER SIX

PIERRE GARDIN HANDED Zoe a card. 'If you're ever looking for more work or experience, give my office a call.'

Zoe bit back an urge to say, *Thanks, but no thanks,* and said, 'Okay. And thank you for giving me a chance.'

'You know your stuff. You say you're self-taught?'

Zoe nodded. 'My father was a photographer.'

'Who was he? I might have met him.'

Before Zoe could avoid answering that question she felt a presence behind her. *Maks.* She'd been aware of him all day on the sidelines, watching carefully.

'If you're finished with Zoe?'

Pierre looked at Maks, a twinkle in his eye. It was scary how he'd transformed from raging to benevolent—a temperamental maestro, indeed.

'Sure, she's all yours, Maks.'

Maks took her hand and led her away. Zoe waved goodbye to the other crew and models, who had all been very sweet with her. She felt buoyed up, fizzing with energy.

When they got back to Maks's car and sat in the back she faced him. 'Thank you so much for giving me that chance. It was terrifying...but amazing.'

Maks's mouth tipped up. 'I've never seen Pierre conduct a shoot without having at least one tantrum directed at his assistant, but he couldn't seem to find fault with you.'

Zoe made a face. 'That could have had something to do with your presence.'

Maks shook his head. 'You're a natural, Zoe, and more qualified than you think. After today, do you still want to do it?'

She nodded. 'Yes. More than ever. Except...' She trailed

off, conscious that Maks might not really be all that interested in what she was saying.

But he prompted her. 'Except what?'

'Except I'm not really interested in promoting the façade of perfection. I'd love to work with models who are unique and diverse. Promote a healthier ideal. Not just size, but skin colour, scars… Handicaps. I really admire the model Kat Winters.'

Maks said, 'She's the supermodel who had the accident and lost her leg?'

Zoe nodded. 'Below the knee, yes. She's inspirational.'

Maks smiled. 'I think the industry could benefit very much from someone like you. Perfection is boring.'

Zoe felt self-conscious. She wanted to divert attention back onto Maks. 'Did you always want to go into the family business? Did you have other ambitions?'

Maks looked at Zoe. He wasn't used to people asking him such direct questions.

As if sensing she'd overstepped, she blushed and said, 'It's okay, it's none of my business—'

But Maks took her hand, stopping her words. She looked at him with those huge eyes, still sparkling with excitement and wonder. Things he rarely saw in anyone any more. The realisation that he felt a level of intimacy with her when they hadn't even slept together should make him uncomfortable. But it didn't.

He said, 'For a long time I wanted nothing to do with the business. I hated my father that much. But I expended so much energy hating him and protecting my sister that I didn't leave much space for figuring out what I wanted. When our father died, my brother Sharif called a meeting with Nikos and me. He made me realise that the business was now ours. And that we had a duty to rebuild the name with respect and honour—things that my father had decimated through greed and debauchery.'

Maks's mouth twisted.

'Even though we didn't grow up together, and I wouldn't call us close, Sharif had done his research, and put us in positions that played to our strengths. Nikos took over the PR and hospitality side, and he gave me the fashion and brand side to work with. I think the fact that he wanted to work with us…trusted us…had more of an effect than either Nikos or I expected. Sharif could have taken over the company alone, but he didn't. And I do enjoy what I do… I enjoy the challenge of dragging this company into the twenty-first century. It's about so much more now than just image. Things are changing, and people like you will be at the forefront of that change.'

Zoe's eyes were wide. Maks felt a prickle of exposure. He'd never told anyone all that before. He'd never really articulated out loud what it had meant for his brother to show such trust in him.

He realised the car had stopped outside the hotel. He hadn't even noticed.

Maks's phone rang.

Zoe blinked.

Maks answered the call as he got out of the car and came around to help Zoe out. Her hand slid into his and fitted there in a way that had him wanting to drag her to a private space so he could shut out the world entirely and expose her need for him. He wanted to feel her under him, all around him, milking his body until he didn't have to acknowledge that she did something to him that no other woman ever had.

But it would have to wait.

He made a face. 'That was Sharif on the phone. I have to call him back and make a few other calls. I might be a while.'

* * *

Zoe battled a sense of disappointment that was mixed with relief. She hadn't expected that conversation just now to reveal so much of herself, or to hear him reveal what he had. It made her feel as if a layer of skin had been pulled back.

She said, as brightly as she could, 'Don't worry about me. I'll probably have an early night—the adrenalin is catching up with me.'

When Zoe got back to her room she leant against the door, taking a breath. Maks was so...distracting. All-consuming. He demanded nothing less than total investment. Even during the day today, when she'd been concentrating so hard on keeping Pierre happy, she'd been aware of him. And now she was actually exhausted. And yet at the same time still fizzing with energy.

She ordered a light supper, hoping that might help dissipate the energy, but when she'd finished she felt the same. Tired but alive.

She'd worked on her first photo shoot today!

A sudden idea popped into her head and she changed into her running clothes. She realised it was too dark to head out onto the streets of an unfamiliar city, so she pulled her hair into a ponytail and went in search of the gym, which was in the basement of the hotel.

At this time of the evening it was empty, and Zoe warmed up before heading towards a punchbag. She hated the gym, but she loved running and she loved boxing.

After a solid ten minutes of throwing high kicks and punches at the bag, Zoe felt her muscles starting to burn and her face was hot. She hadn't heard a sound, so when a voice came from behind her to say, 'Fancy a sparring partner?' she almost jumped out of her skin.

She whirled around, breathing heavily. Maks was standing a few feet away, with a small towel around his neck, in sweatpants and a T-shirt that left little to the imagination.

'Um…' It was hard to speak when she was hyperventilating. 'I need a break and some water…you go ahead.'

On wobbly legs Zoe went over to a nearby water machine and took off her gloves, poured herself some water. She took a big sip before she dared to look around again. Maks was squaring up to the other punchbag, gloves on his hands.

He said over his shoulder, 'I rang your room but there was no answer, I figured you were asleep.'

Zoe made some kind of incoherent breathless mumble in response and drank him in greedily while he wasn't looking. Lord, but he was beautiful. All taut, coiled energy. Graceful, too, for such a big man. His technique was perfect—he was clearly experienced.

When she'd cooled down a little, Zoe put her gloves on again and went back to her punchbag. Maks was still pounding his bag, lost in his own world. Zoe almost felt she was intruding.

She got back to her own workout, but was too aware of Maks in her peripheral vision. He stopped and she heard him breathing. She tried to pretend that every cell in her body *wasn't* swivelling towards him like the bud of a flower opening to the sun.

'You're good.'

She stopped and turned around. She shrugged. 'Not in your league. There's a boxing gym near me. I started to go there after—' She stopped, feeling the creeping shame she always felt when she thought of her weakness.

'After your ex-boyfriend?'

Maks's voice was like steel.

Zoe nodded. 'I went to learn self-defence, but I found sparring and boxing surprisingly satisfying.'

Maks tugged off his gloves and picked up a couple of punch pads. 'Come on—practice on me.'

'I'm not that good...really.'

Maks started to move around her. 'Come on, Collins, show me what you've got.'

Zoe rolled her eyes but took up her stance, trying to remember to stay on the balls of her feet and mobile. Maks started off easy on her, but as she matched him he got faster and more unpredictable, forcing her to duck and react more quickly.

Finally he stopped and stepped back. They were both breathing heavily. Zoe more than Maks. She wished she could take off her top, but she only had a sports bra underneath.

As if reading her mind, though, Maks put down the pads and pulled off his own shirt. He must have seen the look on her face. 'Do you mind?'

Zoe shook her head as a roaring sound drowned out everything else. It was the blood in her body rushing to every erogenous zone. She'd seen men in states of undress in the gym—it was normal. But never one like this...

Maks was not human. He was too beautiful to be human. His powerful torso was a finely etched work of art, ridged with muscles. Not an ounce of spare flesh. Hard. Unyielding. Mesmerising.

She dragged her gaze up and looked at him suspiciously. 'Are you trying to distract me?'

He looked innocent. 'Me? No. Only as much as you're distracting me.'

Zoe nearly guffawed, but then Maks's gaze narrowed on her and drifted down, taking in her heaving chest under the clinging Lycra of her top, down over her belly, hips, thighs and lower legs to where her three-quarter-length jogging pants ended. Normally she worked out in a bra top and shorts, and even though she was more covered up right now, she felt naked.

Wanting to push back against the easy way Maks could manipulate her body, Zoe knocked her gloves together. 'Ready for round two, Marchetti?'

This time he put on his own gloves and started dancing around her. 'Sure, bring it on.'

Zoe launched a few jabs, but Maks ducked them. She knew he was going easy on her, and that only spurred her on. She took advantage of a split second's hesitation on Maks's part to throw a quick right-handed upper cut. The last thing Zoe expected was to make actual physical contact with Maks's jaw. But she did. And, not expecting it either, he stumbled back and fell over a stool, sprawling onto his back.

Zoe wasn't even aware of taking off her gloves or moving. She was on her knees at Maks's side, her hands on his face. His eyes were closed. 'Maks? Oh, my God, Maks... I'm so sorry. I didn't mean to actually hit you. Are you okay? Where does it hurt?'

'All over,' he growled.

His eyes opened and suddenly his hands were on her arms. The air between them was so charged Zoe was sure she could smell electricity in the air. All she could see was hard sinew and sculpted muscle.

She focused on his jaw, which looked red. 'Your jaw... let me get some ice, or something...'

Maks shook his head. 'Don't need ice.'

He was urging her down and towards him, until her chest was pressed against his.

'What are you doing?'

Maks moved his hand from her arm up to her shoulder and then to the back of her neck. He lifted his head. 'Kiss me better and we'll call it quits.'

Zoe's heart hammered. She realised she'd been waiting

for this moment ever since she'd agreed to come on this trip with Maks. She bent forward and avoided his mouth, pressing a kiss against his jaw.

Maks said, 'I didn't mean there.'

Zoe raised her head. There was something heady about being over Maks like this, even though she was aware of the strength in his body and knew that within a split-second she could be on her back with him overpowering her...

'I'm aware of that.'

He arched a brow. 'Are you, now? I'm not getting any younger, Collins.'

She smiled. She hadn't expected this either. Lightness. Flirting.

She bent down, her mouth so close to his that she could feel his breath feather against hers. She stayed there for a moment, relishing the sense of power she had...but every cell in her body was screaming for contact, so she lowered her head and pressed her mouth to his.

At first it was tentative. He was letting her explore... move at her own pace. But she could feel the tension in his form. As if his muscles were swelling against her.

Then all of a sudden, even though she was still on top, she was being kissed. Maks's hand was in her hair, urging her closer, enticing her to open her mouth, allowing him access. It would have been impossible to resist and she breathed him in, tasting him, letting him taste her.

Her blood ran hot and fast. She was very aware of the steel-like muscles under her breasts and instinctively she pressed closer, seeking to assuage the ache building at her core.

Maks drew back and Zoe cracked open her eyes. Everything was blurry. She realised that she was sprawled on top of him and his arousal was pressing against the top of her thighs. She'd been moving against him like a needy little kitten.

Mortified, she tried to slide off him, but he held her fast, hands on her hips.

'Where are you going?'

She didn't want to go anywhere. She wanted to stay right here. 'Nowhere…?'

Maks shifted slightly and grimaced. 'Actually, I think we need to move somewhere more comfortable. When we make love for the first time it's not going to be on the floor of a gym under fluorescent lighting.'

Zoe's heartrate picked up. 'Make love?'

Maks looked at her. 'Sweetheart, we're halfway there already.'

He shifted against her subtly and his erection teased the apex of her legs. Damp heat flooded her core. She almost groaned. He was right. *This was it.*

He moved and stood up in a fluid movement, pulling her up with him. Zoe couldn't take her eyes off him. He let go of her hand briefly, to bend down and put on his T-shirt. Then he took her hand and led her out of the gym and into the elevator.

He turned to her as they ascended. 'Are you ready for this?'

Not, *Do you want this?* Because they both knew it was a foregone conclusion. Was she ready?

On one level she didn't think she'd ever be ready for Maks. Could she possibly live up to what he expected of her? Nerves assailed her. It would be so easy to say *No, not yet.* She knew he wouldn't push it. But he also wouldn't wait around for ever.

She nodded.

'I need to hear it, Zoe.'

Damn him. She lifted her chin. 'Yes. I want this. I'm ready, Maks.'

It should have felt unsexy to be spelling it out like this, but the way he was looking at her was so…intense.

* * *

The elevator doors opened with a soft *ping*. Maks almost didn't notice, he was so fixated on Zoe. His body was tight with a need he couldn't remember experiencing for a long time.

Once inside his suite, he pushed the door closed behind him. He'd let go of Zoe's hand and she turned and walked into the room. His gaze tracked down her body, lingering on every dip and hollow. He wanted to taste her on his tongue. He wanted to taste her when she came apart.

She turned around. Her hair was up, exposing her neck and slim shoulders. She looked vulnerable.

Maks held out a hand. 'Come here.'

She hesitated a moment and Maks held his breath. Then she walked over, took his hand. He turned them so that her back was to the door. He cupped her jaw, traced his thumb over the scar above her lip. Then he bent his head and pressed a kiss to it. And then higher, over her other scar, high on her cheek, where it disappeared into her hairline.

Zoe whispered, 'Why are you doing that?'

Maks drew back. Her scent wound around him, through him. Musky. Sexy. 'Because they made you a warrior. Don't forget that.'

Sudden emotion made Zoe's throat tight. She cursed him again silently for his ability to see right down to her most vulnerable spot. She could still feel the imprint of his mouth on her scars. They tingled. She swallowed the emotion and reached up, wrapping her arms around his neck, bringing her body flush with his.

'Make love to me, Maks.' She couldn't disguise the huskiness of her voice—she only hoped he hadn't noticed.

Maks looked serious all of a sudden. 'If you want to stop at any moment, that's okay, Zoe.'

The emotion was back. 'It's okay. I trust you.' The words

came out before she even had time to process their full significance.

Maks bent down slightly and then Zoe was being lifted against his chest as if she weighed no more than a bag of sugar. He took her into the bedroom, bathed in the golden glow of a few small lamps. The bed looked massive.

Maks put her down on her feet. He put his hand to the back of his T-shirt and pulled it up and off, over his head. Zoe felt dizzy from his scent. Citrus, and something much deeper and darker.

'Take off your top.'

Zoe pulled her Lycra top up and off. She suddenly felt self-conscious in her very plain sports bra. Conscious that she was less than well-endowed.

She almost brought her arm up, but Maks said roughly, 'Don't do that. Turn around.'

Zoe turned around and felt him undo the bra at the back. He slipped the straps down her arms and it fell to the floor at her feet. She kicked off her trainers.

Maks stood behind her, the heat from his body making her shiver with awareness. Not cold. His hands were on her shoulders, moving down her arms. On her waist, spanning it easily. Then up, under her breasts. Zoe's breath was choppy, and it stopped completely when his big hands cupped her breasts. Her nipples pebbled against his palms into tight points of need. She bit her lip.

Maks's mouth pressed a kiss to the spot where her shoulder met her neck. One of his hands moved down, over her belly, teasing at the top of her jogging pants before tugging them down, over her hips. Meanwhile his other hand was massaging her breasts.

Her head fell back against his shoulder. She could feel the smattering of hair on his chest abrading the skin of her back. She wanted to turn around and feel it against her breasts. Her skin. Except she couldn't turn around because

Maks's hand was exploring under her lace panties, and further, to the place where her legs were tightly clamped together.

He said in her ear, 'Let me feel you, Zoe. Let me feel how much you want this.'

She relaxed, and Maks's hand slipped between her legs, his fingers coming into contact with the seam of flesh that hid the beating centre of every nerve-point in her body. He touched her there, until she was helpless but to relax even more, opening herself up to his wicked fingers.

She gasped when he found the moist evidence of her desire. She felt him tense against her, even as he stroked her flesh until she wasn't sure how she was still standing.

His movements became more rhythmic and Zoe's body responded, moving against his hand, willing him to explore deeper. He was a master of sorcery, penetrating her flesh again and again while he stroked that sensitive cluster of cells. Then, on a cry that came from some guttural place as his other hand squeezed her breast, Zoe's whole body tightened like a vice, before a rushing pleasure exploded outwards and upwards, washing everything she'd ever known away and replacing it with a pure kind of satisfaction she'd never felt before.

She wasn't aware of collapsing against him. She was only aware that he was laying her down on a soft surface and resting over her on both hands.

'Okay?'

She could barely nod. Her whole body was suffused with pleasure. She could feel her inner muscles still pulsating in the aftermath.

She watched through heavy-lidded eyes as Maks took off the rest of his clothes, revealing a body that was densely packed with muscles. He had a boxer's body. Immensely strong, but graceful.

Her eyes drifted down and widened when she took in the

most potent part of him. Long and thick. Hard. She could see moisture beading the head and her mouth watered at the thought of running her tongue along his shaft, tasting that moisture.

Somewhere else, where her brain was functioning, she wondered who she had become. She had thought there was something wrong with her after—

Maks came down alongside her. 'What are you thinking?'

Zoe's face flamed at her outrageous fantasy. Her hair had come loose. 'Nothing important.'

He put a hand on her belly. 'You're incredibly responsive. You seem surprised… You didn't—?'

She cut him off. 'No, not with him.' She wanted to get *him* out of her head. She turned towards him. 'Kiss me, Maks.'

He pulled her close, and as he did so he reached for her underwear, pulling it down and off completely. Now they were both naked. His mouth covered hers and she fell into the deep, drugging pleasure of it.

Maks's hand went between her legs again and, emboldened, Zoe explored his body. Tracing his pectorals, the small disc-like nipples, the ridges of muscle that led down to a flat lower belly, and further…to the pulsing heat of him. Strong but vulnerable. Silk over steel.

She wrapped her hand around him, moving it experimentally, up and down. She felt the moisture against her palm and pressed her thumb there, spreading it over his head.

He reared back, putting his hand over hers.

Instantly she felt gauche. 'What is it?'

He looked tortured. Stark. 'Later we can play…you can torture me all you want. Right now… I need to be inside you.'

Her inner muscles clenched at his words, as if her body

was already ahead of her. She took her hand away and lay back, watching as he reached for protection and rolled the latex along his length, sheathing all that silk and steel. For a second she lamented that barrier, and bit her lip.

He came over her, nudging her thighs apart with his. He was all sinew and hard lines and those silver eyes... 'Zoe, I meant what I said. If you want to stop—'

'I won't.' She reached up, overcome with a dangerous rush of tenderness for his consideration.

Maks notched the head of his erection against her. She could feel how slippery she was, and might have been embarrassed—but it was too late for that.

Zoe held her breath as Maks slowly joined his body with hers. She could see the strain on his face. 'I'm okay. Keep going.'

In one cataclysmic movement Maks thrust deeper, and Zoe sucked in a shocked breath at the sudden sharp pain.

Maks stopped. 'Zoe...?'

She felt impaled, as if she couldn't breathe. The force of Maks's body deep inside hers was so alien and yet...utterly *right*. She moved to try and escape the sharpness and it subsided. She breathed out on a shuddery breath. 'I'm okay...honestly.'

Maks moved again, pulling back before seating himself deep again. He did this over and over, letting Zoe's body get accustomed to his.

At one point he said, 'You're so tight...are you sure I'm not hurting you?'

She shook her head, a feeling of awe and wonder moving through her as she felt flutters of sensation eclipsing the sense of discomfort. Tension was spiralling inside her, adding to a hunger that made her move restlessly under Maks. There was no pain now, only a delicious sensation of building pleasure, deep at her core.

Maks's movements became harder, faster. He reached

under her and tipped up her hips, and she gasped when he touched her so deep inside she saw stars. She was overcome with a primal need that only this man could fulfil. She was almost sobbing, begging him for something she knew only he could give her, and that was when he reached between them and touched her, just where his own body was moving powerfully in and out.

That was all it took. A featherlight touch and she flew apart into a million brilliant shards of ecstasy.

It was only when Maks felt Zoe's body climaxing around his that he was able to let go. It had taken superhuman strength not to spill as soon as he'd entered her tight, slick body, but somehow he'd managed it. His whole focus had been on making this good for her.

And now…as his own climax ripped him apart, inside out…he knew that he'd never experienced anything as good as this.

CHAPTER SEVEN

WHEN ZOE WOKE, dawn was just a faint pink trail outside. Maks was sprawled beside her, on his front, legs and arms splayed. Every inch of his magnificent body was no less powerful in repose. His buttocks were two perfectly taut orbs, and Zoe felt hot when she thought of all that power thrusting between her legs.

He was facing away from her, and she was glad of that tiny respite. Even in sleep she was sure she would feel as if he could see right into her...to where she was freaking out as the full enormity of what had happened last night sank in.

She'd slept with Maks Marchetti. She was no longer a virgin.

She'd allowed herself to be intimate with someone. Blindly. Without a moment's hesitation. And not just because she'd wanted him so desperately—although that consideration had wiped everything else out—but also, and far more worryingly, because she'd trusted him.

She went cold inside when she recalled saying that to him. *I trust you.* She hadn't even noticed. Not really. Too intent on the hunger clawing inside her, too intent on achieving satisfaction.

But as that sank in now she went colder than cold. All her precious defences, which had protected her even when Dean had gone too far, had crumbled like a flimsy house of cards in the wake of Maks's expert seduction.

She'd allowed him access to her most deeply secret self. Where she was most vulnerable. Where she'd hidden all her insecurities and fears. And now...she had nowhere to hide.

Maks moved minutely beside her and she held her

breath, but he didn't move again. Terrified he would wake before she was ready to deal with him, Zoe moved off the bed silently. She found a robe hanging on the back of the bathroom door and pulled it on. Then she picked up her strewn clothes and stole out of his suite, hurrying back down the empty corridor to her own.

When she'd closed the door, she let out a long, shuddery breath. *What had she done?* She went into the bathroom and caught her reflection and winced. Her hair was a wild tangle. Her face was still flushed. Her eyes were bright and sparkling. Belying her inner turmoil.

She remembered him kissing her scars.

Zoe stripped off the robe and dived under the shower, lamenting getting rid of Maks's scent from her body even as she scrubbed herself. She saw the faint red marks where his stubble had grazed her skin. The faintest bruise on her thigh where he'd gripped her as he'd thrust deep.

He'd marked her as primally as if they were animals. And she thrilled to it even as she might try to deny it. *You want to be his woman.* She rejected that outright. There was no way, after initiating a virgin, that Maks would be hanging around to repeat the experience. She'd been a novelty from the start, that was all. And now it would be over.

When Zoe was out of the shower she dried herself perfunctorily and went into the bedroom, dragging out her meagre little suitcase. She dressed in jeans and a shirt and packed the rest of her things, ignoring the stunning yellow evening dress hanging in the wardrobe. The sooner she got out of this fantasy land, the better, before she—

She stopped herself. *Before she what?* Fell for Maks Marchetti?

At that moment the doorbell chimed. Zoe's heart stopped. It chimed again. She went and opened it, not prepared to see Maks on the other side, dressed in jeans and a dark shirt, tucked in. He was clean-shaven and his hair was damp.

Zoe instantly felt weak at the thought of him in the shower, water sluicing over that taut, powerful body.

'Maks? Did you want something?'

His face was expressionless, but she could see that his jaw was tight. 'You could say that. Why did you leave my bed?'

My bed. She shivered at the way he said that. It was so arrogant and possessive.

'I wasn't aware I had to ask permission.'

'What's going on, Zoe? Not long ago you were—'

'I know exactly what I was…doing.' Her face grew hot. She wished she could be more suave about this.

Maks came into the room before she could stop him. The door closed behind him. He looked over her head and she realised he could probably see into the bedroom, where her case was on the bed.

He walked around her and into the bedroom.

She walked behind him.

He turned to face her. 'Going somewhere?'

'I thought I should get back to London.'

Maks was in uncharted territory. He was used to women using intimacy as a means to foster a deeper intimacy. He'd never had a woman leave his bed and try to leave the country.

His insides curdled as a possibility struck him. He turned around to face her. 'Did I hurt you, Zoe?'

He cursed himself. He'd been so careful to make sure she was with him, but he knew at some point he'd been taken over by sheer lust and the whole experience. He'd believed she was with him all the way. He could remember the strength of her untried body clamping around his so powerfully, sending him into orbit. But maybe—

She was shaking her head. 'No. *No.* You didn't hurt me. At all. It was…amazing.' She looked shy all of a sudden. 'I didn't know it could be like that. I thought something was wrong with me.'

Maks had a strong suspicion about where that notion had originated, and felt an urge to simultaneously beat that other man to a pulp and to protect Zoe.

He moved towards her, snaked a hand around the back of her neck. Needing to touch her. 'There's nothing wrong with you—absolutely nothing. You're a passionate woman. I saw the fire in you the first time I met you.'

She looked at him. 'You did?'

He nodded. How could she not see that? But then, he knew how people could be made to feel insecure—his sister was a prime example.

She pulled back, dislodging his hand, avoiding his eye. 'I think it's for the best that I leave. You're hardly still interested after last night.'

'I know you're not someone who fishes for compliments, but last night was not like anything I've experienced before.'

She looked at him, her cheeks going red. 'That's just because I was a virgin. A novelty.'

'Oh, was it, now? I happen to think it was much more than that. We have incredible chemistry—last night was proof of that. Or are you saying you don't fancy me any more?'

Zoe would have spluttered if she could have. The very notion… Her every cell was aligned towards Maks right now, as if he was true north and her blood was full of iron filings.

'No, I'm not saying that. But maybe it's better to just… end it now before it gets too…' She trailed off.

'Complicated?' Maks asked, and then he said, 'I won't

let that happen. I'm not in the business of allowing things to get complicated.'

He sounded so sure of himself.

'Last night felt pretty intense. I'm not experienced, Maks. You do this all the time, and you move on. I'm afraid I won't be able to and that scares me.' Zoe bit her lip and then continued, 'You called me a warrior last night. I'm not a warrior, Maks. Anything but. I'm terrified of everything. That's why I don't commit to anything.'

Maks took her hand and sat down on the bed, pulling her down onto his thigh. 'Your whole family died in one moment, Zoe, it's no wonder you're scared. But you survived. You're a survivor.'

Zoe bit her lip for fear she'd let something else tumble out. The truth was that Maks didn't know the half of it. How guilty she felt for having survived. How her whole life revolved around that guilt and how it had informed all her decisions. She wondered if she'd ever feel free to move on and live a life of her own.

In one way, she *was* safe from becoming emotionally invested in Maks Marchetti. She'd never allow herself to wish for something like happiness with him because he wasn't offering it. And because she didn't deserve it.

Maks spoke, scattering her thoughts. 'I'm not offering long-term anything, Zoe. I'm a loner, and I've been reliably informed that I'm emotionally unavailable. You're confusing emotion with sex. What we shared was intense, but it was purely physical.'

Zoe felt the hardness of his muscles under her buttocks. He smelled of citrus and something more potent. An exotic mix.

'I can prove it to you if you like?' he said.

His hand was on her back, fingers seeking and finding the gap between her shirt and jeans, exploring, finding naked skin. Already she was melting. Breathless.

'Can you?'

She couldn't even really care that she sounded as if she desperately wanted him to prove it to her.

He nodded. His fingers were on the clasp of her bra now, and it was undone before she could take another breath. He pulled her closer, reaching around to cup one bare breast under its lace cup. She sucked in a breath. Her nipple was trapped between his fingers, stiffening into a sharp point of need.

With his other hand he cupped her jaw, drawing her face to his. 'Let me show you how it can be…trust me, Zoe.'

Trust me.

Like last night, those words should be restoring sanity to her brain like a bucket of cold water, but she couldn't seem to make herself care. Maybe Maks was right and all this was purely physical. It would burn out and they would go their separate ways. Right now, Zoe was all too tempted to just trust in Maks—again.

A weakness. She ignored the voice.

She touched his jaw with her hand, before spearing his short hair with her fingers. 'Okay, then, let's do this.'

What was it about him that seemed to ignite some spark within her, an urge to rebel, throw caution to the wind?

She knew she didn't really want to explore the answer to that as Maks's mouth covered hers and he pushed the suitcase off the bed.

It fell to the floor, spilling its contents. She wasn't going anywhere.

Maks looked at Zoe, sleeping on the bed. Morning had turned into afternoon, and he was in danger of forgetting about the outside world entirely. She was on her back, the sheet pulled up to her waist. Her skin was still slightly flushed. Breasts plump, with those small, tight pink nipples. His body reacted to the memory of how they'd felt on his tongue, how they'd tasted. How he could make them harder by sucking…

Dio. What was happening to him? He never, *never* encouraged a woman to stay beyond one night. If they saw each other again it was strictly while their mutual chemistry lasted and through no encouragement on Maks's part. That was why he'd always chosen discreet, independent women.

But he'd never met one as independent as Zoe.

She would be on her way back to London right now if he hadn't woken up, incensed to find her gone. For the first time he hadn't been secretly relieved that a woman had left his bed. He'd felt…irritated. Exposed.

What was happening here was way off the charts of Maks's usual modus operandi. But then Zoe was different. And this chemistry… He'd never experienced anything like it.

They'd spent the morning in bed, and it had eclipsed the previous night ten times over. Maks had never come as hard. Or as often. And he didn't know if he'd ever get used to seeing the look of wonder on Zoe's face when she climaxed—as if she'd discovered some ancient secret wonder.

She was a novice, reminded an inner voice. *Her awe will fade. The chemistry will fade. She's just a woman.*

As if hearing his thoughts, she stirred on the bed and it had an immediate effect on Maks's body. She opened her eyes, slumberous. He watched as she registered where she was, and who she was with, when her eyes landed on him. They narrowed on his chest and then moved down to where his body was reacting forcibly under her blue/green gaze.

She moved over onto her side and rested her head on her hand. For a second she surprised Maks with how assured she looked. But then she smiled, and it was all at once shy and bold. She pulled the sheet back and he could see the curve of her body, the cluster of curls at the top of her thighs. 'Where are you going?' she asked.

He smiled. 'Nowhere.'

The outside world was overrated.

Zoe put her camera to her eye and focused on the stunning mosaics in the ornate cathedral. She'd ducked in here after spending the last few hours walking the streets, taking pictures of people, unnoticed.

She understood why she liked photography so much—it kept her removed. And she was losing herself in photography right now to distract herself from the enormity of letting Maks persuade her to stay when she would have fled. Back to her safe little life. Changed for ever. But safe again.

Really? asked a small inner voice. *Would you have been able to put Maks Marchetti behind you as if it had never happened?*

No. Zoe wasn't self-delusional enough to tell herself that. She would never forget Maks now. He was imprinted on her mind and on her body in a way that truly terrified her. Which was why she'd wanted to run.

Except it hadn't taken much to persuade her to stay. They'd spent a whole day in bed yesterday, ordering from room service. Maks had disappeared in the evening—presumably to catch up on the work he was meant to be doing. Zoe had been too sated and exhausted to do anything but have a shower and go back to bed.

Maks had woken her a few hours later, sliding into her bed, wrapping his hard, naked body around hers. She'd turned to him instinctively, more than shocked to find how accustomed she'd already become to having him in her bed.

He hadn't said a word, but he had used his mouth to communicate an urgency and desperation that she'd matched. Rising above him and taking him inside her, moving up and down experimentally at first, and then with more confidence when she'd seen the look of absolute absorption on his face.

The sensation of being in control had been heady. Until

Maks had said, *'Witch...'* and put his hands on her hips, holding her so that he could pump powerfully into her body, showing her that any sense of control had been brief and illusory. But by then she hadn't cared, because every point of her being had been fixated on chasing the ecstasy only he could bring.

She groaned softly at the memory and a nearby tourist looked at her. Mortified, Zoe walked back out into the late-afternoon sunshine, blinking as her eyes adjusted to the light. Autumn was arriving and the city was taking on a golden hue. It was more beautiful than she would have ever imagined, with the multi-coloured turrets of the church standing out against the bright blue sky.

'Here you are.'

Zoe would have dropped her camera if not for the fact that it was around her neck. She whirled around, her joy at seeing Maks taking her by surprise before she could stop it.

He'd been gone when she'd woken this morning, but had left a note.

I can't keep avoiding meetings—much as I'd prefer to. My driver will take you wherever you want to go, except to the airport.

You promised to be my date tonight, don't forget...
M

His date. For another event later this evening. She'd avoided thinking about it till now.

'How did you find me?'

Maks held up his phone. 'I called the driver—amazing what modern technology can do these days.'

Zoe made a face. He turned her brain to mush. Especially when he was dressed in a dark grey three-piece suit that made his eyes look even steelier.

He said, 'I've arranged for the designers in the showcase to send over some dresses for you to choose from for this evening.'

Zoe walked with him back to the car. He'd told her about this event—a fashion show to showcase up-and-coming Russian designers, get them noticed on the world stage. Insecurity lanced her.

'But I'm not a model—I'm way too short. The dresses probably won't fit.'

'I've given them your size and height.'

Zoe stopped before they reached the car. 'I wouldn't want to let them down, though…what if I choose a dress and it looks awful on me? That's hardly fair on the designer.'

Maks turned to Zoe. She looked genuinely concerned. When he could well imagine other women being incensed at the thought of wearing an unknown designer, she didn't want to let them down. He felt a curious sensation in his chest.

'Let me be the judge of whether or not you'll do them justice, hmm? After all, it's my reputation on the line—and the Marchetti Group's.'

She bit her lip and Maks had to fight back a wave of desire. He'd found it hard to concentrate today, wondering where she was. How she was after their indulgent day. And night. She'd been innocent. She must be tender.

That had unleashed another wave of desire.

He took her hand and said, with a rough edge to his voice, 'Stop biting your lip. It's mine to bite.'

Instantly her cheeks went pink. She released the plump flesh, moist from her teeth and tongue. She was a novice with the wiles of a siren. An erotic combination that Maks couldn't resist and had no intention of resisting until he was well and truly sated.

Zoe had never exposed so much flesh before. Acres and acres of pale skin. But the dress… It was like a dress straight out of a fantasy she'd always had but had never acknowledged before.

Never allowed herself to acknowledge.

She'd always believed she wasn't 'girly', deliberately avoiding dresses or anything too flouncy, but after a few days with Maks Marchetti Zoe's inner girly girl was unleashed and there was nothing she could do to stop it.

The dress was an exquisite confection of pink silk and tulle. It had a deep vee to her waist in the front, and two slim straps criss-crossing over her back, holding the dress up. A thick waistband encircled her waist, and a layer of sheer tulle fell to the floor over the silk underskirt, all in the same dusky pink colour. And when she moved the dress sparkled from the thousands of tiny sequin stars sewn into the fabric by hand.

The designer had brought accessories, and friends to do Zoe's hair and make-up, and she was even further out of her comfort zone now, with her hair pulled back into a rough chignon. For the first time she wasn't as acutely aware of her scars as she normally was. Even though they weighed nothing, they were a part of her and they'd always felt like a burden. Something she had to carry.

There was a delicate silver chain around her neck that hung down into the deep vee of the dress, between her breasts. And that was it. Simple. Understated. Elegant. She hoped.

There was a knock on her door and her heart thumped. She picked up the clutch bag from a nearby table and opened the door.

Maks was wearing a white tuxedo jacket and shirt with a black bow tie. The snowy white made his skin look darker. Zoe's mouth dried. That dark grey gaze swept up and down, resting on her chest before moving up. His eyes were wide, his expression arrested.

Immediately Zoe's fledgling sense of confidence threatened to crumble. 'What is it? It's not appropriate, is it? It shows too much…'

Maks let out a sound halfway between a laugh and a groan. 'You could say that.'

Then he must have seen something on Zoe's face. He put out a hand. 'No, it's fine. You'll probably be more covered up than most people there. It's just…you're more than beautiful, Zoe. You're breathtaking.'

'Oh…' She felt her confidence slowly return, along with shyness. She touched her hair self-consciously. 'They put it up…'

Maks reached out and touched her jaw with a feather-light touch. 'I told you…you don't have to hide.'

This was too huge for Zoe to analyse right at that moment—that a man like Maks Marchetti should be the one who was seeing all the way into her and not turning away in disgust or disdain.

She picked up the short blazer-style jacket to accompany the dress and said, 'I'm ready.'

As the elevator descended to ground level, Maks thought to himself that he was glad one of them was ready, because as soon as she'd opened her door and he'd seen that dress he'd wanted to walk her right back into the room, strip it off her body and bury himself inside her until the rush of blood in his brain cooled down enough for him to think straight again.

A short while later Zoe flinched minutely under the barrage of flashbulbs and shouts directed at her and Maks. Before, at the ballet, he'd ignored them and gone straight into the venue, but here he was stopping for a minute to let them get pictures.

She could feel his tension. He resented it. She thought of what he'd experienced at the hands of the media when he'd been younger. They'd fed off his and his sister's pain. No wonder he despised them and their invasion of his privacy.

When they were inside the building—an old disused warehouse on the outskirts of the city—Zoe looked up at Maks. His jaw was tight.

'Maks… *Maks*.'

He looked at her. Blankly for a second. As if he'd forgotten she was there. It made a shiver go down Zoe's back.

'You can let go of my hand.'

Something flared back to life in Maks's eyes and immediately he released her hand. 'Sorry.'

She shook her head. 'Why did you stop for the photographers just now?'

Maks looked at her. 'Because, as much as I loathe them, they also help promote our business. Suffice to say they'll never get anything more from me than a few seconds.' His mouth quirked. 'If Nikos was here and not a newly married father he'd probably still be outside, preening for them.'

'What about Sharif?' Zoe was glad to see him relax, even as she didn't welcome how much it meant to her.

'Sharif has a similar attitude to the paps as me. When our father kidnapped him—'

Zoe gasped. '*Kidnapped* him?'

Maks nodded. 'His mother took him back to her Arabian home when she realised our father had only married her for her dowry. Sharif lived there with her for nine years, until our father went after him because he was coming of age. As the mysterious eldest son of Domenico Marchetti, half-Arab, half-Italian, Sharif was subjected to an intense scrutiny that has never let up.'

Zoe absorbed that. But before she could ask Maks any more, they were approached by a waiter carrying glasses of champagne.

Maks took two and handed her one. *'Na zdorovie.'*

Zoe tried to wrap her tongue around that. *'Nostrovia…?'*

Maks smiled. 'Good enough.'

He clinked his glass on hers and they each took a sip. Zoe felt warm under his gaze, and it was an effort to break eye contact and look around.

It was a huge old warehouse—very industrial chic. Catwalks were set up all through the room, with models walking up and down. People in elegant finery milled around, looking at the models, consulting brochures. Zoe spotted her dress designer in the distance, standing near a catwalk and presumably showcasing her designs. Zoe recognised the whimsical romantic nature of her dresses.

A couple of people approached Maks, and that started a constant stream of people over the next couple of hours. Zoe was happy to hang back, but he always drew her forward, introducing her even though his conversations were invariably in Russian or another European language so she couldn't really participate.

Hanging out with Maks made her feel very conscious of the fact that she hadn't gone to university. *But you could have*, pointed out a small inner voice. Zoe knew it was irrational, and probably very stupid, but she'd always felt that if Ben, her brother, hadn't had a chance to go to university and fulfil his potential, then what right had she?

'Okay?'

Jolted out of her momentary introspection, Zoe looked up at Maks. He was alone, his legion of fans and sycophants having melted away. She nodded, and pasted a bright smile on her face. 'Fine.'

He took her hand. 'Liar. One day you'll tell me what you're thinking of when you disappear like that.'

The fact that he'd noticed made her feel alternately warm inside and fearful. Maks saw everything. And she did have secrets. Secrets that she worked hard at ignoring.

Zoe said brightly, 'I hate to disappoint, but I wasn't thinking of much at all.'

Maks made a sound to indicate how much he believed that, and said, 'Ready to go?'

'Can we?'

Maks smiled. 'I'm an expert at showing my face, talking to the right people and then leaving.' His gaze swept her up and down. He suddenly looked hungry. 'Anyway, I've been fantasising about snapping those far too flimsy straps so that you're naked and on my bed in the shortest time possible.'

Heat curled inside Zoe's lower body, flames licking at her core. Breathlessly she said, 'You'll do no such thing. I promised Oksana I'd take care of her dress.'

Maks arched a brow. 'Oksana?'

'One of the designers you're showcasing and supporting?'

Maks rolled his eyes. 'Fine—I won't damage the dress.'

Zoe felt like giggling. She wasn't used to feeling this... light. Bubbly. Emotion gripped her and she pushed it back down. It had no place here. This was just physical. Not emotional.

Maks tugged her towards the entrance. 'Come on—it's our last night in St Petersburg. I want to take you to my favourite late-night café.'

Zoe let Maks bundle her into the back of his chauffeur-driven car and they were whisked across the sparkling city. Soon they pulled up outside a tall, ornate building. Huge oak doors were opened by a man in a dark suit wearing an earpiece. He nodded at Maks, clearly recognising him.

Inside it was dark and mysterious. Zoe saw alcoves with velvet banquette seats. Candles flickered over faces, half-hidden. Low music played. A sleek blonde woman met them and showed them to one of the booths.

Zoe had never felt more transported in her life. They could have stepped back in time to the playground of the decadent Tsars. And that feeling was only compounded when a selection of food was brought to the table. Small baked puff pastries filled with cheese. Blinis rolled and filled with caviar. And desserts: layered honey cake and balls of dark chocolate. All washed down with sweet sparkling wine.

Zoe was drunk on the wine, the food, but most of all on Maks. He sat beside her, feeding her morsels, not satisfied until she'd tasted a little piece of everything. One arm was stretched out behind her and his fingers grazed the back of her bare neck. Making her skin tight and hot. Making her breasts ache and her nipples tighten with need.

He lifted a tiny piece of toast with caviar. Zoe shook her head, laughing. 'I can't. I'll burst.'

'Fine. I'll have it.'

Maks popped it into his mouth, smiling as he ate. The lightness Zoe had felt earlier still infused her. It was heady. Maks had undone his bow tie and it hung open rakishly, the top button of his shirt was undone too, revealing the bronzed column of his throat.

Zoe saw his gaze drop and rest on her chest. She looked down to see the dress was gaping slightly, showing the curve of her bare breast. The blood pulsed between her legs, hot and heavy. She looked back up and saw Maks was reaching for her, cupping her jaw and angling her head to take her mouth in a kiss that sent her hurtling over the edge of all restraint.

She strained towards him, her arms around his neck. His hand slid into the front of her dress and closed around one breast, squeezing her flesh, trapping a nipple between his fingers. Zoe gasped into his mouth.

He said roughly, 'I want to taste you, right now.'

She drew back, shocked at how desperate she felt. 'Okay.'

Maks smiled and took his hand off her breast. He somehow communicated to the discreet staff that they were leaving, and when he'd paid the bill he led her out on shaky legs to the car.

The journey back to the hotel was a blur. Zoe didn't feel drunk any more. Everything was crystal-sharp.

As soon as they got into Maks's suite he pulled off his jacket and shirt, reached for his trousers. Zoe kicked off the sandals she was wearing. Maks's hands were now on his briefs, pulling them down, releasing his arousal.

Zoe's mouth watered. Feeling bold, she dropped to her knees in front of Maks, the dress billowing out around her on the ground, a cloud of silk and tulle. But she was oblivious to that.

'Zoe…what are you—?'

Maks groaned as Zoe took his erection in her hand and came close. She darted her tongue out, licking the head. Tasting the salty bead of moisture.

'Zoe, you don't have to—'

But she didn't hear what he said because she was taking him into her mouth, running her tongue around the ridge below the head experimentally. She felt Maks's fingers in her hair and she put her hands on his thighs as she explored the silky heat of his body, marvelling at how powerful she felt when she was the one on her knees.

She could feel the tremor in Maks's hand, and the way his hips were jerking as if he couldn't control himself. She took him deeper, relishing his essence, her hands tightening on his thighs as he jerked into her mouth.

Then he was pulling back, out of her mouth, and she looked up. Maks emitted a curse in Italian, or Russian— she wasn't sure which—and then he was hauling her up, reaching under her dress to pull her underwear down.

He lifted her against the door, saying roughly, 'Put your legs around my waist.'

And then he was thrusting up, right into the heart of her. His big, slick body was embedded in hers so tightly

and deeply that she saw stars. Zoe clung to Maks as he effortlessly held her, thrusting deeper and deeper, harder…
Until Zoe had nowhere to go except over the edge, crying
out as her whole body shattered around Maks's.

She was barely aware of him pulling free and the hot
splash of his release against her belly, under the dress.

Maks lifted her into his arms and carried her to the bedroom, stripping off the dress and then taking her by the
hand into the shower, where she would have sunk to the
floor in a state of sated bliss if he hadn't held her up as he
lathered soap all over her body and shampooed her hair.

Afterwards he dried her with a huge soft towel. Then
he took a robe from the back of the door and wrapped her
in it, leading her to the bed, where she lay down, unable
to move a muscle.

A few hours later Zoe woke with a start. She sat up,
becoming aware of the voluminous robe, and then she remembered that desperate coupling against the door. The
taste of Maks's body on her tongue. *In her mouth.* Her inner
muscles squeezed at the memory.

The bed beside her was empty. She went out of the bedroom, passing a chair with the beautiful dress draped over
it carefully. Her face felt hot when she realised she couldn't
even remember Maks taking it off her.

She walked down the corridor, making no sound on the
plush carpet, and found Maks standing at the window, looking out at the sleeping city, its lights twinkling in the distance. He was bare-chested, but had pulled on his trousers.

He turned around when he heard her. She walked over,
feeling shy, and stood beside him. She sensed tension.

He said, 'I apologise for earlier… I'm not usually so…
uncivilised.'

Zoe turned to face him, surprised. 'You didn't hurt me.'

Maks's mouth firmed. 'Maybe not, but—'

Zoe reached out, touching his arm. 'I liked it.'

Very much.

She blushed, and was glad of the low lighting that disguised it.

He looked at her, and then reached for her, pulling her into his side. 'You did?'

Zoe ducked her head against him, not wanting him to see how much she had liked it. His skin was warm, his muscles hard. She nodded against him, embarrassed by the depth and strength of her own desires.

He tipped up her chin. He still looked serious. 'You're small. I was afraid I'd taken you so quickly that you hadn't had time to be ready, or even to say no...'

Zoe's heart swelled dangerously. He was so much the opposite of her ex-boyfriend, who had ultimately been prepared to use violence to get what he wanted.

She shook her head. 'Honestly, you didn't hurt me. I was...ready.'

And she was ready again. She could feel her body softening, ripening. Just from being near him.

'You're sure?'

She came around in front of him and reached up. Putting her arms around his neck. Bringing her body flush with his. 'Yes. I'm sure. I'm not delicate, Maks.'

She had a sense, then, of her own innate strength. An awareness that was new and revelatory. Maks had given her this, and it was more priceless than any jewel.

He looked at her for a long moment and then he brought his hands to her hips. She could feel his body harden against her and she shifted against him. The serious look faded as his eyes blazed with renewed heat. Zoe still couldn't believe that she had such an effect on him.

He said, 'This...between us...isn't over, Zoe. Not by a long shot. We have to leave here tomorrow, but this isn't over...'

Zoe blinked. She hadn't even thought about tomorrow.

She'd happily let the cocoon of Maks's world enclose her in a timeless bubble. But now something flickered inside her. *Hope.*

'What are you saying?'

He caught a lock of her hair and wound it around a finger. He said, 'I have to go to Venice, and if you want my plane can take you on to London. But I'd like you to come to Venice with me for a couple of days.'

Zoe felt a yearning rise up inside her. It would be so *easy* just to acquiesce. Even though she knew the sensible and smart thing to do would be to end this now. Go back to her regular life. To reality. Which was far removed from this man and his world, where he clicked his fingers and things manifested themselves as if by magic.

But…would it be so wrong to indulge for just a little longer? It wasn't as if he was lulling her into a false sense of security. She knew he was only offering a finite affair. And she didn't want anything more either.

Liar, whispered that small voice.

She ignored it. She was getting good at that. At ignoring her conscience. At ignoring that yearning feeling. Yearning for something she'd shut out for years. *Love. A family.* No. Those things represented loss and pain. She wasn't going to risk that ever again. This wasn't about that. Not remotely. So she was safe.

'Okay. I'll come with you.'

Maks smiled. 'Good.'

And then he bent his head and covered her mouth with his, and she leapt straight back into the fire that was so effective at burning away the voice of her conscience.

CHAPTER EIGHT

ZOE HAD SEEN pictures of Venice her whole life. Who hadn't? But pictures couldn't have remotely prepared her for that first view down the Grand Canal from the water taxi. For once, she didn't even feel the urge to look through the lens of her camera. It was just so…beautiful. Timeless. Iconic. Familiar and yet totally new at the same time. Trying to capture it digitally would inevitably do it a disservice.

The crumbling ancient *palazzos* had romantic balconies, and windows that winked like eyes as they passed by. Zoe couldn't help but wonder about the people who had lived in those places….who lived there now. It was like a fairy tale place.

'You're impressed.'

Zoe heard the smile in Maks's voice and glanced at him, feeling gauche. 'Sorry, you're probably used to a more blasé, sophisticated reaction.'

He reached out and caught her hand, tugging her into him where he stood near the driver at the wheel, behind a pane of glass. 'What I'm used to is not necessarily good. It's a privilege to see Venice again through your reaction.' Maks looked at the buildings over Zoe's head. 'I'd forgotten how amazing it is the first time.'

Zoe was glad he was not looking at her as she blushed at his reference to *the first time*. It had indeed been amazing.

The water taxi veered smoothly towards one of the impressive buildings. It stood on its own, with an area of greenery to the side, a massive balcony on the first floor. The taxi pulled up to a wooden walkway and a man in a uniform rushed towards them, helping first Zoe, then Maks, out of the bobbing boat.

They were led up to the foyer of the hotel and welcomed as if Maks was returning royalty by a fawning manager, who came with them in the rococo-inspired elevator up to the most sumptuous, luxurious suite of rooms Zoe had ever seen.

There were chandeliers, gold-painted frescoes on walls and ceilings, acres of Carrara marble, Murano glass vases and lamps, oriental rugs on parquet floors.

When the manager had left, and she'd managed to pick her jaw up off the floor, she asked, 'Do you own the place or something?'

Maks looked a little sheepish.

Zoe's jaw dropped again. 'You own this hotel...' She couldn't quite compute that information, so she walked over to the open double doors that led out to the balcony. She looked down over the Grand Canal and shook her head at the incongruity of *her* in this unbelievable place.

Maks came and stood beside her. 'What are you thinking?'

She looked at him. He had his hands in his pockets, nonchalant. 'I'm thinking that it was naive of me not to just assume you owned this hotel. It must be amazing...'

'What must be amazing?'

Zoe shrugged. 'To walk into a place like this and know that it's yours... It's kind of incomprehensible to me, and yet it's all you've ever known?'

Now Maks shrugged and looked away, out to the view. He put his hands on the balcony. 'I've had great privilege. I would never deny that. But if I could swap what my sister and I experienced for a far less privileged existence then I would, in a heartbeat.'

'It was that bad?'

He glanced at Zoe, his face stark. 'It was bad enough.'

Somehow Zoe knew exactly what he meant. It had been just 'bad enough' to blight both their lives for ever. Like hers had been blighted—albeit by very different circumstances.

She said, 'I only had eight years with my parents and my brother, but they were wonderful years.'

So wonderful that she couldn't bear to contemplate experiencing having a family again, only to have it ripped away from her.

Maks turned his back on the view. 'You lived in Dublin?'

Zoe nodded and smiled. 'We had a beautiful house on the coast, just south of Dublin city, overlooking the Irish Sea. I used to love sitting in the conservatory and watching the weather change over the sea, especially on stormy days. I'd watch how it rolled in with such a fury, and yet I felt so safe and protected...as if nothing bad could ever touch me.'

What an illusion that had been.

Maks reached out and cupped her face. His thumb traced the scar above her lip with such a light touch she was afraid she was imagining it.

He said, 'And yet it did.'

Emotion tightened Zoe's chest and throat. Maks must have seen it, because he pulled her into his chest and wrapped his arms around her. But Zoe was too scared to let the emotion bubble up and out, terrified it might never stop. So she swallowed it down and pushed out of Maks's arms, avoiding his eye.

'I think I'll go and freshen up.'

Maks watched Zoe walk back into the suite, pick up her bag and disappear into the bathroom. He rubbed at his chest absently. The raw emotion in her eyes just now had hit him squarely in the solar plexus. Normally, any hint of emotion made him shut down in response, but he hadn't been able to ignore Zoe. And she'd been the one to push *him* away.

He turned back to the view of the canal, barely registering it. Which only made him think of Zoe's comment about his jadedness.

Porca miseria. What the hell was going on with him? It was as if as soon as he'd laid eyes on Zoe something inside him had realigned into a new configuration.

Immediately an inner voice said, *Ridiculous. It's physical desire, pure and simple. Unprecedented. Raw. Insatiable. But just desire. A chemical reaction. Not emotion.*

He heard a sound behind him and turned around. She'd changed into cropped jeans and a fresh shirt. Her scuffed trainers. Hair down. Minimal make-up. She looked young and fresh and achingly beautiful. Without even trying.

She was holding her camera and lifted it up. 'I might go out and take some pictures. You probably have meetings to attend?'

Her dogged independence made Maks chafe, when he usually abhorred a lover trying to monopolise his attention. Something rogue inside him made him say, 'Actually, I'm not under pressure today. I'll come with you.'

Zoe couldn't stop the rush of pleasure, even though a moment ago she'd actually been relishing the thought of some space from Maks. He saw too much, and he made her feel too much, but now she felt as giddy as a kid again.

'Are you sure?'

'Unless you don't want me to come with you?'

Zoe just managed to refrain from rolling her eyes at that suggestion. 'No, I'd like it.'

Several hours later, Zoe was drunk again. But not on anything more than Venice, some pasta followed by gelato, and Maks. He absolutely belonged in this milieu, against the dramatically beautiful backdrop of such an ancient and iconic city.

She'd taken a sneaky snap of him on a bridge, and she'd bet money that he'd been a Venetian prince in another lifetime. Albeit one in faded jeans that were moulded to his powerful thighs and taut behind and a dark polo shirt that did little to disguise the lean musculature of his chest.

And aviator glasses that made him look like he'd just stepped out of *Vogue Italia* for men.

Zoe sighed. Whatever anomalous moment or thing had led to Maks finding her attractive, she was sure it wouldn't last for much longer. He turned to her and held out his hand and Zoe's heart constricted.

She was in so much trouble.

As she took his hand and let him lead her into the labyrinthine streets, she knew that against all her best intentions and instincts she'd done the thing that she feared most in the world. She'd fallen in love with Maks. And she knew now that whatever she'd believed she'd felt for Dean had been nothing in comparison. Less than nothing. It had been driven by loneliness, and the fact that she'd known him from her past.

This had nothing to do with loneliness or weakness. It was wild, untameable and elemental. And she knew that whatever pain she'd felt before, even when she'd lost her entire family, would pale into insignificance compared to what Maks would do to her. And she was afraid it was already too late.

Maks looked at Zoe where she stood in the small *osteria* near one of Venice's many bridges. She sipped at a small aperitif. He noticed men looking at her and instinctively moved closer. He'd never felt possessive before.

Zoe looked up at him. 'What was the house that you grew up in like?'

Maks thought of her evocative description of watching storms rolling in over the sea and felt wistful. 'Not like yours. No view of the sea. It was a grand *palazzo* in Rome. Beautiful, but austere. We weren't allowed to touch things because they were all priceless antiques. Once, Sasha and I were playing and she knocked over a vase. I'm pretty sure it was Ming.'

Zoe put a hand over her mouth, eyes wide, sparkling.

'Our father came out of his study and saw it. He took off his leather belt and asked who was responsible.'

Zoe's hand came down from her mouth. Now she looked horrified.

'Sasha stepped forward. She was nine. I think she thought he wouldn't dare, if he knew it had been her fault. But I knew my father by then. I knew what he was capable of. So I pushed her behind me and told him I had done it.'

'He beat you with the belt?'

Maks pulled down the collar of his polo shirt and Zoe looked at where he was pointing, to a faded scar just over his collarbone. A rough ridge of skin. She reached up and touched it. Her finger was feather-light against his skin, yet it burned.

She frowned. 'I didn't notice it before.' She sounded almost angry with herself that she hadn't.

Maks swallowed. 'My father stopped when I grabbed the belt off him and started to hit him. I was fourteen by then, and almost as tall as him. He didn't do it again.'

Zoe took her hand down and Maks missed her touch.

She asked, 'How did you know he would be capable of hitting a young girl?'

Maks's insides felt like lead. 'Because I'd seen him hit one of our young maids. And I'd seen him hit our mother when I was much younger, before they divorced.'

'I'm sorry you experienced that.'

Maks took her hand back and kissed her fingers, relishing their coolness. 'I think I would have liked your house.'

Zoe smiled, but it was sad. 'I never saw it again after

the crash. It was dealt with by lawyers and the state. They offered to let me go back and get my things, but I couldn't bear to… Everything was put in storage for me, but I've never visited the storage unit.' She shrugged and looked down. 'I'm a bit of a coward.'

Maks's chest felt tight. He tipped up her chin and saw her eyes were like two oceans of green and blue. 'You're not a coward, Zoe. Far from it.'

Zoe looked up at Maks. He should be the hardest person in the world to talk to, but things that she never spoke of to anyone tripped off her tongue with an ease that shocked her.

He threw back the rest of his aperitif and said, 'Come on, let's go.'

Go where?

Zoe didn't even want to ask, not wanting to burst the incredible bubble of being with this man in this beautiful place. She felt like a miser, wanting to hoard every tiny moment.

After turning a dizzying number of corners they emerged into a small quiet square with a large ornate church at one end. Maks was leading her through to another street when she heard it. The sound of singing.

Zoe stopped. She walked over to have a closer look. Posters advertised an opera, due to take place the following evening. The singing was more audible now, coming from inside, and she looked at Maks, who shrugged and followed her into the dark interior.

People were up on a stage in costume, but no make-up. She whispered to Maks, 'It must be the dress rehearsal. Can we stay a while?'

He nodded. She was about to sit down at the back, but Maks grabbed her hand and led her up a flight of narrow winding stairs. They came out onto a balcony on the upper level that had a view of the whole church and stage.

They were rehearsing one of Zoe's favourite operas, *La Traviata*. The music swelled and washed over and through her. She was captivated. But not captivated enough to be oblivious to Maks beside her, his long legs stretched out carelessly.

The opera company stopped for a break. Zoe sighed as the echo of the music lingered in the church walls and rafters. She glanced at Maks, who was looking at her and smiling. She felt wary. 'What?'

He snaked a hand to the back of her neck and tugged her towards him. 'You constantly surprise me. They'll be coming here tomorrow in ballgowns and tuxedoes, but I think you prefer this, don't you?'

He saw her. Damn him.

She nodded. He pulled her closer and pressed his mouth to hers. The fire ignited instantly. Voraciously. It was only a discreet but forceful cough that made them pull apart.

A priest was standing in the aisle below the balcony, looking up. Zoe went puce. Maks raised a hand to indicate that they were leaving. When they got outside, Zoe broke into a fit of giggles. Maks caught her, and her giggles stopped abruptly when he kissed her again, stealing her sanity. *Stealing her soul.*

He stopped the kiss. 'Let's go back to the hotel.'

Zoe nodded. She couldn't speak.

He led her down to the canal and they took a gondola. As they entered the Grand Canal from a smaller one the sun was setting behind the huge *palazzos* and bathing everything in a rosy golden light.

It was so beautiful that Zoe's breath caught. She lifted her camera, even though she knew that to try and capture it would fail miserably. But she needed to have some record of this moment, even if it would be infinitely inferior. Because she knew it wouldn't happen again.

When they arrived back at the hotel Maks barely ac-

knowledged the manager who leapt to attention. Zoe shot
him an apologetic smile as Maks pulled her into the elevator with indecent haste.

As soon as they got to the suite he closed the door and
looked at Zoe. For a charged moment neither one moved.
Zoe had no idea who moved first, but she was in Maks's
arms, her legs wrapped around his waist, her mouth on
every bit of exposed skin she could find as he walked them
into the massive bedroom.

The French doors were open, and the curtains moved
gently in the warm evening air, but Zoe was oblivious to
everything but the spectacle of Maks's body being revealed,
inch by delicious inch, as he stripped off his clothes until
he was naked.

'Now you...'

He started undoing her shirt, pushing it open, pulling
the lace cups of her bra down so he could cup her breasts
and push her nipples into pouting peaks, begging for his
hot mouth. Zoe clasped his head in her hands as his wicked
mouth tended to her sensitive flesh, his hot tongue leaving a trail of fire.

Her shirt and bra were dispensed with. Shoes kicked
off. Trousers opened and pulled down. Underwear ripped.
She didn't care. She just craved contact. Mutual desperation fuelled their movements, and they took a simultane-
ous breath of relief when Maks entered her on a smooth
thrust.

But the relief was soon replaced with urgency as the tension built and built, until Zoe was begging incoherently for
Maks to release them both... And even though she'd been
begging for it, when it came she still wasn't ready.

She was tossed high, and then fell deep down into a
whirlpool of pleasure so intense that she couldn't breathe.
Couldn't speak. Could only hold on as the storm racked
Maks's body too and only then the tumult subsided.

Maks slumped over her body, still embedded deeply, and Zoe wrapped her legs around him and wished that this moment would never end.

When Maks woke, the bedroom was filled with the pearlescent light of dawn. He felt drunk, but it wasn't from alcohol. It was from an overload of sensual pleasure. Zoe lay curled into his side, one arm thrown over his chest and one leg over his thigh, her foot locked behind his knee, as if to stop him from going anywhere.

He extricated himself carefully from her embrace, the nerve-ends in his body firing to life as he touched the plump curve of one breast and felt the indentation of her waist…one silky thigh.

She curled up on her side, saying something in her sleep. Maks pulled a sheet over her. She was adorably slow to get going in the morning, sleepy and sexy.

Naked, he went to the open window and stood there for a moment, relishing the cool morning breeze on his overheated skin. He felt utterly sated, and yet a delicious tendril of anticipation coiled in his gut.

He heard movement behind him and looked around, a smile curving his mouth, his blood already heating at the thought of waking Zoe up in a very explicit—

Click. She was sitting up in bed and she had her camera lifted to her face. She was taking pictures.

At first Maks's smile stayed in place. 'What are you doing?'

Click. It was as if the sound of the shutter woke him from a trance. He was naked. She was taking pictures.

His smile faded. He said it again. 'What are you doing?'

Zoe lowered the camera. Not even her bare breasts could distract Maks from the sudden cold rush of reality. And the feeling of intense exposure.

'I woke up and you looked so beautiful in the light… I just… I didn't think…'

Maks shook his head. 'Don't do that.'

She put the camera down in her lap. Her eyes were wide. 'Maks, I'm sorry. I wasn't thinking. You looked so beautiful in the light… I just acted on instinct.'

A sense of vulnerability prickled over his skin. A sense of waking out of a deep dream. He felt cold, all of a sudden. He needed to get away from Zoe's huge eyes.

'I'm taking a shower.'

'Maks…?'

But he didn't turn back.

He stood under the hot spray a few seconds later, but it couldn't melt the block of ice that had formed in his gut. He didn't have to look at his phone to know that it would be blowing up after he'd rescheduled a whole day of meetings yesterday.

His brother Nikos had been renowned for this kind of behaviour—going AWOL and then turning up in the tabloids, falling out of a club with two women on his arm, in a different city to the one where he'd been due to attend meetings.

Sharif was a little more circumspect, but recently he'd been at the mercy of some unfavourable kiss-and-tells after one of too many discarded lovers had had enough.

Maks did not do this. Maks had had a well-honed instinct to keep out of the limelight after his parents' toxicity had blighted his and his sister's lives. He'd always been the solid brother. The one who never failed to turn up to meetings and was discreet in all matters.

He knew he and Zoe would be all over the papers by now, because they'd been seen together at more than one event. And if he wasn't mistaken he was pretty sure a paparazzo had been following them yesterday. He hadn't even cared all that much.

And yet it had taken *her* lifting a camera to her face to wake him up. He hadn't been able to see her face. He'd only seen that lens. It had made him realise just how far under his skin he'd let her burrow.

All the way.

No. Maks rejected that thought as he stepped out of the shower. He slung a towel around his hips and saw his face in the mirror over the sink.

What was he doing? Letting a woman get under his skin like this? When there was no way it was going to last?

The most important person in the world to Maks was Sasha, his sister. As soon as he'd been old enough he'd taken Sasha out of his father's house and had become her guardian. His father had died soon after, and anyway he hadn't even noticed that his daughter was gone from his care. Because she hadn't even been his.

Their experiences had fostered an unspoken agreement between them never to repeat the mistakes of their parents.

What he felt here, now, with Zoe, was some kind of lust-induced craziness. He knew better than this. He knew not to send mixed messages. And that was exactly what he was doing. Telling her one thing but behaving in the completely opposite way. When he thought of the previous day, wandering around Venice, hand in hand, taking a gondola—which no self-respecting Italian would *ever* do—he cringed.

Maks and his sister had been the flotsam and jetsam in the wreckage of their parents' toxic marriage, and while Sasha had no interest in the Marchetti Group, Maks did. He'd made it his priority to ensure that he helped to build a legacy that would prove to be far more stable and durable and lasting than any marriage.

That was what mattered. Not the illusion of something that didn't exist.

He knew this was an unprecedented situation. He'd never

wanted a woman for longer than a couple of dates. So it would be hard to do what he had to. But he would do it because he couldn't offer Zoe anything more.

Zoe sat on the bed for a long moment after Maks disappeared into the bathroom. She didn't have to be a genius to figure out that something seismic had just happened.

She shouldn't have taken those pictures.

But when she'd woken and seen him standing by the gently fluttering drapes she'd wondered if she was dreaming. Not awake at all. He'd looked like a living sculpture of a Greek god. Every line of his body perfectly proportioned and muscled in the light of dawn, bathing him in a kind of golden celestial glow.

Zoe had had only one impulse—to capture his beauty. She'd barely been aware of reaching for her camera and lifting it to her face. Much like the first time she'd taken his photo.

Realising that she was sitting in some kind of a stupor, waiting for him to emerge, she scrambled out of bed and took some clothes with her, washing and changing in the suite's other bathroom.

When she was drying herself afterwards she was aware of a tension she hadn't felt in days. She'd become so engrossed in Maks's world. In his masterful seduction. To the point where she'd almost forgotten that a far grittier world existed for her outside of all this…fantasy.

She'd almost forgotten that this wasn't normal. When she'd woken at first, before she'd opened her eyes and seen Maks in all his naked glory, she'd been feeling such a sense of contentment. And peace and safety.

A brief fantastical illusion.

Hard to forget, though, when the after-effects of Maks's body moving over hers, in hers, still lingered.

A cold finger traced down her spine. She hadn't felt that

sense of happiness or safety in a long time—not since before her world had been torn apart and she'd lost everything
she'd loved and known.

She heard Maks's voice in the suite, low. Her pulse
throbbed in reaction even as she realised that this was her
wake-up call. She'd allowed no one close enough to hurt
her—not even Dean, who she'd *known* and believed she
trusted.

She threw on some clothes, a knot in her belly at the
thought of facing Maks. But for a moment, before she
walked into the main room of the suite, she was gripped
by a fantasy.

Maybe she was being paranoid. Skittish. Maybe Maks
wasn't really that annoyed about the photos and maybe he
was even now making arrangements to reschedule his work
so they could spend another day together… And maybe
she was safe. Maybe he hadn't got so close that he would
burn her alive.

But when she entered the main room and saw Maks
pacing back and forth, his cell phone clamped to his ear,
dressed in a three-piece suit, she knew something had broken.

He was remote, barely glancing at her. Speaking Italian. He gestured to where breakfast was laid out on the
table. Fresh coffee, pastries, fruit, cereal. But Zoe wasn't
hungry.

Newspapers. Something caught her eye in one paper
and she picked it up, her blood running cold. There was a
picture of her and Maks at the ballet in St Petersburg. And
another of them at the fashion event. And one from yesterday, here in Venice. She was holding his hand and looking
up at him, smiling. No, laughing.

Zoe sank down into a chair. She felt sick to see herself
plastered across the newspapers. But she'd been incredibly
naive not to expect this. She recalled seeing those pictures

of Maks's brother's new wife—Maggie?—in the papers. She'd had a similar deer-in-the-headlights look.

Maks terminated his conversation. Zoe looked at him. He had a stern expression on his face. One she hadn't seen for some time.

She put down the paper. 'Is everything okay?'

Maks put his phone in his pocket. 'Not exactly, no.'

Zoe stood up again, trepidation prickling over her skin. 'What is it? Did something happen?'

Maks ran a hand through his hair, making it messy. Which only made him look sexier.

He gestured to the papers. 'I should have warned you what might happen.'

Zoe looked down again. 'It's a bit of a shock to see myself in a national newspaper…but it's not the end of the world, is it?'

'Of course it's not. But it won't happen again.'

Zoe looked at Maks. He stood only a few feet away, but he couldn't have been more remote. The little fantasy she'd entertained that he might be rearranging his day so they could spend time together mocked her now.

'What do you mean?'

Maks's grey gaze looked silver in the light. Impenetrable.

'What I mean is that this ends here and now, Zoe. It's not fair to string it out…generating more pictures and headlines…for what? The sake of another few days? Weeks? I have to go to New York today for a meeting with my brother Sharif,' he continued. 'I can arrange for you to get back to London, or wherever you want to go.'

Something like desperation filled Zoe's gut. 'Maks, I'm sorry I took those photos. I can delete them—'

He waved a hand. 'This isn't about that. It's just…time for this to end. Like I said, I'll make sure you're taken wherever you want to go.'

Zoe felt cold. 'I can make my own way back.'

Maks said, 'You should call Pierre Gardin, the photographer from the shoot in St Petersburg. He doesn't encourage people to get in touch unless he rates them. He liked you. I know he's not a particularly pleasant person, but this is an opportunity for you to get into the business.'

Zoe was too stunned to respond straight away.

Maks looked at his watch. 'I have to go. My plane leaves within the hour. I'll leave instructions for the hotel to arrange your onward transport. Please let them take care of you, Zoe.'

He came closer, and for a second Zoe thought she saw a flash of something in his eyes, but she told herself she was imagining things. He reached out and ran a knuckle across her jaw. Her traitorous body sizzled with awareness.

'I had fun, Zoe. More fun than I've had in a long time— I won't deny it. But this was never going to go any further. I lost perspective for a short time. But better that it ends here. Now.'

Zoe's brain wouldn't work. She felt pain—incredible pain—deep inside. The kind of pain she'd only ever felt once before. The kind of pain she'd vowed never to feel again. Yet here she was. Being eviscerated.

Her instinct was to get away as fast as possible. Curl up into a ball and push the pain back down.

He got too close. He's doing you a favour.

Somehow she managed to formulate words, to sound normal. 'I think you're right. Better for both of us to put this behind us and move on.'

Maks smiled, but it was a kind of smile she'd never seen before. Tight.

'Goodbye, Zoe.'

He walked to the door, picked up a small bag and didn't look back.

Zoe wasn't sure how long she stood there, breathless

from the speed at which Maks had ruthlessly cut her out of his life.

She walked over to the balcony and marvelled at how, within twenty-four hours, this view that had felt so full of promise and wonder now felt tawdry and mocking.

She turned back into the suite. Empty. No trace left of the man who had dominated it so easily.

No, his trace was left inside her. A wound that would be added to her other wounds and which would, in time, become a scar. But not visible, like the scars on her face. Invisible.

Anger rose inside her. Anger at herself. For stepping into the blazing centre of a fire that she had *known* would consume her.

She'd already learnt a lesson at the hands of Dean Simpson—a lesson in not letting herself be weak. How could she have let it happen again? So soon? So fatally?

Because Maks didn't make you feel weak, said an inner voice.

He'd made her feel strong. Empowered. And yet even now she could hear Maks's voice in her head, denying that he'd given her those things, those feelings. They'd been within her—all he'd done was encourage her to find them.

And he'd not held back from telling her what his life had been like. Why he had no interest in a relationship or anything more permanent. He'd been scarred too. Except, unlike Zoe, he'd not let himself get lost in a fantasy. He'd not let his innate weakness rise up to drown him. Again.

CHAPTER NINE

'ARE YOU TAKING Nikos's place in the tabloids now that he's an apparently happily settled married man?'

Sharif's tone was mocking. Maks curbed his urge to scowl at his older brother.

Downtown Manhattan was laid out all around them, visible through the huge windows, people were like industrious ants on the sidewalks. But it was wasted on Maks.

'I hardly think a couple of photos in a few tabloids is up to Nikos's standards. Or yours, I might add. You're racking up quite the tally of kiss-and-tells. Not the best judge of women who can be discreet, hmm?'

Now Sharif did scowl. Not that it marred the handsomeness of his dark good looks. 'Who is she, anyway?'

Maks bristled at his question. 'You don't need to worry about who *she* is. It's over.'

Sharif cocked an eyebrow. 'Pity. The board are still skittish, in spite of Nikos's reformation. If you were to settle down too…?'

Maks waited for the inevitable sense of rejection that usually accompanied any suggestion or notion of permanence, but all he felt was hollow. Irritation made him say, 'There's as much likelihood of that happening as of *you* getting married.'

To his surprise, Sharif didn't immediately rebut that statement. When Maks looked at him, his brother's expression was one he couldn't read. Almost…resigned.

Maks frowned. 'Sharif?'

The expression passed as if Maks had imagined it. And a familiar mocking arrogance animated his brother's face again as he said, 'That's enough gossiping, let's get on with it.'

'By all means,' Maks responded, more than happy to focus on work.

A few hours later, in his hotel suite in Manhattan, Maks nursed a whisky as he looked out over the glittering lights of the city that never slept. He felt as if *he* might never sleep again. Restless under his skin. Hungry in his blood. *For her.*

He still wanted Zoe.

He'd never wanted a woman for longer than a brief period.

A tantalising prospect struck him. Maybe he'd been too hasty? Maybe he could come to an arrangement with her in which—?

No. He ruthlessly shut down that train of thought. She wasn't that kind of woman. Sophisticated. Who knew the rules of the game. He'd been her first lover. *She'd just got under his skin.*

All he had to do was remember Zoe's reaction earlier, when he'd broken things off. The way she'd gone so pale. Her eyes huge. Stricken. It had only confirmed for him that he was doing the right thing. They had no future. As it was, he'd already dragged her into the public eye. After accusing *her* of being a paparazzi! The irony was not welcome.

But he couldn't regret seducing her—not when it had been so earth-shatteringly satisfying.

He had no right to give her any hope for more. She'd been a brief aberration. A temptation he shouldn't have succumbed to. A temptation he wouldn't succumb to again.

Three weeks later

Zoe was gritty-eyed after another broken night's sleep. Broken by dreams about Maks. And nightmares. In the latest one she'd been in Venice, endlessly wandering the narrow labyrinthine streets, searching for him, only to catch a tiny glimpse at the last second before he disappeared around another corner.

She hated herself for being so weak. He'd dumped her.

She told herself yet again that he'd done her a favour as she walked to her local corner shop for supplies.

There was nothing like being back in the grittier end of London to remind her of where she belonged. So when she looked down and saw the pictures on the front page of the tabloid newspaper she had to blink several times, wondering if she was still dreaming. Or hallucinating.

It was Maks. He was naked. He was smiling intimately at whoever was taking the picture. Drapes fluttered behind him. For a second Zoe felt as if someone had skewered her with a red-hot poker, but then she realised that these weren't different pictures. These were *her* pictures. Just after she'd taken this picture his demeanour had changed utterly. And then he'd dumped her.

She hadn't even looked back at those photos herself since that day. Not wanting to see the moment when his face had gone from dreamy and sexy to icy cold. Yet now they were plastered all over these grubby tabloids for all the world to see.

'I don't think it's a good idea, Miss Collins.'

Zoe tried not to sound as desperate as she felt, after a long day of trying to track Maks down. He'd ignored all her attempts to call or text him. But she knew he was here, at his townhouse.

'Hamish, please. I need to speak to him.'

Maks's housekeeping manager looked as if he was about to close the door in her face, but then he stood back and said tersely, 'I'll ask him. Wait here.'

Zoe stood in the hall of the stunning townhouse. It was

a very different reception from the last one she'd received here. Now it couldn't be frostier.

After a long moment Hamish returned. 'He'll see you for a few minutes. Follow me.'

Relief flooded Zoe, followed quickly by trepidation. She'd been trying to get to Maks all day, but now that she was here she wasn't even sure what she would say.

Hamish led her into a room she hadn't been in before. A large study. Dark wood-panelled walls. Shelves. Modern technology. A TV on the wall with the news on mute.

And Maks. Standing behind his desk in a shirt and dark trousers. Sleeves rolled up. Hands on hips.

To see him again in close proximity almost made her stumble. She locked her legs.

The door closed behind her and Maks walked over to a drinks cabinet, pouring himself a drink. He didn't offer her one. He turned around. He looked calm, but Zoe could feel the tension.

'Why did you do it, Zoe?'

She felt sick—she'd been feeling sick all day. 'I didn't.'

He ignored her denial. 'How much did you get? If you'd offered them to me first, I might have given you more.'

A sense of desperation flooded Zoe, eclipsing the nausea. 'I didn't sell the photos, Maks, I swear. I have no idea how the papers got them.'

Maks put his glass down and perched on one corner of his desk, for all the world as if this was a civil conversation and as if she hadn't just spoken. 'I mean, I shouldn't be surprised. After all, you have form. The first time we met you were taking my picture and trespassing.'

Zoe's cheeks grew hot. 'This isn't the same.'

'No, it's not. It's worse.'

His voice was like the crack of a whip. Zoe's insides were clenched so tight she almost had a cramp.

'I know how much you hate your privacy being invaded. You know me…you know I would never do something like this.'

Maks just looked at her, no expression on his face. Those silver eyes cold as mercury.

'I thought I did. I thought you were an open book. I thought you were different. But you weren't at all. I knew you weren't happy when I broke things off,' he continued. 'But I had no idea you'd stoop so low to get back at me. Or that you were so mercenary. You had me fooled with your apparent lack of interest in anything material. Your humble but cosy flat.'

Zoe flinched inwardly. How could he think that had all been an act? But her conscience pricked hard. In a way he was right. It *wasn't* the whole truth of her existence. But Maks would never want to hear about that. Not now.

All she could say was, 'I didn't do this.'

Maks stood up straight, folded his arms. 'Stop with the lies, Zoe. They make fools of both of us. We know the money went into an account in a bank right beside where you live.'

Zoe stared at Maks, absorbing his words. Shock, dismay and confusion made her head throb. Who could have done this to her? To him?

Maks's arms were locked so tight across his chest that Zoe could see his biceps bulging under the thin material of his shirt. The blood quickened in her veins. Even now, in the midst of all of this, when he was looking at her as if he wanted to—

His lip curled. 'Take the grubby money that you got from the papers and get out. You won't get anything more from me, so if that's why you came it's a wasted journey.'

'Maks, I swear. I didn't—' But she stopped talking. Maks was a cold, remote statue. Not interested. Convinced of her guilt.

She felt incredible hurt that he could be so quick to mis-judge her.

'Get out,' he said. 'I never want to see you again.'

Something cracked apart inside her, breaking into a thousand pieces. She'd thought she'd protected herself so well, but she hadn't protected herself at all.

It took a few seconds for the red haze to fade enough in Maks's head for him to realise that Zoe had left. For a stomach-plummeting second he thought he might have actually imagined that she'd come here, that she'd stood in front of him protesting her innocence. Hair down. Those scars visible against her pale skin. Her eyes as big as he remembered. Her mouth as lush. *As tempting.*

No.

He unlocked his arms from his chest and unclenched his jaw. She *had* been here. He could smell her scent in the air and had to resist the urge to breathe it deep.

He picked up his glass and drained it in one gulp. He didn't even wince as it flamed down his throat. He barely felt it. His fingers gripped the heavy crystal so tightly he had to relax them for fear of cracking it.

His skin still crawled when he thought of the look on his executive assistant's face that morning when he'd arrived at the Marchetti offices shortly after dawn—and the fact that he hadn't been sleeping well for the past few weeks was *not* something he wanted to associate with the women who had just left.

His assistant hadn't been able to meet his eyes as he'd cleared his throat and said, 'Have you seen the papers yet, sir?'

Maks, feeling irritable, had replied, 'No. Why?'

'There's something you should see.'

His assistant had laid out a sheaf of the main tabloids on

his desk and it had taken Maks a moment even to understand what he was looking at. *Himself. Naked.*

His first reaction hadn't even been anger. Or shock. It had been to remember that morning, with the sun coming up on the Grand Canal in Venice, the breeze cooling his overheated body. The sense of contentment and sensual satisfaction that had oozed through him. Along with that delicious pique of anticipation.

The picture in the papers had captured that moment when he'd looked around and caught Zoe with her camera raised to her face. He'd smiled. Not minding in that first instance that she was taking his picture. And then reality had hit like a bucket of cold water. He'd realised just how lax he'd been. How blinded by lust. To let someone get that close! Close enough to steal his very soul.

The thing that burned and roiled in Maks's gut most was that a lifetime of cynicism had let him down. He never would have suspected Zoe of having the kind of wherewithal to do something like this, and yet up until he'd met her he would have assumed anyone was capable of anything. No matter how innocent they looked or acted.

He thought of all the little moments when he'd doubted she could really be that gauche, that innocent. Naive. No, not naive. Unjaded.

For all he knew she could have faked her virginity—she'd told him beforehand, so of course that would have made him less likely to question if she really was or not. He knew what good actors women were; he'd seen his mother lie over and over again about her numerous affairs until she hadn't cared any more and had freely admitted to them, to taunt his father.

That was when he'd hit her.

They'd divorced soon after that.

But maybe even worse than all that was the fact that when he'd woken today, after weeks of sleepless nights and sexual frustration eating him up inside, he'd been seriously tempted to get in touch with Zoe again.

And say what? He hadn't even been sure, but he'd just wanted her. Badly.

He could blame her for making a fool out of him all he wanted, but in the end *he* was the fool.

Two months later

Nikos clapped Maks on the back as they walked into the exclusive Marchetti Group hotel bar in Paris. 'I should have posed naked years ago. I always wanted to be named Sexiest Man of the Year—and, let's face it, I'm way sexier than you.'

Maks gritted his jaw, which seemed to be in a permanent state of grit now. 'I didn't *pose*.'

Nikos ignored him. 'You could have gone into modelling, Maks. Wasted opportunity.'

Maks opened his mouth to unleash another diatribe at Nikos, who was insufferably happy all the time now, but at that moment he saw his oldest brother, Sharif, taking a seat in a discreet corner booth. Sharif caught his eye and Maks nodded in his direction, steering Nikos towards the table.

It was a rare occurrence that they were all in Paris at the same time, and an even rarer occurrence that they were meeting for a drink.

When they were seated around the table with their drinks, Nikos addressed the elephant in the room. 'This is serendipitous, indeed—all the brothers around a table that isn't twelve foot long and full of other board members. Something to tell us, Sharif?'

Their eldest brother looked as unreadable and unflappable as ever. 'Can't we at least pretend we're a normal family?' His tone was mocking.

Maks let out a spontaneous snort of laughter. 'Normal? What's that? None of us can lay claim to knowing the first thing about what it's like to be normal.' That was followed by a far too familiar sense of hollowness in his gut.

Nikos said, 'Speak for yourselves. I'm a happily committed married father of nearly two children.'

Nikos's wife was pregnant with their second child. It had just been announced in the press.

Sharif said darkly, 'We'll see how long that lasts.'

Maks felt Nikos bristle beside him. He put a hand on his arm. 'He's just jealous.'

Now Sharif made a snorting noise.

They all took a sip of their drinks, tension bubbling under the surface, but it was tempered by something far more tenuous and delicate. *New.*

Maks realised that, as much as they might be wary of each other, they respected each other at least.

Then Sharif, sounding uncharacteristically *un*-mocking said, 'Actually, I wanted to let you know that the group has seen the best returns in a decade. And that's down to us all.' He looked at Nikos. 'The news of your marriage and fatherhood has stabilised nervy shareholders.'

Nikos grinned, lifting his glass. 'Happy to help in any small way I can.'

Sharif went on, glancing from Nikos to Maks. 'I know we all have our reasons for investing our time and effort into this company, and that none of us had to accept this inheritance. God knows, our father didn't inspire loyalty in any of us, but I'm glad we're in this together. I think we can take the Marchetti Group above and beyond anything our father ever imagined, and in doing so we can forge a new beginning.'

Nikos frowned. 'That almost sounds like you've got something planned, brother.'

Sharif shrugged, but Maks noticed that he was watching them carefully. He said, 'I'm just saying that there is no limit to what we can achieve now we're united.'

At that moment Nikos's phone buzzed. It was on the table, and Maks saw an image of Maggie's smiling face and their son Daniel's, close to hers. Daniel was grinning cherubically, with the dark hair and eyes of his father.

Nikos picked up the phone, looking at his brothers. 'Are we done here, or do you want to sit and braid each other's hair some more?'

Sharif rolled his eyes, but his mouth twitched. 'No, go— play happy families. Enjoy it while it lasts.'

Nikos was already up, answering his phone with a sexy growl. '*Moro mou,* you were meant to call me an hour ago…'

Maks knew Maggie well enough by now to know that she'd probably be rolling her eyes at her husband, and a curious little ache formed in his chest at the thought of Nikos and his growing family unit. At his very obvious adoration for his wife. It was such an alien thing to witness.

All of sudden Maks realised that in spite of everything he didn't share Sharif's cynicism. He had a sense that whatever Nikos and Maggie had, it was very real.

Sharif's phone rang. He answered it and went still. Then he said, 'I'm making the most of a set of circumstances set down many years ago. It'll be in all of our interests to take advantage of this opportunity. Let them know I'll expect things to happen within the next couple of months.'

Maks looked at Sharif when he had terminated his call. 'That was cryptic. Anything you want to share?'

Sharif fixed his dark gaze on Maks. For a moment Maks had the impression that Sharif wanted to share something but all he did say was, 'It's nothing that concerns you. Stay in touch, brother. And forewarn me next time you decide to pose naked for the papers. It was rather more of my little brother than I cared to see over my breakfast.'

Sharif got up to leave and Maks rose too, gritting his jaw again. 'I didn't *pose*.'

But Sharif was already striding out of the bar, with a couple of assistants who'd been hiding in a corner chasing after him.

Feeling irrationally irritable and irritated, Maks moved to a stool at the bar, ordering a drink. He noticed a few women on their own. One met his eyes. She was beautiful. Willowy, blonde. Confident. Exactly the kind of woman whose clear invitation he would have accepted before. Except he felt nothing. No stirring of interest. *Nada*. Zilch.

He turned to his drink. His libido only seemed to come to life at night now. When he woke sweaty and aching all over after explicitly sexual dreams featuring a treacherous liar and a thief—

'Maks, you dark horse! Are congratulations in order?'

Maks looked up and to his side, to see the smirking face of photographer Pierre Gardin. Another reminder of Zoe that he didn't need. 'What are you talking about, Pierre?'

'Your girlfriend was working with me this week, and the rumour on set was that she's pregnant. She kept disappearing to the bathroom, but she's still the best assistant I've had in a long time. I hate to admit it, but I think she's got real potential to—'

Maks swivelled around on his stool. He could see Pierre's mouth moving but the sound was muffled. He wanted to shake the man.

He cut through whatever he was saying now. 'What did you say?'

Pierre stopped talking and cocked his head, eyes narrowing on Maks. 'Actually, Zoe never mentioned you. Maybe you're not together any more? Maybe the baby isn't yours? I can't keep up with these young people and their love affairs...'

Baby. Pregnant.

Maks was having a hard time getting his brain to absorb those words. It was so nonsensical.

And then Maks had a mental image of Zoe in bed with another man and his brain went white-hot.

'Where is she?'

Pierre frowned. 'I have no idea. She went home—back to London, presumably.'

Maks's brain was melting.

Pregnant.

Yet she hadn't called him.

Do you blame her? asked a caustic voice. The words he'd last thrown at her reverberated in his head: *Get out. I never want to see you again.*

Was he even the father?

'Maks, are you okay?'

No. He wasn't. For weeks now he'd been avoiding thinking about Zoe's stricken face when she'd come to his townhouse that night, and her entreaty, *'You know I'd never do something like this.'* Avoiding the niggling question as to why she would have come to his house if she'd really leaked the photos and been paid for them. Surely that wasn't the action of a guilty person? Surely she would have just disappeared with the money?

His conscience pricked. His team had offered to look deeper into the leak of the photos. To confirm beyond doubt that it had been Zoe. But Maks had stopped them, telling himself that he *knew.*

But now he wasn't so sure at all.

Within twenty-four hours Maks was standing outside Zoe's door. Not used to waiting for much, if anything, he had to curb his impatience as she seemed to take an age to open it.

When she did, and he saw the shock on her face and the

way her eyes widened, he couldn't stop the rush of blood and instant jolt of lust.

He still wanted her.

As if he hadn't already known that.

'Why didn't you answer my texts or calls?' His helpless reaction made his voice harsher than he'd intended.

She pulled an over-large shapeless cardigan tighter around her. Maks looked down. He couldn't see any visible signs of pregnancy, but she did look pale.

'Maks. What are you doing here?'

He moved into the apartment and shut the door behind him.

'We need to talk.'

She didn't look so shocked now. She moved back. 'You said you never wanted to see me again.'

'That was before…'

'Before what?'

Suddenly Maks was reluctant to ask if she was pregnant, not ready to have that conversation yet, so instead he said, 'Did you sell the photos, Zoe?'

'I told you I didn't, but you refused to listen to me.'

'I'm listening now.'

Zoe said nothing for a long moment, and then, 'You've actually saved me a phone call. I was going to ring your office today.'

'About what?'

'I know who did sell the photos.'

Maks frowned. 'Who?'

'I was hacked by my ex—Dean Simpson. He works in IT and my passwords wouldn't have been hard to crack. I upload all my pictures to an online storage facility. It's a reflex—something I learnt to do long ago, to make sure I don't lose work.'

Maks refused to let go of his cynicism completely. He folded his arms. 'Why would he hack you?'

Zoe paced away to the window. She looked very slight under the voluminous cardigan and in her loose pyjama pants.

She turned around. 'He must have seen the pictures of us and acted out of spite and jealousy. I didn't tell you everything about him—about why he…attacked me.'

A sense of unease prickled over Maks's skin. 'Tell me now.'

She faced him properly. Her scars stood out against her pale skin. 'The reason we broke up was not just because he wanted an intimacy that I realised I didn't want. It was because he wanted something else from me. He hadn't looked me up in London just because he happened to be here—he'd targeted me.'

'Why would he target you?'

For a long moment she said nothing, and then, 'Because he found out who I was and what that meant.'

Maks frowned. 'What are you talking about? Who *are* you?'

Zoe started to pace back and forth. Maks tried not to let his gaze drop to where the vee of her T-shirt dipped low enough to reveal a hint of breast. Even that tiny hint of provocation had heated blood rushing to his groin.

'Zoe,' he snapped, in response to her effect on him. 'I don't have all day for this.'

She looked at him, eyes huge. He saw her jaw set.

'I didn't ask you to come here. If you have more important things to be doing then by all means leave.'

Maks forced his blood to cool. 'Go on.'

She took an audible breath. 'I didn't tell you who my parents were. My father was Stephen Collins, the photographer and author, and my mother was Simone Bryant, the heiress.'

Maks shook his head as if that might clear it, trying to better assimilate this information. He knew her father's name—anyone with even a passing interest in news and current affairs would have heard of Stephen Collins, the world-renowned photojournalist who'd covered some of the grisliest wars. And Simone Bryant had famously been the last remaining heiress to a vast fortune built from one of Ireland's oldest breweries. Maks had a vague memory of a golden society couple…

He focused on Zoe again. 'You lied to me about who you are.'

Zoe bristled visibly. 'I didn't lie. I just didn't tell you exactly who I am. Collins is a common name…'

'Your father won a Pulitzer prize for his non-fiction and then he became a bestselling crime author. I have his books on my shelves.' He stopped, recalling how Zoe had been looking at the books on his shelves in London. She'd probably been laughing at him the whole time. *Dio.* 'Why the hell would you hide who your parents were?'

Maks looked at her as if seeing her for the first time. He felt ridiculously betrayed that Zoe had kept this information from him. But he could also see now where her talent came from. She had it in spades. It was evident in every picture hanging on the walls of this tiny flat.

She just looked at him with those huge eyes.

Maks frowned as something else sank in. 'Your parents were wealthy.'

Zoe nodded. 'Very. When they died, my inheritance was kept in trust for me till I turned eighteen.'

Maks looked around. 'And yet you live like an impoverished student.'

'Because I never wanted to touch that money.'

He was taken aback at the stark tone in her voice. 'Why not?'

Zoe's throat moved as if she was struggling to say the words. 'Because it was blood money. Money that I never should have had. I got it at the expense of my parents' deaths. My brother, who never got to live his life. Of course I wasn't going to use it. I've given most of it away to charity.'

Maks felt a pain near his chest as he thought of the fact that Zoe blamed herself for the accident. He pushed it down.

'What has Dean Simpson got to do with any of this?'

Zoe sighed. 'When I was eighteen I left Ireland for London. I'd always wanted to follow in my father's footsteps, and he started his photography career here. Also, there was nothing for me in Dublin. No family. No ties. Just grief and bittersweet memories.'

Maks was still reeling from all this information and what it meant about the woman in front of him. *If* what she was saying was true.

He said, 'Go on.'

She looked at him. 'I never expected to see Dean Simpson again. When he came to London and tracked me down I realised I was lonely. I trusted him. We'd been in the same foster home. He was my first boyfriend. We had a shared past. What I didn't know was that he'd somehow found out about my background, and my inheritance, and had come to pursue a relationship with a view to getting his hands on it. When Dean brought it up I was shocked. I told him what I've told you—that I wanted nothing to do with the money, that I'd given most of it away to charity—and that was when Dean got angry with me...when he realised I'd been getting rid of it.'

Zoe lifted her chin.

'If you don't believe me you can check the bank account where the money from the pictures was lodged. It's in Dean's name. He didn't even try very hard to cover his tracks.'

Maks looked at Zoe, a small obstinately cynical part of him refusing to give in to what his gut was telling him—

that she was innocent. Always had been. In more ways than one.

'How do I know you weren't working together? That you haven't spent your entire inheritance and you're looking to make more money at my expense?'

Zoe went so pale that for a moment Maks thought she might faint. Instead, she stalked past him and went to the door, opening it.

She looked at him. 'Get out, Maks.'

A lead weight seemed to be stuck in his gut. And then he remembered. The reason why he'd come here in the first place.

He said, 'There's something else. I bumped into Pierre Gardin. He told me that you might be pregnant. Is it true?'

Zoe looked at Maks. She forced herself to breathe, to let oxygen get to her brain. Anger, betrayal, and so many other emotions roiled in her gut that she felt light-headed. All mixed up with a clawing need to throw herself into Maks's arms and wind herself around him like a vine.

She forced all that out. The urge to self-protect was paramount.

When she felt as if she could sound calm she said, 'That's the most ridiculous thing I ever heard.'

'Pierre said you weren't well.'

Zoe's face grew warm and she avoided Maks's eye. 'I had a bug, that was all.'

'So you're not pregnant?'

She gripped the handle of the door. 'Please leave, Maks. I have an English class to teach today and I'm already late.'

Maks sounded frustrated. 'Zoe…if you are, you need to tell me.'

She finally looked at him, focusing on anger to block out all the other disturbing emotions. 'Why? When I know exactly how you feel about having a family? You're the last man I'd choose to be the father of my child.'

'If you were pregnant with my baby I would take responsibility. You wouldn't be alone.'

The thought of Maks having to *take responsibility* for her made bile rise inside Zoe. She said, 'Even if I was pregnant I wouldn't come to you, because I don't need to. No matter how much money I give to charity, the interest alone on what's left keeps me rich beyond anything I know what to do with. So *if* I was pregnant, which I'm not, I wouldn't need you anyway.'

CHAPTER TEN

PLEASE LEAVE, ZOE begged silently, just wanting to escape Maks's far too probing eyes. Relief moved through her when he finally walked to the door and stepped over the threshold.

He turned around. Grim. 'If what you say is true then I owe you an apology. Simpson victimised you as much as me.'

Hurt gripped her again at his reluctance to trust her. 'You don't owe me anything.'

Zoe shut the door and stood in a stupor for a long moment, staring at her closed door. She heard the sound of the main door closing heavily. The throttle of a powerful engine.

In spite of her brave words just now, she knew it wasn't the last she'd see of Maks. Not by a long shot. Not just because he might come back to apologise, as his integrity would demand. But for another far more pressing reason.

Her hand went to her belly. She'd lied. Unforgivably. Blatantly. She *was* pregnant and her little bump was growing every day. But the shock of having Maks here in her space, confronting her, suggesting she might have been colluding with Dean Simpson, had decimated any urge she might have had to tell him today.

Of course she would tell him she was pregnant. When she could do so on her terms. When she could prepare herself for the inevitable distaste she'd see on his face. When she would be able to stand in front of him and tell him calmly and rationally that she was prepared to do this on her own and didn't expect him to *take responsibility*.

Terrified, but filled with a sense of focus and a determination to get over her fear of loss and grief, she knew she owed it to her baby to do her best to try. To create a secure life for them both. To shield them from the fear she would feel every day.

It was time to reassess her experiences and do things differently. She had a child to support now. She couldn't continue like an out-of-work student, skirting around the edges of life, ignoring the fact that she had the means to live well. It wasn't just about her and her guilt any more.

Maks felt sick. It had taken the most rudimentary of internet searches to find the news reports on the tragic crash that had killed Zoe's family. Leaving her the sole survivor. There'd been pictures of the car wreckage that had made him feel weak, and pictures of Zoe, taken before the crash.

Her father had been tall and dashingly handsome, her mother blonde and beautiful. Like Zoe. There'd been pictures of a three-year-old Zoe holding her baby brother, grinning proudly. And a lot of breathless speculation about the young, tragically orphaned heiress.

It also hadn't been hard to find the philanthropic foundation she'd set up to donate money anonymously to various charities. Set up—Maks suspected—on her eighteenth birthday.

He recalled how she'd sounded almost bewildered when she'd mentioned the fact that no matter what she did the interest kept growing on her remaining inheritance. He'd never met anyone before who'd actively tried to get rid of money.

The way she'd denied herself out of a sense of guilt and grief made Maks's chest feel tight.

A knock sounded on his home office door. Hamish stuck his head around it. 'Lunch, boss?'

Maks didn't feel hungry. He stood up. 'No. Can you get

my assistant to meet me here? And call my legal team. I have some information for them.'

'Sure thing.'

Hamish left and Maks walked over to the window, looking out unseeingly. Zoe wasn't pregnant. And even if she was, as she'd pointed out, she didn't actually need his support.

He should be feeling relieved. She was right. A family was the last thing he'd ever wanted. A baby. No matter what kind of ache he might have felt when he'd thought of his brother Nikos and his family. An ache that was still there now.

He'd misjudged Zoe badly. And any sense of betrayal that she hadn't told him about her family was fading fast. He could understand why.

A mixture of complicated emotions roiled in his gut. He didn't usually judge people out of hand. He was actually far less likely to jump to conclusions than either of his brothers. But with Zoe... She'd pushed his buttons from the moment he'd first seen her. And at the first sign of an opportunity to believe the worst about her he'd jumped at it.

The worst thing was, he knew exactly why he'd reacted like that. Because he hadn't been prepared to admit that he still wanted her. That he wasn't ready to let her go. And more. Much more.

Zoe stood on the stony beach and looked out at the Irish Sea. It was a blustery day with leaden skies. Typical Irish weather. She turned around and looked up to the cliff behind her, where a distinctive yellow house stood out. That had been her home. The family home where she'd felt loved and safe and as if nothing could touch her.

A deep sigh moved through her as the wind whipped her hair around her face.

She'd spent the last few days in a storage facility, going

through her family's possessions, and she felt wrung out but also a little lighter. As if a weight was finally lifting off her shoulders.

She faced the sea again and tried to ignore the dull pain that dogged her every step. *Maks.* Every time she thought about him she forced her mind away again. But, like a well-worn groove, her mind kept going over all the reasons why she was so reluctant to contact him and reveal the truth about her pregnancy: he'd never promised her anything but a finite affair; he believed that she'd betrayed his trust, which just confirmed how little he'd really thought of her; he didn't want a relationship or a child or a family.

And, even more damningly, she now knew why he'd appeared on her doorstep in London.

He hadn't really wanted to verify her guilt or innocence. He'd been there to see if she was pregnant. Because the last thing he wanted was more adverse publicity.

She cursed herself again for letting him close enough to hurt her. *Devastate her. Fatally.*

No, she told herself now. Not fatal. She was still here. Whole. *Pregnant.*

She would have to tell him sooner or later and deal with the fact that he would be in her life in some capacity for ever…but not today.

Zoe turned around to walk away from the sea, back up towards the hotel where she was staying while she went through her family's things.

She'd only taken a few steps into the lobby when she heard her name being called.

'Zoe.'

She stopped. The voice was deep. Hypnotic. She didn't want to turn around. *It couldn't be.* And yet no one knew her here.

She turned around. Maks was standing a few feet away in dark clothes. He'd never looked more beautiful or sexy.

Zoe felt weak. 'What are you doing here? How did you know where I was?'

Maks took a step towards her. She stepped back—a self-protective reflex. She saw his jaw clench and felt ridiculously like apologising.

'I went to your flat in London. Your neighbour told me you'd moved out and that you were taking a trip to Dublin. It wasn't hard to track you down.'

Not for a billionaire with means at his disposal, Zoe thought to herself. She could feel herself responding to his proximity. She wanted to drink him in. She wanted to reach up and pull his head down and feel that hard mouth on hers. Every part of her body tingled with awareness and she vaguely wondered if it had anything to do with being pregnant.

Pregnant.

She wasn't ready. Not today.

Coward.

Feeling desperate, she asked, 'Why are you here, Maks? I thought we'd said all we had to say.'

'Can we go somewhere more private?'

Zoe looked around. People were practically tripping over themselves when they saw Maks Marchetti in this very mediocre hotel lobby. Zoe felt like rolling her eyes. He literally was too beautiful to be out in public without causing an incident.

'You have a room here?'

Zoe's mind seized at the thought of him in her small suite. But there was nowhere else private and, as much as she didn't want to tell him about the pregnancy, she knew she had to.

Reluctantly she walked over to the elevator, without waiting to see if he followed her. But she could feel him behind her. Tall. Powerful. His scent was exotic. Musky. *Sexy.*

The tension crackled between them when they were in

the elevator—so much that Zoe got an electric shock when she pushed the button for her floor. It was a relief to get out and walk down the short corridor to her room.

She went in and immediately went over to the window, crossing her arms, looking at Maks warily as he followed her in. She noticed more now. His hair was longer. Jaw stubbled. He looked tired. Dishevelled.

Her heart squeezed with an unbidden urge to know if he was okay. And then she lambasted herself for being weak. She hated him. His betrayal of her was far worse than anything she'd unwittingly done to him.

But when he looked at her she could feel herself aligning towards him. Her head and body at war. She was melting. Aching.

She didn't hate him at all.

'Maks, what do you want?' Her voice was sharp. Panicked.

You. Maks just restrained himself from saying it. Seeing Zoe up close again made him feel primal. Her lithe petite form. That honey-blonde hair, wild and messy from the wind. Cheeks pink. Eyes like two stormy oceans.

He forced his brain out of his pants. 'I came to say I'm sorry. I should have given you the benefit of the doubt. I knew you better than that.'

The pink faded from her cheeks. She looked pale now.

'You've got proof that Dean hacked into my account and sold the pictures.' Her voice was flat.

'No, I didn't need to. I should have trusted you. I gave his name to the authorities. They informed me that he was picked up in Spain yesterday, and he's admitted everything. They're extraditing him back to Ireland to face charges. I won't hold back from bringing the full force of the law down on him, Zoe.'

'Oh.'

It shouldn't surprise Maks that Zoe looked troubled at that news. She probably felt sorry for her ex.

She said, 'You didn't have to come all the way here to tell me that, but thank you.'

He nodded. 'Yes, I did. The first time I saw you I accused you of being something you weren't. You...you have an effect on me. Normally I can be rational, but with you... that goes out the window.'

Zoe bit her lip. 'I can't help that.'

Now she sounded injured. Maks cursed himself. Shook his head.

'You got too close, Zoe. Closer than I've ever let anyone get. The only other person who knows me as well is my sister. That's why I let you go in Venice. When you took my picture, and when it didn't immediately feel like a violation...it was like a wake-up call. I panicked.'

His forced out words through the weight in his gut.

'And then, when the pictures came out, I jumped on any excuse to damn you...so I wouldn't have to acknowledge how much you'd got to me. How much I wanted you. How much I still want you now. Pushing you away was easier than being honest with myself.'

Zoe's eyes went wide, colour flooding her cheeks. He could see the pulse at her throat beating hectically.

'I don't... I don't want you any more,' she said.

He moved closer. Unable not to. Zoe looked at him as if in a trance. 'Don't lie, Zoe.'

She moved back. 'So what if I do still want you? You dumped me, remember?'

Maks stopped right in front of her. Her scent, fresh and sweet, wound around him. He smelled the sea too. Salty. Something in him calmed for the first time in weeks.

'Maybe that was a mistake.'

She'd been looking at his mouth. Now her eyes met his.

'What's that supposed to mean? What do you want from me?'

All Maks knew was that what he really wanted was too huge and terrifying to articulate. Far easier to focus on the hunger that had been eating him up for weeks.

He reached out, put his hands on her arms. He felt the tension in her body even as she swayed towards him.

'I want *you*. We both want this. We can talk later, hmm…?'

Zoe was drowning in a sea of rising lust. The urge to just sink into Maks, allow him to seduce her again, was overwhelming. She desperately wanted to forget everything for a moment…forget the need to think about what he'd said, about what it might mean.

She wasn't sure what signal of acquiescence she gave, but Maks was tugging her towards him and saying, 'Are you sure?'

Zoe just nodded, her eyes fixed on his mouth, silently begging him to kiss her. And then he was, and for the first time in months she felt as if she could breathe again.

It was fast and furious. Clothes were dragged off, thrown aside. They only stopped for a moment when they were naked. Zoe touched Maks reverently, feeling emotional. She'd thought she wouldn't see him like this again.

He pulled her down onto the bed and she sank into him, her whole body melting and on fire at the same time. She gasped when his fingers explored her, testing her readiness.

He moved over her and she welcomed him into the cradle of her body, breathing deep as he moved inside her, deeper and deeper, until she couldn't breathe any more and her whole body tightened before the exquisite release.

Zoe fell down into a warm comforting blanket of peace and satisfaction, only vaguely aware of the rush of warmth inside her.

* * *

When Zoe woke a few hours later the sun had started dipping in the sky. She had her back to Maks. They touched at every point where he spooned her. Her bottom was tucked against the potency of his body—no less potent now, even in sleep.

His arm was wrapped around her, his hand splayed across her. Zoe went cold. His hand was right there...on the thickening swell of her belly.

Panic gripped her. She moved as stealthily as she could, dislodging his hand, moving out from under his arm.

He stirred and said a sleepy, 'Zoe?'

She mumbled something and fled to the bathroom on jelly legs, closing the door behind her. She looked at herself in the mirror. Her eyes were sparkling and her face was flushed. She didn't have to look further to know the evidence of Maks's touch would be all over her body.

She took in everything he'd said before they'd made love. He'd apologised. He hadn't even sought proof of Dean's guilt. He finally trusted her. *He still wanted her.*

That could be the case—and she couldn't stop the hitch of joy and relief inside her at that fact—but she had to remember what was at stake here. She was pregnant, and as soon as Maks knew that everything would change again.

Like that morning in Venice, he'd go cold. Let her go. Because he didn't want more.

She couldn't do this—not now...not when she felt so raw.

But she had no choice. She had to let him know.

She went back into the bedroom and steeled herself, not prepared for the deflation she felt to find Maks still asleep. She looked over his body greedily. She noticed that he had shadows under his eyes. As if he hadn't slept for a while. Wishful thinking that it might have anything to do with her.

She dressed quickly, quietly, wanting to be ready to face him.

Maks stirred again, and those grey eyes opened. He looked for her and found her. Came up on his elbow, smiled sleepily. Sexily. Held out his hand. 'Hey, come back here.'

Zoe teetered on the brink of blurting it all out. She had to tell him. *Now.* But in this moment before she said anything, before she ruined it with reality, a different future shimmered between them. A chance to go back into that Maks bubble, where time stopped and became magical.

Zoe wished she could go back there even as she knew it wasn't really what she wanted. Because she'd suddenly realised here, just a couple of kilometres from her old family home, what she *did* really want. And she couldn't bear to have Maks lay it to waste. Not just yet.

Instead of blurting out what she should be saying, she said, 'I'm sorry, I can't do this. I can't just go back to what we had for as long as it might last. I want more, Maks.'

She turned before she could see his expression change and fled the room, heading blindly downstairs and back out of the hotel, down to the stony beach.

Zoe felt Maks's presence before she saw him. She was sitting on the beach, knees pulled up to her chest. He sat down beside her. She didn't look at him.

He surprised her, asking, 'Is this near where your house was?'

She nodded. 'It's the big yellow house up on the cliff behind us. This beach is where we used to come and play.'

'It's beautiful here. You were lucky.'

Zoe felt a pang to think of Maks's toxic childhood. At least she'd known happiness and love for a while.

Knowing that she couldn't delay any longer, Zoe stood up.

Maks rose fluidly beside her. She tried not to be so aware of his body.

'Maks, I—'

'There's something—'

They both looked at each other. Maks's mouth quirked. 'You first.'

'No, you—please.'

Coward, an inner voice mocked her. She pushed it down.

Maks huffed out a breath of air, ran a hand through his hair, making it stick up messily. Sexily.

'Okay. I want to say that when I came to your flat and found out you weren't pregnant I expected to be relieved. After all, having a baby is the last thing I've ever wanted. A family...'

'You told me.' And she really didn't need reminding. Not now.

'But the truth is that I wasn't relieved. What I felt was a lot more ambiguous.'

Zoe's breath stalled for a second. She looked at Maks. 'What are you saying?'

He shrugged minutely. 'Just that I realised I'd changed. Seeing Nikos with his family...seeing how happy he is... it made me realise that not all families are toxic.'

'Mine wasn't,' Zoe said, almost to herself. 'My mother and father adored each other—and us...'

It had been so perfect and she realised now that a part of her had always afraid she'd never attain that level of perfection, more than she was ever afraid of loss or grief. If she was brutally being honest with herself.

Maks continued. 'It made me realise that perhaps a baby wouldn't be the worst thing in the world...'

Zoe stumbled backwards so abruptly that Maks reached out as if to steady her. She ducked out of his reach, dreading him touching her for fear he'd see his effect on her.

'Why would you say this now?'

Dear God. Did he know? Could he tell? He'd always been able to read her mind.

He frowned. 'Believe me, it's the last thing I ever thought I'd hear myself admit to anyone.'

Zoe shook her head. 'You know, don't you…? You're just saying that now because…' Her breaths came choppy and fast.

Maks frowned. 'Know what? Zoe, what is it?'

She turned away, but Maks caught her arm, turning her back. He was close. Too close.

'Zoe, what the hell is going on?'

The words tumbled out—finally. 'I *am* pregnant, Maks. I lied in London because it was too much, seeing you in my flat. You were saying that stuff about me colluding with Dean, and I couldn't believe you still didn't trust me, and I just… I was so hurt. I couldn't tell you then.' She stopped.

Maks was looking at her. His face stripped bare of expression. She saw when her words sank in. He let her arm go. Stood back.

'You are pregnant?'

She nodded, and braced herself for his inevitable reaction, in spite of what he'd just said. Surely the reality would remind him of how he really felt… But what she saw was dawning anger.

'When *were* you going to tell me? After you'd had the baby? When it was three months old? The way Nikos had to find out about *his* son?'

'No. I don't know. I was going to tell you soon… I just…'

How could she articulate what she'd been afraid of? First that he would reject his unborn child and now that he would reject *her*?

'Maks, I'm sorry. I should have told you that day in London.'

He looked at her for a long moment, a slightly shell-shocked expression on his face, and then he said, 'This changes everything.'

Zoe looked wary. 'What do you mean?'

'We're a family now.'

Zoe was shaking her head. 'No, we're not. That's a ridiculous thing to say.'

So why did it make treacherous hope bloom?

She thought of something and hope dissolved. 'I saw those photos of you in Paris with your brothers. That's why I held back from telling you even when you arrived here. I read the speculation in the papers that you're all under pressure to settle down and prove that the Marchetti Group is stable. That's why you've suddenly decided that maybe it wouldn't be a bad thing if I was pregnant, isn't it?'

Maks shook his head, as if that would make Zoe's words make sense. He had no idea what she was talking about. And then he remembered. That drink in Paris with his brothers. Someone had taken surreptitious pictures with their phone and sold them to the tabloids.

'No, Zoe. *No.* That's not what happened.'

But she wasn't listening. She was backing away again.

'I won't do it, Maks. I won't pretend to be a happy family when we both know it would be a lie. You came here to rekindle an affair, not to make a family. I won't let you use our baby like this.'

Maks was still reeling at the news that she was pregnant. Reeling and filled with something else—something that was spreading out to every cell in his body, filling him with resolve.

'Zoe, I came here because I couldn't stay away. You've haunted me for over a month. I can't look at another woman.'

She shook her head. 'That's just lust. You don't want a family. Stop pretending you're okay with this.'

All the jagged edges that had rubbed inside Maks all

his life were finally slotting into place. He just had to convince Zoe.

He thought of something and pointed out, 'We didn't use protection just now.'

Zoe looked confused, and then understanding sank in. She blushed.

Maks said, 'If your cycle is regular, and if you weren't already pregnant, then I think it's safe to say we took a great risk today. It didn't even occur to me to use protection, because when I'm with you I can't think straight. I want you so badly that all the things I thought I believed in and wanted suddenly don't matter any more. You're the only thing that matters.'

Zoe wasn't sure what Maks was saying, but walls were collapsing and dissolving inside her. Walls she'd erected long ago to keep pain out. Walls that had also kept joy out.

Emotion rose before she could stem it. Emotion she'd been suppressing for years. For ever.

Brokenly, she said, 'I can't have a family, Maks. I won't do it.'

He came close. Too close. 'Then why didn't you just get rid of the baby if you feel so strongly about it?'

The very thought made her feel sick. She put a hand on her belly. 'I never even contemplated doing that.'

'So you're happy to have it be just you and the baby?'

Zoe nodded. She could manage that. She couldn't manage more. She couldn't manage what Maks seemed to be suggesting with his presence, and with a look in his eyes that sent far too dangerous yearnings deep into her soul, where she knew what she wanted but was too scared to articulate it out loud.

Maks shook his head. 'That's not how this is going to work. I won't let you keep my child from me, Zoe.'

'But you never even wanted a child.'

'That was before it was a reality. That's before I realised that I didn't actually know what I wanted.'

Zoe didn't want to ask the question, but the words fell out of her mouth. 'What *do* you want?'

'You,' Maks said simply. 'Us.' He put a hand down on hers over her tiny, barely there bump. *'This.'*

'Why are you saying this?'

Maks's steel-grey gaze locked onto hers. 'You don't get it yet?'

She shook her head, terrified of the emotion simmering too close to the surface, threatening to break free.

He smiled, and Zoe was almost too distracted to notice that it lacked his customary confidence.

'I love you, Zoe. I came here to pursue an affair, but deep down I knew that there was no way I could let you go again. I knew I wanted more than that. And it's not just because of the baby. I won't lie and say it'll be easy. It won't. The thought of being a father terrifies me. But I know I want to do it differently from my father. I want to give my child all the love and support I never had.'

Hot moisture prickled behind Zoe's eyes. She desperately tried to stem the flow, but her cheeks were wet before she even realised she couldn't stop the tears. Silent sobs racked her body.

Maks cursed and pulled her into his chest, wrapping his arms around her, holding her tight. Not letting go even though Zoe clenched her fists against him, as if that could stop him offering comfort.

He said gruffly, 'I'm not letting go, Zoe. Ever.'

When the storm had passed, and Zoe was numb from the release of emotion, she pulled back. Maks looked down and cupped her face, wiping her cheeks with his thumbs. She sniffed. She could only imagine what a sight she looked. Puffy eyes. Puffy cheeks.

'Do you really mean it?'

Maks's mouth quirked. 'That I love you? Yes, I do. The whole damn world knows it too, if they care to look at my expression in that photo rather than at the rest of my body.'

Zoe realised she'd seen it that day, through her view-finder, but she'd been too scared to believe it for a second.

'I know you love me too, Zoe. So don't try and deny it.'

She looked up at Maks. A sense of futility washed through her. She did love him. She'd loved him from the moment she'd trusted him enough to let him make love to her.

Still, something stubborn inside her made her resist taking the final leap of faith. She said, 'It's just the baby.'

Maks shook his head. 'No, you don't get to use the baby as an excuse not to trust me, Zoe.'

'But how can we do this after everything we've been through? I'm scared, Maks. Scared to allow myself to love you or to feel happy. Because I know how quickly it can be snatched away.'

And because she didn't deserve it.

Maks raised a brow. 'Is that a good enough excuse to half-live your life? In a perpetual state of fear and misplaced guilt?'

She looked up at Maks, but before she could respond he said, 'There's something else you need to know. I meant to tell you earlier…but you distracted me.'

'What?'

'You've never looked up anything about the crash in the press, have you?'

Zoe shuddered at the thought. 'No, why would I?'

'So you've never known that the reason your father crashed wasn't because he was distracted. It was because a couple of joy-riding kids had stolen a car and were driving on the wrong side of the road…'

Zoe searched Maks's face for signs that he was just making this up. But the faintest glimmer of a memory was coming back to her. People talking in hushed voices as they looked at her with pity. She'd blocked out so much of that time, and she'd been so young…and then she'd never wanted to think about it.

That moment when her father had looked back at her just before the crash had been crystallised in her mind, but maybe…

'Zoe, even if he'd had his eyes on the road he wouldn't have had a chance. It was too narrow to escape them. You need to know that. It wasn't your fault.'

This was huge. Too huge to take in fully right now. But even as she thought that she felt something shift inside her, like a knot loosening.

Maks said, 'We're different, Zoe. Things can be different for us. I'm willing to take the risk if you are.'

Could she do it? Hand herself over to this man whom she loved but didn't have the guts to say it out loud to yet?

And then it hit her. She simply didn't have a choice except to move forward. For the sake of their baby as much as for her own sake. That was why she'd come back here. That was why she'd never contemplated anything but having her baby.

Maks turned her around to face the water and wrapped one arm around her while pointing out to sea with the other. The clouds were parting to reveal blue sky. And a rainbow.

He said, close to her ear, 'We can't do anything but trust in each other and weather whatever comes our way, but I wouldn't want to do it with anyone else. I love you.'

The rainbow shimmered and glistened, beckoning her to put her trust in this man. She had a sense of her family around her, urging her on. Urging her to finally let go of the guilt that had dogged her whole life. The guilt that she'd used like a shield to stop herself from getting hurt.

It hadn't been her fault.

Zoe felt a sense of peace wash over her. Acceptance.

And a rush of love so intense that she turned around, rose up on her toes and wrapped her arms around Maks's neck.

She'd thought it would be hard to say the words, but in the end it was the easiest thing in the world. 'I love you, Maks.'

'Say that again.'

'I love you.'

Joy flooded her being when she saw the awe she felt reflected in Maks's eyes.

He said, 'Will you marry me? Not for the baby or for any other reason except that I know I want to spend the rest of my life with you and I want everyone to know you're mine. And because I love you.'

Zoe bit her lip, scarcely believing what she was hearing. Slivers of lingering fear and guilt—for wanting what her parents had had and hoping that her life could be different—that it wouldn't be cut so tragically short-threatened to rise and drown her again.

But Maks brushed her hair back and said, 'I know, Zoe. I get it. I'm scared too—believe me. I only saw meanness and selfishness. I'm afraid I don't know how to be a good father. But I know I wouldn't want to do this with anyone else. So will you? Marry me and take the biggest risk of your life?'

The fear and guilt receded, banished finally by the naked emotion she saw in Maks's eyes. A giddy happiness flooded her whole body.

Zoe smiled through her tears. 'Yes, I will. I love you, Maks.'

The risk was huge, but she knew that the reward would be even greater.

He covered her mouth with his, taking her breath and taking her soul and her heart for ever.

EPILOGUE

Four years later. London.

'THERE'S MAMA! LOOK!'

Maks hushed his three-and-a-half-year-old daughter Luna as they walked into the huge, cavernous studio where the photo-shoot was taking place.

'Yes, I see her, *piccolina*. But we can't say hello just yet—she's working.'

'Okay, Papa.'

His daughter wrapped her arms around his neck and buried her head in his neck, and his heart swelled at the easy, instinctive gesture.

Luna had eyes that were an unusual mix of green and grey, and dark blond hair like her father.

Never, not for a moment, did Maks take the love of his daughter or his wife for granted.

Zoe looked around at that moment, saw them, and smiled. Her hair was up in a loose topknot. She never used it to hide her face any more. She sent them a small wave and a kiss. Maks sent her an explicit look that she clearly recognised, and when she blushed in response, he smirked. Even as his own body reacted to that blush. Still.

Time and the reality of family life, terrifying and exhilarating all at once, hadn't dimmed their desire or their love. It had only compounded it, turning it into something Maks had never believed existed. Trust. Harmony. Endless love.

Zoe turned back to finish photographing the model for a magazine cover. The model was striking—one of the hottest at the moment. Zoe had actually spotted her on the street and nurtured her herself. Originally a refugee from

Angola, the girl was stunningly beautiful, yet her face was marked with the scars of war. But she wore them proudly and they'd become a trademark of her look, thanks to Zoe.

Pride filled Maks as he watched his wife at work. There was a quiet buzz of activity in the studio, but also a serenity—a trademark of Zoe's method. She'd already made a name for herself as one of the world's most in-demand photographers, but what had earned her even more respect was the fact that she'd insisted on working her way up through the ranks. Biding her time and learning with the greats. Not using her contacts to get ahead.

Once people had become aware that she was *the* Stephen Collins's daughter, which had inevitably come out once their engagement had been announced, the press had had a field-day rehashing old stories of the tragic crash and her glamorous lineage. And that vast inheritance. But they'd weathered the public interest together, until it had died down again.

Finally, Zoe was done. She loved knowing that Maks and Luna were here, waiting for her. She never felt fully at peace unless she was close to them. She said her goodbyes to her team and the rest of the crew, and to Sara, the model, who had become a good friend.

Zoe only worked with companies and models that promoted an alternative view of the fashion industry. She knew that locked her out of a lot of lucrative work, but she wasn't doing it to make money. She was doing it because she loved it.

Everything in her life was motivated by love now. And nothing more so than her love for her family.

She walked to Maks and Luna, sliding into their arms like a missing jigsaw piece. Luna's small arms wrapped around her neck and Zoe took her, pressing kisses all over her face, making her giggle.

Maks pulled her close, glancing down at her very distended belly. 'Please tell me now you're officially on maternity leave?' He sounded mildly exasperated.

She'd been due to take maternity leave a few weeks ago, but jobs had kept enticing her back. She smiled up at Maks and wrapped her free arm around his waist. He was in full protective Alpha male mode, and she had to admit she found it beyond sexy.

'Yes, finally. And I need a foot rub so bad...'

He smiled, and it was wicked. 'Just a foot rub?'

To Zoe's chagrin, she blushed. Still! After all this time. She smiled back. 'You're insatiable.'

Maks affected a wounded look. 'Me? I seem to recall this morning that you were the one—'

'When is Ben going to come?'

Luna's small voice interrupted their private moment.

Zoe looked at her daughter and her heart swelled. 'In a couple of weeks, sweetie, when he's ready.'

They were having a son, and had decided to call him Ben, after her brother.

Luna clapped her hands. 'Can we go and buy him some presents?'

Zoe sent Maks a dry look. Their daughter was far too smart for her own good. She'd figured out that presents for the baby meant presents for her too.

Maks plucked her out of Zoe's arms. '*One* present—*if* you eat all your dinner tonight and go to bed early and let Hamish read you a story.'

'With his funny voice?'

'With his funny voice.'

Maks took Zoe's hand and lifted it, kissing the palm of her hand while Luna chattered on happily.

Their life was about to expand and get even more hectic. If Zoe stopped to think for a moment she felt breathless. This much love? This much happiness? It was a risk, for sure, but it was a risk she would take over and over again. Because the reward was beyond anything she could ever have imagined.

'Home?' Maks asked.

Zoe looked up and saw their world reflected in his loving gaze. She deserved this. They both did. And everything would be fine.

She smiled. 'Home.'

* * * * *

AN HEIR
CLAIMED BY
CHRISTMAS

CLARE CONNELLY

For readers of romance and lovers of Christmas—
some of my favourite people!

And for the real-life Dimitrios—
thank you for inspiring the name of my hero.

PROLOGUE

'WHAT EXACTLY AM I looking at?' Dimitrios's scorn for journalists was evident in the tone of his voice. Always somewhat intimidating, he reserved a particularly gruff response for the man on the other end of the phone.

'My email?' The reporter's smugness was unbearable.

Its subject was: Call me to discuss.

The only text in the email read:

Article running in the weekend papers.

Attached was a photograph of a young boy.

It was a bizarre enough email to prompt Dimitrios's response. There was something in the child's face—his eyes—that was familiar to Dimitrios, and a spark of worry ignited.

His twin brother, Zach, was renowned for his startlingly brief affairs. Was it possible he had, somewhere over the years, fathered a child?

It was just the kind of scandal the papers would love, dragging their family name—and that of the media empire Zach and Dimitrios had worked their backsides off to protect since inheriting the multi-billion-dollar corporation from their father—through the mud.

'Is there another reason I would have called you?'

Ashton worked for a rival newspaper based out of

Sydney. Dimitrios could have—and would have—pulled strings to have the story killed in his own papers but he knew nothing he said would deter Ashton.

'So? Do you have a quote?'

Dimitrios sighed. 'How can I? I have no idea what response your cryptic photograph is supposed to elicit from me. Recognition? Fear? Sorry to disappoint, but I feel neither.'

He would need to speak to his brother, find out if he knew anything about this. Surely Zach would have mentioned having had a child? Unless he didn't know? Although, wasn't it far more likely this journalist was grasping at straws?

'What about if I give you the name Annie Hargreaves?'

Dimitrios's whole body responded. Staring out of the window of his top-level office at the morning sun that coated Singapore in a golden glow, past the iconic towers of Marina Bay Sands towards the strait, he felt as though a rock had been dropped on his gut.

'What did you say?'

The question was asked through bared teeth. He didn't need Ashton to repeat the question. Everything about Annabelle Damned Hargreaves was burned into his memory. Her body. Her kiss. Her innocence. The way she'd looked at him the night they'd made love, as though it had meant something important, something special. As though he could have given her anything—as though he were that kind of man! Instead of understanding what it actually had been—an outpouring of mutual grief after the death of his best friend, her brother.

He thought of the things he'd said to her after they'd slept together, after he'd taken her virginity. Words that even at the time had been calculatedly cutting. He'd followed the old adage of being cruel to be kind, understanding that she wanted more from him than he would ever be able to give. Knowing he needed to destroy any childish fantasies and hopes she might have had that he, Dimitrios Papandreo, could be the kind of man to give her some kind of mythical happily-ever-after. He'd never been that way inclined but, after Lewis's death, the reality of life's cruelty had been made abundantly clear to him.

None the less, having her name come out of nowhere sent a pulse of raw feeling through his body, scattering any ability to think rationally. Every one of his senses went on high alert in a response that was pure survival instinct.

'Miss Annie Hargreaves, twenty-five years old, of Bankstown, Sydney. Six-year-old boy. Single mother to a little boy named Max. Now do you care to comment?'

Dimitrios gripped the phone more tightly, his whole body coursing with a type of acid. His gut rolled, every muscle on his lean, athletic frame tensed as though he were preparing for a fist fight.

Six.

Max.

The facts exploded through him like sticks of dynamite.

He swore inwardly, standing abruptly and stalking towards the windows, bracing one arm against the glass, pressing his forehead to it, staring directly beneath him. The sense of vertigo only compounded the spinning feeling he was already combatting.

Lewis had died seven years earlier. The anniversary of his death had just passed—a day Dimitrios and Zach marked each year. The three of them had been inseparable, more than best friends. Lewis had been like a third brother. His death had destroyed Dimitrios and Zach. His loss had been shocking—how someone so healthy and strong could simply cease to exist, all of his life force and energy just…

gone. Dimitrios had known pain in his life, but never that kind of grief, and it had torn him in two.

His eyes swept shut as he thought of Lewis's little sister. Annabelle...

It wasn't possible.

'Rumour has it you two hooked up one night, about nine months before this little boy was born.'

Rumour? No. A source. There was no rumour about a child of his or he would have heard it much sooner. Somehow, this man had been given the information from someone who knew way too much.

Annabelle?

He rejected the idea immediately. If she'd wanted anyone to know, she would have come directly to him. Wouldn't she?

'Don't you get it, Annabelle? I was drunk. I came here because I was thinking about Lewis, and I was missing him, and I wanted to talk to someone who would understand. That—' he'd pointed to the bed '—was never meant to happen. I would never choose to go to bed with you. Surely you can see that?'

'So?' Ashton pushed. 'Any confirmation? Have you met your son, Dimitrios?'

His son. It was as if the dynamite kept sparking and exploding, reigniting and exploding all over again. His arm took most of his body weight. His symmetrical face looked as though it had been sculpted with a blade. Tension radiated from his pulse points.

'Look after her for me, Dim. Annie's going to be devastated. She won't cope with this. Please check in on her. Make sure she's okay.'

Guilt nauseated him, as always. The sense that he'd failed his friend, and broken the death-bed promise Lewis had extracted from him, all because grief had driven his body to seek consolation in the one way he knew how. He'd failed Lewis and he'd never forgiven himself for that misstep.

And what about Annabelle? his brain demanded, reminding him that she had been grieving too. And he'd taken advantage of that, seeking solace in her arms, in her body, irrespective of the damage he might have been doing to her already tender heart.

'Annie Hargreaves is a long-time friend of the family,' he muttered, knowing it was the worst thing to say. It was feeding the flame with oxygen.

Ashton's laugh made Dimitrios want to snap something in half. 'A bit more than that, by the looks of it.'

Instincts took over, a ruthless streak turning his voice to stone. 'You do realise you're about to ruin a child's life for the sake of circulation?'

'And *you* claim to have a problem with that?'

Dimitrios couldn't respond. Zach and he had seen their world-wide viewership and readership treble in the last decade. He couldn't—wouldn't—trivialise the work journalists did. He'd long since given up any hope that his life could be played out privately. Despite his personal wishes, he was considered to be someone of interest, a public figure, and his life—to some extent—was a free-for-all.

He ground his teeth together, the whole situation one that filled him with a sense of dark impatience.

'Let me get back to you.'

He hung up the phone and jammed it into his pocket, pushing away from the window without taking a step back from the glass.

'You must know how I feel about you, Dimitrios...'

'How you feel? Christ, Annabelle, you're little more than a child. I haven't thought about you or your feelings except for the fact you're Lewis's little sister.'

The little sister he'd promised Lewis he'd look after.
She'd winced.

'Then let me tell you now. I like you. I think I...no... I'm sure that I love you.'

It had been like having a gun pushed to his temple. Sheer panic flooded his nervous system. He'd made a mistake and it was going from bad to worse. He'd had to disabuse her of any idea that he could do this. He'd had to make a clean break, remove any hope she might have had that he could offer her more.

'You're deluding yourself. Nothing about this was "love". It was sex, plain and simple. And you know what the worst of it is? I was so drunk I barely even remember what we did.'

Her face had scrunched in pain and he'd been glad. He was pushing her away to punish himself—she *should* hate him. He deserved that.

'I have a life. A girlfriend.'

All the colour had drained from her face.

'And you are a mistake I'll always regret.'

Hell. Even now the words had the power to reach through time and make him feel a powerful sense of self-disgust. He'd done the right thing in pushing her away so forcefully, but seeing her heartbreak so clear on her face had made him feel like the worst kind of person. It was a feeling that had never really let up.

He crossed back to his desk, moving the mouse to stir his computer screen to life. The photograph was there, as large as it had been a moment ago, but it took on a whole new importance now.

He'd thought the boy looked familiar, but not in a million years had he considered that he might be the father.

And Annabelle the mother.

Shock began to morph into something else.

Anger. Disappointment. Disbelief.

Why had she kept this from him?

'You'll always regret what we did? Well, I'll never forgive you for that. Just get out. Get out! Leave me alone. Don't ever contact me again.'

Had she been so angry she'd decided to keep their son from him? He'd wanted to push her away for good, but maybe he'd gone too far. Was this some sick form of payback? He couldn't believe it, yet the facts were there, staring right back at him. Annabelle had borne a child, and Dimitrios would bet his fortune on the fact he was the father.

Dimitrios ground his teeth together, his jaw set in a forbidding line as he reached for his desk phone and buzzed through to his hard-working assistant.

'Have the jet fuelled. I need to get to Sydney. Immediately.'

CHAPTER ONE

'THAT'S OKAY. I ate earlier.'

At six, Max was far too perceptive. His huge eyes lingered on Annie's face, as if studying her to see if it was true or not.

'I'm fine,' she assured him, curving her lips into a smile. 'Eat your dinner.'

He returned his attention to the plate in front of him, doing his best to hide the disappointment at the fact he was eating meatloaf for the third night in a row. He speared a piece with his fork, sliced it and lifted it. She watched him, her lips pursed.

'Are you working tonight, Mummy?'

She cast a glance at the laptop propped on the other end of the table. 'A little.'

He nodded, spearing another piece. Pleasure replaced worry. He was growing so fast, eating so much. It was just a growth spurt. He'd settle down soon enough. And hopefully the grocery bills wouldn't bankrupt her in the meantime.

She reached behind her and switched off the kitchen light, then took the seat beside Max, her hands curling around her mug of tea. The warmth was a balm.

'You can work now if you need to.'

Her heart turned over in her chest. 'I'd rather talk to you.'

'But then you'll have to stay up so late.'

She frowned. 'Why do you say that?'

He lifted his shoulders. 'You do, right?'

These last few nights she *had* been burning the candle at both ends. There'd been extra work to do in the firm and she'd put her hand up for it, glad of the additional hours. It wasn't the most highly paid work but the ability to do it from home meant she could be flexible for Max. When he'd been a baby, that had been imperative, but even now, with him at school, the number of holidays children took meant she needed to be able to care for him. There was no one who could help her—no nearby grandparents, aunts or uncles—and the cost of childcare was prohibitive.

'Sometimes. I like it, though. How's the meatloaf?' She winced at the conversation change—the last thing she wanted to do was remind him of the boring dinner he was being made to eat. She kept a bright smile pinned to her face, though. He matched it, nodded then reached for his drink.

He was so like his father.

Pain lanced her. She had to look away. Worry followed pain. A month ago, Max had asked about him. Not like when he'd been a younger boy and he'd become aware that children often had two parents. That had been an innocent, 'Do I have a daddy?' question that had been easy to palm off. This time, it had been laced with meaning. 'Who's my daddy, Mummy? Why haven't I met him? Does he live near us? Can I see him? Doesn't he love me?'

Difficult questions that had required thought and composure to answer. She'd always sworn she wouldn't lie to him, but answering his queries was a minefield.

Not for the first time, guilt at the way she was raising their child spread through her. Not just the relative poverty in which they lived, with Annie having to scrimp and save to afford even the most basic necessities, but the fact she was doing it alone.

A lump formed in her throat, the past heavy in her mind. The night she'd gone to tell Dimitrios the truth had been one of the worst of her life. Seeing him three months after they'd slept together was something she'd had to brace herself for. She'd dressed in the most grown-up outfit she owned, hoping to look not just sexy and glamorous but mature as well, as though she belonged in his world with him. She'd had her speech all worked out—how he didn't need to be involved if he didn't want to be, but that he deserved to know.

But arriving to discover him surrounded by his exclusive, glamorous crowd in one of Sydney's most prestigious bars—and with the gorgeous redhead pressed to his body, all flame hair and milky skin—had sent Annie running. At eighteen, it had been too much to bear. Her pride had been hurt, her heart broken, and the precious kernel of meaning she'd taken from their night together had burst into flames, never to be recovered.

Lewis's death had left Annie completely alone. An already tenuous relationship with her parents had been irrevocably destroyed by their grief—an event that might have drawn them closer had pushed them apart, as Annie's mum refused to see that anyone else except her was hurting. Sleeping with Dimitrios had been the fulfilment of a long-cherished crush, but it had been more than that. Annie had been pulled out of the vortex of her pain and loneliness and put back together again in Dimitrios's arms. Being made love to by him had made her feel whole in a way she'd thought impossible, even if that pleasure was fleeting.

His words the next morning had robbed her of that sense of comfort, plunging her back into darkness and despair. She'd been eighteen and it had all been too much. Lewis's death, losing her virginity to Dimitrios and all that night had meant to her, his harsh rejection of her the next day, discovering she was pregnant and her mother's anger at that, the subsequent estrangement from her parents... Her emotions had been all over the place then but now, as a twenty-five-year-old, she wondered if she'd made the right decisions.

Was keeping Max from Dimitrios something she could still defend?

'What's wrong, Mummy?'

Whoops. She'd let her smile slip. She pushed it back in place. 'Nothing, darling. Keep eating. It's late. You need to get to bed.'

Bedtime, though, had become something of a mission in the past six months. Gone were the days when Annie had been able to read a picture book, tuck the covers to Max's chin, kiss his forehead and slip from the room. It took an hour to settle him these days.

Tonight there was a story, answering a thousand and one questions, letting him have another sip of water, then a trip to the bathroom, then back to be tucked in again, then at least one call of, 'I'm scared, Mummy!'

At that point, Annie compromised and patted his back, even though all the parenting books seemed to suggest it was the wrong thing to do. At this point, it felt like the proverbial straw that was breaking the camel's back, anyway. She'd probably done so many little things wrong—what was one extra?

With a sigh, she crept from his room, pausing in the door frame to give his sleeping figure one last look. Love burst her heart. She was exhausted, worried and stressed but so full of love.

With a wistful smile, she clicked the door shut and moved back to the table. Her laptop beckoned. Cracking it open, she was glad of the distraction of work to keep her mind off the fact she was, actually, starving. She told herself she'd work for an hour and then have a cup of tea

and an oat biscuit—her one indulgence. It wasn't usually
so austere, but with Christmas just around the corner she
needed to try to save enough to buy Max something. He
did without so much for most of the year, while all his little
friends were getting spoiled with books, sports equipment
and anything their hearts desired. She wanted him to have
something for Christmas.

Loading properties on to real-estate listings was work
she could do without too much mental computation. She
cross-checked the photographs with the property name
and the description the various agents had attached, making sure each had uploaded correctly before moving on to
the next.

Almost an hour after starting, a loud knock sounded
at her door. She startled, quickly pushing her chair back.
There was no worry that Max would stir—though he was
difficult to get to sleep, once he was down for the night he
slept like an immovable log. Nonetheless, the noise was
loud and she needed to work.

It was probably a delivery for the flat upstairs. The house
she lived in had been carved up by an industrious landlord many years earlier. Six small flats had been created
and hers was the one at ground level; she often had deliv-
eries intended for other residents simply because she was
accessible.

'Just a second.' She closed the laptop and paused to flick
on the kettle sitting on the peeling laminate bench top before unlocking the door. The peephole had been damaged
years earlier and the landlord had never got round to replacing it, though at her insistence he'd added a chain lock.
She slid it across now and opened the door as wide as the
chain allowed.

Then had to fight every impulse she possessed to stop

herself from pushing it shut again. Self-preservation and a thousand other impulses slammed into her.

Oh, damn.

Was it possible she'd somehow conjured him up? That her overactive mind and memories had willed him into her life again? What the hell was Dimitrios doing here?

She threw a guilt-laced look over her shoulder at her tiny, threadbare apartment.

'Annabelle.' His voice was like warm butter on brioche. He was one of the few people who used her full name. Her stomach clenched at memories of the way he'd said her name that night, of the way he'd touched her, the way he'd…

'I had half a bottle of whisky before coming here, Annabelle. Do you think I would ever have done this if I was in my right mind? I've never even looked at you before. You're just a kid, for God's sake. A teenager—and a naïve one at that. Don't mistake sex for anything of substance. This meant nothing.'

Recalling his words, and the hurt they'd inflicted, was exactly what she needed. She pulled herself to her full— admittedly not very impressive—height of five and a half feet and levelled him with what she hoped passed for an ice-cold glare. Inside, though, her heart was racing, making a mockery of any notion that she wasn't affected by him…

Max.

Their son.

He was asleep only a dozen metres or so away, behind a flimsy white wall. Panic surged through her.

'We have a problem.'

We. Just hearing him use that word sent a flood of warmth down her spine. It had been a long time since she'd been a 'we' with anyone except Max. The cold ache of loneliness was something with which Annie was completely familiar. She lifted one brow, unaware of the way his eyes followed the gesture, not noticing the frown that crossed his face.

'May I come in?'

She stared at him, belatedly realising she hadn't said anything to so much as acknowledge his presence. She was simply standing, staring, her heart in overdrive, her panic centres in full swing. She shook her head urgently, jerking it so hard it could well have snapped from her spine. 'Um, no. I— What are you doing here, Dimitrios?'

'That's something better discussed in private.'

She frowned. Beyond him was a Sydney cul-de-sac. No one was around, that she could see. 'Seems pretty private out there to me.' She reached for her key, hanging on a hook beside the door, then drew the door open further so she could step out.

She knew as she did so that it wasn't just the risk of him discovering the truth about Max. She was ashamed. Her apartment was far from luxurious—heck, it was far from *comfortable*. She'd done her best but there was always something more urgent to buy or pay for. Trendy cushions and throw rugs were way down her list of priorities.

Stepping outside, though, brought her toe-to-toe with a man she'd told herself she'd *never* see again. And even though she'd been coming to realise that was unrealistic— that their son deserved better—she hadn't been prepared for *this*! To see him tonight—here, at her place—was too much, too soon. She wasn't ready; she wasn't mentally prepared.

We have a problem.

'What are you doing here, Dimitrios?'

She registered the response her saying his name had on him. His eyes flickered with something she didn't comprehend. Annie looked away, crossing her arms over her chest. It had been a warm day, but the night had cooled off, and she was wearing only a thin T-shirt and yoga pants.

She'd almost forgotten how handsome he was. His face, so symmetrical, had the effect of having been sculpted from granite. Every line and shift was intentional—nothing had been left to chance. Cheekbones, a patrician nose, a determined jaw and a cleft in his chin that she remembered teasing with her tongue.

Her skin flushed with warmth. His eyes were a steely grey, blue in some lights, and his brows were flat and long, making him look every bit as intelligent as she knew him to be. She'd never known him without facial hair—stubble that grew over his chin and above his lip, but which she doubted was intentional, more the result of a man who was too busy to trouble himself with shaving regularly.

Her stomach lurched as other characteristics threw themselves into her mind. The memory of his hard chest, so chiselled and firm, each muscle drawing her attention and making her worship at the altar of his hyper-masculine beauty. His tan, a deep brown, the colour of burned caramel. His arms, strong and slim, the way they'd clamped around her and held her body close to his as she'd fallen asleep. And she'd fallen asleep believing the promises his body had made hers—that the experience they'd shared was the beginning of something meaningful and special. In the midst of her grief, the sadness that had filled her soul with the sudden death of her older brother, Annie had felt as though she'd come home. She'd believed everything would actually be okay.

'Why didn't you tell me?' He answered her question with one of his own. A *frisson* of danger moved down Annie's spine. The question wasn't the kind of thing you asked. This was no fishing expedition; he knew something. Or, he *thought* he knew something. But what? Hopefully, she racked her brain for anything else it could be—hopefully.

But there was nothing. The only secret she'd ever kept from him—from anyone—was the existence of Max.

Anxiety turned to adrenaline; she shivered.

'Tell you what?' she heard herself ask, her voice a little higher in pitch than normal.

'It's too late for that, Annabelle.' He expelled a breath that could almost have passed for a sigh except there was too much anger behind it; bitterness, too. 'A journalist knows. We have a son together.'

She sucked in a sharp breath, pressing her back against the door in an effort to stay upright. It barely helped. She felt as though the four walls were closing in on her—as though the atmosphere of the planet was being sucked out into space, as though an enormous weight was bearing down hard on her belly.

Why had she thought she could get away with this? Of course he should have known about Max. What had she been thinking?

All the reasons that had seemed so valid a little over six years ago blew away from her like dust in the wind. She stared at him, but the accusation and anger in his face made it impossible to hold his gaze for long. She angled her face away, concentrating on breathing. Her lungs burned. Shame made her cheeks flame.

Her eyes hurt.

A second later, she was aware of his curse, and then nothing. She wasn't sure how long the nothingness lasted, only that his hands were around her waist, lifting her easily as his fingers dug into her pocket to remove her keys. She was groggy—too shocked to protest. He pushed open the door to her apartment and it wasn't within her capability to feel even a hint of embarrassment in that moment—at least, not at her décor.

He carried her to the sofa and laid her down, his footsteps retreating for a moment. She heard squeaking as he opened cupboards and then slamming as they closed heavily. Once, twice, thrice, a fourth time, and then the running of water. He returned with a glass and held it out to her. 'Drink this.'

God, what she must look like to him! She scrambled into a sitting position, holding a shaking hand out for the glass. After she'd had half of it, she sat with it cradled in her lap, fighting the sting of tears.

'So it's true?'

She lifted her face to his, wishing he would sit down or that she could stand up, but her knees were as stable as jelly. And, given the tiny size of her sofa, she didn't actually want him to sit down, because that would bring him way too close to her, and she was already spiralling from the remembered sensation of his strong arms carrying her so easily when she'd passed out.

His voice was throaty and deep, raw and guttural. 'Annabelle, damn it. Tell me. Is it true?'

Except he didn't really doubt the truth, did he? She saw that in his expression, the tautness of his face, the anger in the depths of his eyes. Her stomach squeezed. She couldn't lie to him—not any more. And she didn't *want* to. Nor did she want to lie to Max.

But, oh, Max. How would she explain this to him? She knotted her fingers in her lap, an old nervous habit she'd never been able to shed, her eyes huge in a face that had grown pale. Her side-sweeping fringe had fallen to cover one of her eyes in a river of shimmering gold and she instinctively lifted a hand to swipe at it, tucking the longer strands behind her ear.

She hadn't really thought she could keep Dimitrios from learning the truth. But it was only having him here, with this accusation, that she realised she'd waited for this day—

that she'd known it was coming and had almost longed for it. What else could explain the relief she felt?

He knew. Finally.

It was over.

No more secrets and lies—at least, not to Max.

'Yes.'

He flinched, his cheeks darkening. Perhaps she'd been wrong about him; maybe he hadn't already known? His jaw tightened, as though he was grinding his teeth together. She looked down at her knees because she couldn't bear to look at him a moment longer. 'He's six and his name is Max. I have photos—'

'Photos?' His voice made thick with emotion. 'Give me one reason why I shouldn't go into his room right now and take him away with me!'

Her heart skipped several beats; her lungs failed to inflate. She reached for the arm of the sofa in shock, gripping it hard, feeling as though her eyes were filling with darkness again. She stood up quickly, shaky legs or not, needing to feel more physically prepared for that kind of challenge.

'I've already seen a photo. The journalist had one.'

That stopped Annie in her tracks. Despite the shock, her rational brain began to assert itself. He'd mentioned a journalist earlier, only she'd been so blindsided by seeing him here she hadn't registered that point. 'What journalist?'

'Does it matter?'

'No one can know about this. It's impossible.'

Dimitrios's eyes narrowed. 'You made sure of that?'

She swallowed, hearing the silver blade to his voice, the undercurrent of displeasure that he had every right to feel. 'Yes.' She had; she was sure of it.

'Not well enough, apparently.'

'It's just not possible.' She shook her head. 'He doesn't share your surname. No one ever knew about...' She stumbled, biting down on her lip, as the traitorous word 'us' had been about to escape. There had never been an 'us'. That implied togetherness. Friendship. A relationship, even. They'd had an ill-thought-out one-night stand. Nothing more meaningful than that. 'What happened that night,' she finished awkwardly.

'You never mentioned it to anyone?' he pushed, and his obvious doubts on that score raised her feminist hackles.

'What's the matter, Dimitrios? Does that hurt your pride? Did you think I would scream what we'd done from the rooftops?'

A muscle jerked in his jaw and she had a sense he was trying very hard not to give into his anger. Only she found she *wanted* his anger—it felt appropriate, given what they'd been through and were now discussing.

He spoke calmly, but she could see how that cost him. 'I thought you were a decent person; I believed you to be like Lewis.' She recoiled at the invocation of her brother's name, at Dimitrios using Lewis against her like that. 'But a decent person would never have kept something like this from me.'

'A decent person wouldn't have said all the things you did to me that night,' she responded in kind, carefully keeping her voice soft, though it shook with the effort. 'A decent person wouldn't have shown up drunk on my doorstep—days after my brother's funeral, might I add—and spent the night making love to me only to throw in my face the next morning how little that—*I*—meant to you.'

His expression was inscrutable, but his body was wound tighter than a coil. 'And so this is retaliation? You wanted to hurt me?'

She shook her head. 'No, never.' Her reaction was instant. 'It wasn't about that.'

Silence fell, barbed. No, not silence. There was breathing: heavy, fast…his, hers…it filled the room like a tornado of emotions.

'You told me you would forget about me in days, do you remember that?'

Somehow, the only shift in his features was a tightening about his mouth.

'You told me you were so drunk I could have been any woman—you'd found your way to my door but that was just happenstance.'

'You don't need to repeat what I said. I remember.'

Something sharp moved in the region of her heart. She was glad he remembered.

'You told me you had a girlfriend,' she reminded him anyway, her hands on her hips, her chin jutting forward. She'd hated him then, for taking what had been an incredible night for her—her first sexual experience with a man she'd already been halfway to loving, the comfort and sense of unity she'd felt—and turning it into something so tawdry and *wrong*. She would *never* have slept with him if she'd known he was with someone else!

'Yes.' No apology, yet she saw something stir in the depths of his eyes, something she didn't understand and didn't want to waste time analysing.

'All of which makes me a bastard of the first order,' he said firmly. 'But that still doesn't excuse you hiding our son from me for six damn years.'

She spun away from him, moving to the window that overlooked the street. She'd tried to tell him. She hadn't wanted to do it this way. But seeing him, his lifestyle, how could she throw something like a child into the midst of that? She'd been terrified. What if he'd sued for custody? And raised her child with another woman? She'd already lost so much—her parents, Lewis—the prospect of their baby was all she had.

Seeing him in his own environment like that had shown her the impossibility of telling him *anything,* and the words he'd thrown at her had been like flames, licking at her feet, tormenting her with how little she meant to him. Why would she ever have believed Dimitrios would act in her best interests? She meant nothing to him—he would do as he wanted, irrespective of her wishes.

Convinced of that, she'd fled, and all these years she'd told herself he'd be grateful if he ever learned the truth.

'How did the journalist find out?' she asked quietly, returning to her original question, her face creased with concentration.

'Beats me. Apparently you must have told someone.'

She shook her head. 'I have no idea how a journalist could have discovered this. I've been so careful.'

'And what about my son? Does he know?'

My son. So possessive, so…right. For years she'd thought of Max as *hers.* He was her child, hers to protect, raise, love and shepherd. Except, the older he'd got, the more he'd started to look like Dimitrios, so that it was becoming impossible to ignore his true parentage.

'He doesn't know.'

Dimitrios's response was a rumble, a curse, a moan, low and quiet. It nonetheless reverberated around the room and pressed deep from his soul and into Annie's. She winced, his pain impossible to miss.

'You haven't even told him about me?'

She shook her head softly. 'He's started to ask, though. I've known for a while that I would need to…'

'And would you then have told me, also?'

She turned back to face him, wishing she could lie, but knowing he finally deserved the truth. 'I don't know.' It was the best she could do. 'I'd like to believe so.'

His eyes bore into hers, as though through the power

of sight he could somehow intuit the truth of her heart. Her blood moved like wildfire and the hairs on her arms stood up.

She waited for him to say something, to react, but he stood there for so long her blood began to rush for another reason altogether. She stared at him. A cacophony of emotions filled her, so she took a small step backwards, needing to break the connection that was firing between them like an electrical current. How was it possible that even in this moment he could have any kind of impact on her?

'I—' She wasn't sure what she'd intended to say. She stopped talking when he shook his head and held up a hand, as if to silence her.

'No.' His brows drew closer. 'No,' he repeated, then turned on one heel and took the five or so steps his long gait needed to get him to the door.

'You're leaving?' she demanded.

At the door, he turned to face her. 'I won't do this now.'

Her jaw dropped.

'If you knew how close I was to saying a thousand things I would come to regret, then you'd understand.' He shook his head. 'If I've learned anything, it's to not react when your emotions are in play.'

She stared at him in disbelief.

'I will come back tomorrow.'

She swallowed. 'Max has school.'

'Good. We should talk without him hearing—it will be easier to make plans if he's not present.'

'Plans for what?' But she already knew what he was going to say. Custody. He was going to take Max away, at least some of the time. How could she live with that? Panic filled her. She felt as if she might vomit.

'For our marriage, Annabelle. What else?'

CHAPTER TWO

SHE COULD HARDLY turn a sow's ear into a silk purse but she'd done the best she could, polishing and tidying, neatening the small apartment to within an inch of its life in preparation for Dimitrios's return. Her whole world felt completely tipped off-balance.

For our marriage, Annabelle. What else?

As though it were a *fait accompli*—a given.

It was *so* like Dimitrios. He was born to command, a Titan of any boardroom he entered, a man people couldn't help but respond to and obey. Naturally it wouldn't have occurred to him that she might not wish to be married to him.

But...hello!

How in the world could he possibly think she'd go along with this? They hadn't seen each other in seven years, and that had been a spectacular disaster. She was still sifting through the shrapnel of that evening, let alone the emotional fallout that had come after.

After he'd left.

After she'd found out she was pregnant.

After she'd gone to tell him.

After she'd seen him with his girlfriend, surrounded by people like him.

After she'd had their baby.

She felt as though she'd boarded some kind of express

train and hadn't been able to pause to draw breath. Marriage? Impossible.

Knots tangled inside her belly.

She moved to the kitchen and wiped the counters for the third time that morning, then pressed the button on the kettle, exhaling slowly as she did so. It was grey outside, gloomy and hot, the kind of late-spring day that typified the tropics. The clouds sat low in the sky, thick like a blanket, holding Sydney hostage to humidity and the lure of rain—a relief that wouldn't come.

Annie caught her reflection in the window, darkened from the outside, and winced. Having seen the kind of women he associated with, she understood why his rejection of her had been so fierce that night.

How could a man like Dimitrios Papandreo ever really be interested in her? She'd dressed with care that morning, pulling on her best pair of jeans and a neat, white linen blouse she'd found in a charity shop about a month earlier. She'd pulled her silky blonde hair into a pony tail, then yanked it straight back out again and brushed it until it shone, before deciding the pony tail was best after all. She'd run through the process a few more times before giving up in frustration and allowing it to fall around her shoulders, unintentionally creating the impression of a golden halo.

She didn't generally wear cosmetics unless she was going somewhere for work—which was very rare—and she didn't really own very much in the way of make-up. But as a concession to their meeting, and out of a desire to feel her very best, she'd dashed some pale-pink lipstick across her mouth and dabbed a bit to the apples of her cheeks, blending it until it just gave a hint of much-needed colour to her pale skin. Her nails were short, her feet bare, and there wasn't much she could do about the expression of worry that had taken up residence on her features.

The kettle clicked off; she reached for a tea cup on auto-pilot, placing it on the bench top, adding a herbal bag and filling it with water. She stared at the swirling waves of steam, trying not to contemplate how completely her life was about to change. One way or another—marriage or not—nothing would ever be the same again.

She'd just taken a sip of her tea when the doorbell rang. Startled, she moved abruptly, spilling a gush of boiling liquid over her shirt. She swore, pulling the shirt from her skin, wincing at the hint of pain and shaking her head at her own clumsiness, before moving in the direction of the door.

She wrenched it open, barely giving Dimitrios more than a passing glance—nonetheless, it was enough to send her pulse into overdrive. 'Come in. Have a seat. I'll just be a second.' She moved down the tiny hallway and into the room she was using as her own—it had been designed as a study, a small adjunct to the single bedroom, but it worked better for Max to have the bedroom. While he didn't have many toys, those he did have were very precious to him. She liked him to have space to play with the train tracks he'd been collecting, as well as the books he brought home from the library.

She pulled a replacement from her wardrobe, a simple yellow T-shirt, and changed quickly. The skin above her breasts was pink from where the water had landed but it didn't hurt. Sparing a brief second to check her appearance before she left the room, she almost instantly turned away again, hating to think about the ways she'd changed since that night.

At eighteen she'd been youthful and, despite the grief following Lewis's death, she'd been full of brightness and spark. Her future had all been ahead of her—choices to be made, a university degree to be attained. She looked far older than her twenty-five years, Annie thought with a frown. She didn't see the way the light picked up the colours of her eyes—sparks of blue alongside silver and green. Nor did she see the way the sunshine-yellow shirt complemented her deep brown tan, or the way her slender frame hadn't lost the curves of her breasts and hips.

When she emerged a moment later into the stillness of her living area, it was to see Dimitrios had overtaken the space completely. Not with anything he was doing, just by the simple act of being there. He was big—large—his frame too much for the room, his presence too dynamic and demanding. Annie worked alone, and sometimes a whole day could pass in which she wouldn't hear another human's voice. Everything about her life was small, quiet and unremarkable. Dimitrios was like a blade of lightning splitting that apart.

'I spilled something on my shirt,' she said quietly, self-conscious about her apartment. He was dressed in a suit that, she would bet her non-existent savings, had cost more than her year's rent. Slate-grey with a light blue shirt, it was clearly hand-made and tailored to his frame.

He nodded once, a crisp movement of his head, and gestured towards the table. 'Shall we get down to business?'

Despite the tension, a smile tightened her lips. Just as she remembered. All command, completely in charge. Well, that didn't hurt. For now, she could let him call the shots. Besides, she was curious to hear just what he was suggesting, even when she had no intention of accepting his ludicrous proposal.

'Of course. I've just made a tea. Would you like something?'

'No, this won't take long.'

How romantic. She bit back the sarcastic rejoinder. She didn't want—nor expect—romance from Dimitrios. It was no surprise he wasn't even pretending to offer it. In a small act of defiance, she moved into the kitchen and grabbed her own tea cup, taking a moment to replenish it with boiling water. She was conscious of his eyes on her the whole time, watching as she added more water and returned the original tea bag to the cup, using a spoon to hasten its brewing and to capture all the flavour she could from the single bag.

When she moved to the table, his eyes followed her, and as she sat down she looked at him properly, catching the frown on his face. No surprises there. He was probably wondering how to politely extricate himself from the parting statement he'd made the night before.

Politely? Who was she kidding? This was Dimitrios Papandreo. Having been on the receiving end of his barbed tongue, there was no need to expect kindness from him. Reminding herself of that, she straightened her spine, regarding him with icy patience.

'Well, Dimitrios?' she prompted, cradling her hands around the tea. 'What would you like to discuss?'

It seemed to jerk him out of his reverie. He nodded, reaching into his pocket and pulling out some sheets of folded paper. The table wasn't large—it could seat four at a pinch. He extended his arm a little, holding the papers to her. 'I've had a pre-nuptial agreement drawn up. Nothing complicated.' He looked around the apartment. 'I presume you don't have a lot of assets, but whatever you do have will of course be quarantined from me, for you to retain in your name only.'

She didn't make any effort to take the papers. She was blindsided that instead of attempting to back-pedal on his marriage proposal he was instead doubling down.

'Naturally, the terms are generous towards you. As for our son, he will inherit what you would expect, as well as have access to a trust fund incrementally—on his eighteenth birthday, his twenty-first and his twenty-fifth.' Perhaps mistaking her silence for gratitude or acquiescence, he paused a moment then continued. 'It's as it was for Zach and me, and for my father. It works well. Better than receiving an enormous amount at eighteen, when you're more interested in alcohol and women than being sensible with investments.'

Annie felt as if a rock had landed at the base of her throat. She couldn't swallow properly; her tongue wouldn't cooperate. She sipped her tea, which helped only a little.

'As for where we'll live, I'm not sure if you're aware, but I relocated to Singapore about four years ago. My house is more than adequate for you and our son and any other children—'

She spluttered, her butter-yellow shirt very nearly another casualty of the tea. 'Hold on.' She took a sip, then deliberately replaced the cup on the edge of the table, her fingertips shaking as the reality of what he was suggesting—and the fact he was clearly serious—overtook her.

'I'm not marrying you, Dimitrios, so please stop making plans as though any of this is actually happening.'

He didn't react. She realised then that he'd been expecting some opposition.

'The amount of your allowance is, of course, negotiable.'

She flicked her gaze to the piece of paper he held, then shook her head. 'There's no price on my head. You can't buy me.'

'No?' His teeth were bared in a smile, but it was born of anger. 'I disagree.'

She stayed where she was even as she felt as though bees were flying into her. 'I'm not mercenary. Not even a little. Don't you think that, if money had been any kind of factor for me, I would have contacted you well before this? Do you have any idea how hard these last seven years have been for me? How I've struggled and sacrificed, all for our son? Who, by the way, is called Max. And don't even get me started on how offensive I find it that you've been here ten minutes and haven't asked me one single thing about him.'

A muscle jerked in Dimitrios's jaw and his eyes stirred with unmistakable anger. 'Do you think I want to hear about my own son from you? No, Annabelle. I want to get to know him, but for myself, not through your eyes. He's my child, and I should have been a part of his life well before now.'

The rebuke was like a blade sliding beneath her rib cage, because he was right. She ignored that, though.

'I see how you've been living, how you've been raising my son. Do you think any of this—' he gestured around the room '—is good enough?'

Hurt simmered in her blood. She swept her eyes shut, so didn't see the way he frowned and pushed back in his seat a little, shaking his head in frustration.

'No.' It was just a whisper. 'But I've been doing my best. So don't come in here and insult me, because I won't have it, Dimitrios. You have no idea what this has been like—'

'And whose fault is that?'

She pressed her lips together, sadness flooding her.

'I can't change the past. If you want to be a part of Max's life, I understand, but there's no way we can just pick up and move to Singapore, nor that I would ever marry you. This isn't the nineteenth-century. There's no morality police set to charge you for having a kid out of wedlock, or whatever.'

'There are my morals,' he said simply. 'And there is my son's future.'

'Your morals are your problem, not mine. And as for Max's future—' she inserted his name with determination '—that's something we can discuss.'

'I'm more than happy to discuss the minor details of our situation, but not the solution. We are getting married, Annabelle, so stop fighting me and start getting used to it.' He leaned closer, bracing his elbows on the table. 'Start preparing for it—be happy. All of your worries will be gone from the minute you become my wife.'

A shiver ran down her spine and instinctively she rejected that. All her worries would just be beginning if she became his wife—why couldn't he see that?

'Why are you being so insistent about this? You seem to have had a string of glamorous, high-profile girlfriends, and you've never married any of them, so I can only presume you feel as disinterested in being someone's husband as I do in being your wife.'

'It's true, marriage has never been on my agenda.'

'Never?'

He held her gaze a long time. 'No.'

'Then why now?'

'Max is a game-changer.'

Max is a game-changer. How true that was! For her, it had been a complete game-changer in every way. No university. No shiny, bright career. No friends—it had been too hard to keep up with them with a small baby at home.

'Max is your son,' she agreed quietly. 'But that has nothing to do with you and me—we can both be a part of his life without having to be a part of each other's.'

'That's not good enough.'

'None of this is good enough,' she agreed with quiet insistence. 'But it's the card we've been dealt.'

He held her gaze for several beats. 'I've organised a town-hall wedding. It's better if we marry quietly, then deal with the fall-out and the press later.'

Annie had the strangest sensation that she was speaking a foreign language.

'The...fall-out? Press? I'm *not* marrying you.' She paused after each word in the last sentence for emphasis, and because she couldn't wrap her tongue around the sounds properly.

'If you would like to have a bigger wedding, we can arrange that in due course. I'll leave those arrangements up to you. As for your life in Singapore, are you working at the moment?'

She stared at him, a frown drawing her brows together, forming a crease between them. It was all so absurd that she found herself answering anyway. 'I— Yes. I have a job.'

'What do you do?'

Her frown deepened. 'I load properties on to real-estate websites. I work for several agencies.' She bit down on her lip. 'It's something I can do from home, so when Max was little it made a lot of sense. Now he's at school, but with the holidays and the short days, and the possibility he might be sick and I need time off, the job still suits me.'

Dimitrios's expression was inscrutable. 'What happened to university?'

A wave of nostalgia passed through her. Not sadness, exactly, because she could never be sad about Max's arrival, even when it had signalled the end of so many of her dreams. No, it was nostalgia for the young woman she'd once been.

'Max happened,' she reminded him. 'I couldn't exactly have a baby and complete a law degree.'

He leaned forward, interlocking his fingers and placing his hands between them. 'You were accepted on to a top course, if I remember...'

She wouldn't allow herself to feel even a hint of warmth at his recollection. Dimitrios was a details man. He'd filed the titbit of biographical information for no reason other than it was what he did.

'It wasn't feasible.'

'Your parents?'

'They moved to Perth.'

His brow lifted. 'When?'

'After Lewis died.' She swallowed hard, the pain of that still difficult to process. Annie had learned then that nothing was stable, or permanent. She'd lost her brother and to all intents and purposes her parents in the space of a few months. Life was a rollercoaster with zero guarantees. 'Mum found it too hard to stay here. Everywhere reminded her of him. She needed a fresh start.'

'You were only eighteen, and you were pregnant. Why didn't you go with them?'

'We never had a great relationship.' She was uncertain why she was confiding in him. 'They weren't awful to us or anything when Lewis and I were growing up, but they fought a lot, and it was tense. I think Mum wanted everything to be different for me. Finding out I'd got pregnant and planned to raise a baby on my own, that I'd never go to university and my future was "over"—as she said—made her furious. She wanted me to put Max up for adoption.'

Dimitrios's face was like a thundercloud. 'You're not serious? Rather than offer to help you?'

Annie shrugged. 'It was a no-brainer. They moved to Perth, I stayed here and had Max. Over time, they've mellowed. They love him. I tolerate them for that reason alone.'

Her smile was bittersweet. 'Besides, everything reminded me of Lewis here too. Unlike Mum, I didn't want to run from those memories. Sometimes I find myself going past his old place, just letting that wash over me—how happy he was the day he moved in, how much he loved his life.' She shook her head sadly. 'I didn't feel like I could leave that—him. Sydney is a connection to him. I suppose that sounds silly.'

Dimitrios's voice was husky when he spoke. 'Not at all. I get it.'

'Do you?'

He nodded once and something dangerous passed between them because it was so reminiscent of their shared grief—a guttural, exhaustive sadness that had drawn them together that night. She looked away, focussing on the wall opposite. Scuff marks she'd become used to now seemed so much darker and worse. Embarrassment filled her but she refused to surrender to it.

His tone softened, sympathy obvious. 'I have an apartment here. We can travel back often. I don't intend to uproot you from your life completely.'

She shook her head. 'You're not hearing me. Marriage isn't the solution here.'

He didn't answer that.

'Why did you call him Max?'

Annie's cheeks burned pink. The sentimentality filled her with shame. She wouldn't tell him the truth—it was too much of a concession, and she wasn't ready to give him so much. Admitting that she'd researched his family tree and chosen his grandfather's name somehow made her feel vulnerable, like the silly eighteen-year-old she'd been, the one who'd cared too much. 'I heard the name and liked it,' she said simply.

'I like it too.'

Silence fell, thick with feeling.

'You can come back to Sydney any time you'd like,' he said with a gentleness that threatened to bring tears to her eyes. 'I understand how this city holds a connection to Lewis for you.' He paused. 'It does for me too.'

Their eyes met and something like mutual understanding weaved from him to her, binding them in an inexplicable way, just as it had that night.

'Max can still come and see his friends. But, for the most

part, your lives will be in Singapore. There's an international school he can attend—it's very good.'

But Annie was shaking her head again, refusing to succumb to the image he was painting. 'What part of "no" don't you understand? I can't marry you.'

'Why not?'

The question surprised her, her inability to answer even more so. She searched for something that made sense, something that would satisfy him, and drew a blank.

'Because' or 'I just can't' didn't feel sufficient.

'What? Do you have a lover? A boyfriend?'

Her cheeks flamed. No way would Annie confess the mortifying truth to Dimitrios—that she'd been alone since that one night they'd shared, seven years earlier!

'Marriage just…isn't something you decide to do on the spur of the moment.'

'Even when a child is involved?' he prompted, gently cajoling.

'Especially when there's a child involved!' Her reply was emphatic, born of personal experience. 'Neither of us wants to subject Max to that kind of marriage.'

'What kind of marriage, exactly?'

She pursed her lips, pushing away memories of her childhood. Memories of her parents, who'd fought constantly, who'd been so out of sync, always worried about money, quarrelling with each other, and, when they weren't together, shouting at their children. 'One where we argue and snap. I don't want Max to think that's what family life is all about.'

'I don't intend to argue with you once we're married.'

'So what do you intend once we're married?'

The question appeared to unsettle him for a moment.

Feeling she'd claimed the sensible high ground, she pushed home her advantage. 'You can't actually picture this, can you, Dimitrios? You and me, husband and wife, for as long as we both shall live?'

His eyes were swirling with the intensity of his thoughts.

'Or is this just an arrangement until Max is a bit older? Twelve? Fifteen? Eighteen? At what point do you imagine we'll walk away from this farce you're proposing and get on with our real lives?'

His Adam's apple jerked as he swallowed. 'I promised Lewis I would look after you.'

Annie had to reach behind her for some form of support. 'What?' The word was just a croak.

Dimitrios's expression was grim. 'Before he died.' He looked distinctly uncomfortable—rife with grief. 'He was worried about you. Your parents, the way they treated you…' He shook his head. 'He asked me to keep an eye on you.'

Annie stared at him for several anguished seconds, tears thick in her throat. It was so like Lewis; oh, how she missed her big brother! 'I didn't know.'

'No.' He grimaced. 'Well, I didn't exactly follow through on what I'd promised him.' She understood then—he felt guilty, just as she did, but his guilt had nothing to do with the awful things he'd said to her, the way he'd rejected her so cruelly. No, his guilt was because he'd betrayed Lewis and the promise he'd made. It didn't make her feel better, but it did make a sad kind of sense of what had happened back then.

'That's why you came to me that night? To check up on me?'

He didn't answer. He didn't need to. It shone a new light on how one-sided their passion had been.

'I promised him I'd take care of you, and I've badly neglected that promise. I had no idea how badly until recently but, Annabelle, I intend to fix this. I intend to look after you.'

Her heart twisted, pride snapping inside her. 'And if I don't want looking after? If I point out that I can do that all for myself?'

He leaned closer and her body tightened in an unwelcome response. 'I can't tell you what our marriage will be like. I'm acting on instinct here, and every instinct is telling me getting married is the only thing that makes sense. I promise you this, though—I will never neglect your needs again, Annabelle.'

She ground her teeth together, knowing the importance of fighting him. 'Stop speaking as though this is going to happen.'

'But it is going to happen.'

'You do realise this is the twenty-first century? And that I'm a woman with my own ability to make this decision?'

'The decision has been taken out of our hands.'

'Why do you say that?'

He pushed back in his chair, regarding her with eyes that were impossible to read. 'What do you know of my life?'

The question was unexpected. 'Not a lot,' she admitted.

'You know my family is wealthy.'

She rolled her eyes. 'You're a Papandreo. Your family isn't just "wealthy". You're richer than Croesus. What's your point?'

'That money brings with it a mountain of consequences.'

'Like never having to work a day in your life?'

He arched a brow. She regretted the waspish comment as soon as she'd said it. Both Zach and Dimitrios worked harder than just about anyone. Casting aspersions on their dedication was just petty. 'I'm sorry. I didn't mean that.' She sighed. 'For the record, that's exactly the kind of snappy comment I don't want Max growing up having to hear.'

His grin melted something deep inside her, filling her with warmth. 'So don't snap at me, then.'

'Easier said than done,' she muttered, taking another sip of her tea.

'From the minute my brother and I went to live with our father, there has been press intrusion in our lives. Paparazzi, ridiculous stories, speculative documentaries asserting all sorts of fanciful "truths".' He shook his head scathingly. 'While we have become used to that nonsense, you're not. Max isn't.' He leaned closer again, and his masculine fragrance tickled her nostrils, causing her gut to clench in powerful response. 'There is no question of keeping this a secret. A reporter *knows*. This story will break soon, and your life will change in ways you can't anticipate. I can't protect you here. I can't protect you unless you're in my home, living with me. I can't protect Max unless he's in my house, where I can see him. Don't you get that?'

She gulped, the reality of what he was saying banging into her hard.

'I—can cope with reporters,' she mumbled not at all convincingly, to either of them. 'I mean, I'll learn to cope.'

'Perhaps. But in the meantime you'll expose Max to unnecessary difficulties and drama, all because you won't be reasonable.'

'Reasonable?' Her jaw dropped. 'Marrying you is the opposite of reasonable! It's preposterous. I haven't seen you in seven years and the last time I did see you was—hardly a success,' she pointed out, shaking her head, then closing her eyes against the deluge of memories threatening to weaken her.

'This isn't about us any more.' His voice rang with certainty. 'Max is my number-one priority.'

'You haven't even met him.'

Dimitrios's expression barely shifted, yet a shiver

ran down Annie's spine. 'A point I wouldn't labour, if I were you.'

She bit down on her lip. 'I only meant that he's also my number-one priority. Don't swoop in and act as if you're the only one capable of prioritising him.'

'With all due respect, Annabelle, when I look around this home I see someone who is proud—to a fault. You described me a moment ago as "richer than Croesus", and yet you have been living here in abject poverty, barely making ends meet.'

'That's presumptuous of you.'

'No, it's not. Your credit rating is in dire straits, you're weeks behind in the paltry rental payments, you don't have private health insurance, you don't have a car, you look as though you haven't eaten in a week…'

She gasped. 'Dimitrios…have you had me investigated?'

'You kept my child from me. Don't you think I had a right to find out how he's been living?'

Annie tried to calm her racing heart but she felt as though she were drowning in the sea of his accusations.

'You could have just asked me.'

His eyes held a silent challenge. He didn't need to say what he was thinking—she could read it in his face. *You might have lied.* Inexplicably, tears filled her eyes. She blinked rapidly to clear them, but one escaped and slid slowly down her cheek, dripping on to the table top.

'This is not the end of the world.' His words were gentle.

She stood uneasily, running a hand through her hair as she moved into the kitchen. She wasn't particularly thirsty but restlessness made her act. She pulled two glasses down and filled them from the tap, before returning to the table.

'I can't imagine how you must feel,' she said softly, shaking her head. 'You're being so calm and reasonable, but you must feel…'

His eyes sparked with hers for a moment and her heart turned over in her chest.

'Yes, I feel,' he agreed gruffly. 'I have missed six years of our son's life—because of a decision you made.' He mirrored her earlier gesture, pushing his chair back and standing, crossing his arms. 'I feel everything you might expect,' he said, his voice lowering, calming, his eyes showing anguish but not anger. 'But what good can come of making you pay for that now?'

His eyes probed hers for several long seconds, as though he was scanning her innermost thoughts, assessing her piece by piece.

'Should I punish you, Annabelle? Take our child away from you, like you took him away from me?'

A shiver ran the length of her spine and she lifted a hand, pressing it over her mouth.

'Should I put you through a legal battle you definitely cannot afford, and which I will undoubtedly win? Should I make sure the press has all the gory details, so that you're branded all over the Internet as the kind of woman who'd keep a child separated from his father?'

She wrapped her arms around her slender frame, her eyes huge in her delicate face.

'Don't think these options didn't occur to me. I left last night because each and every one of them was running through my mind, begging to be thrown at you, hurled in a way that could cause the most damage. Surely you deserve that?'

Pain tore through her.

'But then I thought of the little boy, and how much he must love you. I thought of how, when he is a man, he will judge me for the decisions I make today. He will look at me as a hero or a villain based on how I treat you—his mother. And so I came here to extend an olive branch I'm not sure you deserve, but that I need you to accept. Because I will do whatever it takes to have him in my life.'

It was too much. Too kind, too reasonable, so full of love for their child—not his, not hers but theirs. Yet there was still the lurking undertone of a threat. She could tell he didn't want to carry his threats out, yet he would. Of course he would! If she didn't comply, he would take Max away from her.

She couldn't let that happen, even when the idea of marrying Dimitrios terrified her.

'Marriage is—' She hesitated, thinking of all the childish fairy-tales Lewis had filled her head with. 'It's meant to be so much more than this.'

A muscle jerked in his jaw. 'Meaning?'

'It's meant to be about love,' she whispered. And, while she felt stupid and naïve, it was also important for her to admit her belief in that. He was asking her to go against everything she knew to be true.

'For some people it is,' he agreed. 'But for others, it's a convenient arrangement. All marriages are an exchange. Ours won't be based on love but that doesn't mean it can't still be good—for both of us.'

Her heart cracked. Not once had Lewis told her about something so pragmatic. She felt a chasm forming inside her, the reality of her situation clear—the rightness of what he was proposing and the reasons she should agree. But the belief she'd always carried in her heart—that one day she'd be swept off her feet by Prince Charming—was smouldering into ashes.

'I need to think about it,' she said quietly. 'Is that okay?'

His eyes held hers for several seconds, each making her heart twist and her pulse throb, but finally he nodded—just once, a shift of his head, a turn of his body. He began to walk; she waited for him to go past her, but as he reached her he stopped, staring down into her eyes, his expression one she couldn't understand.

'Think fast, Annabelle. I've waited six years. I won't wait much longer to be his father.'

'Yes. He's my son.' Dimitrios's tone gave little away. The admission was already more than he ideally wanted to concede, yet using the press to his advantage made sense, given the circumstances. If Annabelle wanted time to think, then she should at least see the full picture. At the moment, the idea of media intrusion was simply hypothetical to her.

'No kidding.' Ashton's laugh was unpalatable. 'Six years old?'

'Yes.'

'And was I right about the mother?'

It was a turning point. Once he confirmed her name, there would be no going back. 'Yes. Annabelle Hargreaves.'

'How did you meet her?'

Dimitrios's lip curled in contempt. 'You're going to have to do some of the leg work yourself. If you want to invade my privacy, I can't stop you, but I'm not going to spoon-feed you the story.'

Another laugh. 'Have you got a statement for me, then?'

He narrowed his eyes, aware that he was crossing a line he couldn't uncross. He thought of their son and leaned forward, knowing he really had no choice. Just as Annabelle didn't. From the moment they'd conceived this child, their futures had been sealed. 'Annabelle and I have known each other a long time. Recently, we rekindled our romance. We were taking it slowly—for our son's sake—but now I'm happy for the world to know. We're getting married—as soon as it can be arranged.'

CHAPTER THREE

THE FLASH EXPLODED in her face like lightning striking. Annie startled, instinctively pulling her hat down lower. There were at least a dozen photographers standing on the footpath, all shouting questions at her. It was hard to discern a single one from the eruption of voices.

'How did you keep the billionaire's love child a secret for so long?'

'Is it true he's never met his father?'

'What are you wearing to the wedding?'

'Can we see the ring?'

'Have you been seeing him all this time?'

'How have you put up with the other women?'

'Is it true there are twins as well?'

Aghast, she kept her head lowered and moved quickly, but they followed behind, hounding Annie as she walked, shouting questions. When she was only a block away from her son's school, she turned, her face pale and drawn. 'Please.' She held up a hand. 'Just leave me alone.'

Silence fell for a moment and then the questions grew louder.

'You don't sound like a woman in love. Trouble in paradise already?'

She spun away and, despite the stultifying heat of the day, began to run. The school gates were her sanctuary—the photographers didn't cross the barrier.

How the hell had this happened? She walked towards her son's classroom, fishing her phone out of her back and loading up a browser.

With a finger that shook, she typed Dimitrios's name. The first article appeared instantly.

Billionaire Reveals Secret Love-Child and Bride-to-Be!

With a noise of disbelief, she clicked the title and scanned the first paragraph.

> *Renowned bachelor Dimitrios Papandreo is leaving the singles market in a move that will shock and devastate women around the world in equal measure. Rekindling a romance with his childhood sweetheart, the magnate is said to be 'looking forward' to his impending nuptials.*
> *'When it's love, you don't want to wait.'*
> *Love is something the tycoon has been seemingly immune to, dating often but never for long, but apparently he's finally met his match—a woman with whom he fathered a secret son six years ago!*

She clicked out of the article and groaned, stuffing her phone back in her pocket. What the hell was he playing at? God, what was she going to say to Max?

Her phone began to ring and she lifted it from her pocket in the same motion with which she answered it.

'Hello?'

'Are you at Max's school?' Over the line, Dimitrios's voice took on a whole new quality. It was darker and deeper, with an even greater ability to reach inside and stir her up.

'Yes. And, thanks to you and that bloody article, I was

followed here by swarming paparazzi. What the hell were you thinking?'

'The story was going to break one way or another,' he said quietly. 'I put a positive spin on it. Wouldn't you prefer our son to think we're a love match, rather than two people who couldn't control themselves?'

That pulled her up short.

'A heads-up would have been entry-level considerate.'

'Yes.' He drawled the word, so she shut her eyes, knowing that he could have said the same to her. Then, she heard him sigh. 'I didn't know when it would run. I was surprised by his efficiency. I suppose he thought I might leak the same story to a journalist from one of my own newspapers or magazines and wanted to be sure he got there first.'

That made sense, but it didn't help. 'Yeah, well, I'm at school, and Max is about to come out of his classroom, and the second we leave we're going to be mobbed by the press. I'm not ready to tell him about this, damn it, but you've made that impossible.'

'He deserves to know about me. You cannot put that off any longer. As for the paparazzi, I've sent a car.'

'What car?'

'A driver with a black SUV. He'll meet you in the teachers' car park. That should be safe from press.'

She looked over her shoulder to the path that led to the teachers' private parking area. 'I suppose so.'

'Take Max there, then go home and wait for me.'

'Wait for you to what?'

'To arrive. What does Max like to eat?'

The question was such a swift change in conversation, she almost felt as though she'd sustained whiplash. 'He's not very fussy,' she said. 'For a six-year-old. Burgers, pasta, sushi. Why?'

'I'll bring dinner. Wait until I've arrived. We'll tell him the truth together.'

He disconnected the call before she could argue—not that she was sure she wanted to. Everything had become so overwhelming and real. She felt as though the wind had completely gone from her sails.

But this wasn't a time for self-indulgence, or reflection. She needed to act now, think later. She closed the distance to Max's class room. When he emerged, she stood still and stared at him for several seconds, her heart in her throat. He was at least two inches taller than the other children, all legs and arms and intelligent eyes. His smile was quick, his face so handsome. She watched with heart-wrenching pride as a younger child stumbled and almost fell and Max, without hesitating, reached out and steadied the little girl, grinning at her before turning away. He grabbed his bag from the racks and then looked around, his eyes lighting up when he saw Annie.

He had no idea how his life was about to change.

'Hello, darling.' She tousled his hair. 'How was your day?' Such a banal question to ask when a thousand little explosions were rioting through her body and brain.

'Good. Mr Peterson said I aced our maths test'

Pride stuck in her throat. He was an excellent student. His reception teacher had suggested his academic potential might warrant skipping a year, but Annie had been of the opinion it was important for Max's social development that he spend at least a few years with children his peers in age.

'I'm not surprised by that.' She took his hand, leading him away from the class room, a lurching feeling tipping her tummy.

'Where are we going, Mummy?'

Max hadn't noticed yet, but Annie was conscious of

the way other parents were looking at her. She had to get Max home.

'A friend is picking us up,' she murmured. 'This way.'

Now she understood why celebrities always wore over-sized sunglasses. What she wouldn't have done to be able to flick something down over her face! She drew Max closer, walking with an arm around his shoulders until they reached the car park.

A big, dark SUV was there, just as Dimitrios had said it would be. As they approached, two men stepped out, one from each side. The blond, wearing the very dark glasses Annie had been coveting a moment ago, moved to the rear door.

'Ma'am.' He dipped his head forward. Annie froze, the gesture of respect completely unexpected.

'Hello,' she murmured, looking into the rear to see a booster seat had been put in place.

'Who are they?' Max whispered, looking to Annie with curiosity rather than fear.

'Friends. In you go.'

She watched Max buckle himself in then crossed to the other side of the car, where the other man held the door open for her. She smiled awkwardly before taking her own seat. The car wasn't a make with which she was familiar, but she didn't need to recognise the brand to know it was clearly the last word in luxury, from the windows that were tinted as dark as night, to an expansive sun roof overhead and seats that were a sumptuous, soft black leather. There were arm rests even in the back seat and, just as Annie was marvelling at this, the man in the front passenger seat said, 'There are drinks in the centre console.'

'Drinks?' Max's expression showed how fabulous he thought that was. He flicked a switch before Annie could stop him, and the console opened to reveal small bottles of champagne, water and juice boxes. She was sorely tempted to open a champagne, anything to calm her nerves, but she knew she needed every wit about her for what was coming next.

'Can I have a juice, Mummy?'

Mummy. It pulled at her heartstrings. She opened her mouth to say no, but then realised that was silly. His world was going to change shape altogether; why deny him a rare treat when it was on offer?

'Of course.' And, to reassure him, she reached for a water bottle for herself, smiling.

She didn't live far from the school, and fortunately the paparazzi were still waiting for Max and Annie to leave the class room, which meant they were able to make a quick retreat and arrive home with no one the wiser. The car pulled up outside the front and, despite the lack of intrusive photographers, the man from the passenger seat moved quickly, coming to open Annie's door and keeping his eyes on the footpath beyond. As soon as Annie and Max were out, he shepherded them to Annie's door, standing by as it was opened. Once inside, Annie saw a dark shadow beneath the door and knew that the man was standing on the other side.

'Your friend doesn't want to come inside?' Max asked.

Annie's smile was distracted. 'No.'

'That was strange.'

'Yes.'

'Do you want to play cards?'

She blinked, the question reassuring in its normalcy.

She was about to agree when the door pushed inwards—no knock this time—and Dimitrios strode in as though he owned the place. As though he owned *every* place. She put a hand on Max's shoulder reflexively, drawing him closer, but her eyes never left Dimitrios. He was wearing jeans today, and a simple T-shirt, white so it that showed off his tan, with a collar that sat perfectly at his neck.

'Is this another friend, Mummy?'

Annie's eyes flared wide.

'Not exactly.' She swallowed. 'Sit down, Max. There's something we want to talk to you about.'

She was conscious of everything in that moment. Of Dimitrios's size and scent as he came close to them, the smallness of her apartment, the dimness of the furnishings, their son's earnest little face, the way his uniform was tatty and faded.

'Max, this is Dimitrios,' she said quietly, taking the seat opposite Max at the dining table, watching his face for the tiniest flickers, nerves making her pulse fire. 'He was very good friends with Lewis.'

'Uncle Lewis?'

'Yes.' Annie smiled encouragingly. 'And, through Lewis, Dimitrios and I met, a long time ago. We became… friends,' she said, stumbling a little as she got closer to revealing the true nature of their relationship.

Dimitrios settled his large frame in the seat between Annie and Max, putting a hand out over Annie's. She hadn't realised until then how badly it was shaking.

'The truth is, Max, your mother and I were more than friends. We fell in love…and made you.' Every cell in her body began to reverberate. *We fell in love.* It was such a lie, but told so easily that it flared to life inside her.

'Made me?' Max frowned. 'As in, you're my dad?'

It was impossible to miss the flaring of pride in Dimitrios's eyes, or how much that statement meant to him. A wave of nausea-inducing guilt flooded her body.

'Mummy? Is that true?'

She found words almost impossible, so nodded instead.

'But you don't live with us.'

'No, I haven't lived with you,' Dimitrios responded.

'Why not?'

'I live in Singapore.' As though it were simple and that answer explained it.

And, to Annie's surprise, Max nodded. 'That's very far away, isn't it?'

'Yes. Have you ever been to Singapore?'

'I've never been on a plane. I don't even have a passport.'

Dimitrios's face angled towards Annie. 'I see.'

That wasn't so uncommon, Annie thought. It's not as though she was the only single parent in the world who'd deprived her child of an overseas holiday.

'I can organise a passport for you. How would you feel about going to Singapore?'

Annie's heart skipped a beat. She put her hand on top of Dimitrios's to quell his line of questions but he resolutely ignored her, refusing to look her way.

'I… Are we going, Mummy?'

Annie tried to smile. 'That hasn't been decided yet.'

Dimitrios leaned forward. 'The thing is, Max, I think it's time for us to be a real family—for us all to live together—and my home and work are in Singapore.'

Max tilted his head thoughtfully. 'What's your home like?'

Dimitrios's smile was pure charm. 'Would you like to see a picture?'

Max's eyes shifted to Annie's. 'Mummy? Do you want to move to Singapore?'

Annie felt Dimitrios's warning gaze, and her stomach looped with feeling. He'd lost so much—wasn't this the least she could do? Besides, her brief run-in with the paparazzi had shown her what her life was about to become. And what about Max? Didn't he deserve everything Dimitrios could give him? Didn't he deserve a father in his life?

'Singapore is lovely,' she said carefully. 'How would you feel about leaving school, though, darling?'

Max frowned, considering that, then turned to Dimitrios. 'Are there schools in Singapore?'

Dimitrios smiled gently, passing his mobile phone to the boy. 'Yes, there are excellent schools.'

'Is this…the school?' She saw Max's little mouth open in shock. Instinctively, Annie angled herself to see the phone better.

'No, Max. That's my home.'

'Your…home?' Max's eyes were huge. 'You mean I'd live there?'

'If you'd like to.'

Max returned his attention the screen. The house was everything Annie would have imagined, if ever she'd put her mind to it—enormous, modern, huge cement-and-glass boxes piled on top of each other surrounded by tropical trees. It was clearly both impressive and expensive. Beyond it, the ocean glistened, and in the far distance, she could make out the distinctive skyline of Singapore.

'Mummy? Look.'

She nodded. She'd seen enough.

'Why haven't I met you before?'

Annie stiffened, looking at Dimitrios, her heart sinking to her toes. She searched for a way to break it to their son, to confess the decision she'd made and the consequences he'd been forced to live with. Having to confess this to Max was something she'd dreaded—and she felt the full force of what she'd been keeping from him, of the decision she'd made seven years earlier.

Dimitrios spoke before she could work out how to put her thoughts into words.

'Sometimes families become separated, Max, but, now that I'm here, I don't ever want to miss being a part of your life. I wasn't close to my dad, but I'm hoping you and I can become good friends.' His voice was deep. As an adult, she could hear the pain that underscored his words, but Max seemed to take them at face value.

Tears at Dimitrios's kindness filled Annie's eyes. How easy it would have been for him to lay the blame at her feet! To begin to drive a wedge between them, to undermine her with Max. But he didn't. If anything, he did the opposite, glossing over the details, smoothing the way for this transition without laying blame anywhere. She stood abruptly, moving into the kitchen and turning her back on them, the very act of breathing almost beyond her.

He was making everything so easy; he had all the answers. It was Annie who was left floundering, trying to decide how she could make this work, what she wanted and whether her wishes even mattered. Surely Dimitrios and Max deserved to have her put them first now, to make the whole idea of being a family work?

'You have a swimming pool?' She homed in on their conversation again, bracing her palms on the bench.

'Two swimming pools.' She heard the smile in Dimitrios's voice and her heart twisted with memories and regret.

It was the same voice he'd used the first weekend they'd met. She hadn't been much older than fifteen. He and his twin brother Zach had come to the small village on the outskirts of Sydney where she and Lewis had grown up, and Annie had felt as though her whole world had got bigger and smaller at once. She'd never known anyone like him in real life. He'd been twenty-one, but as big as a much older man, and he'd dressed like one too—expensive, classy, easy. He'd smiled at her and something inside her had changed for ever.

'Why does anyone need two swimming pools?' Max was saying with a little laugh.

'One is indoors, part of my home gym. It's for swimming laps. The other sits on the edge of my property, overlooking the bay and the city. That's more for relaxing.'

'And diving?'

Dimitrios's laugh was like warm honey running down Annie's spine. She turned quickly, needing to trap the sight of him laughing, to hold it close inside. 'Yes, for diving.' He winked at Max then his eyes moved quickly, finding Annie, and the smile on his face shifted and morphed. It stayed in place but the warmth in his eyes dropped.

Her heart turned cold.

She pulled a pint of milk from the fridge and poured Max a glass, then put a small biscuit on a plate, carrying them both back to the table.

'Do you have a suitcase?' Dimitrios was asking him.

'Mummy? Do I?'

Annie's heart squeezed with vulnerability. 'No. But we have bags,' she added, missing the look that crossed Dimitrios's eyes.

'It doesn't matter. I'll have boxes brought.'

'What for?' Max's curiosity was, as ever, insatiable.

'Packing.'

Annie startled. Packing made it all sound so real, so imminent.

'I don't have too much to pack. Mummy has hardly anything, do you, Mummy? How do we pack the sofa in a box?'

Dimitrios looked towards the small piece of furniture.

Annie cleared her throat. 'The sofa came with the apartment, dearest. It will stay here when we go.'

'Oh.' He frowned. 'But the train tracks are mine?'

Tears threatened to mist her eyes so she nodded and quickly tilted her head away. The train tracks were nothing special, but to Max they were the world.

'Why don't you go and put everything you'd like to bring on to your bed? That will make it easier to box up.'

''K.' Max finished drinking his milk then stood, smiling as he left the room.

Air had always seemed to be a stable commodity to Annie but when Dimitrios was around it developed a changeability that took her breath away. It grew thin, making it hard to focus when they were alone again. She found it difficult to meet his eyes.

'He looks so much like me.'

Annie nodded softly. 'I know.'

'I will never understand how you could choose to keep me out of his life.'

Annie's eyes swept shut. 'It wasn't an easy decision.'

'Yet you made it, every day. Even when you were struggling, and I could have made your life so much easier.'

That drew her attention. 'You think this is going to make my life easier?' A furrow developed between her brows. 'Moving to another country, *marrying* you?'

His eyes roamed her face, as though he could read things in her expression that she didn't know were there. As though her words had a secret meaning.

'Yes.'

For some reason, the confidence of his reply gave her courage. One of them, at least, seemed certain they were doing the right thing.

'What if we can't make this work, Dimitrios?'

His eyes narrowed a little. 'We will.'

It was so blithely self-assured, coming from a man who had always achieved anything he set out to, that Annie's lips curled upwards in a small smile. 'Marriage is difficult and Max is young—only six. Presuming you intend for our marriage to last until he's eighteen, that's twelve years of living together, pretending we're something we're not. I don't know about you, but the strain of that feels unbearable.'

'You're wrong on several counts, Annabelle.' He leaned forward, the noise of his movement drawing her attention, the proximity of his body making her pulse spark to life with renewed fervour. 'I intend for our marriage to be real in every way—meaning for as long as we both shall live. As for pretending we're something we're not, we don't need to do that.'

Her heart had started to beat faster. Her breath was thin. 'What exactly does a "real" marriage mean?'

'That we become a family. We live together. We share a bedroom, a bed, we raise our son as parents. It means you have my full support in every way.'

It was too much. Too much kindness and too much expectation. She'd thought he would be angry with her when he learned the truth, and that she could have handled. If he'd wanted to fight, she could have fought, but this was impossible to combat. The idea of sharing his bed...when she knew what he thought of her?

You're little more than a child, Annabelle.

He'd all but called her unsophisticated and dull, right after taking her virginity. Heat bloomed in her cheeks and she shook her head automatically.

'Sharing a home is one thing, but as for the rest—'

'You object to being a family?'

He was being deliberately obtuse.

She forced herself to be brave and say what was on her mind. 'You think I'm going to fall back into bed with you after this many years, just because we have a son together?'

His smile was mocking, his eyes teasing. 'No, Annabelle. I think you're going to fall back into bed with me because you still want me as much as you did then. You don't need to pretend sleeping with me will be a hardship.'

Her jaw dropped and she sucked in a harsh gulp of air. 'You are so arrogant.'

His laugh was soft, his shoulders lifting in a broad shrug. 'Yes.' His eyes narrowed. 'But am I wrong?'

Deny it! Deny him! How ashamed she'd been of how easily she'd fallen into bed with him. She hadn't put up any resistance, hadn't asked him any questions. He'd come to her apartment, pulled her into his arms, and she'd simply folded herself against him, lifting her tear-stained face to be kissed better.

'You're wrong if you think I don't have more self-control than I did at eighteen,' she said quietly. 'So, far as I'm concerned, this marriage is for Max's sake alone. I don't need anything from you. I don't *want* anything from you. Behind closed doors, we'll be as we are now. No one needs to know it's all a sham.'

'Do you want it to be a sham?' he pushed quietly. 'When we know that we have the potential for this to be, in some ways, great?'

It surprised her. She didn't respond—couldn't—and waited for him to speak instead.

'Our chemistry is still there.'

Her throat felt thick; she struggled to swallow. He was just saying this to make things easier—he probably thought she'd be as easily seduced now as she'd been then. And maybe he was right. If she let him touch her, kiss her, hold her, her self-control would probably crumble into nothing, just as it had then. Which was all the more reason she had to be strong in the face of this.

'It doesn't matter,' he said after a moment, and the wave of disappointment that formed like a tsunami inside Annie showed her what a liar she was. She still wanted him every bit as much as she had then—and to him, it didn't matter.

'Sex is beside the point. But for the sake of appearances,

you will be in my bedroom. Max is a child, and children talk. I don't want him going to school and telling his friends that we sleep in two separate rooms. It will expose him— and you—to the kind of gossip I'm trying to avoid.'

'But giving a journalist the scoop on Max and me is fine?'

'He already had the scoop, I simply took the opportunity to control the narrative.'

She accepted that—even the great Dimitrios Papandreo couldn't have a story in a rival newspaper pulled just because he didn't like the content.

'Then we'll have separate beds in your room. I only need a single…'

He laughed, but it wasn't a warm sound, so much as a harsh, scoffing noise.

'We will have one bed—my bed—which is big enough for you to cling to the edge of, if you're afraid I won't be able to resist reaching for you in the middle of the night.'

She felt ridiculous. Embarrassed and completely childish. And she also felt that his claim that they shared any kind of chemistry was predicated on his need to get her into his life—for the sake of Max.

He reached into his pocket, removing a small black box that he slid across the table. Annie was so caught up in her reflections that she reached for it automatically, cracking the lid with a lack of any fanfare or ceremony.

The ring deserved more.

'Wow.' She stared at it, blinked, and stared some more. 'What—is this?'

'An engagement ring.'

She lifted her eyes to his, her stomach in knots. 'It's way, way too much.'

And it was. In every way, it was ridiculously over the top. A solitaire diamond, at least the size of her thumb-

nail and shaped like a teardrop, sat in a four-claw plati-
num setting, with more diamonds running down the side
of the ring—each large enough to be an earring, at least.
It sparkled even in the dull light of her Sydney apartment.

'It's nothing—just what the jeweller had on hand. If you
don't like it, you can choose something else.' His voice was
nonchalant, as though it didn't matter to him. It was the
strangest proposal Annie could imagine being a part of.
This whole situation was bizarre.

'I like it,' she responded with a small shift of her head.
'It's just—how much did this cost?' Then, another shake of
her head. 'Never mind, don't tell me. I don't want to know.'
She pursed her lips, searching for words. 'Can you see how
difficult life has been for me? I've scrimped and saved to
be able to afford the things Max wants, and even then always had to buy him second-hand or cheap copies, and you
swoop in here with something like this… It's going to take
me a while to get my head around it all.'

'You should have contacted me.'

I tried. She kept the fact buried inside herself. It would
feel like revealing too much of her feelings, as they'd been
then. She didn't want to discuss the past in that kind of
detail.

'The pre-nuptial agreement.' He pulled it out of his other
pocket and slid it across the table top. 'You should consult
a lawyer, of course, but they won't find anything wrong
with it. The terms are very favourable to you.'

'I can't afford a lawyer,' she said with a groan of frustration. 'I barely know how I'm going to pay for our electricity bill so please just…' She shook her head, not sure
what she'd wanted to say. 'Explain it to me.'

A muscle jerked at the base of his jaw but he nodded.

'It's simple. Max's trust fund is detailed in the first two
paragraphs. The next deals with what happens if I die—

how my wealth is distributed into trusts for him and any other children we might have.' Heat ran like lava through her veins. 'Finally, there's the matter of your allowance and settlement in the event of a divorce.'

Her eyes focussed on that paragraph. Divorce. Her head was spinning. Just like that, it was a foregone conclusion that she would marry him, and he was even planning how they'd deal with a possible divorce.

She forced herself to read the terms carefully, then blinked up at him. 'This looks like I get a ridiculously generous allowance for as long as we're married, and not a lot if I decide to leave you.'

His eyes were business-like. She remembered an article she'd read a few years back, calling him 'a ruthless tycoon'. It was the perfect description for him in that moment.

'That's the point.'

'What is?'

'Your life, as my wife, will be beyond anything you can imagine. You will have whatever you want, whenever you want it.'

It was what he *didn't* say that sent a shiver down her spine. 'And if I leave you I get nothing, and have to live like this again?'

He looked around her apartment, his eyes narrowed. 'You will never live like this again.' His anger was unmistakable. 'But you will definitely find it undesirable to walk away from me.'

'You plan to keep me as what—some kind of economic prisoner?'

'I won't reward you for leaving our marriage; that's not the same thing.'

She swallowed a curse.

He reached across, putting his hand on hers, surprising

her with the touch. 'I want our marriage to last a lifetime, for Max's sake.'

What did any of this matter? If they divorced, she wouldn't want any of his money. Pride wouldn't allow her to take it. She'd sooner live in a tiny flat like this again than exist on hand-outs from Dimitrios.

Tilting her chin in a gesture of defiance, she nodded. 'Fine. I'll sign it.'

His eyes flared with victory. Keeping one hand on hers, he used his other to lift the ring from the box and slowly push it on to her wedding finger.

'It's the right decision.'

Dimitrios stared out at Sydney CBD from his penthouse apartment right at the top of Papandreo Towers, a frown on his handsome face. It was the right decision. There was nothing else he could do. *Support her financially?* an inner voice challenged him. *Sure. But then what?* See their son only occasionally? Be an absent father or, worse, force Annabelle to be an absent mother? Neither option was palatable, and he didn't have to dig very deep into his psyche to understand why.

It was history repeating itself. When he'd walked into her tiny, insalubrious flat, he'd been reminded of the first ten years of his own life, spent living in abject poverty with a mother who'd tried her best but still hadn't been able to keep them afloat. His childhood had been punctuated by contrasts. When his father had occasionally appeared in Dimitrios and Zach's life, he'd whisk them away for a week of luxury and grandeur—everything they wanted was theirs, only to have it all disappear when they'd returned to their mother's. The visits were always fleeting, unpredictable and, as Dimitrios had got older, infuriating. How could his father have so much and leave their mother with so little?

It wasn't as though Dimitrios had ever consciously promised himself he would avoid that situation but, finding himself in his father's shoes, he was determined to act in a way that was in complete contrast to his father's behaviour. He wouldn't see Annabelle suffer. He wouldn't see her worry about money for another moment.

And their son would never feel that he had to love either his father or his mother, but never both. They would be a united front for the sake of Max.

Annabelle might want to resist that, but Dimitrios understood something she wanted far more. It was in her eyes when she looked at him, in the way her body swayed towards him when they were close, in the way her breath grew rushed and her cheeks pink.

She wanted him just as much as she had the night they'd conceived Max—and Dimitrios intended to remind her of that, night by seductive night, until their marriage of necessity developed into something that would bind them in a more meaningful way. Bit by bit, he'd remind her of what they'd shared, and make it impossible for her to contemplate leaving him. All for the sake of their son.

CHAPTER FOUR

Nineteen years earlier

'WHAT HAPPENED THEN, *Lou-Lou?*'

'*I've asked you not to call me that.*' Her older brother softened the admonition with a gentle shoulder-nudge, then grinned.

'Lewis,' Annie corrected, practising the eye-roll she'd been working on.

Lewis laughed. 'Better.' He lay back on the bed, flexing his hands behind his head. 'Well, let's see. The Princess escaped the tower and rode the dragon to safety.'

'Uh-huh. And the dragon promised not to burn her?'

'Because she's a princess.'

'Uh-huh.'

'So that must just leave the bit with the Prince.'

Six-year-old Annie lifted up on her elbow, pouting as she studied Lewis's face. At twelve, he could have been busy playing football, or reading the books he loved, but instead he always told Annie a personalised bed-time story. It was their ritual.

'Yes?' Annie asked, waiting.

'Well, the dragon brought the Princess down to a field—'

'What kind of field?'

'Does it matter?'

'Flowers? Wheat? Corn?'

Lewis grinned. 'Flowers.'

'Okay. Purple flowers?'

'Sure, Annie. Purple flowers.'

She smiled at that, flopping back on to the bed and looking up at the ceiling. Her eyes felt heavy.

'He brought her into the field and there, waiting for her, was the Prince Charming she'd heard so much about. Now that she was free from the Evil Queen, nothing could stop them from getting married and ruling the kingdom side by side. They lived happily ever after.'

Annie smiled. They always lived happily ever after.

'Lewis, are princesses and princes real?'

'Sure they are.'

'But I'm not really a princess?'

'You are to me.'

She smiled, her eyes sweeping closed.

'And will I grow up to marry a prince?'

'Well, he might not be a real prince, but he'll treat you like a princess or he'll have me to deal with.'

'I saw it.' Dimitrios's lips were set in a grim line. His brother looked back at him from the screen of the tablet.

'Has Annie?'

Dimitrios cast an eye towards the newspaper folded on his dining table. The headline was like all the others—proclaiming the secret relationship and love child. But the article had been a barely concealed attack on Annabelle, calling her everything from 'frumpy' to 'ordinary' to 'struggling single mother'. Of course, they'd chosen a particularly unflattering photograph of her, taken the day before. Even then, Dimitrios found his eyes lingering on the picture, noticing all the things the journalist had obviously missed. The elegance of her neck as she spun to address the paparazzi, the sheen of her hair—so shimmering it was like gold—the poise and determination in the strength of her spine, the fullness of her lips, the depth of her eyes.

He pushed the paper aside and gave Zach the full force of his attention.

'Well?'

'I don't know.' Dimitrios ground his teeth together. 'But, either way, she'll have to get used to that kind of crass reporting. It's part and parcel of being a Papandreo.'

'And she's okay with that?'

Dimitrios paused, his brother's hesitation pulling at something inside him. 'What's that supposed to mean?'

'Come on, Dim. You might have the rest of the world fooled with the "sweethearts reunited" bit but not me. You guys were never an item.' Zach laughed softly. 'Well, with the obvious exception of one night.'

Dimitrios instinctively recoiled from discussing Annabelle, even with his brother.

'That's irrelevant. We have a son together.'

'And I can't wait to meet him, but you can't let Annie be torn apart in the media like this. She doesn't deserve that.'

Dimitrios fought an instinct to point out that Annabelle had kept his son from him for six years. 'No,' he agreed. 'I have very little control of how rival media outlets decide to spin this story, though.'

'You have control of a lot more than you realise. You just need to make it much harder for her to be criticised; take the wind out of their sails. Change the story, Dimitrios, for Annie's sake.'

Annie woke with a start, a terrible feeling in her gut that perhaps she'd overslept. It was just like in high school, when there had been an exam or assessment and she used to wake in the mornings convinced she'd missed it. But there was no exam. Just the rest of her life waiting for her. And the anxiety she felt was like a whole ball of wool knotted in her belly. She pushed out of bed and was crossing the apartment to the small bathroom when there was a knock at the door. A glance at her watch showed the time to be almost seven.

She was about to open it when she remembered the intrusion of the press the day before, and Dimitrios's parting warning: 'They will be waiting for you tomorrow. I'll send a driver, but be aware—there will be questions.'

At the door, she paused. 'Who is it?'

'Henderson, ma'am. I drove you home yesterday.'

Surely it was way too early for the driver to take them to school. She flicked a glance at the clock and groaned. It *wasn't* too early. She *had* overslept. With a small yelp, she pulled the door inwards, keeping her pyjama-clad body concealed behind it. 'We just need a few minutes, okay?'

'Of course.' He nodded.

'Would you like to come in? Help yourself to some water or tea?' She thought longingly of the last two teabags sitting in the bottom of the canister.

'There's coffee in the car, ma'am.'

Coffee! Her heart leaped at the promise of caffeine. She smiled. 'Thank you. We won't be long.'

She ran across the apartment, throwing open the door to Max's room. And it hit her the second she saw the plastic grocery bags filled with his dearest possessions.

This was happening.

They were leaving.

Pushing away all the consequences that came with that, she moved to the bed, pressing a kiss to his forehead. 'Time to wake up, Max. We're late.'

'Are we?' he mumbled, so beautifully sleepy, her heart clutched.

'Yep. Can you get dressed straight away?'

'Yes, Mummy.'

She readied herself quickly, throwing on a pair of jeans and a loose-fitting black shirt, noting that it was a little looser than usual. *You look like you haven't eaten in a week.* She frowned as she took a few moments to look at her reflection in the mirror. She had lost weight lately. Too much weight, and not as a result of trying. Her teeth bit down on her lower lip. She tucked the shirt in. That was even worse. She pulled it out, leaving it loose, and added a big bright necklace she'd bought at a charity shop around the corner.

Slightly better.

Hair pulled into a topknot, a piece of toast thrust into Max's hand to eat in the car, and they were ready.

Except—how could they ever *really* be ready? The second they stepped a few feet from the apartment, flashes went off and the questions began again—this time, directed at Max.

'Max, how do you feel about your dad?'

'Are you looking forward to the wedding?'

'Have you spent much time with him?'

'Is it true you have twin brothers as well?'

At that, Annie sent a scowl to the journalist and leaned down closer to Max. 'Don't answer them, dearest. Just go straight to the car.'

Henderson put a strong arm around the pair and shepherded them to the waiting SUV, standing to block the photographers' view as they stepped in. With the door closed, they were protected by the darkly tinted windows.

'That was weird,' Max commented, wrinkling his nose.

Annie burst out laughing. 'Yes, that's one word for it.' She kept laughing because it felt good, and because she was glad for her son's resilience and calmness. She reached across, squeezing his hand.

'Look, Mummy,' Max said as the car pulled out from the kerb. 'There are drinks again.'

'Coffee,' she remembered. 'And that looks like a hot chocolate for you.'

'Really? Are you sure?' His eyes darted nervously towards the front of the car.

Her heart tightened in her chest. 'Yes, I'm sure.'

His eyes lit up as he reached for the cup, blowing across the top before taking a sip. His smile was the only response Annie needed. He ate his toast and drank his hot chocolate, clearly feeling very special as they drove to school. At the gates, Annie walked him in as normal, though nothing *felt* normal. Parents—even parents she considered her friends— were regarding her strangely, and Max's teacher looked as though she wanted to ask a thousand and one questions.

Annie's manner was not expansive. She crouched down, lifting a hand to Max's face, brushing away his thick, dark fringe.

'It's probably best if you don't talk too much about all the changes, Max. There'll be plenty of time to explain to your friends, but why don't we let the dust settle first?'

He nodded. 'Okay.' His nose wrinkled. 'I don't think I'd know what to say, anyway.'

Something inside her ached. She felt his vulnerability in myriad ways. 'No,' she said quietly, roughing his hair. 'You know you can ask me any question at any time, don't you?'

He nodded thoughtfully. 'I know.'

Annie kept her head ducked as she left school, not wanting to engage in conversation with anyone. Henderson was waiting beside the car, arms crossed.

She strapped herself in, pushing her head against the leather head-rest, her eyes closed.

It took a few moments before Annie realised the car was travelling in the wrong direction. She frowned, leaning forward. 'Where are we going?'

'Mr Papandreo asked me to bring you to him.'

To bring you to him. As though she were a possession. 'It would have been nice for him to ask *me* first,' she said under her breath, though a quick glance in the rear-view mirror showed the remnants of a smile on Henderson's face—confirming he'd heard her comment.

She sighed softly. How was she going to avoid snapping at Dimitrios when he was so…so…overbearing? Most people would naturally seek approval before organising someone's schedule, but not Dimitrios. He told a member of his staff to 'bring her to him', without considering that she might have other plans or might simply not want to 'go to him'.

Her eyes fell to her tightly clasped hands sitting in her lap, and the enormous diamond on her finger sparkled brightly.

It was rush hour, and traffic was thick, but the SUV dug through the cars, drawing Annie deeper into a gridded city cast into shade by the glass-and-steel monoliths that towered overhead. She didn't come into the CBD often, so found it hard to get her bearings. Eventually, the car stopped—she thought she caught a glimpse of a sign that read 'Castlereagh Street'. The door was opened and Annie stepped out, breathing in that unique city smell of bitumen, leather, engine exhaust and corporate toil.

'This way, ma'am.'

She smiled hesitantly. 'Henderson, if you're going to be driving me regularly, would you consider calling me Annie?'

He didn't respond.

'After all, you look about my age. It feels ridiculously stuffy for you to be calling me "ma'am".'

'Is it making you uncomfortable?'

'Honestly, yes. It really is.'

He laughed softly. 'Fine. Miss Hargreaves.'

'No.' She shook her head. 'Just Annie. I'm begging you.'

He lifted his sunglasses so she could see his eyes—one was blue and the other brown. 'Fine, Annie. If you insist.'

'I do.' It was a small victory, but it felt important that Annie should hold on to the essence of who she was for as long as possible. 'Thank you. Now, where's Dimitrios?'

With a nod, Henderson gestured to a pair of shiny black glass doors. Annie stopped walking, her breath hitching in her throat as she read the word boldly emblazoned in the signage above. The name was world-famous, synonymous with luxury and prestige. It was the kind of shop she'd never even walked past, far less thought of entering.

'Why?' she asked Henderson, a tone of pleading in her voice.

Henderson smiled, but didn't respond.

Annie stifled a groan but started walking once more, one foot in front of the other, until they reached the doors. Henderson lifted his hand to a buzzer, pressed it and then they waited.

It took only a couple of seconds before the doors whooshed inwards, revealing a shining floor made of large marble tiles, high ceilings, ornate chandeliers dangling from the ceiling and an army of at least ten staff standing in a group. And beside them, Dimitrios, impeccably dressed in one of his custom-made suits with shining shoes, dark hair waved back from his brow, eyes on Annie with a singular focus that made a hint of perspiration form in the valley of her breasts. She was grateful then for Henderson at her side.

'Annabelle.' Dimitrios strode towards her, drawing her into his arms. His eyes glittered with hers, giving Annie only a moment of warning before he dropped his head and crushed his lips to hers, kissing her with an excellent approximation of fierce possession.

She knew it was just for the benefit of their audience, but that didn't change anything. She felt the flicker of desire in the pit of her stomach and, before she could stop it, full-blown need was coursing through her veins. Her arms lifted of their own accord, one hand pressing to his chest, the other curling around the nape of his neck, her fingers teasing the dark hair there, holding him where he was. His tongue expertly duelled with hers, reminding her of his mastery over her, the ease with which he'd driven her senseless with longing all those years ago.

That should have been enough of a reminder. It should have made her put an end to the kiss. But her body was in complete control and it wanted him with a ferocity that was too hard to bear.

His arm curved around her back, as though he knew she needed his support, and he held her there as he lifted his head, his eyes boring into hers, his expression impossible to interpret. But his cheeks were darker than normal, slashed along the ridges of his bones, and she knew he had been as stirred by their kiss as she had been.

'What was that?' she asked, wishing she felt angrier, more outraged, when all she could muster was disbelief that it had ended so quickly.

'Remember, *agape*,' he said quietly, then lowered his head so only she could hear the rest of his sentence. 'All the world believes this is a love match. Try to play along.'

It was the ice water she needed, the stark dose of reality to bring sense back to her addled mind.

'Of course, darling.' She mimicked his tone, forcing an over-bright smile to her face.

'Thank you for meeting me here,' he murmured, taking hold of her hand and weaving their fingers together.

'Did I have a choice?' she queried, without letting her smile drop, her voice just a whisper.

His eyes held a warning. 'Not really.'

He began to walk towards the staff, who had been discreetly looking away from the couple. A man stepped forward. 'Madam, it is a pleasure to meet you. My name is

Gustav and I am the manager of the Sydney store. Mr Papandreo has asked me to help you this morning with anything you might require.'

Annie wrinkled her nose, looking around the high-end boutique with a burgeoning and unwelcome sense of inadequacy. 'Honestly, I don't know how you can help me,' she said quietly. 'I don't really shop in places like this.'

'Then that has been our loss,' the manager inserted charmingly. 'Now, let's get to work.'

All the staff scattered except the manager, who asked Annie, 'Now, champagne and an almond croissant?'

It was on the tip of her tongue to point out that it was just after nine o'clock in the morning, when she thought about how welcome a glass of bubbly would be, given the over-wrought state of her nerves. 'Just a little,' she conceded, nodding a little.

'Excellent. And for you, sir?'

'Coffee.'

'Very good.'

When the manager disappeared, they were completely alone, Henderson waited by the doors with his arms crossed, the last word in forbidding.

'Where are all the other customers?'

'The store isn't open yet.'

'I beg to differ.' She gestured to the staff working to pull dresses, shirts and shoes from racks, transporting them all through a pair of silver velvet curtains.

'They've opened early.'

'For you?'

'For *you*,' he corrected.

'Dimitrios.' She sighed, biting down on her lip. 'Why are you doing this?'

His hand reached for the collar of her T-shirt, pulling on it gently. 'Because your clothes are somewhat the worse for wear, and because I can. Because you're going to be my wife and you will need to dress like it. Because I get the feeling you've sacrificed every comfort for yourself over the years just so that my son can have what he needs most.'

She looked up at him, finding his answers strangely breath-taking. She was both embarrassed that he thought so little of her appearance and touched that he understood how miniscule her budget was for her own clothes.

'It's been hard,' she said quietly. 'But this is too much. I don't need…' She reached for the nearest piece of clothing, a pale-pink blouse made of silk with pearl buttons. The price almost made her fall sideways. 'Dimitrios, this is ridiculous. Who pays this for a shirt, for goodness' sake?'

He unfurled her fingers from the fabric, then drew her to his side. It was all an act, for the benefit of the staff, but his nearness set warm arrows darting through her body.

'Don't think about the price. Just buy whatever you want.'

She shook her head. 'But I don't want anything. I know my clothes aren't exactly glamorous but they're perfect for *me*. For my lifestyle. I work from home. I take Max to school. And, whether we're here or in Singapore, I can't see that changing.'

'Last week, the American President came for dinner,' he said, his voice devoid of emotion. 'I entertain guests like him regularly. Tell me, Annabelle, what do you have that you would wear to a meal with the President?'

She forced herself not to show how awed she was by that. He was trying to scare her into obedience but that made it all the more important that Annie remember who she was. 'I'd wear whatever I had that was clean, and a smile on my face, and I'd ask him about his trip to Singapore and his family, and that would be the end of it.'

Admiration showed on his face. 'I'm not asking you to swan around the house in ball gowns.' His tone was now one of gentle coercion. 'Just try a few things on...see what you like. If you decide you don't want anything at the end of the morning, then that's fine.'

Gustav returned with a glass so full of champagne it had formed a meniscus. He carried it on a small silver tray. 'Madam.'

'Please, call me Annie,' she insisted as she took the champagne.

'Yes, Annie. And coffee, sir.'

Dimitrios nodded curtly as he took the cup, making the fine porcelain look unspeakably tiny in his tanned, masculine hand.

His eyes held both a question and a warning. Annie could stand there and argue some more or she could just surrender to this process, try a few dresses on and then tell him thanks, but no thanks. After all, she wasn't his charity project. She could take her admittedly meagre savings to a department store and buy some new clothes, now that she knew her immediate worries—such as having food on the table—were taken care of.

It was clear that the sales assistants were skilled professionals. The first thing Annie tried on was a linen dress in a colour just like lemon curd. She was only doing it to be obliging, but the second she slipped the dress over her body she felt something click in place. She stared at her reflection for at least ten seconds before reaching for the glass of champagne and taking a large gulp, unable to shift her eyes away.

She looked...like she used to look. She'd never worn anything this beautiful, of course, but the dress brought out the youthfulness of her complexion, reminding her that she was, in fact, only twenty-five.

She stepped out of it quickly, feeling as though the beautiful dress had betrayed her intention not to want any of these designer clothes. White trousers were next, and they were just as flattering. A black-and-white spotty dress followed, then a silk camisole paired with a denim skirt, showing Annie's slim, tanned legs. An hour passed in a flurry of silk, linen, cotton and chiffon and, unbeknownst to her, a diligent Gustav was piling each outfit she'd tried on beside the cash register. When Annie finally emerged from the sumptuous fitting room—back in her regular clothes—her champagne was empty and her resolve was beginning to soften just a little.

'Well?' Dimitrios approached her with a knowing look on his face. 'Let me guess. You loved them all?'

She *had* loved them all, but she knew to buy all of them would be unspeakably extravagant. 'I did. But I particularly loved the yellow dress,' she qualified, moving towards it and running her fingers lovingly over the fabric. 'It was…beautiful.'

For a moment, she thought she saw surprise in the depth of his eyes.

'Then you'll have it.' He removed it from the rack. 'Why don't you wear it today? It's appropriate for your next appointment.'

'Next appointment?' Despite his generosity, something bristled inside her at his high-handed management of her schedule.

'A day spa.'

If she'd had champagne in her mouth she would have spurted it everywhere. Her scepticism must have showed because he leaned closer, murmuring, 'Try it. Just this once. For me.'

She was about to scoff at that but the fact they were being watched meant she had to alter her natural response. 'For you, darling? Anything.'

He dropped his head closer, his eyes warring with hers in a way that set her pulse racing. 'Careful, Annabelle. I just might hold you to that later.'

CHAPTER FIVE

SHE'D RESENTED HIS control-freak ways but, deep down, Annie had to admit that, up until a moment ago, she had also felt a mixture of gratitude and appreciation for Dimitrios. She'd thought the day spa was a gesture of great kindness and compassion, and she'd even let herself enjoy the experience—a full-body massage, a manicure, a pedicure and finally an appointment with the country's top hairstylist. Her natural blonde mane had been given a few foils then toned to a glossy gold and trimmed a little so that the edges were soft, and the layers gave her hair more bounce.

She emerged from the spa feeling a million times better than she had before.

But when Henderson drove her back towards Sydney, he bypassed the turn-off to her suburb completely, causing Annie to lean forward and question him.

'Boss's directions.'

Boss's directions? She sat back in her seat, crossing her arms over her chest, and waited to see what Dimitrios had in store for her next.

'But Max—'

'He's being picked up by one of my colleagues.'

Annie's chest squeezed. In all of Max's life, she'd never once missed a school pick-up. The thought of doing so now filled her with a sense of disbelief.

'But…why?' She shook her head. 'Don't tell me. Dimitrios.'

'Sorry, miss—Annie.'

He drove the car into an underground parking garage, dark despite the fact it was a bright afternoon. She caught a brief glimpse of a sign that read 'Papandreo Towers'.

Henderson accompanied her in the lift but when the doors pinged open on the very top floor he remained behind.

'You're not coming in?'

'No, Annie. Good evening.'

It was strange that she'd come to think of his company as reassuring, but somehow knowing he was just like her—a normal person, rather than someone born into this kind of wealth—made him a touchstone to the real world.

Dimitrios Papandreo was definitely not that.

She stepped into the penthouse and felt like a fish a thousand feet out of water.

'Oh, wow.' She stopped still, standing where she was and angling her face to take in the details of the incredible space. Floor-to-ceiling windows framed one of the most dramatic views of Sydney she'd ever seen, and the ceilings had to be at least treble normal height. There was a polished white marble staircase in the centre of the room that swept elegantly towards a mezzanine level; she presumed bedrooms were up there. A baby grand piano stood in one corner. The artwork on the walls was priceless, and the kitchen looked as though it belonged in the pages of a glossy magazine.

Then, there was Dimitrios, so perfectly at home in the luxurious setting, despite the fact he'd discarded his suit jacket and tie and had unbuttoned the top of his shirt to reveal the tanned column of his neck.

She'd been annoyed at him a moment ago, hadn't she? Yes! *Hold on to that.*

'Why did you bring me here?'

It wasn't exactly what she'd meant to ask but it was a start.

'It's going to be our home until the wedding.'

More high-handedness! She ground her teeth together. 'I already have a home.'

He made a noise of disapproval. 'I made arrangements. Your landlord was happy to end your lease early, given our circumstances.'

'But—' She stared at him, gobsmacked. 'You've spoken to my landlord?'

'Of course.'

'No, *not* of course!' She sighed in exasperation. 'He's *my* landlord. It's *my* lease. *My* home.'

Dimitrios took a step towards her. '*My* son. *My* fiancée. *My* responsibility.'

His responsibility. In a way, it was just what she needed to hear, because all day she'd been wondering why he was going to so much effort, spoiling her with a day spa and a shopping spree. But of course—he felt guilty. He saw her as his responsibility and in some kind of moralistic way felt as though he'd let her down these past six years by not supporting her more. When the opposite was true—she'd let him down by not allowing him a chance to know his son.

The fight left her as guilt rose within her chest.

'Okay.' She nodded once. 'Fine. We'll live here.'

His frown was a whip across his face. 'I expected more of an argument.'

Her smile was just a whisper. 'So did I.'

Her response had clearly made him uncertain, but then, this was Dimitrios Papandreo, and uncertainty wasn't something he did very well. A moment later, he shrugged, evidently taking her decision as a win. 'Great. Your things have been moved into my room upstairs. Max has a room down the corridor from us. In Singapore, there's more space than this; you can have your own sitting room and court-yard for privacy. Max will have a sitting room too.'

'More space than this?' And suddenly, Annie was laugh-ing, because it was all so preposterous. 'This place is... Don't you see, Dimitrios? It's like a palace.'

'That's relative,' he said with a small nod. 'To you, it would seem that way.'

She felt instantly gauche. She sobered, moving into the kitchen, opening drawers and doors on autopilot, though not looking for anything in particular. When she saw the kettle in a cupboard, she lifted it out and filled it with water, simply because it felt good to have something to do with her hands.

'Who's collecting Max from school?'

'My driver, and a nanny.'

'A nanny?' Her head jerked towards his. 'What do you mean, a nanny?'

'Don't look at me like that. I'm not seeking to replace you in his life. I thought an extra pair of hands would be useful during the transition. There'll be a lot of changes. Her name's Francesca and she'll help both of you...adapt.'

The sound of the kettle boiling filled the room. Annie stared at the wisps of steam that lifted from it, her mind reeling. This was all happening so fast; she felt as if she'd barely drawn breath since Dimitrios had reappeared in her life. Had it really only been a matter of days?

'I thought we could use this time to discuss the wedding.'

The knots pulled tighter. 'If you'd like.'

She heard his exhalation of breath but didn't turn to face him. 'Would you like tea?'

'I'll make coffee.'

She nodded, busying herself preparing tea, working beside him in the kitchen in what was a bizarrely ordinary task of domesticity. It was as if they were long-term partners, undertaking such routine, normal duties as though they did them often.

When her tea was made, she propped her bottom against the edge of the kitchen bench, her huge blue eyes framed by thick black lashes, her cheeks pink, her newly styled hair sitting like a pale, fluffy cloud around her face. He mirrored her action, standing opposite her, coffee cup in hand, eyes on her face.

The silence was far from comfortable. She felt every second that passed pull harder on her nerves, until they felt stretched near to breaking point.

'So?' she prompted eventually, when she couldn't take it any more.

'So.' He dragged his free hand through his hair. 'I've arranged the wedding for Friday. Zach's coming. I know you're not close, but I presume you'd still like your parents to be there?'

Annie's stomach dropped. 'My parents?'

Dimitrios studied her. 'Yes.'

'No.' It was a knee-jerk response. 'They don't need to be involved in this.' Her tongue darted out to lick her lower lip. 'They're over in Perth and we're here...'

'You're sure?'

She nodded jerkily. 'Let's just keep it small. A quick, private ceremony.'

His eyes didn't leave her face. He watched her for several long seconds.

'Like ripping off a sticking plaster?' he prompted, with a hint of mocking amusement.

'Yes.' She was relieved, though.

'I know this isn't what either of us would have chosen, but it's the right thing to do.'

Butterflies rampaged through her belly. She nodded, almost convinced he was right.

'So why do you look as though you're about to have a root canal?'

Her eyes flew wide. 'Do I?'

'Or worse,' he said quietly, straightening and taking a step towards her. 'Is the idea of marrying me really so appalling to you?'

Her eyes scanned his face, her heart slamming into her rib cage with the force of a freight train. Annie contemplated it, trying to find words to express how she felt.

'It's just very sudden,' she said eventually.

'For us both,' he pointed out, closing the distance between them, coming to stand toe-to-toe, bracing his arms on either side of her, his body caging hers. Her heart moved faster and harder for a different reason now, reminding her of how it had felt to be in his arms at the boutique that morning, pressed hard against him, his mouth on hers. Her gaze dropped to his lips and her own parted in memory and need.

'There's so much I don't know about you.'

'And what you do know, you don't like?' he suggested.

Her pulse fired. He was right. She had been angry with him for a long time—her heart broken, her feelings hurt. But that all seemed so long ago. Seven years was a long time in anyone's life but for Annie, with all she'd had to keep her busy, the trials she'd faced every day, it had been like a lifetime.

'The truth is, I barely know you.'

Was that really the truth? Standing like this, she felt as though he was familiar to her in an elemental way. Memories of the night they'd spent together were hovering on the brink of her mind, as though they'd happened only a night or so ago, not seven years.

'You'll get to know me.'

'And to like you?'

'That would make our marriage easier,' he said with a tight smile.

Perhaps. Perhaps not. The difficulty, though, wasn't in liking him—it was in liking him too much. She needed to keep some perspective and remember that this was all for Max's sake. Whatever girlhood infatuation she'd felt for Dimitrios, that was in the distant past. The last thing she should do was let her physical response to him make her forget the truth of their situation.

'What time will Max be home?'

His eyes narrowed. 'Soon.'

She was glad. Max was a talisman of reality. 'We should get this over with, then.'

He lifted a brow and she realised the way he could misconstrue her words. Heat flamed in her cheeks. 'Firming up on the details, I mean.'

'Of course.' His response was tongue-in-cheek. She felt as if he was mocking her.

'So the wedding will be on Friday?'

He nodded, apparently back to being business-like, but he didn't move his body. Traitorous feelings made her glad.

'In the morning. I thought we'd fly to Singapore straight after lunch.'

Her breath snagged in her throat. 'So soon?'

'Why delay? Unless you'd prefer we took a honeymoon first?'

A honeymoon conjured exactly the kind of imagery she wished to avoid. She shook her head quickly. His smile showed he understood.

'Are you afraid of me, Annabelle?' His fingers caught

her chin, gently lifting her face towards his so he could read her eyes.

Her lips parted, words trapped inside her.

'Or are you afraid of wanting me, even after all this time?'

Her eyes widened at his perceptive powers. Or perhaps she was just that painstakingly obvious.

Her throat moved as she swallowed. 'I'm not afraid of anything.'

His laugh was silent, just a movement of his lips and a release of his warm breath. It fanned her temple. Her insides shifted; her lungs squeezed.

'When I kissed you today it felt as though no time had passed.'

That was exactly how it had been for her, too!

'It was just playing a part,' she reminded him, but the words came out high-pitched.

'No, it was more than that. It's the saving grace of what we're doing. You don't know me, and I don't know you, but our bodies are in sync, and that's something. It's enough, for now, to base our marriage on. Don't bother denying that you feel it too.'

Was that what she'd been doing?

She shook her head a little, losing herself in the magnetic depths of his eyes. 'I don't want to feel anything for you,' she said quietly.

'Why not?' His thumb padded her lower lip, sending little shivers of desire through her.

'Because.'

One side of his lip lifted in a curl that could have been amusement or cynicism. 'That's not really an answer.'

'I know.'

'You're still angry with me for what I said to you seven years ago?'

Old wounds festered deep inside her. 'I'm not still angry,' she said quietly. 'But I'm smarter now than I was then. I learned my lesson.'

'What lesson is that?'

'Play with fire and you're bound to get burned.'

'Am I fire?'

'You were for me.'

'And I burned you?'

His head was moving closer with every word he spoke, so his lips were only a hair's-breadth from hers. 'You changed me,' she said quietly.

'How?'

She could hardly think straight. 'You taught me not to take things at face value.'

'Why?'

'Because I thought you wanted more from me than just—sex.'

His frown was a slash on his features. 'I wanted to share our grief.'

'Yes,' she agreed. 'But you didn't really want *me*. Any woman would have done for that.'

His response was to move his whole body closer, so she felt his hardness against her, his arousal against her belly. Her stomach looped.

'And you already had a girlfriend,' she added quickly.

'No,' he said.

'But you said—'

'I said what I needed to make sure you got the message. At the time, I thought I was looking out for you, pushing you away for your own good. I didn't want you thinking there was any future for us so I told you what I thought would scare you off.'

Surprise shifted her features. 'You lied to me?'

His expression was impossible to interpret. 'And that

lie cost me. If I hadn't said that, would you have tried to tell me about Max?'

The world was falling away from them; Annie felt as though she were standing on an island with only Dimitrios, their history forming a swirling, raging ocean on all sides. She lifted a hand, curling her fingers in the fabric of his shirt, feeling the warmth of his body through her fingertips.

She'd intended to push him away but, just for the moment, the proximity and warmth of him flowed through her, his strength pushing into her body.

'I did try to tell you.'

The words were softly spoken, so Dimitrios had to focus to make sure he'd understood her. *I did try to tell you.* Was she lying, to justify the fact he had a six-year-old child he'd only just learned about?

'After I found out I was pregnant, I came to tell you, but…'

He was finding it hard to breathe. 'But?'

'I saw you with all your friends, and some woman—who I presumed to be your girlfriend—and I just couldn't do it.' Her voice was hollow, as though she were speaking to him from a long way away. 'You were so sophisticated, it was like you belonged to a whole other universe than the one I lived in. I was only eighteen, Dimitrios. I was scared and embarrassed, and I had no idea what you'd say, but I knew you already had a pretty low opinion of me.'

His gut tightened. 'Where was this?'

'At some bar. I'd seen in the papers that you were going to the opening. You'd been involved in funding it or something.'

He remembered. It was a place on Circular Quay. 'I wish I had told you then.' He could hear the sincerity in her voice and it pulled at something inside him. Whatever anger he was still nursing towards her shifted. 'If it happened now, I would.'

'You were young,' he pointed out.

'Like the child you accused me of being?'

That had been wrong. At the time, she'd felt like a child, but so much of that had been tied up in his guilt. Guilt at sleeping with Lewis's younger sister. If Lewis had been alive, it would never have happened. Lewis would have killed Dimitrios. He'd adored Annabelle—or 'Annie'—and had spoken of her often. Dimitrios had been aware that she had a bit of a crush on him, but he'd never planned to do anything to encourage it. So why the hell had he found his way to her door that night? Why had he pulled her into his arms and kissed her until all thoughts of Lewis, death and sadness were obliterated from his mind?

She didn't wait for an answer. 'I did want to tell you. But then I saw you with that woman and I was—hurt. Jealous.' She shook her head, not quite meeting his eyes. 'I know I had no right to feel that way…'

He lifted his hands, cupping her face. 'Whatever else we were, I was your first lover. It's natural that you felt something when you saw me with another woman so soon after that night.'

Her lower lip trembled, and he groaned, because he didn't want her to cry. He needed her not to.

'I thought I'd be ruining your life because I'd fallen pregnant. Then I thought you might insist on taking the baby away from me. I was hormonal and alone and it was hard to know what to do. But, the more time that passed, the more I felt I'd done the right thing. Until he was born…and he just looked so much like you, Dimitrios. His eyes were exactly like yours.' Her voice was hoarse, thickened by emotion.

'I thought about telling you then. I even picked up my

phone to call you, but the things you'd said to me that night kept going around and around my head.'

He stiffened, anger at the past making his body grow tense.

'I don't mean that I wanted to keep it a secret to punish you. But you were so cold that night. I felt like you…hated me. What if you hated our baby, too? What if you hated me even more for having him? I honestly felt like my only option was to keep him secret and raise him on my own.' A tear slid down her cheek, and finally her wet eyes lifted to his face. 'I'm so sorry for what I did to you—to you both.'

'Don't.' His voice rumbled from the depths of his soul. 'Don't apologise to me. I blamed you when I first found out, but how can I blame you now?'

He moved closer, needing to comfort her the only way he knew how. He brushed his lips over hers and felt her shuddering breath as she exhaled. 'I'm the one who's been in the wrong. I was wrong to go to you that night, wrong to push you away so hard afterwards, saying whatever I needed to make you realise how wrong I was for you. I was wrong not to contact you afterwards. You weren't a child, but you were so much younger than me, and considerably less worldly.' His hands splayed over her cheeks, drawing her closer, his lips on hers now. 'I'm sorry.'

She sobbed. He caught her anguish with his mouth, then he kissed her, slowly at first, gently, his mouth apologising to her. But then her small groan ignited something deep in his soul so, without his intention, his kiss deepened, conveying urgency and need, his hands moving to her hips, lifting her to sit on the edge of the bench, his hands curving over her bottom, holding her pressed to arousal, his kiss a demand and a promise. The spark that had ignited between them earlier that morning had caused a full-blown explosion now.

He continued to kiss her as his hands began to roam her body, and hers did likewise, pushing at his shirt, her fingers working the buttons slowly but determinedly, undoing the top two before she made a sound of frustration and simply lifted it from the waistband of his trousers. Her fingertips explored the muscular ridges of his abdomen, following the lines there until she reached his hair-roughened nipples and touched them so tentatively, he wanted to let out a guttural oath.

It was like the breaking of a dam, the beating of a drum that couldn't be contained. He lifted her from the bench, wrapping her legs around his waist, carrying her from the kitchen without breaking their kiss, and her hands continued to roam his body hungrily, each touch like a promise of what was to come. He needed her in a way that made no sense, yet it also made all the sense in the world.

She pushed at his shirt as they entered his study. He was rarely in Sydney so the space, while beautiful, was devoid of the clutter in his Singapore office. He carried her to the large white sofa, laying her down and following after her, his body weight on hers, his kiss dominating her as his hands found the hem of her dress and pushed it upwards, just as he'd wanted to do when she'd shown it to him on the rack. He'd imagined her wearing it, imagined himself removing it. A heady rush of achievement flooded his body.

This would be the silver lining to their marriage—the one thing they could build a relationship around. He pushed at the dress, lifting away to remove it from her completely, and then he stopped. He didn't kiss her again, even though he wanted to, because there was something he wanted to do so much more desperately.

He wanted to look at her. To see her. See the body he hadn't been in the right frame of mind to fully appreciate the night they'd made love, yet still remembered well enough to see the changes made by a child, a few years. Despite her slim frame, her breasts had grown rounder, her hips too. He cupped her breasts possessively, as though he had every right, as though she were his in every way, his mouth finding hers once more, his fingers teasing her nipples, making her arch her back and moan in a way he understood on a primal level.

'Yes,' he promised, though she hadn't said anything. She didn't need to. 'Soon.'

Her fingertips stilled for a moment, then gained momentum, moving up his back, dragging down, her nails pushing into the waistband of his trousers and curving into the top of his bottom, dragging him closer to her, lifting her hips at the same time, as though trying to unite them.

'Too many clothes,' she said breathlessly. It was a sentiment with which he one hundred per cent concurred.

'Way too many.'

He pushed to standing, his eyes burning into hers as he stripped himself of fabric completely before dispensing with her underwear. Once again, he could only look— the sight of her was so intoxicating, like a drug he'd never known he was craving. The curls of hair at the top of her thighs, the fullness of her breasts, their creamy skin and the pinkness of her nipples. She had matured into a woman's body, and he wanted, more than anything, to make her his.

A voice in the back of his mind was shouting at him, reminding him he'd already acted on his own selfish impulses where Annabelle was concerned, taking her because it had suited him, regardless of what had been right for her. But this was different, wasn't it? They were getting married. They already had a child together.

His arousal was straining so hard, it was painful; he could feel heat building up inside him, begging to be released.

Any woman would have done.

That wasn't true. He'd needed Annabelle that night, just as he needed her now. He didn't know why she had this power over him, but she did. That didn't absolve him of his obligations, though, his duty to do the right thing by her. If anything, it made it so much more imperative that he did so.

She wasn't just the mother of his child, she was still Lewis's sister, and he owed them all more than just the animalistic indulgence of his urges.

'Please,' she whimpered, her fingertips moving to her breasts, cupping them so he swore under his breath, the temptation almost too much to bear.

'God, Annabelle, I want this.'

'Me too.' She pushed up to sitting, reaching for his hand and yanking him back to the sofa. He went even when he knew he should have fought her. He sat and she lifted herself up to straddle him, her cheeks pink, her eyes fevered.

'But we can't do this,' he muttered, shaking his head in disbelief at what he was saying. His arousal begged him to reconsider.

'What?' she murmured, as though she'd misheard him. Her hand dropped between them, cupping his masculine strength, the pad of her thumb brushing over his tip. He dropped his head back, his eyes squeezed shut as a bead of moisture escaped.

'We should wait. Until we're married.'

'What?' This time it was higher-pitched, rife with disbelief. 'You have got to be kidding me.'

Her beautiful body jack-knifed off him, her eyes showing surprise, then hurt.

He stood, moving towards her, but she lifted a hand, stilling him. 'Don't. Just let me… You're saying you don't want to sleep with me?'

And, despite the seriousness of that moment, his lips

curved in a sardonic smile. 'Does that look like what I'm saying?' He gestured to his rampant erection, and felt a flood of warmth at the innocent blush that spread over her cheeks.

'Annabelle, seven years ago I made a selfish decision that has completely changed your life. If we have sex right now, I have no reason to think you're not going to regret it, and that you're not going to think I've taken advantage of you.'

'But—you're the one who said you want this to be a real marriage.'

He rubbed his hand over his stubbly jaw. 'I do want that. I want us to find some common ground, and right now the fact we obviously still have this chemistry is a great start. But you're completely blindsided by all this—I'm not going to take advantage of you in what could just be a moment of indecision or uncertainty.' He ignored her lifted hand, moving closer, so he could lace his fingers with hers.

'I want you. I want you more than I have words to express, so believe me when I say it's taking all my willpower to walk away from you. But it's what I should have done seven years ago.'

Her eyes were huge, hollowed out. 'You regret it that much?'

He shifted his head, surprised by her interpretation. But it was accurate. 'Yes,' he said with a nod. 'I do. Not because that night wasn't great. Not because I didn't want you. But because I should have been strong enough to understand that we weren't well-matched. You were nothing like the women I usually see. You still aren't.'

She spun away from him, dragging her hand free. Her back was trembling.

'I know that.'

'No, you still don't understand. You're so beautiful, Annabelle, but you're also so innocent. So inexperienced and naïve. For me, that night was just sex, and for you it was… what? Love?'

He saw her flinch. 'Whatever I thought it was then doesn't matter now.'

'But it does. If we're going to have a physical relationship, we need to define the parameters of that first. I won't hurt you again, Annabelle. I have regretted hurting you for seven years—I can't remember that night without a deep sense of shame. I won't let that happen again.'

She'd turned back around and was staring at him as though he'd just said, 'I kill kittens for fun.'

How could she not see what he was doing? That this was a sacrifice and a half? Did she have any idea how much his body was screaming for her?

'Seven years ago, I thought you cared for me,' she whispered, and that same sense of shame and guilt fired inside him once more. 'I was stupid and naïve, just like you said.'

'I did care for you, Annabelle.'

She rejected that. 'You cared about Lewis's sister, not about me as my own person.'

'I cared about you enough to push you away—hard—so you wouldn't waste any more of your time fantasising about me.'

She held up a hand again to silence him. 'I'd built you up in my mind to be something you weren't. I had all these ideas about you, and I know it was stupid. It was a crush. I don't feel any of those things now.'

He wondered why that bothered him so much. Ego, he thought, with a shake of his head.

'I've had seven years to wake up and smell the coffee. I get it. I was just someone for you to have sex with, nothing more meaningful. You're someone who lives your life in a certain way. I don't have any problem with that, and you shouldn't feel bad about it. My expectations were just way out of step with the reality of what you were offering. But they're not now. I get what the parameters of this are. I get that sex is probably the only thing we'll ever have in common.'

'And that's enough for you?' he asked, carefully keeping his voice devoid of emotion.

She sighed. It was all he needed to hear. He moved closer, coming to stand in front of her.

'I'm not going anywhere.' He lifted his hand to her arm, slowly running a finger down it, his gaze following the gesture, noting the goose bumps that followed in its wake. 'Let's take it slow and make sure you don't get hurt this time around. Okay?'

CHAPTER SIX

ANNIE RAN HER fingers over the rows and rows of designer outfits, shaking her head as she moved around the walk-in wardrobe. Could it still be called a wardrobe when it was the size of her old apartment? she mused, pulling a drawer open and gasping when she saw that it was filled with neatly organised handbags—also boasting designer names. She shut it again quickly.

This couldn't all be for her, surely?

Everything she'd tried on that morning and loved was there, but there was much more as well. It was as though someone had taken her impressions and used them as the building blocks of her fantasy wardrobe. There was everything from casual—jeans and yoga pants—to sophisticated and glamorous—slinky silken dresses, and even a couple of ball gowns, as well as trouser suits and blouses. It was the kind of wardrobe a teenaged Annie would have fantasised about.

With a small smile, she pulled one of the dresses up and held it against herself. Just as in the boutique, she saw how beautiful the dress was, and how much it suited her. She imagined that when she wore it she would look, and feel, a million dollars.

Speaking of which, all the price tags had been removed, which was a saving grace, because if she could easily tally up what he'd spent she'd *never* let him keep them. That, though, was a technicality. She could estimate the expense and it didn't change the fact that her heart had lifted at the sight of so many beautiful things, and all for her.

Ordinarily, she might have gone to lightly chastise him, and then to thank him, but what had happened between them earlier had caused Annie anxiety all evening. Max had arrived home not long after Dimitrios had put an end to their passion so she'd been able to busy herself with the important job of helping him assimilate this dramatic change in his circumstances. Fortunately, Max was a grounded kid and—mostly—he took it on the chin. His room was enormous, and he found the idea of a nanny interesting, but having his familiar books and train set waiting for him in his room seemed to assuage any concerns he might have had.

They had dinner together—burgers that Dimitrios ordered in, which Max ate with gusto, earning many beaming smiles of pride from Dimitrios. Annie had watched their interactions with a sense of sadness—at what the two had lost because of her—and pleasure—because it clearly wasn't too late for them to build a meaningful relationship.

That was why they were doing this and, whatever personal sacrifice that required Dimitrios and her to make, it was completely worth it.

As for their own personal relationship, maybe he was right. Maybe they shouldn't rush into bed together. A day ago, Annie would have laughed off the suggestion, but Dimitrios's appeal was as magnetic as ever. She was going to have to work extremely hard to fight it.

But did she even want to?

I don't want you to get hurt again.

Once she skipped over the mortification of how much of her heart was being worn on her sleeve, his thoughtfulness was pretty reassuring. She'd been a teenager the last time they'd had sex, and he *had* hurt her. By design! He'd aimed to break whatever illusions and hopes she'd built up thanks to one night of passionate sex. He'd said what he needed to—the harshest things he could think of—to push her away. It had worked. She'd been devastated, and furious, but he was doing everything he could to avoid her going through that again.

She could have told him he needn't have worried. His diatribe that night had spawned something new in Annie; she was no longer the person she'd been then. She'd never be that woman again.

The fact he'd been her only lover didn't change how she viewed sex now—it was purely a physical act. It didn't mean anything. Just because they desired each other didn't mean their feelings were—or ever had to be—involved. It was only passion. Respect and friendship had to be worked on separately.

And what about love? a little voice inside her demanded. *What about the fairy stories and the idea of a happily ever after?*

Childish nonsense, Annie thought, pushing that little voice deep inside her as she walked back through the bedroom and into the hallway.

She was looking for Dimitrios, to thank him for the clothes. What she hadn't expected to find was him in their son's room. She checked her watch; it was half an hour after Max's bed time. Dimitrios had said he'd tuck him in and, given how much he'd missed, and the fact Max had seemed fine with it, Annie hadn't objected. She slowed down as she approached the door, the deep rumble of Dimitrios's voice setting goose bumps along her arms.

'This one is from when I was a boy, not much older than you.'

'What happened?'

She wanted to peer round the door to see what Dimitrios was talking about, but she knew then that they might see her and stop talking.

'My brother—your uncle Zach—you'll like him.' She could hear the smile in Dimitrios's voice. 'He liked to go to the Rocks, just down there.' Annie closed her eyes, picturing Sydney's famous Rocks area. 'There's an old bridge and a set of steps. We used to climb half way up them and then jump down, pretending we could fly.'

His laugh filled Annie's tummy with butterflies.

'Really?'

'Mmm,' he said. 'But we couldn't fly, as it turns out. I got this scar when I fell and hit my arm on the footpath. My mother wasn't very pleased.'

There was silence and she tried to imagine what the expression on Max's little face would be like. Eventually, frustrated, she moved just a little, shifting to peer round the door. Her heart cracked wide open. Dimitrios was propped up on the bed beside Max, his large frame just a grown-up version of Max's. Max had his left arm out and she presumed the one scar he bore—from when he'd fallen off his scooter as a two-year-old—had been the initial subject of the conversation.

'Is that my grandma?'

'Yes,' Dimitrios confirmed, his voice neutral.

'Where does she live?'

'Right here in Sydney.'

'How come I've never met her?'

Dimitrios looked around the room; Annie shifted backward, out of sight.

'You'll meet her soon. At the wedding.'

'Does she live with you?'

'No. I live in Singapore, remember?'

'Oh, yes.' Max tilted his head to the side, lost in thought.

'I'd miss my mummy if she ever didn't live in the same house as me.'

Perhaps some sixth sense alerted Dimitrios to her presence, because at that exact moment he lifted his gaze and pinpointed her immediately, his eyes latching on to hers.

'You won't have to worry about that.' His lips curved in a small smile; she found herself returning it. 'You're going to be stuck with your mummy and me for a very long time.'

She moved a step backward, into the hallway, tears stinging her eyes. He'd said that he didn't want to hear about their son from her. He wanted to get to know Max all on his own. She was watching that happen and it was an act of beauty and magic.

'Now.' She heard the natural authority in Dimitrios's voice, even when it was softened by affection. 'It's far later than I realised. You must get to sleep, Max.'

Right on cue, Max yawned. 'Okay, Dimitrios.'

Her heart twisted. Soon, that would change to Daddy.

At the door, Dimitrios emerged, his eyes finding Annie's. But Max called out, 'Wait! You forgot to tell me about the one on your chin.'

Annie watched as Dimitrios lifted a finger and pressed it to a small scar that ran along the ridge of his jaw line. It wasn't a new scar; she remembered it from the night they'd... She couldn't think of that. Her body was still tingling from the kisses and touches they'd shared earlier today.

'Remind me at breakfast.'

'What will we eat?'

Dimitrios's smile flicked towards Annie, warming her belly. 'What would you like?'

'Pancakes?'

Dimitrios laughed, the sound reaching inside Annie and setting something free.

'How about eggs?' he suggested instead.

Max paused. 'Okay, I guess so.'

Annie was impressed. It would have been easy for him to agree to Max's request for pancakes, but Dimitrios had instinctively known not to indulge Max's every whim, especially not with junk food.

By silent agreement, they moved further down the corridor before speaking. 'You're great with kids,' she said honestly, lifting her face towards his as they walked.

'I have good friends who have children. I've spent some time with them.'

It was a curious thing to contemplate—his life now, what it looked like. They'd known each other years ago. Dimitrios had been twenty-four the last time they'd slept together, and his lifestyle had probably been quite typical for someone his age. Now, in his early thirties, what did his social life look like?

'That surprises you?'

She smiled wistfully. 'I guess I had imagined you still going on as you were then. You know, partying and all that. But it's been seven years.'

He stopped walking, his brow furrowed as he looked down at her. 'That was never really my scene, Annabelle. Zach, yes, but for me I generally used to go for a drink then head home to work.'

She lifted her shoulders, indicating it didn't really matter, but in contradiction to that heard herself ask, 'Is that really true?'

'Why would I lie to you?'

'You wouldn't,' she said instantly. 'It's just the papers...'

'Yes, I know. Zach and I are tabloid fodder.'

'As am I now, apparently.' She chewed on her lower lip, thinking of the mortifying article that had run the day before. She stopped walking, lifting a hand to his arm to stop him. 'That's why you took me shopping this morning, isn't it? Because of that piece about me being dowdy and unsophisticated?'

A muscle jerked in his jaw and he looked as though he was quite capable of strangling a bear with his bare hands. 'I didn't know you'd seen it.'

'Yeah, a friend emailed it to me.'

He was studying her thoughtfully, his eyes roaming her face. 'You're not upset?'

She shrugged. 'I mean, it wasn't the nicest thing I've ever read, but it's not like I'm under any illusions here. I know what I am, and what you are. That article's probably been the closest to the truth since our "whirlwind romance" was announced.'

That caused his frown to deepen.

'You're not dowdy.'

'Well, I'm probably not now, after your whole Cinderella treatment today,' she said with a small laugh, and began to walk again, but it was Dimitrios who caught her wrist this time, holding her still.

'You never were. I didn't arrange that because I thought you needed to change.'

She lifted a brow, his denial unexpected. 'No? So why did you?'

He lifted a hand as though to cup her cheek but dropped it again. 'Your poverty made you an easy target. I didn't like to see you being bullied like that. I don't like to think of Max hearing that kind of thing said about his mother.'

Ah, Max. Of course. All good deeds came back to Max—just as they should. And, though he hadn't referred to Lewis, she was sure that promise was there too—a desire to look after her simply because she was Lewis's sister.

She smiled again but this time it felt a little brittle. 'Well, thank you. I didn't expect to find a wardrobe the size of my old apartment here, nor that it would be stocked with such incredible clothes. It was very generous of you.'

His eyes wouldn't shift, though. They stayed locked to hers so swirls of emotion spun through her belly.

'It wasn't generous, so much as appropriate. You must start thinking of yourself as my wife—all that I have is yours.'

'For as long as we're married,' she couldn't help quipping, but she said it with a wink, to show she was joking. 'And thank you again. It's going to take me some time to get used to that. Actually, I'm not sure I'll ever get used to that, but I do appreciate you trying to make me feel comfortable in this palace.' She gestured around them, her eyes following the lines of the room. 'It's just—' she added and then stopped.

He put a hand on the small of her back, guiding her deeper into the lounge and across it, to where a bar was set up.

'Yes?' he prompted as he opened a decanter containing an amber liquid and poured two measures, handing one to her. She expected the fragrance to be an assault but it had a honey-like quality that was gentle.

'A week ago, I was furiously budgeting to work out how I could get Max what he wants for Christmas.' Her voice was rueful. 'I know that must seem strange to you, but it's why the last few months have been so tough. He's such a smart kid and I don't want him to miss out on stuff because I can't—couldn't—provide him with the material things a lot of his friends have.' She lifted her slender shoulders in a shrug. 'It's not as though he'd asked for anything extravagant, but for me even normal things are hard to afford. So, yeah, this is going to take some getting used to.'

'What did he ask for for Christmas?'

'A remote-controlled car and a train for his tracks that

has a motor, so he can set it going and watch it travel in circles.' She smiled indulgently. 'What can I say? He's an automobile kind of kid.'

Dimitrios's eyes glowed with something she didn't understand. 'You don't need to worry about anything like that ever again. Whatever you think he should have, consider it done.'

'But I don't want him to be spoiled,' she said quickly.

'No.' Dimitrios sipped his drink then gestured towards the deck. It was a beautiful night, the stars twinkling above Sydney, the Opera House gleaming like a pearl in the moonlight.

She walked beside him, wondering at the surreal nature of this. Why did it feel so natural for them to be together like this? There was a level of comfort between them that she hadn't been prepared for.

'What is Christmas usually like, for you and Max?' Dimitrios prompted conversationally, guiding her to a bench seat that overlooked the view.

'Quiet,' she said thoughtfully. 'We go to church in the morning, then come home and Max opens his presents. I can usually pull together enough to buy him two or three— just small things. Mum and Dad send something—though it's usually practical, like clothes, because they know he's growing like a weed.' She breathed out so her side-swept fringe shifted, catching the moon's golden light across her hair. 'I make something special for lunch, something we don't have any other time of year—salmon or turkey—and then we watch a movie and have a little piece of pudding each. Pretty normal.'

Then, with a smile, she turned to face him, crossing one leg over the other. 'Though, I suppose "normal" is a very relative term. Your Christmases are probably very different to mine.'

He smiled, but it was constrained. 'Actually, our Christmases are usually quiet too. Zach hates Christmas—always has, probably always will. And Mum has her step-kids, who make a huge fuss of her, so she generally lets us skate by without expecting us to visit or anything.'

Nerves spread through Annie like wildfire. Somehow, for some reason, she'd thought of Dimitrios as existing in some kind of void. She hadn't followed through the idea that, by keeping Max from Dimitrios, she was also keeping him from Zach and their mother, and any other family members who might feel that they wanted to get to know Dimitrios's son.

'Is she angry about me keeping her grandson from her?'

Dimitrios took a sip of his drink. 'No.'

Annie found herself leaning closer, though she'd heard him fine. 'How can she not be? After what you've lost, and what she's lost?'

'Because I'm marrying you, and she knows better than to complain to me about my choice of bride.'

'Ah.' Annie's smile was instinctive. 'So she's afraid of you?'

Dimitrios shook his head firmly. 'Not at all. She knows that once I've made a decision I'll stick to it, come hell or high water. What would the point be in questioning me, or you?'

'That doesn't mean she's not angry.'

'Would you feel better if she were?'

Annie considered that. 'In a way, yes.'

'Why?'

'Because I think I probably deserve it.'

Dimitrios stared at her for several seconds, his eyes showing a hint of frustration but his voice was gentle.

'You tried to tell me about him. And, since then, you have sacrificed everything to raise our child. I wish things between us had been different but, after the way I treated you, I have only myself to blame.'

'You're being so understanding…'

'I'm not an ogre.' He frowned. 'Though I can see why you might think I was.'

'You *were* pretty brutal that night.'

He dipped his head forward in silent agreement.

'I can't believe we're getting married in two days.'

He turned to face her thoughtfully. 'You can't believe it as in, it's not what you want?'

She considered that, lifting her shoulders. She remembered the way he'd been with Max, and the things Max had said about wanting to live with his mother for ever, and she found herself shaking her head. 'I think we're doing the right thing. Max is worth it.'

His eyes held Annie's for several seconds and then he nodded. 'Yes. He is.'

CHAPTER SEVEN

'YOU'RE NERVOUS.'

Her eyes lifted from her lap to his face, then shifted to the window behind him, and the view that sped past as the car moved. Her fingers were clasped in her lap, her features drawn. Annabelle Papandreo looked beautiful, wealthy and untouchable. Her blonde hair had been clipped to one side, and for their wedding she'd worn a stunningly ornate headband that invoked a nineteen-forties vibe. Her gown had been similarly timeless, art nouveau lace meeting silk, hugging her body all the way to the floor.

'Is that silly?' she asked.

He shook his head, finding it hard to look away from her face. Some time after boarding the flight, she'd taken all her make-up off and slipped into a change of clothes, far less glamorous than the wedding outfit but every bit as striking—a black linen singlet paired with a pair of silk trousers.

Dimitrios had found the flight a unique torment, his fingers itching to reach out and feel the different textures for himself.

'It's just been a big day,' she pointed out, referring to the whirlwind of their brief morning ceremony, the lunch with his family and a few select friends—only those he thought she'd like best—and then the flight to Singapore.

The moment they'd stepped off his private jet and on to the tarmac, the sultry night heat had wrapped around them.

Max hadn't seemed to notice, nor mind, but Annabelle had fanned her face with a magazine as they'd walked, then turned the air-conditioning up in the limousine as soon as they were inside. It was like an ice cube now, but again, Max was impervious to the climate—he was fast asleep in his car seat, opposite them.

'You did very well.'

She spun back to face him, her eyes scanning his face for sincerity. How could she doubt his words? It had been a big day, just as she'd said, yet in every way she'd carried herself with pride and grace. He had known she was nervous about seeing his brother and meeting his mother and yet she'd embraced them, taking time to speak to them at length, showing them who she was and making inroads into forming a genuine relationship with both of them.

There was nothing about her that had seemed unhappy, or had spoken of the unusual terms of their marriage. To anyone watching, they would have seemed like a perfectly normal couple on their wedding day.

If Zach thought Dimitrios's about-face with regard to marriage was strange, he'd had the manners not to say as much on Dimitrios's wedding day. But Dimitrios had decided a long time ago that he wasn't interested in love or marriage—he'd seen what 'love' had done to his mother and it had been a salutary example of what he never wanted to become.

Which was why this marriage was so damned perfect.

As he'd advanced in years, one part of his plan hadn't sat well for Dimitrios—the lack of children. He'd felt a yearning to continue his lineage, but he'd still been reconciled to not having that, given that he didn't want a traditional marriage.

And here Annabelle had presented him with all the pieces of a marriage he wanted—if he could have cherry-picked the perfect situation, it would be exactly this. He desired her, he respected her and she'd already borne him a son, so it was likely they'd have more children when they were ready. Yeah, he was feeling pretty damned good about things—especially because he'd also taken great pains to make sure he was looking after her feelings this time round.

Relaxed, he stretched an arm along the back of the leather car-seat, his fingers dangling tantalisingly close to the exposed skin of her shoulder.

'So what are you nervous about?'

Her brow furrowed, her eyelashes sweeping down and hiding her expression for a moment. She had a little dimple in her cheek that deepened when she frowned and pursed her lips like that. Out of nowhere, he imagined leaning forward and pressing his tongue to it.

Later.

'I mean…' She darted a glance at him and then looked down, twirling her engagement ring around her finger. He'd already spotted that habit she'd developed. 'This ring, the private jet, now a limousine…and I can't help noticing that these houses are kind of enormous.' She gestured to Ocean Drive as they moved round it.

'You've already seen a photo of my house.'

'I know. It's just hitting me that this is where we live now.'

'You'll get used to it.'

'What if I don't?'

'Then we'll move back to Sydney.' The quickness of his response surprised him—his willingness to leave the life he had here was something he hadn't known he felt. Then again, he'd expected Annabelle to simply pick up and leave her life, and all that was familiar to her. Why should it be any different for him?

'I think a big part of it is making sure Max settles in

well. So long as he's happy at school, then I'm sure I'll be happy.'

He heard the determination in her voice and admired her for it. She really wanted to make a success of this.

'When did you move here?' she asked a little uneasily as the car turned into the section of road that led to his home.

'Four years ago.'

'Right, you said that.' Her tongue darted out, licking her lower lip. 'Why Singapore?'

'We spent a lot of time here—our teenage years. It feels as much my home as Australia. And then, a few years back, we expanded into a television network and a masthead of magazines and newspapers. I moved here first, but Zach spends around half his time here now too—we both love it, to be honest. It's a convenient springboard to anywhere in the world.'

That made a lot of sense. 'It was good to see Zach again. He hasn't changed.'

'No.' Dimitrios laughed, but there was a hint of worry at the back of that laugh, a worry he generally didn't express to anyone. Yet, despite that, he found himself saying, 'To be honest, when that journalist sent me a photo of Max, my first thought was that Zach must be the father.'

It seemed to distract Annabelle from her anxiety. Her eyes moved to Max and a small smile curved her lips. The first since they'd boarded the jet, he realised.

'Why?'

'Well, he bears more than a passing resemblance.' Dimitrios tried to make light of his admission, but Annie shook her head.

'Well, you *are* twins,' she responded in a droll tone.

Dimitrios nodded.

'So why, then?'

'Let's just say the rumours about me are generally exaggerated.'

'You mean you don't go through women like most men go through underwear?' she prompted, and though her voice was calm she was watching him with an intensity that told him to be careful—he didn't want to give her false hope about him.

'I'm not a saint,' he said with a lift of his shoulders. 'I've been with women. But I'm careful. You are the only woman I've ever lost control with.'

She looked towards Max, perhaps double-checking he was still asleep.

He moved the subject off himself. 'Zach is more…carefree. We're twins, yes, but we're very different. If either of us was going to accidentally get a woman pregnant, I would have put money on it being him.'

Annabelle tilted her head to one side, considering that, but whatever response she was about to offer, it wasn't to be. Her attention was caught by something behind him, and her lips parted, so he turned to see his house from her perspective. The size of it was impressive but it was more than that. The car paused at enormous gates that swung open on their approach, then it swept up a long drive, past ancient trees with huge canopies that provided much-needed shade on summer days.

'This is it, then,' she said, but quietly, more to herself than him. He wanted to wipe the worry from her face, to give her courage, so before he could second-guess the wisdom of his intentions he leaned forward and pressed a kiss to her lips. It was only meant to be brief, just a boost of strength, a distraction, but the second their lips connected he felt a surge of adrenaline coursing through his veins. His body moved closer, pressing hers back against the car, kissing her until her hands lifted and tangled in the collar of his shirt and she made that sweet little moan of hers. He swallowed it deep inside himself, thinking how addictive her noises were, how much he liked hearing her make them, how she was unlike any woman he'd ever known.

And she was—because Annabelle was now his wife. Mrs Papandreo.

The door to the limousine opened. He fought a wave of frustration at the interruption. What had he been hoping for? To have his way with her here in the back seat of the car? Their son was asleep only a short distance away. Where the hell had his self-control gone?

'What was that for?' Her eyes were enormous, her lower lip full and dark from the pressure of his kiss.

'To distract you,' he said. 'Did it work?'

She shifted, casting a glance towards the house then turned back to face him. 'For about three seconds.'

And, despite the fact he was the one who'd called a halt to the physical side of their relationship, he found himself saying, 'I might have to be more inventive, then.'

Her intake of breath was audible. He smiled, loving how easily he could arouse her, tease her—but that wasn't a one-way street. When he stepped out of the limousine behind Annabelle, he was conscious of how badly he wanted her.

'Max is exhausted,' she observed, the nervousness back in her voice.

'There's been a lot going on recently.'

'Yes. And he was so excited to be on the plane, he barely slept.'

He'd noticed that. Max's curiosity had been insatiable. He'd wanted to understand everything he could about planes—the atmosphere, engines, jet fuel, air traffic control. Dimitrios had answered all the questions he himself would have had as a boy, but he knew there'd be still more to follow from Max.

'He's very intelligent,' Dimitrios murmured.

'Yes. There was some talk of putting him up a year, but I decided to hold him where he is for now.'

Dimitrios straightened, midway to reaching into the car. 'Why?'

'You don't agree with my decision?'

'That's not what I said. I'm just curious. I would have thought most people would be thrilled by the possibility of that.'

'Not me. I know he's a smart kid. He'll do great things as he gets older. But he has to develop socially too, and putting him up an academic year or two could be really hard for him to juggle. He's happy—he was happy—with his peers. I thought I'd see how he was doing in a few years and then decide if it's worth considering.'

Dimitrios reached into the car to unbuckle Max, lifting him easily and carrying him over one shoulder. 'I'll get Max into bed and then show you around.'

Her head was spinning so fast, it truly felt as though it might come off altogether. She'd seen the outside of his house and she'd seen his penthouse in Sydney so she'd known to expect grand. But this was a whole new level of grand. While the house was some kind of brilliant tribute to modernism, with the appearance of concrete cubes all stuck together to form different spaces—including several rooms that seemed to be both outdoor and indoor at the same time—it also boasted an incredible array of antiques, all Singaporean, ancient and fascinating.

She found herself wanting to ask question upon question about each one, but instead contented herself with admiring them from a distance—a sculpture here, a fountain there, a tapestry, a vase. The ceilings were high, the floors marble and tile, polished to a high sheen. In the background there was an army of servants, all wearing black uniforms, the women in white aprons, moving silently and almost unseen—except Annie *did* see them. She saw everything—with a mixed sense of awe and fascination.

It was hot, too—far hotter than in Sydney—though inside was blessedly air-conditioned. She looked around the room he'd brought her to. It was technically their bedroom, but it was so much more. At least four times the size of her apartment, it boasted a bed carved from wood, large and ornate, and a sofa that was covered in velvet, a beautiful shade of apple-green. The floors were timber with a large brightly coloured rug, and wooden French doors opened out on to a balcony. Curtains billowed from it.

Fascinated, Annie moved in that direction, aware of Dimitrios's eyes following her progress, and then his body walking behind hers. The steamy heat hit her like a wall when she emerged, but she breathed in deeply, the air inexplicably tropical. Her hands curved around the railing as she took in the new, unfamiliar skyline. Lights shone brightly in one direction, including the Marina Bay towers she'd seen on television. In the other, it was sheer darkness.

'The bay,' he explained, pointing from behind her, so his arm brushed hers. 'In the morning, you'll see it for yourself. It's beautiful.'

She shifted her face a little, looking up at him. It was a mistake. He was closer than she'd realised and in moving she'd brought her lips within reach of his cheek. The compulsion to press forward and kiss him was overpowering.

Our marriage won't be based on love, but it can still be good.

Everything about this whirlwind was like a fairy story, except for that. Annie and Dimitrios knew what no one looking in from the outside could see. It was all fake. The vows they'd spoken to one another, promising to love and honour, were a lie. A lie born out of love—but love for Max, and even Lewis, not for each other.

She sighed, looking away from Dimitrios, focussing on the towers across the water. 'They're beautiful.' Her voice was hoarse, and she swallowed to moisten her mouth. 'I've seen them in movies, but in real life, they're huge.'

Had he moved even closer? In the sultry night air, she caught a hint of his masculine aroma, and her stomach clenched in automatic response.

'An excellent spot for Christmas shopping.'

She wrinkled her nose, well aware that the shops in a building such as that were bound to be incredibly high-end.

'I see your hesitation, Mrs Papandreo,' he said quietly, the words a caress against her ear. Her pulse lifted. She felt an ache deep inside, a need to push backward a little and lean against his broad chest, to feel his closeness and have his arms wrap around her. She wanted to pretend, just for one night, that their marriage was a *real* marriage. That this was a normal wedding night, and the passion that flowed between them had roots in love, as well as lust.

But Annie knew the risks inherent in such pretence. She had to stay on her toes.

'Perhaps,' she said with a little lift of her shoulders. 'I didn't see a Christmas tree in your house.'

Dimitrios stayed close and she was glad of that. 'It's still three weeks away.'

Annie turned to face him then. 'That's soon.'

'Then I'll have a tree brought in.'

'Do you have decorations?'

'They'll bring those too.'

She shook her head, a smile tickling her lips. 'Life really is different for you.'

'Is that a complaint?'

'On the contrary. I'm starting to think I could get used to this.'

* * *

'We're so high up, Mummy! I feel like I could fly.'

'Don't you dare. Don't even think about it.' She reached out and grabbed Max by the back of his shirt, her heart rate accelerating at the very idea of him pitching his little body over the railing.

Dimitrios laughed, leaning closer so he could whisper in her ear. 'I don't really think he's going to jump, do you?'

Embarrassed, she threw him a look. 'We're so high up.'

'And perfectly safe.' He nudged her shoulder then reached down, taking Max's hand in his. 'Now, no more giving your mother a heart attack.' He winked at Annie and began to walk off, the two of them so similar that she stood where she was for a moment, high above Singapore, enjoying the vista of the Supertrees and the walkway that linked two of them. The view was incomparable, the air cool and fresh up there. And, more than that, Max was in seventh heaven after a whole day spent exploring Bay South with Dimitrios.

The sun was lowering in the sky, casting the world in shades of orange, and a moment later Dimitrios slowed to a stop and turned back towards Annie.

'You coming?' he mouthed, their eyes sparking even at this distance.

She swallowed and began to move, catching them easily. Dimitrios reached for her hand and she let him, the sense of rightness spreading through her as they walked.

'This is like magic.' Max's voice was filled with wonder. Annie couldn't disagree.

'You should see it at night.' Dimitrios gestured to the Supertrees that made up this man-made grove. 'The trees light up like big sparklers.'

Max's face showed suitable awe.

'It sounds breath-taking,' Annie murmured. Dimitrios stopped walking and stared at her. His look was so full of admiration and intensity that her heart warmed, her cheeks turned pink and she felt a thousand and one things.

He lifted a hand, brushing his thumb across her cheek, and then he smiled, a smile that reached right inside her and made her feel special and perfect.

'What's that, down there?'

Annie followed Max's gaze. 'It looks like some kind of street performance. A magic show, perhaps?' Nestled amongst the trees on street level, a group had set up, and a crowd had formed to watch them.

'Cool! Magic! Can we go see?'

Annie had been about to distract him, but Dimitrios spoke first. 'Sure, buddy. It's on the way home.'

Home. Her heart shifted gear; she did her best to tame it into submission.

Hours later, a weary Max was carried through the doors of their house by his father. Annie was too alive to feel weary. The day had been one of the best of her life. A spontaneous suggestion to show Max some sights had led to a picnic lunch by the water, and an afternoon spent at the Gardens by the Bay, the skywalk and then finally a pleasurable hour watching talented magicians wow their crowd.

'He's exhausted,' she murmured as they approached the door. Dimitrios ruefully caught her eye over Max's head.

'Perhaps I pushed it too far today.'

'No,' she denied. She'd never forget the sight of Max and his dad playing soccer together—such a simple act, but one that had spoken of love and togetherness, something she hoped to see repeated often. 'It was perfect.'

Their eyes held and her heart sparked once more, rioting in her chest.

'I must admit, I had an ulterior motive in keeping you out so late.'

Annie frowned. 'You did? What?'

'What's an ulterior motive?' Max mumbled sleepily.

Dimitrios pushed the doors open and stood back to allow Annie to enter ahead of him. She did so and then froze... the decorations almost too enormous and over-the-top to process.

'Oh, my goodness. What have you done?'

She whirled around to find Dimitrios watching her carefully.

'Do you like it?'

His question was casual but his voice was deep.

Her expression was lightly mocking. 'No, I hate it.' She pushed lightly at his arm. 'It's incredible.'

He put an arm around her, drawing her close to his side. Magic and mistletoe were so thick in the air, she had to work to remind herself that this was all just pretend. All of it except how much they both loved Max, who was rubbing his bleary eyes and no doubt trying to understand why his father's house now resembled a department store. It had been completely decked out with Christmas finery—all while they'd been out for the day.

'Why?'

'You wanted a Christmas tree.'

'*A* Christmas tree!' she exclaimed with disbelief, lifting a finger. 'As in one. Somewhere. Something small to sit around on Christmas morning and put Max's presents beneath. This is...' She searched for the right word, her eyes saucer-like. 'Spectacular.'

'You deserve spectacular,' he murmured, kissing the tip of her nose, sparking a kaleidoscope of butterflies deep in her tummy. *It's not real.* Somehow, despite all the mistletoe and magic, she *had* to remember that.

CHAPTER EIGHT

'I DIDN'T KNOW there were butterflies in space.'

'Hey, who's telling this story?' Lewis pressed a finger to Annie's nose, his wink crinkling one side of his face.

'You.'

'Right, so let me tell it.'

'Keep going.'

'Yes, ma'am. A whole army of butterflies lifted way off the surface of the planet, their wings all silvery and shimmering, so that even in the darkness of space they shone like tiny little stars. Princess Annie put her hand out, like this...' He reached forward and arranged Annie's hand so it was at a funny angle. She giggled. 'And they came to sit on her arm, and her fingertips, and her hair. They were nice butterflies, not the kind that bite you—'

'Butterflies don't bite.'

'Some do.'

'Do not.'

'Annie,' he warned.

She bit down on her lip. 'Okay, keep going.'

'Only two butterflies bit Annie.'

'Hey.' She punched his shoulder.

He grinned.

'They lifted Annie far away from the planet and carried her out into space. The End.'

'Wait a second.' She shook her head. *'That's not a happy ending.'*

'Isn't it?'

'No, and you said there's always a happy ending.'

'Ah, so there is.' He stood up from her bed, and Annie wriggled down, arranging her head on the pillow. Lewis pulled the quilt up under her chin, then stroked her head. *'How about this, then? The butterflies carried Princess Annie through space, all the way to her home planet, where she was met with rose petals at her feet and jubilant cries from her adoring public.'*

'Better,' she murmured, her eyes heavy.

'She was brought to the palace in a golden carriage, shaped like a pumpkin but with butterfly wings, and there the prince she'd fallen in love with as a child was waiting—he'd never forgotten her. They got married and lived happily ever after.'

Annie smiled, sleep almost claiming her. *'And the Zap Aliens?'*

'They never bothered her again.'

Annie woke with a start, a disorienting confusion seeping into her, so she pushed up and blinked, trying to remember where she was. Not in the small bedroom she'd grown up in, and not with Lewis telling her bed-time stories. Not in her home in Sydney, where she and Max had spent the last six years. Something spiky caught her attention, and then the hint of pine-needle fragrance, and it all came whooshing back.

She lifted her hand to be sure, eyeing the enormous diamond.

Dimitrios. Their marriage. Singapore.

She moved a little, looking at him sleeping, her heart hammering against her ribs. God, what was she doing?

Dreams and memories of Lewis had formed a lump in her throat; she stepped out of bed as quietly as she was able, padding gently across the room to the door, which she opened silently, slipping downstairs and into the industrial kitchen.

She silently made a cup of tea and carried it through the downstairs of the sprawling mansion. One of her favourite rooms was a sunken sitting room that seemed to jut out of the house itself. She liked it because there were enormous trees in front of it, so she felt almost as though she were perched in a bird's nest in a rainforest. She pushed the windows wide open and breathed in deeply. It was raining—a heady, tropical rain that smelled of heat, thunder and papaya.

The furniture in this room was dark wood, the cushions colourful. She curled up on a corner of the sofa, cradling the cup in her hands, staring out at the falling rain.

'It's early.' His voice was roughened by sleep. She turned towards the door, bracing herself to see Dimitrios—but nothing could have braced her adequately for the sight of him in only a pair of boxer shorts, his toned, taut abdomen calling for her attention. She looked away quickly.

'I couldn't sleep.'

He walked across the room, taking a seat down the other end of the sofa.

'Did I wake you when I left?'

'Must have.' He shrugged. 'I'm a light sleeper.'

'I'm sorry.'

'Don't be. I like getting up early.'

'This early?'

'Not generally.'

She sipped her tea.

'What woke you?'

There's always a happy ending for you, Annie.

Emotions flooded her. She traced one of the ornate patterns on the rim of the cup, lost in thought.

'I have these dreams.' She sighed. 'More like memories. Of the bed-time stories Lewis used to tell me.'

'What kind of stories?'

Her smile was nostalgic. 'Oh, about dragons and castles and magical caves—stories that would take you to a far-away world or a different star system. There were always monsters and I was the only person who could save the world. I wish he'd written them down—though I'm probably the only one who'd appreciate them.'

Dimitrios was quiet for so long, she shifted to face him.

'You must miss him a lot.'

Annie nodded. 'Yes.' What else could she say? After Lewis died, she'd been completely alone. Her parents hadn't factored. Briefly, there'd been hope—Dimitrios—but whatever comfort she'd gained from their night together had been very, very short-lived.

'Me too.' He tapped his fingertips against his knee, his eyes distant, as though he had travelled back in time. 'He was my best friend. I couldn't believe it when he died.'

'No,' she murmured, taking another sip from her tea. 'It was so sudden—but that was merciful, given how much he hated being sick.'

Dimitrios nodded. 'He had so much potential; what a cruel twist of fate to lose him at only twenty-four years of age. So young.'

'So young,' she agreed.

'I notice Max talks about his Uncle Lewis.'

Annie nodded. 'I've made sure he knows about him. Being an only child, that sibling bond is quite foreign to him.'

Dimitrios reached out, brushing a hand over her hair,

then letting it drop to the back of the sofa. 'Would you have liked more children?'

'I always thought I would have more than one,' she said with a little lift of her shoulders. 'I loved being a sister. I liked having someone to tell my secrets to, and Lewis was—a great brother.' She cleared her throat. 'What about you?'

'I never even thought about having children, up until a few years ago.'

'What happened a few years ago?'

'Nothing in particular. Actually, it was hot on the heels of this.' He gestured to their feet. 'Expanding our operations in Singapore. I was on such a high—I felt like Zach and I could do no wrong. We inherited this business that our grandfather built from the ground up, and we've worked so hard to make it bigger and better, but for what? Who's all this for? With no kids, where does it go?'

His fingertips traced an invisible circle on her bare flesh, sending goose bumps along her skin.

'I've never wanted to get married. I've always, always known that about myself.'

Annie's chest felt as though it were being tightened.

'I appreciate how strange that must sound to you—my wife—but our marriage is different. I didn't want to have the emotional pressure of being married. A wife who loved me and needed my love in return.' He grimaced. 'And, as you wisely pointed out, most marriages are based on a presumption of love.'

'Not ours, though,' she said quietly, surprised her voice sounded so stoic when the admission did something strange to her insides.

'No.' His agreement was swift, his nod a further confirmation of that. 'I didn't want to raise a child as I was raised—going back and forth between a mother and father.

So I felt my options were pretty limited. Until I was contacted about Max and everything fell into place.'

A dart of something like resentment moved down her spine. It was all so convenient for Dimitrios. Oh, missing six years of Max's life wasn't ideal, but presumably that was a small price to pay for having a ready-made heir waiting in the wings, and a woman he could draw into exactly the kind of marriage he wanted.

'Why are you so against marriage?' she asked, keeping her voice devoid of emotion.

'Not all marriages,' he quipped with a grin, gesturing from him to her.

'I meant, genuine marriage.'

That lessened his grin, for a moment turning it into a hint of a frown. 'It's not marriage so much as the idea of love,' he said thoughtfully. 'I saw how my dad treated Mum, how he treated us, and I guess it just solidified for me how bad an idea it was to care too much for someone.'

'Why? What happened between them?'

'Nothing. It was a whirlwind affair. She got pregnant. He didn't want kids so he got on with his own life, leaving her in total poverty to raise two boys.'

Annie's stomach turned over. Everything began to fall into place. 'I see.'

His eyes narrowed, and he nodded tightly. 'Yes. Just like I left you.'

Her gaze softened. 'You didn't know.'

'That changes nothing about how much you've been struggling.' His lips tightened with self-condemnation. 'My father saw no intrinsic value in Zach and me until he got married again and my stepmother couldn't have children. She badly wanted them and so he brought us here to Singapore. Our mother was devastated.'

Annie gasped. 'How could he do that to her?'

'He didn't care about her at all,' he said succinctly. 'Theirs was a brief affair and it meant nothing to him. He never thought of her again.'

Annie found it impossible to look at him. She spun her face away, pain wrenching through her, because those exact same words could have applied to her relationship with Dimitrios.

'It's not the same as us,' he said thickly. 'I have thought of you many, many times since that night, Annabelle.'

Something shifted. Hope. The absence of pain. 'Oh?'

'I pride myself on always being in control. I have never done something I regretted, something I felt happened beyond my control, except for that night with you. After I'd promised Lewis I'd look after you, I did *that*.'

Her eyes swept shut at that admission. 'That's not thinking of me, that's thinking of yourself—and your own perceived failings.'

'It's thinking of you, and wondering what it was about you that drove me over the edge of sanity. Lewis's little sister.' He shook his head. 'What power you held over me.'

A rush of something like pleasure expanded in her chest but she ignored it—there was no power here, no victory. He was talking in the past tense and, even if he hadn't been, it was obvious he resented whatever he thought her source of power was.

'I think it was just shared grief,' she said simply.

'That was definitely a catalyst,' he agreed, moving closer still. 'But you'd wanted me long before that night.'

Her lips parted at the statement, her cheeks growing pink. 'You looked at me as though you thought I was the second coming. What red-blooded man wouldn't have responded to that?' he asked.

'I was too young to know how to respond to you,' she said with a soft exhalation. 'I'd never met anyone like you.'

'It was a long time ago.' His fingertips found the thin strap of her singlet top and pushed beneath it, his exploration so soft and gentle that it was almost as if he didn't realise he was doing it. 'You're more experienced now.'

Her cheeks glowed with more warmth. 'Am I?'

She didn't need to look at him to know that he was frowning. 'I presume so.'

'More experienced with men?'

'It's been seven years.'

'More than six of which I've spent single-handedly raising a child,' she pointed out, her defensiveness making the words sound more caustic than she'd intended.

'You're saying you haven't been with anyone since me?'

She lifted the cup to her lips, needing a minute. Her brain was going haywire.

'Annabelle?'

God, how she loved that he used her full name. He always had done. She forced herself to look at him, her eyes raking his face. 'You're the only man I've ever been with.'

He flinched a little, clearly shocked by this. 'But it's been seven years.'

'We just discussed that.'

'But you're… How have you gone so long without sex?'

She laughed; she couldn't help it, but sadness flooded her because it was obvious from his response that such an idea was anathema to him. How many women had he been with since her? She didn't want to consider that.

'That night was— I'd been drinking.' He dragged a hand through his hair, moving closer. 'Honestly, I can't even remember if I was as attentive as you deserved. I just know it was your first time and that I hadn't expected that.' He brushed his finger down her arm and she drew in a shuddering breath.

'You were…attentive.'

His hand moved towards her wrist.

'Even drunk, I guess you knew what you were doing. Like you've already said, it didn't matter who you were with, it was just sex.'

His lips compressed. 'I should never have said that.'

'It was the truth, though, right?'

He frowned, his handsome, symmetrical face shifting into something approximating a grimace. 'I needed...a human connection.'

She shifted a little, and her knee brushed his, a thousand sparks shooting through her. 'And I was there.'

He shook his head, lifting a hand to her hair, stroking it. 'You were so brave at the funeral. I was watching you and the way you stood, the way you comforted your parents and were strong for them.' His voice was low and husky and it did something to Annie's insides. 'And all I could think about afterwards was how you must be feeling. Who was comforting you?'

Her heart trembled.

'I'd promised Lewis I'd look after you, but it was more than that. I wanted to make sure you were okay too. But that was all, Annabelle. That's why I went to you. And then you opened the door and a need I couldn't...wouldn't...control overtook me. I have spent the last seven years hating how weak I was in that moment, but maybe it was bigger than weak or strong. Maybe it was just...right.'

Had he moved, or had she? They were closer now, and she breathed in, tasting him on the tip of her tongue. 'It felt right.' It had. Right up until the morning, when he'd left and reality had come crashing down on her.

'You're Lewis's sister.'

She nodded slowly.

'You're the last person I should have gone to, should

have slept with.' He groaned. 'You were a virgin, and I was drunk. Everything about it was wrong.'

'No.'

It was a simple answer, straight from her heart.

'It really wasn't.' She put her hand on his knee and he frowned in response. 'Stop torturing yourself for that night. I could have stopped it at any time. I could have pushed you away, told you to wait. I knew you'd been drinking and I knew you were as emotional about Lewis as I was.' She lifted a finger to his lips, silencing anything he might have said in response. 'If either of us was selfish, it was me. I'd had a crush on you for years and I couldn't let you walk away. I took what you offered because I needed it. I wanted you to be my first.'

His eyes flashed with comprehension; something moved deep in their depths.

'But you didn't want to get pregnant,' he growled, still obviously blaming himself.

'No,' she agreed. 'But when I found out I was pregnant I was happy, Dimitrios. The idea of having your child was never a disaster for me. Even when I saw you at the club, and realised it was something I'd probably need to do alone, I was okay.'

'How can that be?'

Her expression was wistful. 'Because I was alone. And so lonely. I never had many friends, and I wasn't close to Mum and Dad. Lewis was…he was my world.'

Dimitrios moved closer, nodding slowly.

'And then you came to me and for one night, one brief, wonderful night, I felt like everything was going to be okay.' She was too caught up in her memories to worry about how much she was revealing. It was the truth, and suddenly she had a burning impulse to unburden herself of it. 'I felt so connected to you and I needed that.' She pressed a hand to her stomach, remembering what it had been like to be pregnant. 'Finding out I was pregnant was a lifeline when I needed it most. A baby bound me to the outside world, to you and to Lewis. A baby was someone to be strong for.'

He moved closer, pressing his forehead to hers. 'You are so strong, Annabelle. The strongest person I've ever known.'

She lifted her shoulders. 'I've been what I had to be.'

His breath whispered against her cheek. 'Seeing the way my mother suffered because of my dad, I can't believe how *you've* suffered.'

'It's not the same.'

'Really? Because I have the strangest sense that history's been repeating itself.'

'Your dad was indifferent to your mum's situation. You didn't know about mine.'

There was silence in the room, just the sound of his breathing and hers mingling, mixing, faster than breathing should have been given that they were sitting down.

'I would have done this sooner if I had.'

She couldn't say why, but his words didn't relax her. If anything, it was a reminder that their whole situation came down to his sense of duty and obligation, rather than anything to do with him wanting to be with her by choice.

'Have you really not had the opportunity to meet anyone since me?'

'I haven't had the inclination,' she murmured huskily. Then, thinking it sounded as though she'd been pining for him, she quickly added, 'I had to be a mum and dad for Max. I wanted him to know that I was always there for him.' She bit down on her lip. 'Between Max and work, I've had my hands full.'

More silence, heavier this time, and with every second that passed Annie felt her awareness of Dimitrios increasing until her blood felt as though it had turned to lava in her veins.

'And you?' she whispered in an attempt to hold on to sanity, to remember who they were and what this marriage was really about. 'I suppose life went on as usual for you.'

A frown briefly marred his handsome face. 'Largely, yes.' There was an uneasiness in admitting that.

Her smile showed a hint of sadness. 'Relax. It was one night. It's not like I expected you to stay celibate afterwards.' She laughed to put him at ease but it sounded brittle, even to her own ears.

'The thing is, I was so full of regrets.'

She flinched a little, but didn't move away.

'Sleeping with you was a betrayal of my closest friend. I'd promised Lewis I'd look out for you and instead I'd done the exact opposite. I was harsher to you than I needed to be, simply because I had to make sure you didn't continue to harbour any feelings for me. At the time, I was sure that I was doing the right thing.' His smile was tight. 'I wanted to forget you.'

Realisation dawned. 'So you did what you could to make that happen? Sleeping with other women to expunge me from your memory?'

His eyes widened. 'Not consciously. And not so cynically. But, yes, Annabelle. I hoped I would simply forget you as time went on.'

She knew that he hadn't, though. He'd already said as much.

His voice was a husky growl. 'I wish I could tell you something different.'

She shook her head. 'Why?'

'Because you deserve that.'

Her stomach squeezed. 'You never made me any promises, Dimitrios.'

'Didn't I?' His smile was ghost-like. He stood, and the distance he put between them was like a yawning barrier she ached to cross. 'Perhaps you're right. But I've made you promises now, Annabelle. I won't hurt you like that again. I will never let our chemistry dictate what happens between us—if we sleep together, it will be because you decide it's right, not because our bodies can't control themselves. And I will do whatever I can to make you happy here in this marriage. Okay?'

CHAPTER NINE

SHE COULDN'T STOP thinking about him. It was as if a switch had been flicked, in the week since they'd spoken in the lounge she preferred, with the tropical rain lashing against the windows. She caught his eyes often and, every time that happened, heat bloomed in her cheeks. She watched him when she should have been doing other things. She imagined him undressed—pictured his abdominals, his tanned skin, his broad shoulders. She found herself daydreaming about him and, when it came to actually sleeping in the same bed as him yet not touching, Annie was fighting a losing battle.

Each night, Annie felt as though she were burning alive, lying only a few feet away from him on their separate sides of the bed. She was so careful not to move, not to stir, not to reach out and drag her nails down his back, cup his buttocks. Temptation was driving her crazy.

It wasn't just sensual heat, though. It was so much more.

Dimitrios was an amazing father. Watching him bond with Max convinced her, every day, that she'd made the right decision. Seeing them together made her feel a happiness she'd never known. It wasn't even as if they were slowly building a relationship. Something had clicked inside Max the moment he'd met Dimitrios. It was easy and natural, as though they'd been together from birth. The night before, she'd watched Max and Dimitrios play cards for hours, while she'd pretended to read a book. But her concentration had been shot, so in the end she'd given up and simply enjoyed the sight of her son playing his favourite game—and winning by no small margin.

Yet every time Dimitrios had lifted his gaze and looked at Annie, her heart had skipped a beat, her stomach had tied itself in knots and she'd felt a surge of need that had had nothing to do with Dimitrios's paternal abilities and everything to do with him and her.

'Good morning.' She startled, shifting in the bed a little, wondering how he'd known she was awake. Usually one of them got up before the other, avoiding the intimacy of speaking while they were lying down side by side. Silly, really, given that they'd created a child together.

She rolled over, wondering why she didn't feel more self-conscious about her natural state—no make-up, hair a mess, wearing only a pair of pyjamas she'd had for years. Annie's lips lifted into a small smile. 'Good morning.'

'Are you busy today?'

Annie shook her head. She'd kept on a few clients, but the workload was much lighter than before, and she'd been able to finish up for Christmas.

'Why do you ask?'

'Francesca is taking Max to that soccer workshop.' He reminded her that the lovely nanny he'd hired had scheduled some holiday activities for Max—many of them with pupils from the school he'd be attending—and he was already starting to make friends. How quickly it was all falling into place!

'That's right. He was so excited about that.'

'Yes.' Dimitrios's smile showed pride, but the way his eyes were roaming over her face made it hard to concentrate on anything except the fact there was only about eight inches between them—and how badly she wanted to close them.

'So,' he drawled, 'I was thinking it would be a good opportunity.'

'For what?' she enquired on a snagged breath.

'To go Christmas shopping.'

It was such a perfect suggestion, she should have been excited, but there was a part of Annie that was screaming in complaint. What had she hoped he'd say—that they stay home and make love all day?

He was waiting for *her* to suggest that. He'd made it obvious it would only happen if and when she said she was ready. And what if she could never screw up the courage?

The idea of that made breathing difficult. What was she waiting for? Why wasn't she telling him how much she wanted him?

'You mentioned you'd been saving up for Max,' he murmured, reaching out and putting a hand on hers. It was a simple touch but it sent a jolt running through her and she visibly startled, her eyes flying wide open. 'You don't need to worry about money. I want you to get him whatever you want. And I want to come—to help choose some gifts for him.'

Her fingers were tingling beneath his. 'That's very... thoughtful. But surely you're too busy?'

His expression shifted a little. 'If you'd prefer to do it alone, I understand.'

'No.' She shook her head, rushing to correct his misunderstanding. 'I didn't mean that.'

'It's fine,' he said gently. 'It's been just you and Max for a long time. I didn't mean to rush you. We can leave things as they have been—you do the shopping. I'll help next year.'

Next year. It was such a promise of permanence and longevity! It was hard to get her head around that. Besides, he was right: this would take time. He was being so reasonable and understanding, so accommodating of her needs.

'It's not that. I'd like you to come. I honestly meant what I said—that I presumed you'd be too busy.' A frown crossed her face. 'I don't want you feeling that you have to rearrange your life for us.'

A pause followed, then he leaned closer. 'I don't feel that I have to. I want to.'

Lightness spread through her; a smile followed. 'Then let's do it.'

At some point since Sydney, he'd stopped thinking of her as Lewis's sister. He'd stopped thinking of her as a mistake from his past and started seeing her as she was. And Annabelle Papandreo was completely captivating. His eyes followed as she browsed the toy aisle, carefully lifting boxes from the shelf, looking at them for several moments, reading the back, then more often than not replacing them in their spot. He was pushing a trolley that remained empty. If it had been up to him, it would be half-full by now. At least.

'What exactly is the selection criteria?'

She turned to face him, her smile like sunshine. His chest compressed in response. 'It's complicated.'

'Hit me with it.'

She grinned. 'Really, I'm just looking for something he'll love.'

Dimitrios bent down and picked up the box she'd most recently discarded. 'And you don't think he'd love this?'

'Oh, he undoubtedly would.'

'So why not get it?'

'Because it's not perfect.'

'And you want to get him just one perfect gift?'

She tilted her head to the side. 'I usually get him a few things. The things he's asked for and something I choose—a book, perhaps some tennis balls.' She shrugged. 'We used to go down to the park on weekends and play tennis, you know. He's actually very good.'

Dimitrios felt pride swell in his breast. Their son was good at many things. Cards, conversation, reading and, yes, he believed sports too.

'And even though you could buy this store ten times over and not see a dent in your bank account?' he prompted.

Her eyes grew round. 'I'd never do that.'

He smiled, moving closer, an urge to kiss her almost overtaking him. 'I know.'

'I guess I don't want him to feel like his life has changed too much.'

Dimitrios bit back a laugh; Annabelle didn't. The sound was self-mocking. 'I know how ridiculous that sounds. I mean, look where we're living. I had to ask the housekeeper to stop making his bed the other day because that's a job Max has always done for himself.' Her smile was rueful. 'I just don't want him to get used to all this. To think it's normal.'

That sent a jolt of warning through Dimitrios. 'What's wrong with getting used to it?' Only, she didn't need to voice the fear she had. It was obvious to him. He moved closer then, pressing his finger beneath her chin, lifting her face to his. 'We're married now, Annabelle. None of this is going away.'

Her eyes were suddenly suspiciously moist. His chest felt as if a bag of cement were pressing down on it.

'I know you say that, but...'

A tear formed on her lashes, making them clump together. He was conscious of holding his breath as she searched for the right words. When she spoke, her voice was barely a whisper. 'Everyone's always gone away.'

Her eyes didn't meet his and he was glad. He wasn't sure what his expression would show, but he felt as though she'd reached into his chest and hollowed him out.

She was right.

Lewis had died. And then her parents had moved to Perth. Then he'd got her pregnant and disappeared out of her life into a world that, to a teenaged Annabelle, must have seemed like a million miles away.

She'd been alone for ever, fighting her own corner, looking after her son all by herself. No wonder she felt as if all this might be transient.

'This is for keeps.'

Her smile was brief. Dismissive. He shook his head and moved closer. 'I don't make promises I don't mean.'

Her eyes lifted to his and he felt a thousand and one things slamming into him. Mostly, he wanted to make her smile again, to make her truly happy. She was the mother of his child, so that was only natural. How could Max thrive if he didn't have a happy mum?

'Think about it, Annabelle. Why would I have suggested we get married if it wasn't a permanent arrangement?'

She nodded awkwardly. 'I know. You could have taken Max away from me without breaking a sweat.' Her eyes were troubled at the prospect of that. 'I'm grateful you didn't.'

'I don't want your gratitude.'

Her eyes held the hint of a challenge. 'What do you want, then?'

Great question. The answer was harder to voice than it should have been. 'I want to take it one day at a time, but I know I want you and Max here with me. Or wherever I am. It just feels…right.'

It was how they'd described the night they'd spent together. It was a word that kept coming up when they spoke. 'Right'. It was right that they'd got married. Right that they'd come to Singapore.

She pulled away from him, nodding vaguely, a smile on her lips that didn't reach her eyes. 'Yes, okay.' She reached out and grabbed a box, putting it in the trolley. 'Maybe this one.'

She hadn't even looked at the gift to see what it was.

Frustration zipped inside Dimitrios. He'd disappointed her. He'd given the wrong answer. What had she expected him to say? What had she wanted?

He ground his teeth together, following just a little behind her, his eyes scanning the rows of gifts.

Half an hour later, Annabelle had chosen a few more, with more care, each assessed for several minutes until, with a small nod, she'd decided they were suitable and had slipped them into the trolley. It was hardly what Dimitrios would describe as a 'haul'. A remote-controlled car, a motorised train for Max's train set and a soccer shirt.

They'd agreed they didn't want to spoil him, yet as Dimitrios's first Christmas with Max he found it hard not to throw every damned toy into the trolley. The idea of Max waking up to see the tree littered with presents with his name on them made Dimitrios feel all warm inside.

But their first instincts had been right. He was a great kid. Kind, generous, loving, happy. There was no need to fill his world with material things. Besides, he was living in a mansion with an army of staff at his disposal, his every whim catered for. Normal life was in his rear-view mirror, and Dimitrios knew for himself how unsettling that change was to make.

'You know,' he said as they left the department store and entered the opulent walkway of the mall, decorated for Christmas almost as thoroughly as his home. 'I've been thinking about your law degree.'

'I didn't get a law degree,' she reminded him.

'You couldn't, because of Max. But he's at school now, and you don't need to work—or not as many hours as you have been. You could study, if you wanted.'

Her surprise was evident, as though it hadn't even occurred to her. 'I could, couldn't I?'

Something lifted inside him, his mood shifting. It was just what she needed to underscore the permanence of this. A life outside him and Max—a life that would fulfil her and make her happy. 'Lewis always said you were the smartest person he'd ever met.'

Her eyes flashed to his, showing happiness. 'Did he?'

'Yeah. Present company included.'

She was smiling properly now, the look on her face making him feel a thousand kilograms lighter.

'I'd want to see Max settled into school properly first,' she was murmuring. 'But after the first term, once I knew he was making friends and doing okay, then I wouldn't feel so bad about doing something for me.'

'And it doesn't have to be law. You could study whatever you want.'

She laughed. 'You don't have to sell me on it, Dimitrios. I get it. It's a good idea.' Her voice was warm and soft. She slowed down a little, and emotion sparked in her eyes once more. 'Thank you.'

'You don't have to thank me.'

She lifted her shoulders. 'It wouldn't have occurred to me. And I love the idea.'

'Great. I'll have one of my assistants look into it.'

She shook her head reproachfully, a smile making her eyes sparkle. 'I can look into it myself.'

Relief flooded him. 'Keep me posted?'

* * *

'Can I open them yet?'

'Almost.' Dimitrios grinned, his hands covering Annabelle's eyes, his body guiding her carefully across the marina.

'I can smell the ocean salt.'

'Very perceptive.'

'You're not going to throw me to the sharks, are you?'

'Not yet.'

She laughed. 'I'm serious, Dimitrios. Where are we?'

'Has anyone ever told you that you're bad at surprises?'

'I've had enough surprises to last a lifetime,' she said in a droll tone that made him grin. He'd been smiling a *lot* today, after the heavy emotion of that morning, when she'd confessed her fear that he'd go away just like everyone else had. They'd strolled the mall, window-shopped and Annabelle had shown utter shock at the price of several things. He loved how down to earth she was and wondered if that would change, given her net worth now. Lunch had been at one of his favourite restaurants, and then they'd gone to a gallery, where Annabelle had shown an impressive knowledge of modern artists.

The idea to come here had been spur of the moment. Deep down, Dimitrios admitted to himself that he hadn't been ready for their outing to come to an end. It was a good opportunity to get to know her better, he told himself.

'Okay, almost time.'

At the premier yacht club of Singapore, his boat stood several feet longer and taller than any other. He brought her to a stop at its stern, then slowly eased his hands away from her eyes, letting them drop to her shoulders and mould to her warm skin.

'Can I open my eyes now?'

He looked down at her and something jerked hard inside

him, a feeling he couldn't place, a sense of importance and need that he had no idea how to rationalise.

'Yeah, open your eyes.' He cleared his throat, moving his hands and stepping to her side so he could see her reaction.

A divot formed between her brows as she scanned the boats before giving his more attention.

'The Patricia?' she asked with a raised brow.

'My mother.'

'Seriously?' Her smile was gently teasing. He nudged her with his shoulder in response.

'What? Not cool enough for you?'

'It's…' She sobered, shaking her head.

Frustration hit him. He didn't want her to close herself off from him. 'It's what?'

'Sweet.' But her tone was reserved; clipped.

He suppressed his impatience. 'Want to go on board?'

She looked at him for several seconds and he felt as though the world had stopped spinning. He waited, wondering when he'd become someone who sat back and waited rather than just calling all the shots. Wasn't he the kind of man who ordinarily would have said, 'Let's go on the yacht?' Nonetheless, he found himself standing there silently, watchful but not speaking, all his attention focussed on Annabelle.

She turned back to the yacht, her expression impossible to interpret. 'Just for a minute.'

His response was to reach down and take her hand, lacing their fingers together as he guided her to the swim platform.

The wind in Annie's hair made her feel as if she could do anything. She gripped the railing, looking back at Singapore with a sense of lightness and happiness that, contradictorily, made her anxious. She was getting too relaxed, enjoying herself too much. She had to remember that this was all pretend. Even when he was being so ridiculously attentive and sweet, and making her feel as though she was the centre of his universe, it wasn't about Annie so much as Max. All of this was for Max.

Dimitrios wanted them to be happy here, and he knew a big part of that was making Annie happy, so he was being accommodating. It wasn't about her. He was doing what he had to do to protect his son.

The lightness disappeared a little and she felt glad. Better to be aware of her situation at all times than to simply relax and enjoy.

'Do you like it?'

She hadn't realised Dimitrios had joined her; she'd been lost in her own thoughts. She startled a little, turning to face him, then wishing she hadn't. He'd changed into a pair of swimming trunks, a turquoise that made his tan glow like gold, and she found it almost impossible not to let her eyes drop to the expanse of his toned chest. Dark hair arrowed towards his shorts and in the periphery of her vision she followed it then felt heat bloom in her cheeks.

'Do I like…what?' Her voice sounded so thick and hoarse. She cleared her throat but knew it wouldn't help.

'The yacht.'

'Oh.' She nodded. 'Yes.'

His grin showed white teeth. She jerked her head away, but it didn't help. His image was seared into her eyeballs. His proximity made her pulse go haywire.

'Are you going swimming?' The question sounded so prim! She closed her eyes for a moment, wishing she could be effortlessly cool and unimpressed.

'If you'll join me.'

She glanced down at the dark ocean. It was a warm day

but the idea of jumping off the back of the boat didn't appeal to her. He lightly pressed a finger to her elbow then ran it down her forearm, teasing her flesh before taking hold of her wrist and lifting it, pointing towards the top of the yacht.

'Up there.'

Closer inspection showed that the top of the yacht had deck chairs, and she could only surmise a pool at its centre.

'You don't think we should be getting back?' They'd been on board for half an hour. 'Just to see the city from a distance.'

'Max is fine. Francesca's with him.'

Dimitrios was right; Annie knew that. Her desire to return to the safety and space of his house had nothing to do with Max and everything to do with the fact she was finding it almost impossible not to obey her body's increasingly demanding needs.

'I don't have any bathers.'

'There are plenty in the bedroom. Come. I'll show you.' He caught her hand once more, pulling on it gently so she collided with his naked chest. Her breath burst from her lips. She stared up at him, her pulse hammering hard, his eyes boring down into hers speculatively.

'Or you could swim without.' The words were said low and deep, a husky invitation that had her knees quivering.

She swallowed a groan, but found she couldn't deny how tempted she was. Apparently, he took her silence as a rebuke, because he squeezed her hand. 'Relax, Annabelle. It was a joke.'

Disappointment seared her. She wanted to tell him she was fine with going naked, that it was no big deal to strip out of her clothes and let him see her as she was, but something held her back.

'How come you call me Annabelle?' She blurted out the question instead, causing him to frown.

'It's your name, right?'

'I mean, when everyone else calls me Annie.'

He lifted one shoulder. 'Maybe I don't like to be the same as everyone else.'

Fat chance, she thought with a smile. Dimitrios Papandreo could *never* be like anyone else on earth, ever.

He began to walk across the deck and into a window-filled corridor, and she fell into step beside him. A bedroom came off it to one side, but not like any bedroom she might have expected to see, had she put any thought into such matters. No, this room was spacious and decorated more like a bedroom in a five-star hotel than on a boat. An enormous king-size bed sat at its centre, a huge mirror framed in pale timber hung behind it, and there was cream-coloured carpet underfoot. The furniture was Scandinavian in style, and a huge wardrobe boasted a selection of clothes—male and female. A wisp of jealousy breathed through her, unmistakable and sharp. Who were the clothes for? Who'd worn them?

'I had a selection sent here after your shopping trip in Sydney,' he said, as though he could read her thoughts. She moved closer and saw that, as with the wardrobe selection then, these had their tags still attached.

It was so thoughtful and unexpected, though it shouldn't have been. If she knew anything about Dimitrios, it was that he was prepared for anything.

'I like to have stuff at each of my places,' he explained. 'Saves having to pack much when I travel.'

She reached for one of the dresses, feeling the silk fabric beneath her fingertips, her lips twisting in a smile that was bittersweet. 'Exactly how many homes do you have?'

'Singapore is my home,' he said, surprising her by coming to stand right behind her. 'But I have properties around the world, mainly in the places we do the most business—London, Madrid, Tokyo, New York, Paris, Dubai, Sydney.'

Her head was spinning.

'Did you come back to Sydney often after—' She forced herself to finish the question, though she wasn't sure where it had come from. 'After that night?'

His eyes flashed at hers, hesitation obvious in their dark depths. 'Not often.'

'But you did come back?'

His nostrils flared as he exhaled, evidently choosing his words wisely. 'We have business there. It's where my mum lives. Yes, I came back.'

Her stomach looped. The idea that he'd been in the same city as Max and not known about him made everything feel so much worse. At that moment, the boat began to move, as though it had come across the wake of another craft, just little shifts in the current that caused it to rock—and to rock enough that Annie lost her footing ever so slightly.

Dimitrios's response was instant, snaking a hand out to catch her elbow, holding her steady. It was the lightest touch, and for an obvious purpose, but it set her pulse skittering wildly. All she was conscious of was his nearness and strength, the warmth of his touch, his overtly masculine bearing, the woody citrus fragrance he wore. And suddenly she was riding a different wave, this one not gentle or slow, but dragging her higher and higher in an inescapable current. Her eyes lifted to his and she felt something lock into place—the culmination of everything she'd been feeling and wanting all day and the certainty that, though she might wonder at her decision, she knew it was the only decision she could make.

Her hands lifted to his bare chest, her fingers splaying wide over his pectoral muscles. She dropped her gaze to them, staring at her fingertips, her mouth dryer than the desert.

'The bathing costumes are in the drawer.' It was gruff. She noticed he didn't take a step backward, though. If anything, he moved slightly closer, so his hips brushed hers, sending a riot of awareness tumbling through her body.

She was scared but she was also bold—she knew what she wanted—and that certainty meant she was going to see this through, come what may. Her eyes held his, a challenge in their depths as her fingers found the hem of her shirt. She lifted it slowly, not looking away from his face, so she recognised the moment his expression shifted and his lips parted on a hiss of breath, his features being pulled tight.

'Help me get changed?' she murmured as she pushed the shirt over her head and dropped it to the floor.

His eyes fell to her lace-clad breasts, his concentration so fierce she could feel heat radiating from him to her.

'Annabelle...' It was a plea. A desperate, aching plea. 'You don't know what you're saying.'

She reached behind her back, finding the bra clasp and undoing it. 'I beg your pardon, but yes, I do.'

She undid the bra, dropping it from the edge of her fingertips so that her breasts spilled out, her nipples taut, begging for his attention.

He swore softly, but everything was magnified; she heard it and it ricocheted through her soul like an earthquake.

'Make love to me, Dimitrios. I don't want to wait any longer.'

CHAPTER TEN

DISBELIEF ETCHED LINES about his mouth but then he shook his head, as though waking from a dream, and a second later crushed his lips to hers, a kiss designed to taste, torment, dominate and give.

She surrendered to it completely, but only for a second, then desperate hunger—starvation—was taking over, ripping her body apart piece by piece, and she was certain he was the only way she could be built back together again.

Her arms wrapped around his neck, pulling her higher up his body and, understanding her silent plea, he lifted her against him, wrapping her legs around his waist as he moved towards the bed, his hands so strong and commanding, his body so warm and masculine. She was melting against him, her insides turning to mush, heat slicking her feminine core, nipples aching for his touch. She arched her back, his name a curse and a spell on her lips, an incantation she offered again and again, her voice barely recognisable.

He kissed through her words, swallowing them whole, his hands working the button at her waist and pushing her trousers down, his fingers lingering tantalisingly on the curves of her calves before reaching her ankles, caressing the flesh there, then the soles of her feet. She whimpered at the lightness of his touch, wanting more, simultaneously relishing everything about this—the desire to stretch it out, to make every second last a lifetime. She wanted to hold on to this.

I'm not going anywhere.

Her heart trilled in her chest. She reached for his shoulders, her nails scoring the flesh there, her back tilting. His lips on her knee surprised her; she startled in response to the unexpected touch and his hands reached for her hips, holding her steady as his mouth made its way slowly, oh, so slowly higher, his tongue teasing the flesh of her inner thigh inch by inch, her breath fast and loud as he went higher still. One hand left her hip, pushing her legs apart, and it didn't occur to her not to comply. She lifted her feet on to the edge of the bed and his mouth came between her legs, his tongue so light she could barely feel it at first, so light it left her desperate—utterly, incandescently desperate—for more.

Still, she wasn't prepared for the experience that was coming—his mouth closing over her most sensitive cluster of nerves and kissing her there until she almost passed out from pleasure. Her fingernails pushed into his shoulders and somewhere in the very, very distant recesses of her mind still capable of thought, she worried she might draw blood.

And yet she couldn't stop.

She couldn't change anything about what they were doing; this was a juggernaut and they were both on board it, just as they'd been that night seven years earlier.

'You're so wet,' he growled, the words so deep they reached inside her and sent tremors of pleasure radiating through her body. His fingers moved to echo his mouth's movements, slipping inside her and finding her raging pulse, until she tipped over the edge of sanity and existence and became a pile of nerves. She cried out as pleasure swallowed her. His name at first, and then just moans, over and over, her body racked with shakes of euphoria.

He didn't give her time to recover. A second later he was kissing his way up her body, his hands still pleasuring her womanhood, his mouth taking a nipple hostage, pressing it hard against his lips, then lightly, so the contrast was too much to bear. She cried out, and he brushed his hair-roughened chin across her chest to the other breast, subjecting that nipple to the same exquisite pleasure-pain.

'Stay here,' he groaned as he reached her mouth, his lips tantalisingly close to hers. 'Don't move.' His eyes bored into hers, as though he was afraid she was going to change her mind. Not a chance in hell.

'Where are you going?'

'To get protection.' A frown creased his perfectly symmetrical brow. 'Unless you want to start trying for another child right away?'

Nothing could dampen the pleasure she was feeling, but his words pulled her some of the way back to sanity. Another child? Another chance to experience motherhood, without the stress she'd known constantly since Max's birth? But, no. That wasn't something you just went into lightly. She needed to think about it, make sure it was the right decision. She shook her head, smiling to hide how tumultuously affected she was by that idea. 'I'm not ready.'

A firm nod from him and then he was gone, walking across the room before disappearing through the door and reappearing less than a minute later, a string of metallic squares dangling from his fingertips, his body now completely naked. His grin showed he wasn't at all affected by her decision about the casually suggested next child, but she barely registered his facial expression. Her entire attention was taken by his physique—his strength, his perfectly honed body, his lithe grace, his easy athleticism, and the impossible-to-miss state of arousal. Her eyes clung to his erection, a hint of panic spearing through her at the idea of *that* fitting inside her.

'God, you're beautiful.' Pleasure spread through her at his compliment. No, not just at the compliment, but the way it sounded—as though it had been wrenched from the heart of his soul, as though he couldn't not say it because he felt it with every fibre of his being. It was though he was marvelling at her, worshipping her, even.

'You've changed since that night. These are bigger.' He reached for her breasts, cupping them in his hands, his fingers brushing over her nipples.

They were. After Max, her breasts had never gone back to their previous size, though they were still modest.

'You're beautiful,' he said again, shaking his head with a rueful grin before bringing his mouth to hers, kissing her until she was breathless and starlight danced behind her eyelids. She groaned, lifting her legs around his waist, holding him tight.

'I was just thinking the same thing about you.'

She felt his smile against her shoulder and then he was pushing up, running his hand over the side of her face, his eyes searching hers, as though he wanted to say something to her but couldn't find the words. She held her breath anyway, her heart beating overtime, and in her mind she knew what she wanted to hear.

Her eyes flew wide but there was no time to process the foolishness of what she was hoping for—the idea that Dimitrios might love her. If she'd had time to consider it, she might have realised how foolish it was to cement their arrangement with this next step, but he was already parting her legs and pushing his arousal against her womanhood, and animal instincts took over, shoving worry, thought and perception clear from her mind.

She tilted her hips, welcoming him even as he pushed deeper, slowly at first, so she dug her nails into his side and groaned, 'Please, now,' until he drove himself the rest of the way, deep, hard and fast, just as she longed for. His length filled her so she needed a second to adjust to the sensation of his possession, but only a second, and then he was moving again, each thrust of his length exactly what she needed, so she found herself tipping closer to the edge of pleasure. Her fingers sunk into the mattress, her hands curling round the soft sheets, ripping them loose from the bed as she surrendered to the moment, lost on a wave of perfection and euphoria.

She rode that intense wave of pleasure until it crashed around her, spreading heat through her entire body, her head thrashing from side to side, her moans filling the luxurious bedroom, the waves rocking the boat nothing to the waves that were rocking her soul.

As with her last orgasm, he waited only a moment for her breath to slow and then he was moving again, expertly shifting her body a little so she was on her side. Each movement he made reached different parts of her, sending new shockwaves of awareness tearing through her; his hands on her breasts was the last straw, each touch of her nipples seeming to light a fire inside her that there could be no hope of extinguishing.

Their faces were an inch apart, his eyes on hers the whole time, watching her, reading her, trying to understand her, and the intensity of his gaze added a whole new level of intimacy to the experience. A tear rolled down her cheek; she was powerless to stop it. He leaned forward and kissed it, then moved his mouth to hers so she tasted saltiness and passion. This kiss was soft, gentle, stirring something deep in her belly, even as heat and passion coursed through her veins.

He growled low in his throat, moved harder and faster and this time, when pleasure wrenched her from Earth and spirited her far into the heavens, he released himself with one deep, passionate thrust, spilling his seed from his body, her name on his lips filling the room, mingling with her fervent cries, a harmony of intense pleasure and need.

Afterwards, there was not silence, so much as music. The rhythm of their breathing, the humming she made as she tried to process the extent of their pleasure, the rocking of the boat like a dance into which they were being drawn.

Tension had been dogging Annie for a long time. Seven years? It was as though it had been building ever since that night and now it had finally broken; like the bursting of a dam, something had been loosened and Annie felt…free. She smiled. It was like a weight being lifted from her chest. She'd come home.

Home.

She lifted a hand to his chest, her fingertips pressing against his sternum, so she could feel the solid beating of his heart. She closed her eyes, a smile tingling her lips as she sighed.

Exhaustion was chasing pleasure. She felt as though she could sleep for a week.

But there was a normal life to get back to.

Max.

Her eyes flew open. Dimitrios was watching her, so her heart rate kicked up a notch, renewed desire firing in the pit of her stomach. And even as his arousal was filling her, she felt as though she wanted him all over again.

She ran her fingers sideways, finding his nipple and brushing it slowly. To her surprise, he made a growling noise, as though the same pleasure that had filled her at his touch was now moving through him.

She wanted to explore this, to learn how to pleasure him. No, she wanted to learn how to drive him crazy, how to make him feel a thousand and one things, including the complete loss of control she'd experienced. For years Annie had lain dormant, the sexuality he'd stirred completely disregarded in her day-to-day existence, but now it was bursting to life inside her, refusing to be contained. She had a hunger; she had no idea if she could ever control it.

But Max...

'I hate to say this, but we really should think about going back.'

His fingertip traced a line from her chin to her shoulder, then across her clavicle to the indent at the base of her throat. It was such a light touch, but his familiarity and possessive confidence was a whole new level of sensuality.

'Why?' he murmured.

A smile shifted across her lips.

'Because we have a son.'

We have a son. It was a statement of fact but the 'we' came so naturally to her lips, and the sharing of Max. They had a son together. Max would always bind them.

I'm not going anywhere.

Euphoria spread through her body, reaching her fingers and toes and everything in between.

'He's with Francesca.'

'But the soccer day will be over by now.'

'So she'll give him dinner and put him to bed.'

Annie frowned. She'd never missed a single night of tucking Max in. Not once. But he wasn't a clingy child, and he adored Francesca.

For six years she'd put him first, prioritising his needs above her own. It hadn't been hard—she was a mother and that instinct had come naturally and with a strength she dared not defy. But for the first time in a long time, lying here with Dimitrios, the waves lapping gently at the side of the boat, she felt a pull to be selfish. To put herself first, just this once.

'You think he'll be okay?' she wondered, seeking reassurance even when she knew he'd be fine.

Dimitrios's smile had the power of a thousand suns. 'I wouldn't suggest it if not.'

Annie relaxed, letting her body go limp and her eyes close, moving closer to Dimitrios so her head was buried in the crook formed by his arm and his chest. 'We'll call him later, though?' she said softly.

'Yes. We can call him later.'

Dimitrios took a moment to let the feeling pass. Panic gripped him, vice-like and hard. Annabelle snuggled against him and he felt as though he suddenly couldn't breathe, as though he was trapped in a place he'd never wanted to be. Married. Intimacy. This was all so new to him.

For many years, he'd promised himself this was a situation in which he'd never find himself. He'd slept with women—of course—but he'd never stayed the night. Even before Annabelle that had never been his inclination but, after their disastrous night, and realising how badly he'd hurt her, he'd taken an incredible degree of care not to inadvertently lead a woman on. He drew clear lines between sex and anything more, making sure he was absolutely open about what he could offer, what he wanted.

But Annabelle wasn't just another woman, she was his wife, and besides, despite his usual proclivities, there was nowhere else he wanted to be than here, like this, with her. Her head against his chest had grown heavy, her breathing steady. She was asleep. He shifted a little, checking the time on his wristwatch, a slow smile spreading over his face. They had all night—and he was going to make the most of it.

'And this is Annie.'

Lewis reached across, tussling his little sister's blonde hair, earning an eye-roll from her. But, as her vibrant blue eyes shifted to Dimitrios and Zach, bright pink colour infused her cheeks and her full lips parted on a husky breath.

'Hey, good to meet you.'

Zach extended a hand, grinning as she took it and smiled in response. Dimitrios, though, stood stock-still. She was nothing like Lewis, who was dark in complexion and colouring, though their eyes had a similar shape. And there was something in the quizzical force of her expression, intelligent eyes that he somehow just knew would miss very little.

'We're heading away for the weekend,' Lewis said. 'Are Mum and Dad home?'

Annie's eyes lingered on Dimitrios before shifting to look at Lewis. 'Dad is—upstairs.'

'And Mum?'

Annie shrugged, but there was tension in those shoulders, a look in her eyes that spoke of pain.

Dimitrios wanted to know everything about that—why was she troubled?

Lewis didn't speak of his parents often. But he talked about his sister constantly. Dimitrios wasn't sure why, but he'd pictured Annie as younger than she was—perhaps that was just Lewis's big brotherly, protective vibe, making it seem as if he had a kid sister rather than someone on the brink of womanhood.

Womanhood? Christ. She was a teenager. Fifteen? But,

yes, she was on the cusp—and why the hell was he notic-ing the fullness of her curves, the sweetness of her smile? He needed to get a grip.

'We should get going, Lewis.'

'Right.' Lewis put an arm around Annie's shoulders, drawing her close. 'Annie, entertain these guys while I go pack. Won't be long.'

Dimitrios watched as Annie and Zach fell into an easy rhythm, chatting about anything, from the local area to her schoolwork, to the law degree she was already set on pursuing.

'I do really well in legal studies,' she said with a small smile.

Dimitrios noticed that she barely looked in his direction. But he looked at her. He found it almost impossible not to.

'Law is so dry, though, so boring,' Zach was teasing, a grin on his face.

'I like boring.'

She laughed, a sound like a bell ringing. Then her eyes dipped furtively towards him and her smile dropped, a frown taking its place before she looked away again quickly—but not before he could see the pink in her cheeks again.

'Would you like a drink?' she asked Zach, but she ges-tured towards Dimitrios too, encompassing him in the in-vitation.

'Nah, we've got water bottles in the car.'

'I'll have a coffee,' Dimitrios was surprised to hear himself say.

Hadn't he been telling Lewis to hurry up only a minute earlier? So why prolong their time in this house?

'O-okay...' She stuttered a little, dipping her head for-ward so a curtain of blonde covered her face. 'How do you take it?'

'Black, strong.'

She lifted her eyes to his then and something fizzed between them—something that made sense of what he'd been feeling.

She had a crush on him!

That was why he was watching her like a hawk, trying to understand her behaviour towards him. She was young, inexperienced and her hormone-driven mind had cast him as some kind of romantic hero. Wasn't that what teenage girls did?

He smiled to soften her nervousness, but it seemed to have the opposite effect.

'I won't be long.'

He startled, shifting in the bed, casting another glance at his gold wristwatch. Only ten minutes had elapsed but he'd dozed off, the past beckoning him, dragging him towards recollections he hadn't thought of in years. The first time he'd met Annabelle she had made an impression on him. Even then there'd been something about her that had got under his skin—and it wasn't simply that she'd had a crush on him. No, he'd found her every gesture intriguing, and he'd wanted to sit there and decode her, to make sense of her. Whenever Lewis had spoken of her after that, he'd listened with extra attentiveness. Particularly when she'd started dating some boy from a neighbouring school two years older than her. Lewis hadn't really liked the guy. 'But it's her life,' he'd said with a shrug. 'And she clearly thinks he's great.'

That had been the end of it. Or so Dimitrios had told himself. Then why had he gone to Annabelle the night after the funeral? It had been more than just checking up on her. It had been way more than his promise to Lewis. He'd felt compelled to see her, as though she was exactly where he needed to be.

He shifted a little in the bed, moving so he could see her, and something lurched inside him.

For whatever reason he'd gone to her, she'd deserved better. He'd had no idea she'd been a virgin; how could he have? She'd had boyfriends by then. Why would he presume a woman of eighteen hadn't had sex when she'd been dating? Would it have changed anything about that night? That was something he couldn't answer with any certainty.

He moved again and this time Annabelle stirred, slowly blinking up at him, the clarity of her eyes jettisoning him into the past at the same time she propelled him into the future, so he was at sixes and sevens with no clear notion of where he was in time or place.

'I fell asleep.' She smiled apologetically, only the slightest hint of the teenager he'd first met lingering in her eyes and on her lips.

'Do you want to sleep some more?' he asked, even as every bone in his body was silently praying she'd say no.

She shook her head, shyness flooding her eyes. 'That's the last thing I want.'

A second later, she'd lifted up and straddled him, her expression showing sensual heat. A second after that and her lips were on his, her flesh pressed to him, so thoughts and memories all burst into flames; there was only Annabelle, there was only this…

CHAPTER ELEVEN

'I DON'T WANT this to happen,' she sobbed, hugging Lewis close, his frail frame in the bed bringing a lump to her throat that she couldn't clear.

'We don't have any say in that.' Even in his weakened condition, he smiled, trying to ease her pain. 'Listen to me, Annie. I'm tired. I don't know how long I'll have, but it can't be long. The drugs make me feel loopy most of the time,' he said, referring to the cocktail of pain medication he'd been prescribed.

'I know.'

She sat on the edge of his bed, stroking his hand. In the space of three months, he'd gone from looking strong and vital to this—pale and barely a skeleton with skin.

'You are my favourite person in the whole world.' He turned over his hand, catching hers. 'You're so smart and so kind and so funny—you are going to live a wonderful life.'

A sob racked her lungs.

'I need you to do something for me.'

She nodded urgently. 'Anything.'

'Live your life for me. Remember how proud I am of you. Remember how much faith I have in you. Remember the stories I've told you about everything you deserve and don't ever settle for anything less. You're brilliant, Annie. You deserve the world.'

* * *

The memory had come to her out of nowhere, hovering on the brink of her mind as she woke early the next morning. Their night had been perfect. After the boat, they'd gone to an exclusive club, where Dimitrios had sat close to Annie she had drunk a cocktail and felt as though she were floating in heaven. Neither of them had seemed to want the night to end. They'd come home in the small hours of the morning and they'd made love again in the bed that Annie now thought of as theirs until her body had been weakened by pleasure and she'd been too tired to keep her eyes open.

Everything was perfect.

Except it wasn't. It just *looked* perfect.

The distinction sat in her gut as she dressed that morning and, despite the corner they'd turned, she felt a sense of panic crowding her.

They'd become intimate but that didn't really mean anything—at least, not in the sense she wanted it to.

Out of nowhere, with the force of a lightning bolt, she remembered the detail of when they'd been making love on the boat and she'd wanted, more than anything, for him to tell her he loved her. How she'd craved those words— words she knew she'd never hear him offer.

Dimitrios went to work and she was glad of that. She needed space to fathom what she wanted next, what their new level of intimacy meant and, more importantly, she needed to work out how to exist in a marriage that included friendship and sex but no love. Weren't the lines getting far more blurred than either of them had intended?

Fortunately, Max was in one of his million-miles-an-hour moods, so it was hard for Annie to focus on anything but him. Even when her mind kept throwing flashbacks at her—reminding her of the pleasure she'd felt the night before, of the man who'd driven her wild—she forced herself to stay in the present. One foot after the other, breathing in and out, until the day was almost at an end.

In the way of children, Max barely seemed to feel the heat of Singapore. He wanted to go out and explore, and Annie agreed, so they asked the driver to take them into the city. They shopped and found a playground, then the driver took them to a food market full of local delicacies. They weren't too adventurous with their selections, but what they did order was delicious, and Annie promised they'd come back another time.

Christmas was everywhere they looked—despite the heat, as in Australia the depictions and decorations were all of a northern hemisphere, wintry Christmas. Trees with white snow painted on their ends, windows that looked snow-covered. Annie bought a packet of gourmet fruit mince pies on autopilot—it was something she'd always loved as a child but had had to do without since Max.

As the evening drew closer, nervous anticipation began to seep into her body. Soon they'd be home and that would mean facing Dimitrios. Annie knew she had to work out what she wanted before then. If she didn't? They'd go to bed together, and again and again, and a pattern would form that would set the tone for the rest of her life. Which was fine, if she could accept what he was offering.

But was it enough?

She looked down at Max and guilt rammed her. How could she even think it wouldn't be? How could she think her feelings mattered at all? This was right for Max, wasn't it?

But her own childhood had been so marred by her parents' unhappy marriage. She knew she had to avoid that too. She wouldn't raise Max in a war zone.

Only, fighting with Dimitrios wasn't inevitable—they could treat each other with respect even if they didn't love one another.

If only Annie could be certain that was the case!

She stopped walking, staring at a glamorous handbag-store as her heart twisted sharply. It *wasn't* the case. They might not love each other but Annie loved Dimitrios. She groaned softly, lifting a hand to her parted lips. She'd loved him as a teenager, but that had been easy to write off as a childish infatuation. This was so different. This was far more adult, far more dangerous, predicated on the way she'd come to know him now, years after they'd conceived Max. He was everything she'd fantasised about back then but so much more, too. He was kind, gentle and thoughtful, considerate and passionate. He was her other half.

'Mummy? What is it?'

She swallowed hard, realisation making her breathing uneven. 'I'm just hot, Maxi.' She reverted to his baby name and he didn't complain.

'We should go home. Or get ice-cream.'

His opportunistic second suggestion brought a vague smile to her face. 'Home for now.'

'Okay.' His voice only sounded a little disappointed. 'It's funny to think of this as home.'

More guilt. What was she actually proposing—that she leave Dimitrios? She couldn't do that to Max, no matter how hard this was for her. But nor could she stay in a sham marriage, could she? She felt as though she were in a small room with daggers on all sides.

'Do you like it here?'

The question was guarded, carefully blanked of any of Annie's own thoughts.

'Oh, yeah. It's great. I love the soccer team, and the school looks awesome. I love the house and the pool and the golf course and my room.'

Annie nodded, difficulties cracking through her mind. 'Good, darling. I'm glad. Now, where's that car...?'

* * *

Dimitrios patted the box in his pocket as he strode through the front door, a smile on his face, impatience making his movements swift. His day had been long, far longer than he'd intended. A crisis had blown up with one of his corporate investments—the kind of crisis that would usually necessitate Dimitrios's personal attention, requiring him to jump on the jet and fly straight to Hong Kong to sort it out.

But he didn't. Instead, he did phone conferences and worked over email to resolve the situation, and in the back of his mind was the certainty that he didn't want to leave Annabelle and Max.

His family.

Max was in bed when he returned home. 'I'm late,' he said to Annabelle, shaking his head. 'I couldn't get away sooner.'

Her eyes didn't quite meet his, reminding him of the first time they'd met, that memory still fresh in his mind despite how much had happened—and changed—since then.

'It's fine. He was tired. We walked a lot today.'

He smiled, but also a kernel of jealousy lodged in his chest. He needed to scale back his hours—he should be joining Max as he got to know his new city.

'Where did you go?'

'Everywhere,' she said. 'Are you hungry?'

There was something in her tone that raised a hint of alarm. Instinctively, he wanted to erase that. 'Sure. But first, I have something for you.'

She froze, her body quite still, her eyes wide as they lifted to his. 'Oh?'

He reached for her hand at the same time he removed the jewellery box from his jacket. The world-famous turquoise would communicate to her that something special was inside. He watched as she lifted the lid, her fingers a little unsteady. The ring shone in the light of the hallway. Large diamonds formed a circlet, and in their centre there was a canary-yellow diamond the size of a fingernail, cut in a perfect circle and set in four shimmering claws. Annabelle stared at it for a long time, as though she'd never seen a ring before.

'It goes on your finger,' he said with a droll smile.

She didn't look at him. 'I know. It's just… Whatever did you buy it for?'

He pulled the ring from the box and took her hand in his, lifting it so he could slip the ring on to her finger.

It was a perfect fit. She flexed her fingers, staring at it, before flicking her eyes in his direction. 'Why are you giving me this?'

He reached for her hand, stroking her fingers. 'Last night felt like a beginning. I wanted to mark the occasion.'

The column of her throat shifted as she swallowed. She looked the opposite of overjoyed. It was as though the ring was some kind of burden. 'Thank you.'

Her reaction wasn't what he'd expected. He spoke carefully, his voice calm, but his every instinct was flaring to life, telling him something was up.

'You don't like it?'

Her white teeth sank into her lower lip. 'It's beautiful,' she contradicted, but so quietly he had to strain to hear. 'It's just…'

'Go on.'

'About last night…'

He braced his skeleton with steel, a sharp rush of wariness making his body tense all over. 'Yes?'

She sighed. 'I think we need to talk.'

And, just like that, he recognised that he'd been afraid of this all day. It was why he'd stayed local, why he'd moved mountains to be able to come home to her tonight. He'd been worried about her reaction.

Regret. Guilt. Shame. Everything he'd felt after the first time they'd been together came crashing back into him. But this was different—he'd been so careful this time, fighting all his instincts to make sure the time was right for Annabelle, that she was ready.

Except something was bothering her, and that was everything Dimitrios had wanted to avoid. He braced himself for whatever was coming. 'Okay. Let's talk.'

Annie poured two glasses of wine and handed one to him, the ring catching her attention. She stared at it for a few seconds, then moved towards the table nearest the pool. The water was a deep turquoise colour and greenery surrounded them—bougainvillea grew rampant like a purple-flowering wall, giving privacy on one side. The city glistened straight ahead, and geranium and succulents formed a lush garden to their left. She breathed in, the fragrance of this place heaven. Except her nerves were too stretched to enjoy it.

'Well?' He was so formal, an air of caution infusing his words. The man she'd made love to for hours the night before was nowhere to be seen. 'What did you want to talk about?'

She ran her finger over the rim of the glass, forcing herself to rip this plaster off, to be brave even when she knew she could just enjoy the good parts of this life and be done with it.

You have to live your life for me now, Annie.

She sipped her wine, glad of the hit of alcohol. 'I need to know if anything changed for you last night.'

He leaned forward, his fingers linked at the front of the table, his eyes boring into hers. 'Such as?'

A weight dropped inside her. She sipped her wine again,

knowing she shouldn't do that—this was definitely a conversation she wanted to be present for, and to have all her brainpower at her disposal. The problem was, if he didn't understand what she was saying then she already had her answer. Nonetheless, she knew she needed to explain.

'You were right about the first time we slept together. It was more than sex for me.'

He stayed ominously silent, and for the first time Annie had a sense of what it would be like to be opposite this man in a combative capacity, of what he must be like in business.

'I think I fell in love with you the first time we met and that never really went away.'

'A girlhood crush,' he dismissed easily, except it *wasn't* easy. She heard the hesitation in his voice, and knew he'd recognised how she felt. How could he have failed to see? She'd worn a huge heart very clearly on her sleeve.

'No, it was more than that. I'd heard Lewis talk about you, so I think even before you and Zach came to our place I was halfway to thinking you were pretty amazing. But something inside me just clicked the day we met.'

'You were fifteen,' he reminded her, a hint of cynicism in his voice.

'Yes. And I tried very hard not to think about you again.'

'Right. You went out with other men,' he pointed out, earning a frown from Annie.

'How do you know who I dated?'

'Lewis mentioned it,' Dimitrios responded tightly.

'Technically, I guess I did date, but really it was just friendships. I didn't ever *feel* anything for anyone. Handsome, intelligent men could chat me up in a bar and I wouldn't have the time of day for them. That's never changed.'

She sipped her wine, looking into the distance, the past pulling at her. 'Even after Max, I'd meet people. In playgrounds and cafés, on the street, and yet no matter who asked me out, the answer was always the same. You're the only man I've ever wanted, Dimitrios.'

He sat very still, his features inscrutable. But in the depths of his eyes she could see emotions—concern, resistance, disbelief.

It was another answer he didn't realise he was giving her. His obvious rejection of what she was saying made it crystal-clear how little he welcomed this confession.

'I was angry at you too, though,' she continued anyway. 'Angry that you were going on with your life, with other women, other friends, and no doubt you'd forgotten all about me.' She shook her head. 'So long went by that somehow I hoped my feelings for you had dwindled into nothing in the intervening years.'

He reached for his wine for the first time, taking a generous drink before quietly replacing the glass between them on the table. 'Go on.' His voice was a growl, scarcely encouraging.

'I can't fight this any more, Dimitrios. I don't *want* to fight it. I'm as much in love with you as ever, and last night just made it impossible for me to ignore it. Everything clicked into place for me. I love you.'

Silence fell, loud with expectation.

She waited, even when she knew that every second stretching between them made the waiting futile.

'Annabelle.' He sighed, standing up and coming round to her side of the table, leaning against it, his long legs kicked out in front of him. His citrusy cologne reached her nose, making her insides clench in instinctive recognition. 'You are…'

He paused, searching for the right words. 'An incredible mother, and a beautiful person. I respect you so much. And there's no one on earth I would rather be married to, raising a child with. But this marriage isn't about love. For both our sakes, we need to be clear about that.'

She nodded jerkily, hating how close he was, hating that his answer was the opposite of what she wanted. Hating and loving him so damned much in that moment.

'You have been very clear,' she answered slowly. 'But now it's my turn.'

He was still, waiting. She reached for her glass, comforted by the feeling of the stem in her fingertips.

'I thought I could do this. Our marriage makes sense and, after what you've missed with Max, I wanted you to have proper time with him.' She drank to clear her throat.

'I'm glad.'

'I married you because I knew that if I said no you might have taken him away from me and I couldn't have handled that. I still couldn't.'

Tears filled her eyes; she blinked quickly.

'But the problem is, you've made everything too perfect.' She looked up at him, seeing him through the fog of her tears.

'And "too perfect" is bad?'

He wiped away one of her tears, but she flinched—the touch was too much. She couldn't bear his kindness; not if she was going to get through this.

'It can be.'

He made a noise of frustration. 'Why can't this work? Everything has been so great. We have fun together. We're attracted to each other. Why does that have to be a bad thing?'

His ability to see it so simply was the nail in the coffin for all her hopes, but still she needed to go through with this.

'You weren't the only one who made Lewis a promise before he died. I did too. I swore to him that I'd live my life for him and for me. He told me I deserved the fairy tale, the happily-ever-after.' A sob made the words thick. 'And this is so close, Dimitrios. You are everything I could ever want, for me and for Max, but if you don't love me too then I can't… I can't just pretend…'

'Shh,' he murmured, pulling her to stand against his chest, his lips pressing to the top of her hair. 'Please, don't cry.'

'I'm sorry, I didn't mean to, it all just hit me today. I think waiting to sleep together was a good idea, but it was also a bad idea, because last night when we made love I knew beyond a shadow of a doubt that for me it really was making love. I knew as we came together how much I love you. What we did means that much to me.' She reached for her hand and dislodged the yellow ring, placing it on the table. 'And for you, it meant something too. It meant having sex. With your wife, a woman you "respect", but that's all, isn't it?'

A muscle jerked at the bottom of his jaw. He didn't say anything, but then he didn't need to.

'This is… Everything is so beautiful.' She looked around, gesturing with her hand in a sweeping motion. 'You've made me feel like a princess in a fairy tale. It's not your fault that I forgot it was all just pretend. You've reminded me. You did everything you could to make me remember.'

He dipped his head in silent acknowledgement of that.

'But we're both trapped in this stunning, gilded cage. You would never have chosen this—me—would you? If it weren't for Max?'

His face was a forbidding mask.

'You don't have to answer,' she assured him, because his silence was answer enough. 'I know how you feel. You're doing everything you can for him, and for me, even though it means you're stuck living a life you would never have opted for.' She shook her head. 'And I'm sorry for that. I wish I could give you what you want—the kind of marriage that would make any of this worthwhile.'

'You think that's why I wanted to sleep with you?' he asked, disbelief etched in his tone. 'God, Annabelle, that wasn't me making the best of our marriage. It was the same insatiable need that drove me to you all those years ago. Everything else about this marriage might be a pretence but that isn't.'

She flinched, even though he was only confirming what she'd just said.

'I get it, but I've realised something today. I can't do half-measures. I can't make love with you when there's no love between us.'

He dropped his head forward, staring at the ground. 'Love isn't—and never has been—something I sought.'

Her smile was bittersweet. 'In my experience, you don't seek love, it seeks you.'

'Not me.'

'No,' she whispered, nodding, taking a step back from him. 'Definitely not you.' She wrapped her arms around herself, the reality of all this forming an ache low down in her abdomen.

'Please, wear this.' He reached for the ring but she held a hand up, shaking her head. 'It was a gift and it suits you.'

'It's very beautiful, but I don't think commemorating last night is a good idea.' She grimaced. 'Let's just…go back to how things were before, okay? We can forget it ever happened.'

Dimitrios wanted to rail against that. He felt trapped. Trapped between a rock, a hard place, an ocean, a tsunami and a wall of fire. He felt suffocated by indecision. He should say that he loved her. Just say the damned words and let this all go away. What difference would it make if he lied to her?

But he'd never do that, not even to relieve her suffering. Annabelle was brave and beautiful, telling him she didn't want a sham marriage. She wanted—and deserved—the real deal.

The guilt of the past few years was back, stronger than ever.

What would Lewis say if he knew what situation they were in—what situation Dimitrios had got them into?

God, what would Zach say?

He closed his eyes, his lungs hurting with the force of his breathing. 'Do you want a divorce?'

When he opened his eyes, all the colour had drained from her face. He ached to pull her into his arms but he knew the importance of the boundaries she was erecting. He had to respect them.

'Is that what you want?'

'No, Annabelle.' He dragged a hand through his hair. 'I don't want a divorce. I told you I wasn't going anywhere, and I meant that, one hundred per cent. But I don't want you to spend your life miserable and duty-bound, as you see it, to live with me.'

She tilted her face away from him, his outburst clearly hurting her. He swallowed a curse.

'I'm sorry. I just wasn't expecting this.'

Her eyes were haunted when they met his. 'You and me both.'

She chewed at her lip in a way he found far too distracting, given their current state of discord. 'I want what's best for Max.'

He frowned. 'I do too.' Uncertainty rippled inside him. 'But not if that's to your detriment.'

Her smile practically hollowed him out. 'Letting myself fall any further in love with you would definitely be detrimental to me. Treat me like a polite stranger and I'll be fine. Okay?'

A polite stranger. He stared up at the ceiling with a pain in his gut that wouldn't go away. A full forty-eight hours after Annabelle's confession, and Dimitrios's mood had gone from bad to worse.

Despite her pronouncement, she'd stayed in his room. 'Max will notice,' she'd said simply when he'd suggested he could move into a room down the hallway.

All of this was for Max. They were both in agreement on that. So here they were, polite strangers lying in his bed, on opposite sides of it, neither moving for fear of accidentally touching the other, despite the fact there was enough space between them to form a chasm.

As for sleep, it was a luxury that fell well beyond his grasp.

He shifted to look at her and something tightened low in his abdomen. He couldn't tell if she was asleep or not. It was possible the same thoughts were tormenting her, keeping her awake, an awareness of him like a form of torture, just as it was for Dimitrios.

But if she was pretending to sleep then it was logical to conclude she would continue to do so even if he moved. Stepping out of bed, he grabbed a shirt from the wardrobe and pulled it on, determinedly not looking back at the bed until he reached the door. Only then did he tilt his face a little, dark eyes that swirled with frustration finding Annabelle, looking for her, hoping to see—what?

She'd rolled over, turning her back on him.

She wasn't asleep, but she was closed off to him, and he suspected he deserved that.

CHAPTER TWELVE

IT WAS IMPOSSIBLE not to feel the contrast with last Christmas Eve. Annie stared around the beautiful living room, with the twelve-foot Christmas tree Dimitrios had organised, and felt a wave of sadness. On the surface, this was perfection. Everything was so lovely, but Annie's heart was more broken than it had ever been.

This house, the decorations, the setting…everything was so stunning. She and Max had spent Christmas Eve the year before watching a children's movie and eating turkey sandwiches, but she'd been…happy.

Not whole, exactly. She knew now that a Dimitrios-sized gap had always been inside her, but it had been easy to live with a gap. His absence hadn't been as bad, because there'd been an element of not knowing. It had been possible to keep some kind of fantasy alive, even when she'd never really given it much thought on a conscious level. There'd been a level of plausibility.

But not now.

Now she'd felt everything he had to give and it had brought her to the edge of who she was, forced her to see him as he was, and she loved him—all of him. His rejection had cut her deeply but, as with everything, Dimitrios had done it so well. No screaming, no shouting, no accusations. It was nothing like her parents' arguments, nothing like the kind of marriage she'd spent a lifetime fearing she'd find herself living in.

Dimitrios was too honourable for that. Too kind. He didn't love her but he cared—not for her, necessarily, but for people in general. He was trying to do the right thing for everyone.

Annie couldn't be the one who ruined this. Max deserved her to try, to put aside her own feelings again, to bottle them up and hold them deep inside herself, just as she had in the past. If she could do that again, then Max could have both his mum and his dad. But with Dimitrios here, a living, breathing person within easy reach, could she be sure she wouldn't weaken and stumble? What if she decided that something was better than nothing and gave into the temptation that was weighing down on her?

Perhaps she should have kept the ring after all—as a reminder of how she'd felt the morning after, a reminder to keep her distance.

Annie brushed her fingertips over the pine needles of the tree, releasing a hit of that festive fragrance into the room. She lifted her fingers, inhaling, a stupid tear wetting the corner of her eye.

The Christmas Eve before, she'd been worried about everything, but her heart hadn't been heavy like this.

'Mummy?'

Mummy. How much longer would he call her that? Surely not long.

She took a second to surreptitiously wipe away her tear then turned, forcing a bright smile to her face. Max stood beside Dimitrios and, in keeping with their current arrangement, she forced herself to give him the briefest nod of acknowledgement before turning all of her attention back to Max.

'I was just wondering where you'd been,' she lied, crossing the room but stopping at least a metre short of the two of them. It was impossible not to notice how well-matched they were. They belonged together. Whatever it cost her personally, staying was the right thing to do. It would be so much harder than leaving. In leaving she would have had the space to heal, but here the cause of her pain was a constant presence. But that didn't matter. Max's smile pushed any sense of grief from her mind for a moment.

'We've been shopping.'

'Have you?'

'Uh-huh. Look.' Max pulled something from behind his back—a small box wrapped neatly in red. 'A present for you.'

Annie's heart turned over in her chest. 'You got something for me?'

'It was Daddy's idea. And Uncle Zach's.' Her heart twisted at the ease with which those two figures had become a part of Max's life—a daddy, an uncle. 'Besides, you always get me something.'

Now Annie couldn't continue to ignore Dimitrios without appearing rude, and she was determined that Max wouldn't pick up on any tension between them. Her own childhood had shown her what that felt like—she wouldn't have Maxi growing up in a war zone.

'That was very thoughtful of you.'

His eyes seemed to lock on to hers, trying to draw something from deep within her. He was silently asking a question, but she had no idea what answer to give him.

'I hope you like it,' Max said, pushing the present towards Annie.

'I'm sure I will.' She held it in her hands, feeling the weight of it, letting that tether her to the present. She would open it in the morning; she wasn't sure she could face it now.

'Daddy has some ideas for what we should do today.'

Annie's heart sunk to her toes. 'Does he?'

'He says we should make a pudding. He doesn't have a traditional recipe, and I told him we don't either, but apparently lots of people do, and we agreed that making a pudding should be our new tradition. What do you think, Mummy?'

Annie was lost. On the one hand, it was such a beautiful idea, a gift for their son to cherish, but on the other it was asking way, way too much of her. She stared at Dimitrios for a moment, all her hopes in tatters at her feet. But this was the life she'd chosen. Hadn't she just been thinking how Max was worth this sacrifice?

'Great, Max.' Her voice was over-bright. 'I just have to send a quick email and then I'll be right with you.'

Annie didn't need to send an email, but she definitely needed a moment to rally her courage before she could come and join the fun family activity Dimitrios and Max had planned.

'Mummy works a lot,' she heard Max explain as she left the room.

'Does she?' Dimitrios guided Max past the tree towards the kitchen, but his mind was on Annabelle with every step he took. Her face. Her eyes. The sadness he saw there. The same guilt that had been dogging him for years was exploding inside him now.

'Yeah, she has to.' Max sighed heavily. 'She always wants me to have stuff, but it's hard. So she works a lot, because that's how she earns money, and it means I get new shoes when I need them and stuff.' He looked down. 'My feet grow really, really, really fast.'

Dimitrios smiled despite the direction of his thoughts. He guided Max into the kitchen.

'I wish she didn't work so hard, though.'

'Oh?'

Dimitrios began to pull ingredients from the pantry. With only a moment's notice, his domestic staff had made sure they had everything they needed on hand for the start of the Great Pudding Tradition.

'Yeah.' Max came to stand beside Dimitrios and, when he pulled a bag of flour out, Max took it, helpfully carrying it to a place on the bench before returning for another item.

'Why is that?'

'Because she's tired all the time.'

More guilt slashed Dimitrios. Guilt and a sense of failed responsibility. But it was more than that. He grabbed for the sultanas and passed them to Max, a frown on his face.

'And I'm loud and busy, and I like to do stuff like go to the playground, but I don't always like to ask Mummy because I know she's tired and if I do ask her she'll say yes.'

Dimitrios nodded. 'You're considerate, Max.'

'Thanks.'

Dimitrios had missed so much. He'd missed so much of Max's life, and he'd missed Annabelle being a mum. He'd missed her tiredness and her happiness, her tears, her pleasure, her everything.

'Do we need aprons? They always wear aprons in cooking shows.'

Dimitrios nodded, distracted. 'Yeah, they're here somewhere. Why don't you have a look?'

Max rifled through doors and drawers and appeared with a pair of aprons a minute later. 'There's only two.'

'Okay, I'll go without.'

Max shrugged. 'Can you help me with mine?'

'Of course.'

He secured it around his son's back, folding it in half to fit, tying it loosely into a bow. They were almost finished measuring ingredients before Annabelle appeared by the door to the kitchen, her expression inscrutable, her hair pulled into a no-nonsense pony tail he found his fingers itched to muss. He looked away with a sense that he was falling off the edge of a cliff.

'We saved you an apron, Mummy.'

She stiffened, and Dimitrios understood—this was the last thing she wanted to be doing. Damn it, he'd regretted hurting her for seven long years, and now what? Their marriage was going to hurt her every single day. He couldn't do that. He couldn't live with this.

But what other option did they have? She was right— they were both trapped in this marriage he'd insisted on, trapped by their love for Max.

'Thanks, darling. I'll just make a cup of tea…'

'I'll make it,' Dimitrios offered, his eyes holding hers until something shoved him right in the gut. He felt it like a physical blow, but it wasn't. Everything around him was shifting.

'That's fine. You keep measuring.' Her smile was brittle but when she looked at Max it softened. 'I won't be long.'

'You know what we need?' Max said happily. 'Christmas carols.'

He was evidently oblivious to the undercurrent of tension flowing between his parents.

'Christmas carols are a great idea, darling. Let me see what I've got.' Annabelle reached into her back pocket and pulled out her phone. Dimitrios frowned at the sight of it— so old and battered. How had he missed that? She pressed a button and some old jazz carols began to play, filling the kitchen with nostalgia and magic. But Dimitrios was only half-listening.

He went through the motions of making the pudding, following to the letter the recipe on his own state-of-thert phone, noticing that Annabelle kept a careful distance from him at all times.

It was one of the longest days of his life. Both adults were doing everything they could to make it special for Max, which meant they spent the whole day together as a family. The tension of being near Annabelle and not being able to touch her, not being able to make her smile, almost crushed Dimitrios.

When Max was finally asleep, he went in search of Annabelle. He didn't know how he knew where she'd be, but something drew him to the Christmas tree downstairs. He found her sitting on the floor with a glass of wine, her legs crossed, her eyes on the present Max had given her, a small frown on her face. She'd showered and was casually dressed, her face wiped of make-up, her blonde hair loose around her face.

His gut clenched again in a now familiar sensation.

He loved Max. That love had been easy and instantaneous. He'd taken one look at his son and known the child was a part of him and always would be. And Annabelle?

Everything inside him ground to a halt. His blood stopped rushing, his heart stopped pumping, his lungs ceased to inflate; he was completely still. Even the world seemed to stand as it was, refusing to shift with its usual motion.

'Annie...'

It was the first time he'd abbreviated her name. She jerked her face towards his, her eyes huge and for a second unguarded, so he saw the pain there, the look of loss.

It was a strange thing to inspire revelation but it was like a lightning bolt for Dimitrios. He looked at Annie and knew in that instant he would do *anything* to make her happy. Not just to make her happy because she deserved to be happy, but because her happiness was suddenly the

most important thing in the world to him. Because, if sh
wasn't happy, he never could be. Because Annie had com
to mean everything to him, and he'd been too mired i
his suspicion of love and marriage to see what was righ
in front of him.

'I was just…' She turned away from him, the sentenc
trailing off. 'I don't know. Sitting here.'

Her sadness hit him in the chest but now his reactio
didn't bother him. He understood why his body had bee
lurching, clenching and feeling so completely different fo
weeks now. It had been so much smarter than his brain.

'Max has had a good day,' he said gently, coming to s
beside her. She stiffened; he felt it. God, he'd been such
jerk. How had he missed something so obvious?

Because he'd been fighting it—Annie—since the firs
moment they'd met, when she'd been fifteen and the littl
sister of his best friend.

'He's had a great day,' she agreed.

'And you?'

She turned to face him, her eyes roaming his face, a
though looking for something. 'It was nice to see Max s
happy,' she said eventually.

He lifted his hand to her cheek; he couldn't resist it, cup
ping her skin there. She leaned into his caress for a momer
and then jerked back, almost knocking her wine glass ove
He reached past her, catching it, then straightened.

'You told me about your parents' marriage, and I tol
you about mine,' he began quietly, knowing he needed t
get every word of this right. 'But I don't know if I ever ex
plained how much my dad's behaviour affected me. I don
know if I made it clear to you that seeing my mum broke
by how much she loved Dad formed a part of me that I hav
held on to my whole life. I had a daily reminder that lov
is bad. Love hurts. That formed my backbone; it change

me. And I have never regretted that; I've never felt that my life was lacking in any way.'

Her eyes were huge. She moved, as if she was about to stand up, to run away from this conversation. He couldn't have that. He reached across, putting a hand on her knee. 'Hear me out. Just for a minute.'

Her eyes swept shut. She wanted to leave, he could tell, but she nodded just once, then reached for her wine glass, cradling it in her fingertips. 'Go on.'

He released a breath he hadn't realised he'd been holding. 'I don't know if you remember the first time we met?'

Her response was another short, sharp nod.

'I found you—'

'Don't lie to me,' she warned.

'I'm not lying. I found you captivating. I found myself thinking about you and, whenever Lewis talked about you, which was all the time—he was so damned proud of you, Annie—I listened with my whole body. I was glad when he said you had a boyfriend, because whatever hold you had over me wouldn't survive that. Except it did. I thought of you often, and I wondered about you, so I did the only thing someone like me *could* do—I went out of my way to avoid you. Whenever you were with Lewis, I steered clear. I controlled my reaction to you completely by not seeing you.'

She looked towards the tree, the shimmering lights catching her face in little blades of gold and silver.

'And then, after his funeral, I was weak for the first time in my life. I followed my instincts. It was *never* just sex for me, Annie. And no one else would have done. I needed *you* that night. Only you could put me back together again. Only you could make sense of the grief that had deluged me completely. I needed *you*.'

Her lips parted at his words but she kept her face averted, as though looking at him would be too much.

'You were so beautiful and innocent—so much more beautiful and perfect than I'd dared imagine. I think I knew even then that you were the one person on earth who could make me forgot how much I hated the idea of marriage and love. You were far too great a risk and I wasn't brave enough to take it.' He ground his teeth together, hating himself for the decisions he'd made then.

'I disappeared out of your life because I knew if I weakened, even a little, I would want all of you—all of you for ever—and I'm not someone who does "for ever". You deserved so much better than me.' He groaned. 'What a coward I was. A foolish, selfish coward. I told myself I was protecting you by pushing you away, by saying all those awful things to you, but I was protecting my own stupid heart, making sure there was no risk you'd ever want me again.'

She turned to him then, her beautiful eyes showing sympathy—a sympathy he had no right to.

'I spent seven years consciously forgetting you, and I mean that literally—it was a conscious effort I made every damned day, not to think of you. Because you were all I wanted to think about, Annie. You're the only person I've ever met who's had this kind of hold over me and now I finally understand why.'

She mouthed the word, 'Why?' but no sound emerged.

'I love you,' he said simply. 'I have loved you since before I even met you, but that day you became a part of my soul. I don't know why, but there is something in you that answers everything in me, and I have fought that harder than I ever want to fight anything again.'

A juddering sound escaped her lips. 'I'm not going to take Max away from you, if that's what you're worried about,' she said quietly. 'I'm not going to ask you for a divorce. I meant what I said the other day. I'm committed to our marriage, because of Max—'

'This isn't for Max,' he interrupted, brushing his thumb over her lower lip. 'I could have moved to Sydney, set up across town from you, shared custody of him. This was never just about Max. It's been about my family—the woman I love and the child that love made. It's about us being together because that's how we belong. It's about you getting every happily-ever-after you deserve, just like Lewis said. This isn't guilt speaking, Annie, it's hope. Hope that you can forgive me, eventually, for the pain I put you through, for my useless foolishness when it came to you. It's hope, a hope that I probably don't have any right to hold, that you can let yourself love me without fear, without pain.'

She stared at him and every second that passed was like a weight being added to his chest.

'I always play to win. You probably know that about me. I told myself I married you for Max. All along I've told myself this is for Max—but these last few days have shown me what a lie that was. Because Max is right here in my home, exactly where I wanted him, but with you being miserable and pulling away from me I can't be happy. I don't just want Max, I want you too, Annie. You're both a part of me.'

She stared at him, tears moistening her lovely eyes, the thick lashes clumping at the base.

'I love you,' he said simply, urgently. 'With all that I am. Not because of Max, not because of Lewis, but because of you, Annabelle Papandreo.'

She made a strangled noise and shook her head, and a part of him threatened to break. He needed to do more, to say more. How could he make this any clearer?

'You called this a gilded cage the other day. Well, yes. It is. I gilded it for you, because I wanted you to have everything imaginable. Because I love you. Every gift was chosen by me for your happiness. I wanted to give you everything because I was too scared to give you my heart—and I see

now that's the one single thing you've ever wanted, the one
thing that would have shown you how much you mean to
me. Now the thing I'm most afraid of is that you won't believe me, or you won't trust me not to hurt you again. The
gilded cage isn't our marriage, it's the idea of living a life
without you in it.'

'Dimitrios—'

'You don't have to answer tonight. We've both waited
seven years for me to stop being so obtuse. I can wait a bit
longer. Just—think about what you want. And know how
I feel about you.'

She closed her eyes; he hated that. He wanted to see her
thoughts, to understand her emotions. But when she opened
them again, she was smiling and shaking her head. 'I'm not
going anywhere.' She repeated the words he'd once said to
her, and his heart leaped.

'What does that mean?'

She laughed softly, tilting her head back. 'I love you,'
she said with a lift of her shoulders. 'And it sounds like you
love me too—a lot—and so, to my mind, that's kind of a
Christmas miracle.'

He looked towards the tree, a grin breaking out on his
face as he relaxed for the first time in a long time.

'Everything has been so perfect, Annie. None of this
was pretend. It was perfect because it was real.'

'Yes,' she agreed, leaning forward and brushing her lips
to his. 'And it always will be.'

'Yes,' he promised, kissing her right back. 'You will
live happily-ever-after. I promise you that now, with all
that I am.'

'I believe you.'

'I was just thinking how perfect this has been.' Annie
smiled as Dimitrios walked into the room. Christmas day

was drawing to a close, and it had been the most blissful day of Annie's life. Max had loved his gifts, and Annie had adored her picture frame—with a photo of Max and her inside it—and the pudding they'd made had been the icing on the cake, a delicious tradition to take forward into all their future Christmases.

When she'd whispered to Dimitrios that she hadn't got anything for him, his eyes had glowed and he'd leaned forward and whispered in her ear, 'You are all the gift I require, Mrs Papandreo.'

But Dimitrios had a look on his face now that had her sitting a little straighter and placing her eggnog on the end table. 'What's the matter?'

'Nothing, I think.' A frown etched its way across his face. 'I just had the strangest conversation with Zach. He's coming over soon.'

'Here?' She glanced at her wristwatch. 'It's eleven o'clock.'

Dimitrios laughed. 'For Zach, that's when the night begins.'

'Of course,' she agreed. 'Well, it will be nice to see him, anyway.'

'I just pray he doesn't stay too long.' Dimitrios grinned, brushing his lips to Annie's. 'I have plans for you, my love.'

'And I hope they last all night...'

'All night? How about a lifetime?'

* * * * *

MILLS & BOON

Coming next month

THE COST OF CLAIMING HIS HEIR
Michelle Smart

'How was the party?'

Becky had to untie her tongue to speak. 'Okay. Everyone looked like they were having fun.'

'But not you?'

'No.' She sank down onto the wooden step to take the weight off her weary legs and rested her back against a pillar.

'Why not?'

'Because I'm a day late.'

She heard him suck an intake of breath. 'Is that normal for you?'

'No.' Panic and excitement swelled sharply in equal measure as they did every time she allowed herself to read the signs that were all there. Tender breasts. Fatigue. The ripple of nausea she'd experienced that morning when she'd passed Paula's husband outside and caught a whiff of his cigarette smoke. Excitement that she could have a child growing inside her. Panic at what this meant.

Scared she was going to cry, she scrambled back to her feet. 'Let's give it another couple of days. If I haven't come on by then, I'll take a test.'

She would have gone inside if Emiliano hadn't leaned forward and gently taken hold of her wrist. 'Sit with me.'

Opening her mouth to tell him she needed sleep, she stared into his eyes and found herself temporarily mute.

For the first time since they'd conceived—and in her heart she was now certain they *had* conceived—there was no antipathy in his stare, just a steadfastness that lightened the weight on her shoulders.

Gingerly, she sat beside him but there was no hope of keeping a distance for Emiliano put his beer bottle down and hooked an arm around her waist to draw her to him.

Much as she wanted to resist, she leaned into him and rested her cheek on his chest.

'Don't be afraid, *bomboncita,*' he murmured into the top of her head. 'We will get through this together.'

Nothing more was said for the longest time and for that she was grateful. Closing her eyes, she was able to take comfort from the strength of his heartbeat against her ear and his hands stroking her back and hair so tenderly. There was something so very solid and real about him, an energy always zipping beneath his skin even in moments of stillness.

He dragged a thumb over her cheek and then rested it under her chin to tilt her face to his. Then, slowly, his face lowered and his lips caught her in a kiss so tender the little of her not already melting to be held in his arms turned to fondue.

Feeling as if she'd slipped into a dream, Becky's mouth moved in time with his, a deepening caress that sang to her senses as she inhaled the scent of his breath and the muskiness of his skin. Her fingers tiptoed up his chest, then flattened against his neck. The pulse at the base thumped against the palm of her hand.

But, even as every crevice in her body thrilled, a part of her brain refused to switch off and it was with huge reluctance that she broke the kiss and gently pulled away from him.

'Not a good idea,' she said shakily as her body howled in protest.

Emiliano gave a look of such sensuality her pelvis pulsed. 'Why?'

Fearing he would reach for her again, she shifted to the other side of the swing chair and patted the space beside her for the dogs to jump up and act as a barrier between them. They failed to oblige. 'Aren't we in a big enough mess?'

Eyes not leaving her face, he picked up his beer and took a long drink. 'That depends on how you look at it. To me, the likelihood that you're pregnant makes things simple. I want you. You want me. Why fight it any more when we're going to be bound together?'

Continue reading
THE COST OF CLAIMING HIS HEIR
Michelle Smart

Available next month
www.millsandboon.co.uk

COMING SOON!

We really hope you enjoyed reading this book.
If you're looking for more romance, be sure to
head to the shops when new books are
available on

Thursday 10th December

MILLS & BOON

THE HEART OF ROMANCE

A ROMANCE FOR EVERY KIND OF READER

MODERN

Prepare to be swept off your feet by sophisticated, sexy and seductive heroes, in some of the world's most glamourous and romantic locations, where power and passion collide.
8 stories per month.

HISTORICAL

Escape with historical heroes from time gone by. Whether your passion is for wicked Regency Rakes, muscled Vikings or rugged Highlanders, awaken the romance of the past.
6 stories per month.

MEDICAL

Set your pulse racing with dedicated, delectable doctors in the high-pressure world of medicine, where emotions run high and passion, comfort and love are the best medicine.
6 stories per month.

True Love

Celebrate true love with tender stories of heartfelt romance, from the rush of falling in love to the joy a new baby can bring, and a focus on the emotional heart of a relationship.
8 stories per month.

Desire

Indulge in secrets and scandal, intense drama and plenty of sizzling hot action with powerful and passionate heroes who have it all: wealth, status, good looks…everything but the right woman.
6 stories per month.

HEROES

Experience all the excitement of a gripping thriller, with an intense romance at its heart. Resourceful, true-to-life women and strong, fearless men face danger and desire - a killer combination!
8 stories per month.

DARE

Sensual love stories featuring smart, sassy heroines you'd want as a best friend, and compelling intense heroes who are worthy of them.
4 stories per month.

To see which titles are coming soon, please visit

millsandboon.co.uk/nextmonth

JOIN US ON SOCIAL MEDIA!

Stay up to date with our latest releases, author news and gossip, special offers and discounts, and all the behind-the-scenes action from Mills & Boon...

 millsandboon

 millsandboonuk

 millsandboon

It might just be true love...

MILLS & BOON

HEROES

At Your Service

Experience all the excitement of a gripping thriller, with an intense romance at its heart. Resourceful, true-to-life women and strong, fearless men face danger and desire - a killer combination!

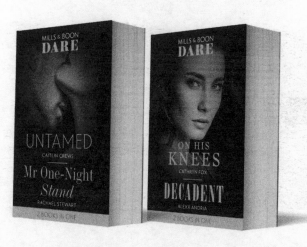